CW00402806

OtherLight

OtherLight

The Quest Continues

Book II

Bruce Campelia

Hardcover ISBN: 979-8-9866656-0-3

PRINTED IN THE UNITED STATES OF AMERICA

This book is dedicated to the Old City of Jerusalem, a sacred location full of ancient memories of human civilization. There exists no better place for us all to visit, discover the roots of our common humanity, and reclaim our true path into the light.

"I give you the end of a golden string,
Only wind it into a ball,
It will lead you in at Heaven's gate
Built in Jerusalem's wall."

–William Blake

Foreword

THERE ARE FEW books for young adult readers that seamlessly weave religion and spirituality with a bit of magic and fantasy. This happens to be one of those books. Over the last two LightPassers volumes, I have been delighted to watch Morningstar, Zack, Liyah, and Kai Li develop into not only characters but multi-dimensional teenagers that I would be honored to know.

This adventure of theirs is a little different than *Quest of the Chosen*, mostly because we've moved into the real world with real problems. The issues that the Light Passers face in *OtherLight* are ones that many teenagers growing up in the world today are faced with: racism, injustice, and world conflicts that they have no choice but to be dragged into. So where can we find similarities with Morningstar (an Indigenous Lakota Sioux), Zack (an African American Christian), Liyah (a Muslim from Palestine), and Kai Li (a Buddhist from Hong Kong)?

The answer to this is found not only in the connectedness they find during their journey but also in the fact that throughout these pages, they realize that they share more similarities than differences. Especially where their religion is concerned. *Mitákuye Oyás'iŋ*: they are connected in their humanity.

In addition to creating characters that we champion, Bruce possesses a shrewd insight into human strength and weakness, hardness and compassion that we acknowledge to be part of our complete makeup as human beings. His knowledge and unparalleled research into the settings and events taking place are the mark of a true craftsman of language and a world traveler. And he takes us right along with him on a tour of Jerusalem.

There were times in this novel when I was on the edge of my seat reading about the still-very-real conflicts with Israel and Palestine, the (admittedly fictional) inner workings of Hamas and Mossad, and how several teenagers can thwart a large governmental plot. But the best thing that Bruce does, is give these teenagers a voice. He shows them—and us as readers—how much they matter; how much of a difference they can make.

I hope you'll share this book with other young readers in your life, and with adults, as well. I believe it will spark not only enjoyment but also some important discussions and maybe, if we're lucky, a paradigm shift or two.

Caroline Smith
Editor
Author, *Shadows in the South*

Acknowledgments

MANY WRITERS WILL tell you that while their first book was an epic challenge, the second one can threaten their sanity. I'm here to bear witness to that.

This book is intended to shift the reader from the background adventure of *Quest of the Chosen*, where the characters and overall series philosophy are introduced, to real situations in this world of ours. On the surface, it might seem easier to write it, since four of the main characters remain the same and there is less focus on complicated fantasy elements, yet I found the opposite to be true. While the first book was a labor of love, for this book I felt some obligation to create an equally meaningful story that would bring the concept and power of the entire series into clear view.

I seem to have forgotten that the first book took almost ten years to create from vague notion to final printing, whereas *OtherLight* had a one-year completion target. That compression of time, combined with the usual and constant self-doubt as an author, played havoc with my mind. And this is why I am so grateful for those who helped keep me on the path, always renewing my faith in my mission, and myself.

In this regard, I would like to take this opportunity to thank the following people for their steadfast belief in this work and their encouragement to make it through this common writer's struggle: Elizabeth Littlefield, my partner, for her unfailing encouragement and patience. Elizabeth, an artist in her own right, edits all my first drafts and helps keep me on message. These books would not have appeared without her, and those many friends, family members, and readers who dropped me notes, asking me when they can expect to get the next book—not because they are pushing me, but because they genuinely love the story and miss the characters they have come to know.

Thanks also to Caroline Smith, my content editor for both books, who challenges me to maintain the highest level of storytelling and weave the many elements together as seamlessly as I can; Abbey Linville and Kathy Greene, the newest and youngest members of my editing team who helped tighten up the wording, and who bring to the table a welcomed perspective of their generation; Liza Marie Garcia and her team at NOW Publishing, who helped bring both books to life; and all of you who have told me you are moved by the Light Passers Chronicles series.

This book is for all of you.

With sincere thanks,
Bruce

ISRAEL
יִשְׂרָאֵל
إسرائيل
LEBANON
Golan Heights
SYRIA
Sea of Galilee
Galilee
Coastal Plain
Jordan Rift Valley
Jordan
Tel Aviv
WEST BANK
(PALESTINE)
Jerusalem
Bethlehem
N
MEDITERRANEAN SEA
ISRAEL
Dead Sea
GAZA STRIP
(PALESTINE)
A.I.A
Beersheba
Negev Desert
JORDAN
EGYPT
ISRAEL

GAZA STRIP
רצועת עזה
قطاع غزة

Beit Lahia
Jabalia
Beit Hanoun
Gaza
MEDITERRANEAN SEA
Deir al-Balah
ISRAEL
Khan Yunis
Abasan al-Kabera
Rafah
Arafat Int'l Airport
EGYPT

LEBANON
SYRIA
MEDITERRANEAN SEA
West Bank
ISRAEL
JORDAN
EGYPT

Characters*

The Light Passers
Morningstar: Lakota Sioux teen
Zack: Black teen from Detroit
Liyah: Israeli teen from Palestine
Kai Li: Asian teen from Hong Kong
Ooray: Mystical being

In Palestine
Khalib: Liyah's younger brother
David Al-Rahim: Liyah's father and owner of the *Filastin Dawn* paper
Rania Al-Rahim: Liyah's mother
Ahmad: Palestinian teen boy
Safir: Muezzin at Al-Aqsa Mosque
Hassan: Hamas leader, part of the drone team
Akeem: Hassan's assistant for drone tests
Jamal: Overall strategist, wireless, and materials lead of the drone team
Murtaza: Hassan's connection for funding
Billy Kane: American Evangelical connected to the church in Bethlehem
Nura: Young mysterious woman supporting the Palestinian cause; part of the drone team
Nasir: Technical lead of drone team
Sayf Yasin: CEO of drone factory
Fahzi: Iranian connection to Hassan and Hezbollah
Yusuf Al-Najafi: Iranian-Saudi Falconer and supporter of Palestine
Dawoud: Yusuf's assistant for falcon training
Taliq: Falcon
Hezbollah: Shiite Muslim political party
Hamas: militant movement and one of the Palestinian territories' two major political parties.

In Israel
Esty: Israeli teen
Dr. Adam Blum: Esty's father and consultant to the Prime Minister of Israel
Lavi Haddad: Minister of the Interior of Israel
Saul Liebowitz: Deputy Minister of Defense for Israel
IDF: Israeli Defense Forces
Michael Korrin: Commander of Israeli Air Force
Aman: Military security agency of Israel, including special ops and cross-agency coordination
Aaron Levi (Major General): Senior Advisor of Aman
Israeli Intelligence Agency: Oversees covert operations
Shabak: Also known as Shin Bet. Organization in charge of general internal security for Israel and its occupied territories
Yossef Cohen: Director of Shabak
Mossad: Called "The Institute"; Agency responsible for Israeli foreign intelligence and counterterrorism
Mabood: Leader of the group holding Khalib captive

*All names are fictional

Other Important Terms and Places to Know:
Muezzin (Arabic *mu'adh·dhin*): the person responsible for the calls to prayer each day
Hijab: Head covering worn by Muslim women
Thawb: Long Saudi robe-shirt
Bible: Holy text of Christianity
Quran: Holy text of Islam
Talmud: Holy Text of Judaism
Zah-re: (pronounced zah-ray), Book of Truths: Fictional summary writings representing universal truths
Jerusalem: One of the oldest cities in the world, and a spiritual center for Judaism, Christianity, and Islam
Old City: The oldest part of Jerusalem located on the Temple Mount
Church of the Holy Sepulchre: Church in the Christian Quarter of the Old City
Dome of the Rock: Islamic shrine located on the Temple Mount
Al-Aqsa Mosque: Mosque compound located in the Old City

Western Wall (sometimes referred to as the Wailing Wall): Ancient wall in the Old City
Gaza Strip: Small, densely populated Palestinian territory on Israel's southern border.
The Negev: Desert in southern Israel
West Bank: Palestinian territory bordering Israel to the East
Yatir Forest: Manmade forest in Eastern Israel, near the Palestinian and Jordanian border
Anim Synagogue: Ancient synagogue used 300-600 years after the death of Christ

One

THE PHONE RANG for a fourth time, before a stately woman, sitting behind the desk in the anteroom to the office, completed her review of the day's activities and then picked it up. She speaks with a steady, professional voice.

"Good morning. Ministry of Interior."

She listens for a moment then speaks again. "He's quite busy this morning…Okay, hold just a minute."

The inner office line buzzed. An overweight man wearing a white dress shirt and dark blue tie pressed the intercom button.

"Yes?"

"It's Mr. Rahim. He says it's urgent."

"Okay, I'll take it."

The man picked up the receiver and pressed the flashing line as he removed his thick tortoise-framed glasses, twirling them between his thumb and forefinger. "Good morning, David! It's been a while."

"Yes, it has indeed, Lavi. We had peace for a bit, didn't we?" replied Liyah's father. "How are you?"

"To tell you the truth, I could be better. These new rocket attacks by the boys in the Strip don't help my blood pressure. I see that our retaliation hit close to you. Sorry…that's the IDF from the Minister of Defense and Prime Minister, you know…not my call."

"Yes, I know. More than close, though. The blast blew out the front of my building. No one got hurt at the paper, but I can't say the same for the new media building across the way." He paused. "Bad situation, Lavi. Seems to be getting worse, not better. I don't like the signs."

"Looking for some financial assistance, David? We don't have any authority in Gaza, except maybe overseeing various passes."

"Actually, no. It's not that," he replied, his tone more somber. "I'm calling about something else."

"What's that?"

"It's my son, Khalib. He's been taken captive by some terrorists."

Lavi Haddad stopped spinning his glasses. "My God, David," he gasped, holding the phone out straight and staring at the receiver as if he could see who was talking, then bringing it back to his ear. "When did this happen?"

"Almost a week ago."

"Is there something specific you need? I'll do anything I can to help. No question."

"I'm really not sure," David responded, drawing out each word. "I've been doing some digging on my side…using my sources here at *Filastin Dawn*. There's a boy who works here who I believe may have some way to get messages to an underground network. I'm hesitant to fully use that leverage until I know more, but all other efforts have come up short. I was hoping you might be able to obtain some information through your channels there at the Ministry, or other government-level groups that monitor terrorist activities."

"Do you have any information I can use?"

"Not really, Lavi. He was taken out of Beit Lahia during the recent disturbance. I would have said it was Hamas, ramping up their local efforts here in Gaza. But the tactics don't match. So maybe a more regional group, like Hezbollah, out of Iran. My investigative team indicated they seem to be getting more influential here lately."

"It's not much to go on, but I'll make some inquiries right away. Hold tight, my friend."

The Minister slipped the receiver slowly back on the phone as he let out a deep sigh. He pressed the intercom button.

"Sir. What can I do for you?"

"So sorry, Devorah. We're going to have to reschedule my morning meetings. Something's come up."

David Al-Rahim spun a half-turn in his chair. He leaned back and placed his feet up on the low file cabinet next to the desk, then started clicking the end of the ballpoint pen in his hand.

There was a knock on the doorframe.

A boy poked his head into the office. "You were looking for me, sir?"

"Yes, Ahmad. Please come in."

Ahmad shuffled timidly into the office, then stood there, hands clasped in front of him.

"Sit, sit. Please," Liyah's dad insisted.

As Ahmad sat down, his boss stood up and moved around to the side of the desk, resting his butt on the edge, one leg over the corner.

He looked down at Ahmad and spoke directly, without hesitation. "Any new word from your connections."

Ahmad swallowed as if forcing down a big bite of a sandwich. "Sir?…I'm n-not sure what you mean."

"Let's not pull any punches here, okay? I wasn't sure if I should speak with you about this, but I'm out of options…and running out of time.

"Options?"

"I think you know what I'm talking about. I overheard Liyah speaking to one of her friends…the day after she came back from the square without Khalib. She said your brother and some of his friends have been getting into trouble lately and they were trying to coax Khalib to join them that day, during the confrontation in the square."

Ahmad wrung his hands, avoiding eye contact. "I really don't know much about it, sir," he replied, keeping his eyes on the floor. "I did hear about the situation from my brother, but he said they lost track of Khalib in the confusion, that he wasn't with them."

"Liyah told me she had helped Khalib get away from the crowd and sent him home. You don't know anything about that?"

"No, sir." Ahmad finally glanced up to meet his boss's eyes. "Really!"

"So, you're telling me you don't know anything at all?"

"No. I mean yes…Sir." He rubbed his hands harder.

"And you have no connections with the terrorists."

"Well…"

"Well, what...?" Ahmad's boss prodded.

"Well, I know a couple of them…just by accident. But I don't belong to any of the groups. I was hoping that, at some point, I could get an assignment to do a story…for the paper." His eyes followed the tall man as he left his perch on the desk and began pacing. On his third pass, he halted, turning to face the young, would-be apprentice again.

"Look, Ahmad. I'm not trying to make you nervous or interrogate you. We're desperate to find out who took Khalib and where he is before something really bad happens, or he gets taken to another country. I feel like all the options are slipping away from me, so I have to try everything I can. You understand, right?"

"Sure, sure. Absolutely. If I knew anything or could help, I would. Of course."

Liyah's dad scratched his chin as he began pacing again, talking to the floor. "What article are you talking about…for the paper?"

"Oh, well, I was just thinking. Maybe if I had a chance to talk to one of these groups, we could do a story about what really drives them.

You know, like you always insist on…a fair account of the conflict, from all the different perspectives."

Liyah's dad placed his large hand on the desk close to Ahmad. "And why would you do this?"

Ahmad's eyes drifted up to meet his. "Because I really want to be a journalist, and because I'll be out of school in a year and will need to find work. And you know how hard jobs are to find around here."

"That's a pretty tall order for a new person like you, especially when my own investigative team isn't making any headway."

"Well, I'd do it. Certainly, to help find Khalib, and also to help lower the temperature around here…things are getting worse for everyone." He paused. "But then there is a complication," he added.

"And that is…?"

"It's dangerous. If they find out I'm really looking for Khalib…and he's there…they might do something to me. But my contacts think I might be able to give them fair representation through the paper, since I *am* young, and people would likely listen to a fresh voice."

Liyah's dad rested his chin in his hand. "Hmm…Yes. It's tricky business, but I'm interested in getting Khalib home safely. I really don't care about local terrorist groups right now, only the one that has him." He began pacing again. "Do you think it would also help if they knew I supported your effort? Could you take a message to your contacts?"

"What kind of message?"

"I'll write one up tonight. Meet me at the Branch Cafe in Gaza for coffee, on Al-Jala before work tomorrow. I'll give it to you then. Okay?"

Ahmad nodded. "Sure. It's on my way in."

There was a long pause as they both stared in silence.

"You're free to go."

Ahmad launched himself up from his seat. "Okay, Mr. Rahim. Sure thing." He hurried towards the door. "See you then."

"But back to work first, right?"

Ahmad turned around, backing clumsily into the hallway, half tripping, then banging into the door jam. "Yes, sir."

Two

Beit Lahia

LIYAH HEADED UP the street, on an errand for her mother to bring back some vegetables for dinner. Her mind wandered—*She probably wants to distract me; to make me more pleasant at home. But why aren't they as upset as I am? He is all I think about. Where are you, Khalib?* she wondered out loud.

She bit her lip as she meandered through the aisles of the outdoor market, her mind growing more uneasy, her stomach beginning to churn. *It's my fault,* she thought. *If I hadn't lost him that day in the square, my brother never would have gone missing.*

She paused in front of a stand that jutted out in her path. Sighing, she picked up an eggplant from the bin and squeezed it gently, testing its ripeness. As she inquired of the vendor about its cost, she caught a glimpse of a boy moving toward her from the corner of her eye. He looked familiar, maybe one of Khalib's friends?

"Liyah?" the boy asked, approaching her. "Can we talk?"

Liyah nodded, and they moved to a quieter part of the market. The boy looked nervous, his attention jumping from her to the market, then back to her, eyes darting this way and that.

As her eyes followed the path of his, her heart started to pound.

"Is there something wrong?" she asked, her eyes now locked onto his. "You're scaring me."

"Sorry," the boy replied. "Things are crazy in Gaza, aren't they? It's out of control. And more people are getting kidnapped." Someone hurrying down the aisle bumped into him from behind.

Liyah waited until the woman moved on. "So, do you know where Khalib is?" she asked, her tone betraying cautious excitement.

"No," he replied, "but I do know something."

Liyah's voice went up. "You do?

"Shhh..." he cautioned, holding his finger to his lips. "What I mean is," he whispered, "someone from your father's paper was questioning a few of us the other day. I told him that I hadn't been with Khalib that day in the square. I…"

"Who?" Liyah interrupted.

"Uh, I don't know his name. But I'd seen him before. Maybe the brother of one of Khalib's other friends?"

"That could be Ahmad."

"Well, anyway, I didn't mention then, that some of my older brother's activist friends had been talking about how other boys had also gone missing over the past few weeks, and no one seemed to be piecing it all together. But the word is that these kidnappings are by a non-Palestinian group; a terrorist organization from another country." He glanced around at the bustling market, stepping aside so that a few others could pass. "These terrorists are indoctrinating and training them at an unknown location, then sending them out on missions to countries in the Middle East and Africa."

The boy pressed a folded piece of paper into Liyah's hand. "Here is a name and address. My brother got this from one of the boys yesterday. He said the man on the paper may have more information about your brother. Don't look at it now. It might seem suspicious…these days you can't trust anyone. I was told the man would be expecting you." He stepped back. "I've got to go."

Liyah nodded. "Okay, I can't thank you enough."

The boy started to leave, then stopped. "Promise not to tell anyone, or else we'll all be in danger…Promise?"

"I promise," she assured him.

He turned, and in an instant disappeared into the throng of people hustling about the market.

Liyah stuffed the paper in her purse, grabbed a plastic bag from the end of the aisle, and completed her shopping assignment.

The next day, she made an excuse to her mother to return to the marketplace, but instead, took a long walk to the address marked on the piece of paper. She worked her way through the oldest part of the city, to a stone-paved roundabout with a fountain at its center—watched over by a statue of a golden eagle. She proceeded along the narrow, crowded sidewalks. She passed the small shops, their fabrics, shoes, accessories, and a host of other goods displayed on tables out in front. Liyah continued, passing restaurants and cafes buzzing with activity, the aroma of morning coffee and pastries wafting through the air. Pausing ever so briefly, she breathed in the delightful smells before picking up her pace.

Leaving Beit Lahia, she entered the outskirts of the town of Jabalia. She glanced at her phone. The GPS indicated her destination was just down and across the street in front of her. But when she arrived, she saw only a mosque at that address, with its narrow stone minaret rising above a large domed roof, both capped in stunning blue tiles.

Two muffled *booms,* like that of back-to-back explosions, jerked her head in the direction of the downtown area, where the *Filastin Dawn*, her father's small but well-known international newspaper offices were located. She stopped for a moment to scrutinize the sky. Two pillars of smoke rose in the distance. *How close to the Dawn?* she wondered. She felt her throat tighten. She pushed the creeping sense of fear out of her mind. *Not now,* she told herself. *First things first.*

Up the granite steps she walked, past the iron gate at the top. She crossed a small garden, then entered the mosque through one of its two enormous hand-carved rosewood doors. She stood there for a moment, observing the vastness of the room before her—its ceiling reached high up into the dome, and the empty floor stretched out before her in both directions, covered by a thick, rich, red and gold carpet. A few people dotted its surface in prayer.

Looking around, she felt at a loss as to what to do next. *How am I going to find the person here?* she wondered. Moving farther into the room, she looked up at the gold and crystal chandelier suspended from the peak of the dome. She stopped at the base of one of the six stunning marble pillars along the edges of the room, thinking it must support a tremendous weight levied by both the chandelier and dome.

She lingered there, looking about, thinking of her brother. *What if he never comes back? What if he dies? How will I ever make up for it?* Falling to her knees beside the pillar, Liyah prayed, then sat back on her legs and started to sob.

Drying her tears on her sleeve, she rose to her feet. A man approached, dressed in a simple white robe. "What is the problem, my child?" he asked. "Certainly, it is a shame to be unhappy on such a beautiful day that Allah has provided for us, no?"

"I am looking for a man," Liyah replied. "I was told to come to this address, but clearly it is not the right one." She hands him the piece of paper.

The man studies it and gives it back to her. "And what do you want with this man?" he asks, in a serious tone.

Liyah shuffled her feet and avoided his direct stare. "He may know where my brother is."

"Is your brother lost?"

"No. But he is missing…since the day of the trouble in the square."

The man's brow furrowed. "And what makes you think this person can help you?"

Liyah thought about her response. *Why does this man ask so many questions instead of answering my simple one? I must find Khalib. Does he, or does he not know the man on the paper?* She took a deep breath. Her confidence began to return. "I was told by a friend he might be able to help. My brother is sometimes an angry young boy. And he can be impulsive. But he has a good heart." She cleared her throat then continued. "He loves his country. I fear he is vulnerable to bad teachings, and that those who have taken him will turn him into something he is not."

"And who is the one who knows this man?"

"I cannot tell you…for the safety of that person and for the safety of this man I seek. Do you know the man on the paper?"

"If you find this man, will you keep his safety in mind too?"

Liyah locked her eyes on his. "I will not tell anyone. It is my brother I wish to help. I will do anything to find him. I will not tell a soul, as Allah is my witness."

The man searches her face. "I am the imam here," he says.

Liyah's eyes shot downward; she bowed her head.

"Oh, I am so sorry. I did not know, my Imam. Please forgive me."

The imam reached his hand out and raised her chin up until her eyes met his again. "And what is your name, my child?"

"Liyah…Liyah Al-Rahim."

"Ah, yes. I know of your father…and your brother. Your father is a businessman of repute. He is a good man. Your brother has been throwing stones, so I've heard."

"He doesn't mean it," Liyah protested.

The imam smiled. "Yes, I know this. I did not say his heart is bad. I only said he has been throwing stones." He smiles again.

"Can you help me find this man? Do you know who he is? Why was I sent here, to a mosque?" Liyah asked.

"So many questions!" The imam laughed. "Yes. I believe I can, young lady, for it is I. I am *that* man."

Liyah's eyes grew large. *How could this kind imam be a man who would know about the kidnapping of my brother?*

"Well…," he continued, "I have your assurances that all that transpires between us will end here." His eyes prompted her to agree. "Yes?"

Liyah, stunned by his words, hesitated. Her voice finally returned, anxious, hurried. "Oh, yes…yes, of course. I have said that, haven't I? Yes…above all…you can trust me…I have pledged to Allah."

He nodded, smiling once more. "I see you have. I am aware of the recent kidnappings in Beit Lahia, but I am not directly connected to them. However, as you might guess from my position in the community, I do know many people, and some are involved in the various sides of the political and religious…shall we say," he waved his hand as if conjuring up the right word, "*discussions* that are taking place in our country these days."

The Imam gazed across the room, then brought his attention back to her. He spoke quietly and deliberately.

"There is a terrorist organization from Iran which people refer to as Nuqi al-Islam. At times they have teamed with Al-Qaeda, the terrorist group that originated in Saudi Arabia. Their mission is to destroy Israel. At all costs.

"While Nuqi al-Islam is from Iran, splinter groups have now formed in many countries. They steal innocent people from their homes, mostly those who already have hate in their hearts, and those, like your brother, who are young and moldable or have something they need, like money, connections, or special knowledge. They take them to different places, sometimes in different countries…training camps in Africa, Asia, and Iran. There, they are brainwashed and taught elements of terrorism, like making bombs, using automatic weapons, infiltrating communities, starting riots and unrest, and other evil notions.

"It is believed that Nuqi al-Islam is the group behind the kidnappings in Palestine, here in the Gaza Strip, where the Israelis have stirred a lot of anger with their actions in recent years. They came here after the bombings several years ago, but have only recently set up the connections to get the kidnap victims out of Palestine, past the Israeli checkpoints."

A look of devastation flashed in Liyah's eyes. "How will I ever find Khalib, then? I thought you could help. Without you, there is no hope." She searched his eyes beseechingly.

The imam extended his hand, and upon receiving hers, cupped his other hand on top of both. "Perhaps there is a reason I was mentioned by your friend after all," he reassured her. "I know a man in Jerusalem who has had strong ties to some of the radical groups in the past. He is a muezzin, the one who calls people to prayer. He is at an ancient mosque in the Old City. He has not been involved with these people ever since many of them turned to even more extreme activity. He doesn't believe in the bombing of innocent people and children regardless of the cause like these terrorists do. But he has many connections, and if anyone could help, he might be the one."

"I will go to him immediately," Liyah replied emphatically.

"It is difficult for a woman, let alone a girl, to travel by herself throughout Palestine, as you well know, my dear. It could be quite dangerous as well if you run into some of these people. Besides, what will you do if you find out where he is? You won't be able to help him by yourself. And I cannot risk my involvement from this side. No one must find out who I am or about my involvement in these affairs.

He's right, Liyah thought. *What could she possibly do by herself?* Her heart sank with the weight of his words. But then she remembered the friends she met only a week ago, and the words of the mystical Ooray about *fearing* and *leading*. She straightened her droopy shoulders.

"Don't worry, my Imam, I will keep your name out of this. I have friends…they will come. I know they will help me and protect me. I will need the name of your contact and how to find him. Can you do this for me?"

The imam studied her face before speaking. "You are a good sister, my young friend, and a brave one. I can see you love your brother very much. I am worried for you…but yes, I will do that. Do you have something to write on?"

Liyah separated the wooden latch of her woven handbag and reached in. She took out a pen and a small piece of paper, handing them to him.

The imam wrote the name of the man and the mosque in East Jerusalem on the paper and then handed it back to her. "You can use my name with him. But no one else."

"Yes, I understand. I really appreciate this. I don't know how to thank you."

"Just bring your brother home safely. These are troubled times," said the imam as he turned to leave. "May Allah go with you."

"And with you, my Imam."

Liyah watched him disappear behind the farthest pillar. She stuffed the paper into her purse, and headed out of the mosque, to the street.

I'm gonna be late, she fretted, quickening her pace along the sidewalk. *I can be home in twenty minutes if I hurry,* she thought, *maybe still early enough to fend off any anger from Mom.*

Halfway home, Liyah heard her phone ring. Without breaking stride, she freed it from her purse and brought it to her ear. "Mom?" There was a long pause. "At the Dawn?" she asked, her voice charged with fear and anxiety. The two explosions and plumes of smoke filled her mind again as a queasiness gripped her stomach. "What? Is anyone hurt?…Yes…I'm almost home. I'll be right there."

THREE

LIYAH TURNED THE corner and saw her mother waiting on the sidewalk in front of their home, looking in the opposite direction. As she got closer, her mother turned and called out.

"Where've you been, young lady?

"I, I..."

"Well never mind," her mother added, in a huff. "There's no time for that. The taxi at the curb is for us."

Her mother's tone seemed more anxious than angry to Liyah. "Tell me more about what happened at the Dawn," she implored, her rising anxiety capturing her thoughts. "Any news?"

"Bombs blew up across the street. At the Media Building."

Liyah gasped. "Oh, no!"

"Yes. I know," her mother acknowledged, opening the door to the cab then sliding in next to Liyah. She caught the driver's eyes in his mirror. "Filastin Dawn, please...Jabalia. Hurry." She turned back to Liyah. "Someone called from the office a few minutes ago. He said the windows of the paper had been blown in, and that your dad was out in the street, trying to help somehow.

Liyah reached for her mother's hand, her voice choking up. "Is he...alright?"

"Well I think so. That's what I was told, anyway."

"But we don't really know then, do we?" Liyah questioned, doubting the reply. "He tends to downplay everything, doesn't he? Remember the time when a bomb went off right outside the paper a few years ago? He ended up in the hospital with glass shards in his legs. He told everyone he was okay then, too."

"Uh-huh. I know, I know," her mom replied quietly, patting her hand. "But your dad assured them."

"He always does, Mother."

The two sat in silence the rest of the way. A block from the offices, the driver pulled the cab to a stop at the curb. He checked the mirror again, his brown eyes searching to connect. "Can't get any closer. Police have it cordoned off." He paused briefly. "That'll be twenty."

Liyah's mom pulled a twenty-shekel note from her purse along with five extra one-shekel coins, passing them forward. The man nodded. "*Shukran.*"

Pushing open the cab door, Liyah wedged her way through the narrow opening. She stood on the sidewalk and turned around, opening the door fully and offering an outstretched hand. Her mom latched onto it and pulled herself up beside her.

Liyah headed swiftly down the street, her mom in tow. As they neared the building Liyah's eyes widened, and her pace slowed. Just ahead she could see plumes of thick black smoke rising from across the street, and blue and red flashing lights from police cars and emergency vehicles. People rushed past, jostling her as they fled the site. A few hustled past her, toward the commotion. *Curiosity seekers? Rescuers?*

It took only a few more steps before the devastation, once blocked by the surrounding buildings, unfolded into Liyah's view. Next to the boarded-up hole that marked the remnants of the recent Israeli attack on the old Media Building appeared the new wreckage of its neighbor, the media's replacement home—a re-purposed six-story cement structure that housed several media outlets, including the local cable TV station and several international news outlets.

Police dressed in dark blue riot gear—heavily helmeted, with bulletproof jackets and Kevlar pants, stood guard in front of hastily assembled precast traffic barriers, while rescue workers combed over giant piles of torn floors and crumbled walls.

Liyah had visited that building with her dad not too long ago. Her mind raced. *Those six, once vibrant stories of activity were now stacked upon one another, just a pile of rubble filling a deep chasm blasted out of the earth.* She looked at the broken concrete slabs, their deformed iron rebar fingers protruding out the ends, stacked like dead soldiers on the battlefield. She studied the rescuers who searched through the devastation, wearing gas masks to guard against the dust that choked the air, still swirling outward into the nearby streets, and swallowing up everything in its path.

She turned her back to the scene, covering her mouth tightly with her hijab. She lowered her head and yanked her mom's hand. Together, they hastily crossed the street and headed a few doors down toward the Filastin Dawn, a much smaller building than the new media building *had been.* It had not been attacked directly, but the concussion from the explosion and flying debris had punctured holes in its façade;

the windows were completely blown in on all three floors, and the large entrance door hung precariously on a single top hinge.

Gingerly slipping past the door, Liyah and her mother made their way into the reception area. Shattered fragments of glass and concrete littered the floor. No one was there. Some of the dust had settled but the finest of the particles remained suspended, slightly clouding her vision. She made her way down the hall, past the executive offices, with her mother following. *Where was her dad? She hadn't seen him outside.*

Entering the middle of the building, she made a left and headed toward the conference room. The door was closed, but through its large soundproof windows, she caught a glimpse of the side view of a tall man standing at the end of the long table, addressing a number of men sitting in swivel chairs along both sides. He had thick graying hair and wore a light blue dress shirt, unbuttoned at the collar, with a red and white striped tie hung loosely around his neck. No mistaking—*It was him!*

Unable to restrain herself, Liyah tapped lightly on the glass with the nail of her index finger.

"Liyah," her mother whispered in a stern tone.

Her dad rotated his head just enough to catch a glimpse of her out of the corner of his right eye, then turned it slowly back toward his audience without giving notice.

Liyah and her mother stepped into the office across the hall, sitting down in the nearest chairs. They waited silently, but impatiently. At the click of the conference room door, Liyah sprang up. She took short, anxious steps toward the door as the room emptied, then forced her way between the last couple of stragglers and into the room. She flung herself at her dad. Tears poured down her cheeks as she hugged him, before finally loosening her grip. She searched his eyes.

"Baba, we were afraid you might be hurt."

He patted her head, then placed his hands on the sides of her face and smiled. Shifting his eyes to his wife who had just joined them, he nodded. "I told them to tell your mother everything was okay."

"Well it seems your daughter is right about you," she replied, her lips narrowing ever so slightly then relaxing.

"And what is that?" he asked, bringing her to him with his other arm, then hugging them both.

"That you're not exactly truthful at times like this."

"But I did tell the truth," he protested. "I'm fine."

"Not the whole truth," Liyah countered, frowning. "The front of the Dawn is a mess…there's chaos everywhere." She glanced at the dirt and cuts on his arms exposed by the rolled-up sleeves of his shirt, and then the layer of dust coating his pants. "And what happened to you? You *are* hurt. Were you in the front when the bomb went off?"

His eyes traced the path of Liyah's, then rose to meet his wife's stare. His countenance turned somber as he addressed her. "It wasn't a bomb. It was mortar fire…two small missiles, actually. One right after another. Both hit the building across the street."

"We saw the damage," her mother replied. "It's horrible. A war zone. We couldn't get near." She looked over at Liyah.

Liyah's face fell as she remembered the two deep muffled sounds she had heard on her way home. "So how did you get so dirty and cut up?" she asked, her voice unsteady.

"Once I knew everyone here was okay at the Dawn, I went across the street to see what I could do. The smoke and dust were so heavy I had to take frequent rests to catch my breath. I helped dig through the ruins and pulled a few people out. Some were dead, many others severely injured, and a few miraculously unhurt but in shock. The police arrived within ten minutes, followed by a rescue team another ten minutes after that."

"That's when you came back?" Liyah asked.

"They cleared the area. It was too dangerous. I came back here to get everyone together and tell them what to do. That was the meeting that just ended. The reporters and video team that were still here are now covering the situation outside. Since part of the front of the building has been blown in, some people will remain here to make sure the rooms are locked up well and all the recent files are securely backed up. Others will place calls to loved ones to reassure them. But news is news…and this is *big* news…so a skeleton staff will remain all night to report the latest on what's happening, and guard against possible looting. I'm free to go home, but I'll have to return very early in the morning and be on call all night. I think–"

"Sir, excuse me, sir," a young man uttered, breathless, as he frantically rushed into the room. He handed her father a ring of keys. "The presses are safe, locked down temporarily. I gave Mahdi the other set. He'll work with the reporters to keep one pod open and ready to cover this story. I'll go see if anyone else needs help." He looked over at Liyah, appearing surprised, as if only then had he noticed there were others in the room.

"You know Ahmad, don't you Liyah?" her dad queried.

"Ah, yeah," she stammered, caught by surprise. Her mind shifted to the dinner party at the house the previous week when Khalib had gone missing. She had been so excited to see Ahmad, even if he didn't know that she had a crush on him. He must have left before she got home. In all the turmoil that followed she completely forgot about him. She looked to the side for a moment to catch her courage, then back.

"Hi, Ahmad. What are you doing here?"

"What, no 'How are you'?" her dad admonished.

"She hasn't been properly introduced, David," her mother responded sternly.

"What?" her husband replied. "They're like acquaintances, aren't they? Well, I thought they were, and besides, what difference does that make? He was at the party last week."

"But Liyah came late," she admonished. "Remember?"

"This is all nonsense these days, isn't it?"

His wife frowned and Liyah jumped in. "Sorry, you caught me by surprise, Ahmad. I wasn't expecting to see you. Especially here."

"No worries. I get it. I only started working here a month ago."

"I hired Ahmad to help out with a few things when he wasn't at school," her father added. "He's the brother of one of Khalib's friends."

Liyah kept her head forward–but let her eyes drift toward her father. "I *know that*, Dad."

Ahmad turned to her father. "Any news on him?" he asked, hesitantly.

"Unfortunately, no."

An uncomfortable silence filled the room. Ahmad stared at his feet, finally bringing his eyes back up, scanning all three of them. "Sorry to hear," he replied, his voice unsteady, balking. "It's awful what happened here isn't it? I've got to go help out." He lowered his head. "Sorry for the rush. Hope to see you under better circumstances, Liyah."

"Me, too," she assured him, as he turned and bolted out of the room and down the hall.

A loud, heavy crash suddenly jolted the walls and blew a cloud of dust through the hole in the front of the building. Her dad rushed toward the entrance, Liyah and her mom following briskly behind.

They stepped outside, gazing across the street. Sirens blared out their *whoop-whoop* alarms. Blue, red, and yellow lights flashed and whirled through the lenses of dozens of police cars, fire trucks, and other emergency vehicles. Several floors of the building on the left of the first pile of rubble had just collapsed. A group of emergency personnel rushed over to assess the situation.

"Oh, Allah. It's awful!" Liyah cried out in anguish, looking across to where the rescue team was working diligently, digging through mounds of concrete chunks, unrecognizable metal objects, fractured pipes, and pieces of *everything*—packed solid under their collective weight…searching for survivors, or bodies, but not making even the smallest perceptible dent in the hills of debris. The horror of it filled her mind. She whispered into the hot, dust-filled air. "It's starting all over again..."

Liyah's mind flew back into the past. She remembered when she was little and was left abandoned under the rubble of her home, and when she fell through the cave floor while she and Morningstar were out gathering food only a week ago. She had overcome all that and was stronger now. *But there are people under this pile…still. And I know that feeling. Maybe I can't help Khalib yet but I can help them.* Her emotions swamped her. She broke out in a run across the street.

"Liyah!" her dad shouted, chasing after her, and stumbling upon the pile of debris before catching her.

"Allah, Allah, Liyah! What do you think you're doing?"

"If there are people under here, they are suffocating, Dad."

He grabbed her hand. "Come. There is nothing you can do here. These people have it under control and are doing their best." He tugged at her arm.

"But Baba…" Liyah pleaded.

"Come, sweetie. We need to concentrate our efforts on finding your brother."

"I can't seem to help him either," she complained, tears appearing under her eyes.

"Come." Her dad coughed as he led her back to where his wife was standing.

"It's all too much," Liyah said as she and her dad stood there, brushing off their clothes.

"I'm afraid you're right, Liyah," he replied. "The times ahead do not bode well. I only hope this doesn't turn into an escalation that can't be stopped. I fear for our country. At least what remains of it."

He led them two blocks away to a small parking garage. While the attendant retrieved the car, Liyah and her mom remained on the sidewalk. They watched in stunned fixation the flight of people to and from the disaster scene and listened to the commotion and chaos emanating from yet another *ground zero*. After handing the attendant a tip, her dad slipped behind the wheel. He eased the car out of the garage, bringing down his window as he approached his wife and daughter. "Sit in the back with Liyah, would you, dear? She's pretty upset."

Once situated, the drive home seemed to take forever to Liyah. Traffic was thick and slowed to a near standstill. Even some of the side streets were clogged. After about ten blocks, things finally thinned out a bit. A short time later, their street sign came into view.

The car pulled up in front of the house and her dad shut off the engine. The quiet calm inside the car, the green of the bushes, and the nicely trimmed lawn lining the side of the walkway leading to the front door seemed surreal to Liyah—the polar opposite of where they had just been with the screaming sirens, mayhem, suffocating dust, and the solid gray cloud everywhere she looked.

No one moved for a few moments, as if there was nothing to entice them out of their temporary shelter. *What was there to look forward to?* Liyah mourned. *An empty house? An only son and brother missing? The beginning of more trouble with the Israelis? More rocket attacks? Bad news on the TV?*

Time had stopped there in the car. *And I am safe,* Liyah thought.

The driver's door of the car snapped open. The spell was broken.

There hadn't been many times recently, if any, when they were able to be together like this, Liyah considered. Her dad worked long hours and had seemed somewhat depressed since Khalib had disappeared, her mom anxious and preoccupied. As for her? Well, she didn't seem to have much time or motivation to chat. Between school and the guilt of not returning Khalib home safe to the party, her mind seemed fragmented, allowing only small thoughts to filter in from time to time. *After all, wasn't it her fault that he was somewhere out there with some terrorists? Wasn't it?*

After entering the house Liyah turned to her mother. "Think I'll read and take a nap."

"Good idea, dear. I'll plan a snack for dusk, something light before we have dinner, to break the fast for today."

Liyah rested quietly on her bed, her head propped up by her pillow. She had no intention of napping; depressing as it was so far, the day had not made her tired in the least bit. It made her restless. She stared at the wood beams traversing the ceiling. She thought about how nice it had been to grow up here, with loving parents, even if they were stodgy *old-school* types at times, especially her mom. *They probably couldn't help it,* she wondered, *trying to hold on to traditional things and beliefs—from serving meals in the formal dining room, fasting every day during Ramadan, and worrying how and when Liyah should be introduced to boys.* They believed Palestine still had hopes of becoming its own state, but that of course was more uncertain than ever in Liyah's eyes.

She traced the beam right above her head toward the far wall, then down to the small painted desk across from the foot of the bed. She remembered the day her dad brought it home, a faded yellow relic, its surface chipped and gouged. He told her he was going to give it *love and attention* so that she could have her own special desk to do her schoolwork. She was only nine at the time; it seemed the next seven years had passed in the blink of an eye. On her tenth birthday, he brought it up from the basement to this room. And it hadn't moved after all these years.

It had been reborn, Liyah had thought at the time. She studied it now. It was as beautiful and elegant as the day he set it there. Its surface was flawless and hung slightly over the face of the drawers—a single wide one in the middle and three down the right side, each with an ornate brass handle. The legs of the desk curved gently outward then returned inward, resting on delicately carved cats' feet. He had painted it light purple, with small swirls of pink floating like clouds across its length. She remembered what he had said the very moment he uncovered it for her: *This desk is like an iris, Liyah, the flower of Palestine. The purple iris, like you, is one of the most beautiful and intricate flowers in the world. It was named by the Greeks. It means rainbow, and it symbolizes eloquence, hope, wisdom, communication, and faith.*

Faith. Liyah's thoughts drifted to her visit with the imam, then to Khalib, lost out there. Somewhere…in danger. Her attention circled back to the top of the desk, and to her purse. Her eyes widened. She sat up with a start. Moving to the desk, she grabbed the purse, unlatched it frantically, and looked inside. It was still there—the piece of paper with the address. There was her bracelet too, the one Ooray had given all of them—her, Morningstar, Kai Li, and Zack.

About a week had passed, and yet she had put much of what had happened on that strange journey with her three new friends out of her mind, too absorbed with finding Khalib. But then there was what she had said to the imam…*not to worry, that she had friends who would help. What friends? These friends…of course.*

Liyah retrieved the bracelet and slipped it on her wrist. She opened the middle drawer of the desk and took out the necklace she had placed securely in the rear corner—the Timeless Teardrop. She lifted it over her head and set it gently down onto her neck. The bright red ruby dangled on her chest, catching the light from the late afternoon sun streaming through the windows. The facets reflected the rays like a red disco ball, glittering on the surface of everything in the room.

Should she contact her friends now? She knew what to do, but not how to do it. She thought of what Ooray had said, that she only needed to think of them while holding onto the necklace. *Or was it the bracelet? Or their specific symbols on the bracelet?*

She paused. *How was she going to explain this to her parents if all three of them showed up? It would probably be tough enough, anyway, to just explain Morningstar's appearance.* To be safe, until she learned more about using the powers of the necklace and bracelet, she would use both objects, she thought. With her left hand she grabbed hold of the bracelet that was Morningstar's symbol—the Web of Life—then lifted her right hand to her chest, touching the ruby with her fingers. She calmed her mind then began thinking of Morningstar. The bracelet began vibrating; she concentrated harder, imagining Morningstar coming to the house, to her. It then started to pulsate, slowly at first, then faster and faster, until it began to hum…then both the bracelet and the ruby suddenly stopped vibrating altogether.

Liyah took her fingers from the ruby and let go of the bracelet. *Was that it? Will she get the message? How will she know?...And when will she come?*

Having missed her opportunity for a nap, Liyah gathered herself together and headed down the stairs to get her pre-dinner snack. *This fasting business is tough,* she said to herself. *It's going to be even harder if Star shows up and I have to watch her eat during the day…while I starve.*

Wednesday Before Easter

FOUR

THE EVENING HAD passed, and Liyah woke to the sound of a blender whirring, its blades beating against the inside of the metal bowl. The room was still dark, but she knew she needed to be downstairs soon for breakfast before the sun came up; otherwise, she'd have nothing in her stomach to sustain her during the day's fast—not until dusk. Instead, she snuggled deeper into the sheets under her warm puffy quilt. *Just a few more minutes,* she thought, before drifting off.

The sun began to rise, prying into the room through the gap in the drapes, striking Liyah's eyes. Her eyelids slowly opened, then blinked several times as her mind began to ease itself into the new day. A fuzzy image appeared before her, its details finally coming into focus.

"What! Who…" she gasped, her upper body bolting upright, resting on her elbows.

"Hi, Liyah. I didn't think we'd see each other again so soon," the voice said.

In the small, soft armchair in the corner of the room, sat a girl. She looked familiar. Liyah's eyes focused more intensely.

"Oh, Allah! Allah! Is it you?"

"Well, who else? You called, didn't you? It's a way different time zone in South Dakota, you know. I looked it up…eight hours difference." She smiled. "I was visiting my grandfather when your ruby stone on the bracelet started flashing. I had to wait until I thought it might be a good time here…but then again, I'm not sure how the *time thing* works in all this. It seemed to stop last week, didn't it? Very strange."

Liyah jumped out of bed and rushed at her. Morningstar had just enough time to stand before Liyah enveloped her in a huge hug. She took her by the hand. "Come. Come. Sit on the bed with me."

Morningstar obliged. They faced each other cross-legged, simultaneously spitting out words at each other like the spattering of machine gun fire, each trying to start the conversation, then stopping, then starting again.

Liyah finally won out. "I almost didn't recognize you," she gushed, breathlessly.

"Must be the one long braid instead of the pigtails."

Morningstar chuckled. "I *should* be pretty much the same, as you might suspect, since everything I owned went up with the tornado. I still have what I was wearing then—my jeans, moccasins, tunic, and red bandana. But I hear that's a popular headdress here." She grinned.

Liyah's mind flashed back to the previous week, when she was swept up into a light that brought her to another world, where she woke up surrounded by Morningstar and the two boys: Zack, and Kai Li. She remembered their dangerous trials, helping each other survive, overcoming their fears, and growing so close together in such a short time. And the mission. It had all come back. Such little time had passed since then, and in all the confusion, she must have put it all out of her mind.

Liyah blinked, forcing her mind back into the present. "Yes, yes! Wow! It's truly you, Star! And of course, now I see the bracelet, and your Web of Life silver necklace." She waved her hands wildly as she rattled off an uninterrupted series of questions without expecting any immediate answers. Then an important one popped into her mind.

"Before I tell you why I needed you, you have to fill me in on your grandfather…your *lala*, as you called him during our strange adventure last week. "Am I hearing you right? He's alive? It seems like ages ago already but it's been less than a week. Can you believe it?"

Morningstar grabbed Liyah's wrists to slow her motions. "I love that you're so excited, but I don't want to be knocked out."

Liyah laughed, settled down, then sat silently. She admired Morningstar's ability to gain control of herself in almost any situation. *She had learned a lot from her in that place,* she thought…*wherever it was.* "Okay, okay. Go on."

They locked eyes. Morningstar quieted her voice, then began. "When I got back home, to where the trailer used to be before the tornado, I learned that he had survived, barely, and was in a hospital. He's still recovering there, and I hope he'll be released soon…some broken bones and a punctured lung. I've been staying in a makeshift shelter with a lot of other people who lost family or are simply homeless because of that storm. When you called out to me, I was sitting next to him in his hospital room. The bracelet vibrated and the Timeless Teardrop pulsated bright red…so I knew it was you."

"What did you tell him?"

"Well, it was actually him. He noticed it first and pointed to it. I didn't say anything. Just that it was a gift, and that I would tell him more another time.

"I don't know what to say about mine, Star. My mom has noticed it, but I avoid answering her questions."

Morningstar nodded. "I don't know if our families are ready yet. I can't say I'm fully ready either. I'm still experimenting with the powers." She flipped her wrist back and forth as she glanced down at the bracelet. "It's mind-boggling. I used both the necklace and the bracelet together, then thought of you to see if it would get me to you. Seems almost like that journey never happened, except for these gifts Ooray gave us, and the fact that now we're together again."

"I know what you mean…and Ooray!" She shook her head in disbelief. "It's crazy. I wonder if we'll ever see him again…or is it her?" A broad smile lit up her face.

"I guess we'll have more time to catch up, so tell me now," Morningstar pressed. "What's the problem? Must be pretty important."

Liyah took in a deep breath, sighed, then grabbed hold of Morningstar's hand. She felt the deep connection again, like at the end of their time together with Zack and Kai Li. Tears started to well up under her dark brown eyes.

"My brother, Khalib, was abducted by terrorists. At least that's what we think."

"I'm so sorry Liyah. I really am," Morningstar said as she squeezed Liyah's hand tightly. "I'd do anything to help. But this is a foreign place for me. I don't know its ways. And I'm not really a spymaster of any kind, you know." She smiled ever so slightly.

The tears formed a trickle, lightly cascading down over Liyah's cheeks. "I know. I know. I just need support, another brain. And you have a good one." She forced a smile. "Maybe we have to contact Ooray again, if we even can? But beyond that, I got the name of a man in Jerusalem who might be able to help. He's connected to several terrorist groups. I told the person who gave me his information that I had friends who would help. He agreed to assist me, only under *that* assurance, and that I would not speak his name."

Morningstar paused briefly before answering. "What about your friends here?"

"I really don't have any. I mean, at least not ones that could help in something like this. It's too dangerous, and girls here don't have as many freedoms as men. On top of that, no one would understand what you and I can do together."

"We don't either, really," Morningstar replied. "I mean *fully*."

"Yes. But we're learning. And you know what Ooray said: *Together we cannot be defeated.*"

Morningstar smiled broadly. "Okay, my friend. You've got me…at least for a short while. I told my *lala* I needed to get out of the makeshift place I was staying because it was quite depressing…go visit a friend, so I wouldn't be back to the hospital for a bit. He'll start wondering at some point, though. Probably in a handful of days." She paused again. "Shouldn't we be contacting Zack and Kai Li?"

"Let's wait until we see what happens, okay? I can only handle so much right now. We're going to have enough trouble explaining *you* when I take you downstairs for breakfast."

Liyah led her to her brother's room, handing her one of her favorite hijabs. "Put this on. You can freshen up in the hall bathroom. There's an extra towel on the rack. I'll be back in five minutes to take you downstairs."

Liyah brought her clothes into her bathroom, threw some cold water on her face, brushed her hair, then put on her jeans and a red mid-length jumper over her white turtleneck. She slid into a pair of flats, donned her hijab, and returned to Khalib's room. She knocked lightly on the door.

The latch clicked and Morningstar slipped into the hallway beside her.

Reaching the bottom of the stairs, she led Morningstar to the archway of the dining room. Her mom and dad were sitting at the table, her dad reading the paper, her mom fiddling with the serving dishes. Three places had been set, a large china plate, a bowl for cereal, a linen napkin and silver utensils placed at each, with a small glass for orange juice and a larger one for milk at the sides. In the middle of the table was a large serving board holding an assortment of foods in bowls: a starchy cereal made from a local whole grain called freekeh, fruits, olives, tomatoes, boiled eggs, peanut butter and banana sandwiches, nuts, cheeses, and a yogurt-like dish. Liyah could see that her parents had finished their meals.

Liyah entered the room, Morningstar a couple of steps behind and not yet visible.

"It's about time you got up, young lady," her mother admonished. "Your father heard noises coming from your room and insisted I reheat this for you, even though you have broken your fast. We ate before the sun came up, as Allah desires."

"I know, sorry mom, but I'm starving. I'll make it up."

"And just how are you going to do that?" her mom replied. She stood up with her back to Liyah and reached across to add her husband's plate to her own, then turned to make her way into the kitchen. As she did so, her eye caught Morningstar standing in the wings.

"Well, what have we here?" She turned to her husband. "David?"

He continued to read, oblivious to her words.

"David? David, I'm talking to you!"

He pulled his head up out of the paper. "Huh?"

She nodded her head in the direction of the girls.

"Good morning, Baba," Liyah offered, cheerily.

"Well, good morning sweetheart. And who do we have here?"

She stepped to the side, gently grabbed hold of her friend's arm, and coaxed her forward. "This is Morningstar."

Her mom rested her fists on her hips, her lips lightly pursed. "Well, Liyah, it would have been nice if you had told us someone was coming over. Luckily, I planned for a special breakfast this morning, so we have plenty of food." She wrapped her robe more fully around her and pulled the sash tight.

"Nonsense," scoffed Liyah's dad, his expression transforming into a giant smile. "Hello to you, Morningstar. Welcome to our humble home."

"Hi, Mr. Al-Rahim," she managed. "Sorry to surprise you."

Liyah whispered in her ear.

"I mean, Mr. Rahim."

Liyah's mom studied both of them. "I didn't hear the front door close, Liyah, or the doorbell for that matter. It's like she floated in from the sky. Is this a new friend? Are you doing something special at school today? Maybe a play? That's quite an outfit you have on, dear."

"Mom! Jeez." Liyah blurted out. "Enough with the questions. Besides, there isn't any school this week, don't you remember? It's spring recess. And it's already Wednesday." Liyah reached out in front of her, her palms to the ceiling, as if wondering how her mom could have possibly forgotten. "I've been off for two days."

The legs of her dad's chair scraped along the tiles like chalk on a blackboard as he pushed it back and stood up. "That's right. Of course," he said, turning to his wife and smiling. "What's gotten into you, Rania? Must be all these missiles and hot tempers." His tone changed from playful to slightly somber. He continued, "got everyone on edge." He walked over and shook Morningstar's hand. "Sit, sit, you two. Eat. So happy to have you join us for *suhur,* our morning Ramadan breakfast before fasting for the day. Let's chat about the day ahead."

Liyah's mom, still looking confused and with unanswered questions, took the used plates into the kitchen and then set a place for Morningstar. She dished out hot cereal, still warm, from the pot, and filled the two small glasses with juice before reclaiming her seat.

"I apologize if I gave you a bad impression just now, Morningstar. I wasn't expecting to see anyone here, otherwise, I would have put on a more formal morning gown, not this old thing." She grabbed hold of one of the terrycloth sleeves, shaking it.

"I don't mind," Morningstar replied, not leaving any space to be questioned. "I mean, really. Liyah has said so many good things about you. She's so lucky to have you. Both of you. I only have my grandfather. My parents died in a fire when I was little. I wouldn't care what they wore if they were here at the table with us in this different place."

Liyah's mom held up a carafe of what Morningstar would later find out to be goat's milk, and passed it to her. "Here you go dear," she offered. "So sorry to hear that. It must have been very difficult for you."

Morningstar poured some milk into her bowl, mixed it into the cereal, then passed it over to Liyah. "I really don't remember them much, except for looking at a few pictures. I was very young. The pictures helped keep them alive for me when their memory would start to fade."

Liyah's mom studied Morningstar, lingering a few seconds on her clothing. "Well, you are certainly welcome here. What did you mean by a *different place*? You don't live here in Beit Lahia? I guess I don't remem…"

"No, she doesn't, Mom," Liyah interrupted. "She's from far away. America. That's why she's wearing her native clothes."

"That's wonderful!" Liyah's dad chimed in. "How long will you be here?"

Morningstar lifted a spoonful of cereal toward her mouth. "I'm not sure. I…"

Liyah cut her off, feeling a touch of panic gripping her. "She's on a tour…to Jerusalem. Uh, it's one of those where they plan formal group things, but you can also do your own thing. She, uh, plans to stay in the area for a few days while the tour goes somewhere else. Then she'll join up again before returning home."

Morningstar stared at the furrows forming on Mrs. Rahim's forehead. She gulped silently, glancing back and forth between Liyah and her mom.

"How long have you two been friends?" her mother asked.

"I…well…We met in the square yesterday when I was doing an errand."

Her mother looked over at her father and then back to her. "Hmm, are you girls…"

"Well, well, well," Liyah's dad broke in. "I suppose you still need a place to stay? You can stay here, of course. We'd love that."

"David, I'm sure she has other plans."

"Nonsense! I won't have it. She can bring her suitcase into Khalib's room." He looked to Rania. "Or stay with Liyah in her room."

"Well, actually Dad…her stuff is on the bus. It, uh, took off before she could get her bag."

Liyah's mom frowned, once more studying the two girls.

Morningstar jerked her head as Liyah's dad smacked the fat of his palms on the table. "Okay then. It's settled."

Morningstar lifted another spoonful to her mouth then glanced over at Liyah's mom, still staring at her husband, who immediately changed the subject. "So, how do you like your cereal, Morningstar? I bet you never had it before?"

"It's very delicious, Mr. Rahim. It reminds me of a dish at home. What's in it?"

Liyah's mom appeared to settle down, obviously pleased with Morningstar's response. "It's made from wheat..."

"Durum wheat," her husband added. "It's famous. "*Native*," he emphasized, "to Palestine."

Liyah flashed a displeased look. "D-a-a-d! Really?"

Morningstar chuckled.

Liyah's mom continued, her face easing into a smile. "Perhaps it's like your oatmeal. I put in raisins and mixed it with a glaze. Very common here."

Morningstar tasted another half-spoon. "It's sort of loose, if you know what I mean, not sticky-creamy like oatmeal. More like our traditional pudding, which is made with corn and molasses." She tasted it again. "But it's very similar…sweet…nice."

"The glaze is made from dates, also *native* to here." She sent a mischievous smile to her husband and daughter. "We boil down the juice so that it's actually very similar to molasses."

"You must still be exhausted from all the traveling," Liyah's dad suggested. "Unfortunately, I have to get going. I'm meeting someone for coffee at the Branch Café downtown. What are your plans for the day, you two?"

Liyah shrugged. "Not sure yet. I thought I'd show Morningstar around a bit."

"Fine. Have fun," he said, grabbing his suit jacket from the back of the chair, and the newspaper from the table. Passing through the hall, he picked his briefcase up off the bureau and made his way to the door. Liyah's mother met him there.

"Something doesn't fit," she said quietly, pointing her head several times toward the kitchen.

"I know dear." He whispered back. "It will be okay. Just make sure they stay in contact with you. There's a lot happening this week with all the celebrations coming up and Khalib still missing. And political tensions are still rising."

He opened the door and kissed her on the cheek. "Can we discuss all this later? I've really got to go."

FIVE

Jabalia

ACROSS THE STREET from the *Filastin Dawn* headquarters, above the pile of rubble, the sun rose over the rooftops in a cloudless sky. Most of the dust from the explosion had settled, but a fine mist of tiny particles still floated about, dimming the morning light. A dozen or more rescuers wandered over the cement and crushed metal hill that was once the new Media Building. A cadre of construction vehicles consisting of small cranes, utility Bobcat excavators, and bulldozers assisted the workers, moving the debris, loading dump trucks, buzzing and beeping. Men in yellow-green safety vests prodded and poked the tangled mess, desperately searching for any signs of life.

A dark form approached the scene and ducked under the yellow tape marked *Do Not Cross* in bold, black letters, delineating the boundary of the crime scene. A nearby policeman narrowed the distance between them, shouting. "Hey! You! This area is cordoned off. You're not allowed here."

The shadowy person continued on, mounting the pile, walking toward the workers, not hearing, or perhaps not heeding, the warning. The officer scrambled up the base of the wreckage, tripping over loose chunks of debris, finally catching up. "Hold it!" he demanded, grabbing the shoulder of the intruder, who halted, then turned to face him.

"Nura!" gasped the officer, taking a step back.

A girl, dressed in a black, double-breasted trench coat, collar up, stared into his eyes. The only visible part of her young face was the mysterious mask formed by her dark, shapely eyebrows, long black eyelashes, and the white that surrounded her light eyes. The rest of her face, head, and neck was covered by a white keffiyeh headdress with a black fishnet design. The keffiyeh was unmistakable: the unification symbol of Palestine. It stood for the history of the region—the fishermen, the original rural settlers, and the trade center of the ancient world. The lines connecting the knots of the net reflected the important trade routes that all passed through Palestine; and the olive leaves, forming the knots, symbolized the resilience and strength of the Palestinian people.

The officer recognized her immediately, although he'd never met her. She was real to many, but also a rumor—a shadowy ghost, appearing when least expected, sometimes in the midst of a riot, or feeding the poor, or soothing the injured. She was a legend already with the women who were fighting for their rights in the entire Arabic region. But many men also respected her, even if threatened by her fearless independence. She was calm and quiet, yet resolute. *Filled with light* those who followed her would say—the very meaning of her name.

"Hello, officer. What can I do to help?" The words poured out slowly, solidly, like melted honey, filling his ears. He was locked into her stare.

"I…I," his voice failed him. He took a breath. "This is no place for you."

"But surely it is exactly the place for me."

"There is nothing left, only the stench that comes with burned flesh. There is only danger here."

"There is no danger here, only hope," she said softly, almost in a whisper, before pausing a moment. "Hope that we may find someone alive. Hope that one day this will all end. Where have they taken the people?"

"You mean the survivors?" He hesitated before giving in. "Several hospitals. Most are at Kamal Adwan."

She nodded, then bowed. "Thank you for your service, sir. Please search until we are sure there are no more. Never give up. And deliver my gratitude and blessings to the other workers if you would be so kind."

The officer watched her, frozen, his eyes glued to her back as she made her way down the mound of death and then along the sidewalk, until she disappeared from view.

The Branch Cafe was not a place Ahmad had been to before, even though it was on his way to work. He still had one more year to complete his secondary education and hadn't yet adopted a liking for coffee. He preferred his American sodas…when he could get them.

But many companies had shuttered their doors in Gaza over the recent years due to the open hostilities. It didn't really matter whether they left Palestine entirely or re-opened in the West Bank. Gaza lost either way: more unemployment, higher poverty, and fewer options. The Branch was also upscale, not something Ahmad could afford anyway.

He entered the cafe and immediately began scouting for Liyah's dad. There was a bustle about it this morning, even after the attacks of the previous day that happened only about a mile away. Or maybe it was because of them? People congregating, getting close, nervous, defiant.

Ahmad had no difficulty spotting his boss standing at the counter. He was almost a head above everyone, well-dressed as usual, and his profile reminded Ahmad of an Egyptian general—strong jaw, close-cut graying beard with a well-trimmed mustache. He made his way over, greeting him with a wave of his hand as he approached.

"Good morning, Mr. Rahim. Sir."

"*As-Salaam-Alaikum*, Ahmad."

"*Wa-Alaikum-Salaam*," Ahmad returned, thinking maybe he should have greeted him first in Arabic, even though English was frequently spoken in the office, as well as in many meetings."

"What can I get for you?"

"Nothing, sir. I'm fine."

"Don't be shy. I asked you here. How about a cappuccino?"

He hesitated, not sure whether to hold his ground or avoid causing any friction. After all, he was still getting used to working at the paper and didn't know his boss that well, even though their families knew each other, his adopted family that is. *Perhaps I should try one anyway*, he thought. *What's there to lose?*

"Uh, okay. Thank you."

His boss turned back to the counter and held out his card. "Two cappuccinos please."

The man behind the counter entered the sale, then processed the card. "Name?"

"David."

"Thank you, David." He passed the slip to the barista and moved to the next patron.

Liyah's dad found a table in the corner and took a seat looking out to the street. Ahmad sat facing him. He didn't say anything, which set Ahmad's nerves on edge even more than they had been in anticipation of coming here. *What kind of message was his boss talking about?* He had a few contacts there in Gaza City he met through some friends, and he knew they were somehow involved in the launching of rockets into Israel at times. But mostly he was trying to find influential people so he could write an article for the *Filastin Dawn*—to impress Mr. Rahim and maybe someday become an actual journalist himself.

He wanted to write about how lopsided the conflict was but without anger or bias. And he especially wanted to write about how technology was used to weaponize both sides, making the companies rich while taking a toll on the lives of his countrymen and the fragile Palestinian economy. But he didn't want to move too fast with these new contacts before he even had a chance to establish a relationship. But then again, he didn't want to disappoint his boss either.

"When we're done here, I'll give you a ride to work."

Ahmad began unconsciously tapping his finger on the table. "No need, sir. I have a car."

"Am I making you nervous, Ahmad?" asked his boss, watching as Ahmad wrung his hands.

He stopped fidgeting and looked at his boss. "Ah…no, sir. Not really, sir. I mean I have a lot on my mind."

"Oh. Do you want to share?"

A voice called out from the front. "Mr. David, Mr. David. Your coffees are ready."

Ahmad rose. "I'll get them, sir." He made his way to the counter, happy to deflect any further interrogation. When he returned, Liyah's dad was on his cell, looking out the window.

"Yes, yes. I see…Ministry of Defense…Hmm, special passes? Okay, that could be helpful."

Ahmad set the coffees on the table and took his seat. Mr. Rahim turned from the window and looked over to him, holding up his index finger. "Okay…right." He nodded. "I see. Well, thanks, Lavi. Let me know if you find out anything else. I'll keep the passes in mind. Maybe my team could use some to gain access to more information. I know my daughter would appreciate a couple anyway, for her and her friend to see the Old City. In the meantime, I'll try to get more information to you as well, to help narrow this down…Yes…Okay. *Ma'a salaam.*"

Liyah's dad placed the phone in his shirt pocket. "Thanks, Ahmad. Where were we?"

"I was just thinking," he replied, gaining a degree of confidence. "I don't want you to be disappointed if I can't help you locate Khalib."

"Absolutely not. Sorry if I came on too strong yesterday. I know you have Khalib's interest in mind, just like my family. I would never think otherwise. Now…let's try the cappuccino." He smiled and lifted up his cup and presented it to Ahmad. Ahmad reciprocated.

Ahmad scrunched up his nose, the bitter taste overpowering him.

"Something wrong with it?" Mr. Rahim asked. "Mine seems good."

"No, no. Sorry," he replied, flushed. "Just not used to it, I guess. I thought the steamed milk would tone it down."

"I see. New to this game, are you?" Liyah's dad winked, then let out a small laugh. "Stick a small cube of sugar in it."

Ahmad retrieved three of the cubes from the center of the table and dropped them in.

His boss laughed again. "That should do it."

As they sipped their drinks, Liyah's dad took an envelope out of his pocket. "I'm looking for any information you could get on Khalib's location. There's a note inside that can help you if you need to use it to get more introductions. Many people know me. But even if they don't, you can use it to assure them everything will be kept secret."

He took a small envelope from the inner pocket of his jacket. "Be careful, Ahmad. I don't want you disappearing on us."

Ahmad placed it in the pocket of his shirt. "I may have to go slowly at first, Mr. Rahim. It's not like these guys are my best friends. I just happen to have access to a few who might know something. I'm also trying to develop connections, you know?"

"Yes, I understand."

Ahmad felt his body tighten as the reality of his mission began to solidify. "I'll do my best."

"I know you will, Ahmad. But don't go *too* slow."

"No, sir…uh…I mean yes, sir. Of course, sir."

SIX

EMERGENCY SIRENS BLARED from vehicles still arriving and leaving at the side entrance of the hospital. It was early morning when Nura pushed her black-gloved hands down on the heavy chrome bar and opened the big glass door. The place was abuzz with nurses and doctors hustling in all directions, yelling orders, moving carts, answering phones, and creating extra spaces in hallways to place patients. The energy from yesterday's physical explosion at the Media Building had simply been transformed into human energy within these walls.

A young receptionist, fishing through papers, caught a glimpse of her out of the corner of her eye. She stopped her activity, focusing now on this person headed toward her dressed in a black raincoat with two rows of large buttons down the front, collar up, sashed around the waist. A gray turtleneck was visible at the neckline, and gray knit pants showed below the knees, with cuffs kissing the top of a pair of black running shoes.

Nura approached the desk, her light eyes, dark brows, and modestly curved nose the only identifiable personal features.

"Can I help you?" the receptionist asked.

"I'd like to see the patients from the blast. The ones that are well enough for a visitor...and the Director, please." Her voice was low and steady.

"I...I'm sorry. That would be impossible."

"Why?" Nura questioned, her voice tranquil, her demeanor confident. "I've been here before."

"Well," the receptionist replied in an unsteady voice, "because I don't know you...and besides, you would need a formal pass to see the Director."

A heavyset nurse wearing a surgical mask, green hair cover, and gloves was passing by the desk and heard the exchange. She glanced at Nura, then slipped down the mask so she could be heard. "It's okay, Beth. I'll accompany her." She turned and nodded to Nura.

Nura's shoes squeaked on the shiny waxed floor as they made their way down the hall. After passing through a set of swinging doors and taking several turns, they entered an open ward of over thirty beds, placed only a few feet apart with minimal screening in between them. The patients were in all different levels of need—some sitting up, some walking around, but most of them lying bandaged, and a few with IV lines hanging off metal posts at the bedside.

The nurse led her to a man standing at the side of one of the beds. He was speaking to a doctor in green scrubs. The man was dressed more like a casual businessman than a medical person, in pressed suit pants, a light blue shirt open at the collar and rolled-up sleeves.

"Excuse me, Dr. Bashar," the nurse said to the man in the scrubs. This young woman would like to speak with Dr. Osman. Her eyes shifted to the businessman. Both men brought their attention to Nura. Neither blinked. The doctor nodded to Nura and then left on his rounds.

The businessman remained facing Nura. She held out her right hand to him. "*As-Salaam-Alaykum*, Dr. Osman."

"*Marhaba. Salaam*," the man replied, shaking her hand. "What can I help you with?"

"I have come to offer my blessings to those injured in the missile attack. And I'd also like to speak with you after. I have something to deliver to you."

"I see. Certainly." He replied, nodding. "Your reputation precedes you. You caused quite a stir here when you visited last year, after the first attack." He nodded his head up and down several times. "I think they're still talking about you. And I've seen your pictures in the press. Some, especially the women, say you are the Muslim Joan of Arc, here to save Palestine and its people—a mysterious dark knight."

"I do not command an army like her, but I do understand the anger of those who use different weapons to oppose their oppressors."

"Some of the pictures capture you in the middle of the fray at times, dressed as you are now."

"Perhaps at peaceful demonstrations which unfortunately turned violent. I condemn all violence against people."

There was an extended pause before he spoke again. "Sorry, I didn't mean to give you the wrong impression. I'm not attacking you, Nura. Quite the opposite. I am simply curious, like so many. I have heard much of your compassion and your assistance to those in need.

Why don't we take care of both things at once? I will accompany you on your bedside tour and we can talk more at the same time."

She nodded. "Thank you, sir."

They began at the bed next to them and circled the entire ward, introducing themselves to each patient. Dr. Osman talked about the hospital and the care each patient would get. Nura held their hands, sometimes whispering closely into the ears of those with heads wrapped in gauze, the mask of her eyes locking in their attention. She wished them well. She spoke of the great tragedy of the history of agony and despair that has clouded their homeland for centuries, not just the recent past. Yet, never once did she speak in anger or hatred. She referred to the pain experienced by both sides, of hope that one day it would end, that all would be united in brotherhood and sisterhood, because Muslims, as well as Christians and Jews, follow the same God, and the great prophets—Moses, Jesus, and Muhammad—all of whom are brothers.

Having completed the round, they arrived back where they started. Nura glanced at Dr. Bashar bending over the patient in the last bed. He was checking on a monitor cable attached to sensors on the woman's chest. A nurse was changing the dressings. As the doctor stood up, the image of a badly burned woman came into view. Some of the lighter burns along her arms and legs were left open to the air to heal. The rest of her body was covered in bandages. She was missing one hand entirely, and parts of both feet. Her head and neck were wrapped in layers of gauze, only her eyes visible. Dr. Bashar explained that she is a nurse and was walking in front of the Media Building, on her way to work at this very hospital when the first missile hit.

The woman was incapable of moving, so it was not possible to tell how much pain she was in, only that she was awake. Tears crept down the sides of her face, wetting the gauze as it absorbed them. It appeared as if she knew this person who now attended to her, this young woman who bent ever so close to her, with eyes almost smiling.

"You are brave," Nura said gently, but loud enough for her to hear through the bandages, words also audible to Dr. Osman, Dr. Bashar, and the nurse. "Braver than the bomb throwers and the missile launchers. You are a better servant than the politicians, and holier than the priests, the rabbis, or imams. You are a saint, the daughter of Allah. I bow to your greatness."

Nura bent her head down, waited a moment, then raised it, once again locking onto the woman's eyes, now flooded with tears.

The only noise that could be heard was the quiet, intermittent beeping of monitors and the shuffle of the nurses' shoes across the floor. Nura faced the middle of the room and spoke so everyone could hear.

"Peace will come! One day. One shining day...to all of us in this cradle where civilization began. And to all across the world. We are all of the same cloth, from the same source." The shuffling of feet faded as the nurses and aides stopped to listen. She paused, raising her arms high above her head and holding the palms of her hands towards the patients. "And you are the light that will bring us home."

A muffled voice came from the blistered, swollen lips of the woman she had just attended. "Nooo-r-aah. Al-lah...Allah yus-allmak."

"Yes," said Dr. Bashar, touching her shoulder lightly from behind. "God bless you indeed, Nura."

A slow muffled sound of "*Noo-rah*" radiated from the beds on either side of the woman, then from all those who could speak, spreading out in two semicircles and meeting at the other side of the room, almost like the wave of cheers at a football match. As Dr. Osman led Nura past the beds to the exit, the chant grew. The mixed voices of old and young, many in pain and straining with effort, became a chorus, ending only after the two disappeared from the room, the swinging doors flapping to a close behind them.

Dr. Osman led her to the main entrance of the hospital and opened the heavy door for her. "I see why there is such a commotion, Nura. It is a *healing* commotion."

"Thank you, Director. I still have something for you, though." She reached into the side pocket of her coat, pulled out an envelope, and handed it to him. "This is for your good work here. Take care of these people, as I know you will."

"I will, Nura. May Allah keep you in health. *Ya'teek el 'afye*!"

"*Salaam*," she replied.

Dr. Osman let the door close as Nura walked down the steps and into the street. He returned to his office moments later and opened the envelope, removing five pieces of paper. Each was a copy of a bank transfer in the amount of 10,000 American dollars, confirming a deposit from a Swiss bank into the main account of the hospital, a total of $50,000. He placed the copies back in the envelope. As he gazed out the window of his office, he caught a glimpse of her dark form in the distance, disappearing into an alley.

The two girls descended the stairs and made their way to the front door. Liyah wore a pair of new jeans and pink sneakers she had purchased during her last visit to the market with her mother, as well as a favorite three-quarter length shift, embroidered with columns of white geometric shapes, and highlighted with pink and green threads. The blue hijab she had worn when she first met Morningstar had been replaced with a dark red one made out of chiffon.

Liyah's mom heard their steps from her chair in the living room. She caught up to them as Liyah swung the door open, stepping outside behind Morningstar.

"Hold on there!" her mother shouted, grabbing the door before it closed. "What's your plan for the morning?" She looked up at the sky then drew her shawl tighter around her body. "Are you going to be warm enough? It might bc sunny later, but it's definitely chilly now."

Mrs. Rahim glanced at Morningstar who turned around to listen and stood with one foot on the bottom stair. Liyah had given her a dark blue heavy-cotton hijab to wear over her head and shoulders, imprinted with white seashells, a piece of Morningstar's red and white bandana still visible at her hairline. Two of Liyah's small, beaded cloth purses hung by leather straps over both girls' shoulders.

"We're good, Mom," assured Liyah. "We'll be fine. I'm going to show Star the market. We'll be back after lunch."

Even though the marketplace was less than a half mile away, Liyah went a round-about way, taking time to show Morningstar the route she had taken that day when she, Morningstar, and the boys ended up in the strange place together. She pointed out the square where the demonstration had gotten out of control, and where she was when she lost track of her brother. It was 11:00 by the time they finally arrived at their destination.

The actual market itself occupied a small number of narrow, intersecting streets. People jostled up and down them as they stopped in front of the kiosks and various other areas where goods were displayed. It was a beehive of activity. *Even more than usual,* Liyah thought. People seemed a bit agitated, or even worried. *Buying up food and other supplies in case there were more missile attacks, perhaps? Or maybe just more people due to spring vacation and other family members in town to celebrate Ramadan?* There was something unusual in the air that she couldn't quite pinpoint.

As they passed a vegetable stand, Liyah watched her friend's eyes widen as she scanned the stacks of squash, cucumbers, red and green peppers, eggplants, apples, and pears. Large boxes and bins overflowed with lettuce, spinach, olives, tomatoes, dates, grapes, and citrus fruits: oranges, grapefruits, tangerines, lemons, and limes. Next to that stand was a family selling prayer mats, used clothing, beads, and bangles of all sorts. At every stall there was something different, and this went on as far as one could see.

They stopped at the end of the next block, where the narrow street met a larger roadway. Liyah was beaming, proud of her homeland, her city, and her people. "What do you think, Star?"

"Amazing. That's the only word I have. I never knew there was this kind of place in the Middle East...especially Palestine. I always thought it was like a desert, with most people living in lean-tos or broken-down houses. Sort of like the Reservation at home. It's exciting!"

"There are much bigger markets in Gaza City," Liyah said. "Come, I want to show you that too."

"We have to be back after lunch, don't we?" Morningstar warned.

"Wow. Aren't *you* the cautious one?" Liyah chuckled. "It was only last week when we were out hunting for berries and you dragged me into those caves...and I was the one begging to go back to Zack and Kai Li."

Morningstar smiled. "Ha! Yes, I remember. Maybe it's just that I'm a guest here, and I don't want to get into trouble with your mom."

"We're already in trouble," Liyah laughed, "Why did you think I brought you here?" She laughed again. "Let's go. I'm supposed to meet someone there anyway. I promise we'll get back in time."

Liyah grabbed Morningstar's wrist and dragged her to the corner, raising her other arm to hail a taxi. As one pulled to the curb, she yanked open the rear door, then slid across the seat, hauling Morningstar in after her.

"Gaza. Café Pasha, please."

Liyah studied her friend who gawked out the window of the cab, taking everything in. *It must be such a new experience for her,* she mused. *Maybe someday I will see her home too. And meet her grandfather. But right now, for me, there is only Khalib.*

SEVEN

Gaza City

LIYAH FIXED HER eyes nervously on the meter next to the driver, watching the fare tick slowly but steadily higher. The taxi wasn't moving much faster than the pedestrians; she didn't plan on it taking so long to go merely a few miles to Café Pasha, located on the edge of the center of the city. But she was still early for her meeting despite demonstrations that were growing organically along the route. Pockets of angry people carrying signs were shaking their fists in the air at reporters and shouting, their voices muffled slightly by the closed windows of the cab.

Beit Lahia was closer to where the missile struck but there was no sign of a gathering storm of humanity when they were at the market. Not like here. *Maybe because people didn't have time to organize yet?* Liyah considered. *Or perhaps simply because Beit Lahia was so much smaller, only about one-tenth the size of Gaza City, and not as densely populated.*

The city held over half a million people, twenty-five percent of the two million living in the Gaza Strip itself, that small section of earth bordering the Mediterranean she knew simply as *The Strip*—the third most densely populated area of land on the planet.

Liyah's fingers fumbled nervously as she unlatched her purse and checked its contents, counting the shekels. *It is going to be close,* she thought. *What if there wasn't enough to get home?* "Right here. Right here is fine," she called out, her voice rising in volume. "We're close enough."

The driver found the first open space and pulled the taxi to the side. Liyah handed him the fare and a tip, then nudged Morningstar to open the door. Once outside, she pushed the door shut and grabbed hold of Morningstar's hand again, desperate not to lose her in the sea of people. They hustled along, passing streets packed with vendors hawking everything under the sun—all kinds of goods from used equipment to toys, toasters, handbags. Even designer-labeled clothes. In the middle of it all, cars crept along, wedging their way through to their destinations.

At one of the bigger intersections at the boundary of the market area, they found some room to breathe. Crossing the street, Liyah checked the numbers on the buildings. Seeing the blue sign with white Arabic scroll, she pulled Morningstar down a small set of stairs and into the café. It was larger inside than she expected given its location, but cramped nonetheless, and dimly lit. Old chairs and small sofas with worn fabric coverings were placed randomly about, some between tables and some alone against the wall, under wooden bookcases stuffed with tattered books. Ceiling fans buzzed above.

Liyah could feel an air of the old Middle East about the place, reflecting pictures she'd seen of past times in Istanbul perhaps, or maybe of Beirut before the tragedy of the '70s where like-minded writers from all over once met to smoke hash pipes and discuss love and politics.

She scanned the surroundings and made her way to a table in the back where a two-seat sofa was placed. She stole one of the nearby, smaller stuffed chairs and dragged it over, placing it opposite the sofa, then captured her friend's attention.

"Have a seat, Star. I'll take the sofa. This should be isolated enough."

Morningstar sunk into the chair. "Isolated?"

"When Jamal gets here, we will have to speak quietly."

"Quietly? Why?"

Liyah slipped her purse off her shoulder as she sat down on the sofa, placing it on the table. She undid the latch and lifted out her cell phone. "We made it with ten minutes to spare."

"Why quietly?" Morningstar repeated.

"I got Jamal's name from a friend of a friend. He moved to Gaza from East Jerusalem about a year ago, after the first missile attack. His parents were killed in it while walking home. He was going to Azrieli College in Israel and studying the Quran there under an imam in East Jerusalem. I'm hoping he might be able to help us reach the person in Jerusalem I'm supposed to contact."

"How do I fit into this, Liyah? How am I going to be able to help you? Like I said, I'm a fish out of water. Even my phone doesn't work here."

"You're funny with the nature references all the time," Liyah said with a smile. "I know, but I don't have anyone I can trust. And it's dangerous here. I have to be very careful letting *anyone* know what I'm doing."

"But why me?" Morningstar protested. "Maybe even together we can't help."

"I need someone to travel with me. I can't travel alone. Not here. And besides…you have *powers,* remember." Her serious tone was replaced with a smile as she pointed to her friend's bracelet.

Morningstar looked down at it, then over to Liyah's identical one. "I've been experimenting like Ooray told us to do, but I haven't had much time or a good place to do it without attracting attention."

"I know what you mean. Same here."

"I don't know Liyah. It seems complicated. A lot of risks. So many unknowns. I might be more of a burden than a help."

Liyah burst out laughing. "What are you talking about? What did you and I just go through with Zack and Kai Li? Nothing could be more dangerous or unknown than that!"

"I still think we should contact them." Morningstar replied. "But it's great to see how much stronger you are, Liyah. I remember when we first met, when you were crying all the time, and Zack called you a 'basket case'. Now, it's me who is off balance."

"Your *off balance* is like a giant skyscraper bending to a tiny gust of wind."

Morningstar laughed. "Well. Okay. Let's see what happens in the next few days. I really need to be back by the end of the weekend. My *lala* will probably start calling around to see which friend I'm supposedly staying with."

"There will be a lot going on here, Star. We can have some fun even if we'll be trying hard to find Khalib."

"Such as?"

"This year's an unusual one. A very rare one. One where Muslims, Christians, and Jews will all have a big celebration of their holiest of holidays at the same time. Jerusalem is maybe the holiest of holy cities. The main activities will overlap during the next few days: Ramadan for us, which began a few weeks ago and lasts thirty days, and Easter and Passover. Passover, you probably know, is the Jewish holiday for when the Israelites were set free from Egypt. It starts this Friday, which is also the day when Jesus was crucified. And of course, that makes this Sunday, Easter."

"What's Ramadan?" Morningstar asked.

"It's a holy period of fasting, when we are supposed to reflect on things, be a better person, and celebrate the Night of Power…the day Allah revealed the Quran, our holy book to Muhammad. I guess you'd say sort of like the Bible..."

"Is that a particular night?"

"It changes. Historically, sometime in the last week or so of Ramadan. This year the formal celebration will be a week from tomorrow. But everything seems to build up to that day, so this weekend in Jerusalem is going to be a mob scene."

"Aren't you supposed to be fasting? Is that why your mom frowned at you when she served us breakfast?"

"Yeah, but don't worry about it. You can do whatever you like, of course." She paused. "During Ramadan, we're supposed to eat something before dawn, then go without food or water all day until we get a light snack at sunset. After that, we have a big meal at night to fully break the fast and renew our energy."

"Every day?"

"Yup."

Morningstar's mouth dropped open. "Wow, I don't think I could do that."

"The fasting is to remind us of the suffering of others. Sometimes I forget. If you do, you're supposed to make up for it by extending the fast or by doing a good deed. Do you remember me telling you that my mom is stricter than my dad about practicing Islam?"

"Yeah. It was why you were shy about bathing in front of me and covered your face from the boys most of the time with your hijab."

"Yes, well you can see I'm not doing it now. I was pretty scared when we first met, I had no idea where we were, and you guys were strangers. I was overly cautious until I got to know you. People in the Arab and Muslim world sort of fit in between opposite poles. For instance, my mother is quite devout, and furious with my dad sometimes because he doesn't follow all the rules. Maybe that's because he's been influenced by the international nature of his job, even though he is still a Muslim."

"What about here?"

Liyah scanned Morningstar's face. She seemed glued to her every word.

"Here in Palestine? Well, it's sort of a mixed bag. Palestine, in general, is more liberal in dress and other things than other Muslim states. But even here, many aren't. And in The Strip, the influence of extremism has risen lately due to the trouble with Israel. Depending on where you are, some groups are demanding stricter adherence to the Quran. It's been getting worse in that way, and women and girls especially, have to be aware of their situation.

"You seem to be sort of in the middle." Morningstar offered. "Are you?"

"I follow the practices of Islam the best I can, but I'm more of a Sufi—Muslims who follow a more mystical side of Islam. They believe in a personal relationship with Allah and are more accepting of other spiritual paths. That's why I could understand what you were talking about…that all things are connected to what you called the Great Spirit. Why Zack believes in the essence of Jesus and not so much the formal sacraments and stiffness of his Catholic upbringing. And why Kai Li follows the Buddhist philosophy of pursuing personal enlightenment. So, we are not so different after all, are we? We learned that in spades together I'd say…huh?"

She watched Morningstar's face light up with a broad grin, her eyes dancing. "Yes, we did." Morningstar acknowledged. "We all got that, didn't we? At least in the end, when we went through everything together. I suspect Ooray may have chosen us because of that, and to teach us."

"I agree, but Ooray also told us that *everyone* is really chosen, and we need to help them find their light so they can pass it on. I did wonder about the whole thing sometimes, though. Like Zack used to say: 'We're gonna wake up and find out it was just a dream.' And I also wonder if we'll ever see Ooray again. Or if we are totally on our own now?"

Morningstar studied the activity in the cafe, then turned back around, changing the subject. "Shouldn't Jamal be here soon? Do you know what he looks like?"

"Oh, my!" gasped Liyah, anxiously pressing the button on her phone to wake it up. "I lost myself in all that." It was just past the half hour. Her eyes darted around the room, settling on a young man leaning against bookcases directly across from them. He was holding a red notebook and looking around. Their eyes met, but he shifted his stare to the entrance.

"He's the one, Star," Liyah said, pointing to him. "I'm sure. I've never met him, but he was to carry a red book for me to recognize him." She lifted her phone and texted him.

Jamal's phone buzzed. He removed it from his pocket, read the message, then surveyed the room until he saw Liyah waving. He made his way to the table.

Liyah studied him as he approached. He was average height and dressed in business casual with slip-on leather shoes, dark khakis, a plaid shirt, and a light blue jacket. *He could pass for a young businessman for sure,* she thought. His eyes were brown and he was clean-shaven, with darker skin than hers. He reminded her of some Lebanese friends of her father's, with his dark eyes and brown wavy hair, askew from the wind. He stood in front of her without speaking.

Liyah blinked several times then brought her mind back. "*Marhaba.* I'm Liyah." She held out her hand. "Nice to meet you, Jamal."

Jamal shook it, bowing slightly and smiling. "*Marhaba.*"

As Jamal then glanced down at Morningstar, his expression turned more serious. She popped up out of her chair and then went over to stand next to Liyah.

"I didn't mean to frighten you…ah…," Jamal began.

"Morningstar," Liyah interjected.

"Morningstar," he repeated, "Interesting name."

Jamal then addressed Liyah. "I thought we were doing this alone."

"Yes, well I'm sorry about that," Liyah apologized emphatically. "But she's going to be helping me locate my brother. Nothing we say will go any further…I promise." She watched as his eyes switched back and forth between her and Morningstar, his expression still serious.

The girls sat down together on the sofa. Jamal, with a look of resignation, took the chair. "Well, okay," he replied, hesitantly. "I'll see what I can do to help without getting into any trouble myself. I might not know anything of value anyway." He tapped the table with his forefinger several times. "So…?"

"So…the thing is…" Liyah said, glancing at Morningstar, her eyes seeking moral support. "We're looking for my brother, Khalib Al-Rahim. He was abducted by terrorists."

"Well, I know that much. You told me that in your first text to me. Are you certain?"

"Pretty certain. There doesn't seem to be any other explanation."

"Maybe he ran away? Boys are always running away from home nowadays to join the cause against Israel. There are a ton of organizations…not all are terrorists."

"He wouldn't do that. Not Khalib. I know that much!"

Liyah watched as Jamal studied her eyes. *It was like he was looking through her.* "I was told you work in Jerusalem and do religious studies in the Old City."

"Yes. That's true."

"Well, the person I need to talk to is there. I'm not supposed to speak his name to avoid attracting attention. And I can't say where I got it from, except to that man. But he may be able to help."

"If you don't say his name then how can I possibly help you?"

"I can't speak it. People may hear. But I think it's okay to show it to you." She fished in her purse and pulled out a small, folded piece of paper, and handed it to him.

Jamal unfolded it. It had the name of a mosque and the name of a man. He looked over at Liyah, to Morningstar, then back again. There was a long pause. Liyah sat motionless as she swallowed the lump in her throat. He returned the paper to her. "Yes. I know this man. But why do you need me if you already have his name?"

"It will be difficult for us to get into East Jerusalem, let alone approach as a woman with such a request. I was hoping you might be able to introduce us somehow."

"Well, I can't get you across the border into Israel. I have a work visa for the technology center that allows me to cross, but you'll need other passes for that. However, I can definitely introduce you to him. It happens that I'm a student of the imam of that mosque, and the man on the paper is the one who calls us all to prayer…the muezzin."

Liyah beamed, grabbing onto his forearm with both hands., then releasing him abruptly. "Oh, sorry," she said to him. "But this is wonderful news! I will get the passes, although I don't know how yet. How can I ever thank you?'

"We'll see if anything comes of it. In the meantime, we can communicate by phone. You have my text number to leave abbreviated messages. You never know who is reading things these days, so be cryptic. But I only talk to a few people on that special number; I modified my phone to have two different numbers." Jamal took a pen from his shirt pocket. "This one is more secure," he said, as he wrote the number on the opposite side of the paper bearing the imam's name, then handed it back to her.

Standing up, Jamal addressed both of them. "I've got to get back to work. Otherwise, I would stay a little longer. Call me when you get the passes, and we can set a time to meet in the Old City."

The girls followed him to the door, and up the cement steps to the sidewalk. The noonday sun warmed the air. Liyah gazed up into the bright blue sky as Jamal turned around to say goodbye. "What's that up there?" she asked, pointing.

Morningstar and Jamal looked up simultaneously, Jamal having to turn slightly to look over his shoulder.

"Drone," said Jamal. "A big one. It's quite common to see them now that hostilities have heated up again. The Israelis are probably searching for the source of the rockets that were fired last night from Gaza City toward Israel in retaliation for their missile strike near you in Jabalia. I have no idea why they bother. It seems no matter how many rockets we fire, it's rare that any get through their defense shield. Then we just get blasted with artillery fire or more missiles."

They watched as the drone hovered high up, almost directly above.

"I've never seen one linger like that, though," Jamal added. He turned and faced the girls again, then bowed. "*Ma'a salaam.*"

"*Salaam*," replied Liyah.

"*Salaam*," added Morningstar, grinning.

Jamal smiled, nodded, and headed up the street.

"Catching on?" asked Liyah.

"Hardly," replied Morningstar.

"Tell you what, Star," said Liyah. "We don't have to be back quite yet. Why don't I get you a little something to eat here? I have enough money left to do that. Then we can skip the taxi and walk home. It's a bit of a walk, but we're used to that I'd say, after that *adventure* we were on last week."

They laughed together under the brilliant morning sun, then made their way back into the café, and to the service counter at the far end. After checking out the pastries, they waited in line a few minutes until it was finally their turn to order.

"Nothing for me," Liyah said to the boy behind the register, "but she'd like some *awameh*...say five of the small ones. And a bottle of water. Make the *awameh* To Go, please."

"Sure," the boy replied, ringing up the sale. He scooped the donut hole-like treats from the bin and placed them in a small bag, handing it to Morningstar along with the water.

They moved away from the counter and into the corner near some bookshelves. Morningstar set down the bottle then took one of the pastry balls from the bag and hungrily shoved it into her mouth. "These are great!" she said, chewing away, her words garbled. She gave Liyah a thumbs up.

"You can eat them on the way. Let's start walking back."

Morningstar popped a second one in her mouth, then closed the bag. As she picked up the bottle of water from the shelf between the bookshelves, a high whining sound filled the room, becoming lower in tone and progressively louder by the second. They looked quizzically at each other. Then...

BOOM!

A sudden explosion shook the café, blowing in the door at the front and knocking a few nearby patrons to the floor. The girls steadied themselves against the bookshelves, eyes riveted on each other. The blast was immediately followed by a stronger one, caving in the wall opposite them and leaving no one standing. Then a third, closer explosion sent out a concussion wave that ripped through the remaining walls that wavered like jelly before collapsing. The ceiling then shattered, sending the large fans spinning to the floor, and pouring down cement chunks from above, as the walls crumbled underneath.

Swirls of heavy dust blew out into the street above. And then there was dead silence.

EIGHT

FANS WHIRRED ABOVE the four aisles inside the huge, corrugated steel Quonset hut that housed part of Aleab Ltd.'s manufacturing operations. On cold winter mornings, the fans circulated the warmth from small portable electric heaters spaced around the room. On summer days, they provided marginal relief by blowing the sweltering heat up through narrow vents in the ceiling. Aleab, as its name indicated, was the maker of games for the Palestinian market as well as for export to other countries, as much as the Israeli chokehold would allow through customs.

Sayf Yasin, the company's CEO, wearing light brown pants and a white shirt with rolled-up sleeves, along with another man in a button-down blue work shirt and green armband, made their way up and down the rows of assembly stations, stopping briefly from time to time.

"This first row of stations, Hassan," said the CEO, "is where we take the raw materials and process them into parts that are restricted by Israel from coming into Gaza. For instance, these stations take in thermoplastic bricks of different colors, melt them at high temperatures, then use an injection molding technique to cast the propeller blades. The next station uses carbon fiber instead of plastic, to form the blades, creating lighter, stronger but more expensive ones."

"At this end station, we use the same types of materials as the previous stations but create the body of the drone as the frame for all the main parts to attach. Thus, we end up with two major types of drones, with one type being more expensive and higher in performance than the other."

Hassan nodded to the workers at the machines as they moved on to the next aisle, walking in the return direction.

"The first couple of stations along this row is where we inspect and test all the small items—electrical components, sensors, antennas, clips, incredibly small circuit boards, and the very latest Lithium Polymer batteries that provide the best combination of power density and lifetime."

"What's that?" asks Hassan, pointing to a tiny black component the size of a fingernail as he scratched his finely trimmed, short white beard.

"A camera…believe it or not. It gets mounted on a gimbal that rotates to give a full 360-degree picture below the drone. For hobbyists, it provides the vision for the operator. But there are other uses that we'll get into later."

The CEO waved his hand toward the large section of stations in front of them, as they completed the run of the second row. "This is where we connect all the subassemblies to form the drone: flight controllers, speed controllers, all solid-state modules, propellers, power system, cameras, sensors, etc." He pointed to the end of the line. "You can see that there are again two main areas, one for the high-end ones and one for the cheaper fun ones for kids and hobbyists. Each work order creates a different style aircraft, based on color, materials, performance, added features, and cost. This allows us to create a host of drone styles within each major group, although only a handful make up the bulk of our sales."

"Is this where mine are being assembled?" Hassan asked as they turned the corner.

The CEO turned and frowned, his eyes lingering on Hassan's. "The *team's,* you mean," he replied, dragging out the words unmercifully slowly.

"Yes, of course," Hassan acknowledged, looking down at his shoes, then moving along to the first station in aisle three.

"This area," the CEO continued, "is where the drones go through final physical inspection." He pointed to the next few stations stacked with completed drones. They walked along, stopping in the middle of the last section.

"And here is where the software is installed and tested, including all the avionics that guide the flight like the sensor readings, optical analysis, power and position monitoring."

"It's fantastic, Sayf!" Hassan acknowledged. "Really quite amazing."

"Thank you. Now, I think we should be going downstairs to the meeting. They may be getting itchy. Been waiting longer than they'd like."

"Of course. But quickly, what about that last aisle over there?" Hassan asked.

"It's the line for the video games we're known for. We have a number of them that are packaged for installation on the major game platforms in the market. I think some are way over the top," he paused, chuckling, "but the kids love them, as do many adults it seems." He shrugged. "Who would have guessed?"

"Is that your main source of income?" Hassan questioned.

"Well, a good bit of it, along with the low-end drones. But we are stuck with serving only the local market with the drones. They cause attention if we try to export them out of Gaza." He paused briefly. "Actually, most of our money is made from the products in a similar building right next door. There, we make all kinds of children's toys, utilizing our expertise in plastics. They sell like crazy, and we can export them more easily. Versions of the cheap plastic propellers you saw are even used on top of funny beanie caps, and as spinners for game boards." He turned. "Let's get to the meeting."

Already at the end of the aisle, they descended a set of stairs that led to the warehouse area below. Hassan followed closely as they walked to the back of the building, passing racks of storage bins filled with parts, subassemblies, and finished products on one side, and across from all that, another assembly line for drones.

The CEO stopped, just before reaching the small conference room at the back. Hassan, scanning the stations, bumped into him. "Sorry, I was looking at this line here."

"Yes, yes. No bother. I was going to show it to you on the way back, anyway. This one is actually the line you referred to as *your line.*" I wanted to hush you because only a few workers up there know much about this. It's basically a line that mimics the high end one upstairs, except the materials are enhanced to provide a high degree of *stealth,* as they say, and the programming is entirely different, using special components."

The door to the conference room clicked open. A young man in jeans and a crewneck sweater without a shirt underneath, walked out. Seeing the two men standing there, he spoke out.

"They are waiting for you, sir."

NINE

NASIR HELD THE door as they entered the room, then closed it securely behind him. Hassan nodded to him as he passed. In the center of the room was a large wood table. The only items on it were five glasses of water, and a small, jet-black drone. Two plastic chairs were positioned on both sides and one at the head. The CEO addressed the man and the woman sitting there.

"I sincerely apologize for keeping you. I wanted to give Hassan a little tour of the factory, since as you know, he is an important benefactor and critical to our success with this operation."

The woman stood up and offered her hand to Hassan from across the table. She was dressed entirely in black with a white keffiyeh with a fishnet design covering her head.

"Hassan Bakir, this is Nura," the CEO indicated, offering the introductions. "I'm sure you know of her. And this is Jamal from the Tech Center."

After exchanging the standard greetings, everyone took their seat, with Jamal next to Nura, Hammad across the table and next to Nasir, and the CEO at the head of the table.

"I want to keep this short but we need to get through some important things since this is Wednesday, and *Operation Swarm* takes place only four days from now. No one is allowed to take notes, and all further conversations must take place in person unless it can't be avoided. First on the agenda is financing. Hassan?"

Hassan glanced sequentially at each of them, then addressed them in a serious tone. "I'm one of the senior members of Hamas leadership." He pointed to his green armband with the white Arabic lettering. "There are only a few people in the Committee who are aware of what is being planned, and they are sworn to secrecy under the penalty of death. We've been placing funds into an account that's only accessible to Sayf, here. He faced the CEO. "I am aware it's not enough to fully carry out this complex and costly operation, but it's all we have available due to other priorities, security considerations, and of course the high risk that this project could fail, with devastating results."

"We completely appreciate that, Hassan," the CEO interjected. "No one outside of this room is aware of our plans. There is a lot at stake here for all of us." He paused, turning to Nasir. "Nasir's salary is covered by the general operations of Aleab. The company also covers some of the expense for various drone parts." He shifted, looking toward Jamal. "Jamal, some of your consulting fees, and the remaining gap in the funds needed to complete the operation, have been covered by a generous donation from Nura."

"I was wondering about your connection to all of this, Nura," said Hassan, looking displeased. "But I accept your contribution to the cause regardless of how you manage to come up with funds to support this, the hospitals, and others."

Nura nodded. "I have my sources."

"Yes, apparently," Hassan agreed, a tinge of sarcasm dripping from his tongue. "But I think it's also important for all of us to be honest here, since there is so much on the line. So, I must say that this is highly unusual for a woman, or should I say *girl* in this case, to be a factor in such an operation."

The CEO turned to him. "What are you getting at, Hassan?"

"I'm saying that our lives are at stake here, should this fail and the Israelis find out. They will track us down and kill us. And you know how capable Mossad is of doing just that."

"So you think she is going to tell someone?"

"I didn't say that, Sayf. It's just that she is a very visible person. We all know that. Not only because she seems to pop up everywhere, but because of what she wears. She could easily be seen here. And on top of that, she's known for her vocal stance against some of our more extreme tactics."

Visibly stiffening, the CEO spoke sternly. "Nura and Jamal came in through the tunnel and will leave that way. No one will see them. We'll make sure of that."

"Mr. Bakir…sir," Nura cut in softly. "Excuse me, but as to any *extreme tactics,* as you put it, you promised there would be no civilian casualties. No deaths at all, if it could be helped. That was my stipulation for the donation needed to complete Operation Swarm."

"Yes, I did agree to that," Hassan replied. "I fear, though, that as a woman, you will go soft if something happens. I make no apology for my beliefs. Like *so many* others, I think that girls should be seen and not heard, and that women should tend to the home and stay away from business and politics."

"By *so many*, you must be referring to men, for many women of *this day*, of my generation, do not share this belief. Perhaps you are indeed right about *fear,* though…but it is you who displays it, not I."

Hassan leapt to his feet, slamming his fist down on the table. "This is blasphemy!"

Nura remained poised, her voice calm. Her eyes locked on Hassan's. "The Prophet of Islam…peace be upon him, said '*women are the twin halves of men.*' He also said they should be honored."

Hassan glared.

"Sit! Sit, Hassan!" the CEO chuckled, laughing lightly to tamp down the temperature in the room. "Don't let your blood boil! It's not good for anyone, especially at our age. Besides, we only have a few days left."

Hassan returned begrudgingly to his seat, still simmering.

Yasin continued. "Let's move on, shall we? Jamal, here, is a brilliant student of materials research and wireless communications. He studied for almost three years at the University until his parents, who helped support the family and his education, were killed in an attack last year. Jamal left school, taking a job at the tech research center. He is also the key strategist who came up with many important aspects of the plan."

He then nodded across the table. "Nasir is our drone expert and head software engineer. The two of them developed the main technological underpinning of the operation. They will lead us through it. Gentlemen…if you would."

Nasir reached to the middle of the table, picked up the drone, then moved to the end of the table, opposite his boss. "I'll start by giving you all an overview of the drone itself."

Holding the drone in one hand, he waved his other hand above it. "We have spent a lot of time making these drones as small and light as possible, mainly to avoid detection, but also to mitigate costs, since we have to produce so many of them. And the less it weighs, the more payload it can carry to its target. This drone is only twenty-five centimeters in its widest dimension. That's about nine and a quarter inches for any of you familiar with the top American drones." He held it flat in his palm while he moved his hand up and down. "And it weighs only two hundred grams—less than half a pound. Its vertical dimension is a little over five centimeters, making the total depth including payload under ten centimeters, about three and three and a half inches. You'll get a better understanding of the importance of this when we discuss targets in more depth at the next meeting."

He took in a long breath before continuing. "This is a quad-copter, so it has these four main propellers on top in a square pattern. They are used for lift. You'll notice it also has two smaller props," he explained, pointing to them, "one in the front and one in the back, used for directional movement and added stability. The structure is made of a unique carbon fiber—light and strong. We kept the central body as low profile as possible. It houses our ultra-flat communication circuitry, sensors, cameras, flight controller, main batteries, etc. The small motors that drive the props are located at the end of each arm under the propellers. Using the highest end, state-of-the-art components, we have been able to shave off substantial weight in the main body, battery, and motor areas."

Nasir returned to his seat, leaving the drone behind. The CEO nodded to Jamal, who rose and took Nasir's place.

Jamal lifted up the drone and addressed the others. "We have been able to incorporate the dramatic improvements in many technologies over recent years, even months, allowing us to create a drone that exceeds even our own ambitious goals. One that is quite small, yet can deliver a highly explosive payload. But we have had to also overcome perhaps the biggest issue of all: detection avoidance. We…Hamas that is," he said, glancing over at Hassan, "have fired hundreds of rockets towards Israel just in the last several days, in retaliation for the missile strikes and artillery fire that killed many unsuspecting and innocent Palestinian civilians." He rotated the drone in his hand. "Not one has hit its target. The Israelis have extraordinary military capabilities. It makes us feel more helpless, wouldn't you agree?"

Jamal observed the nodding heads around the room. "At the same time, we don't have artillery, or Phantom jets, or tanks, or even the ability to deflect what they throw at us," he said, his jaw tensing, his tone more acidic.

He began pacing back and forth. "Are we really so weak?" he asked, scanning the eyes of his audience as they locked in on his movements, anticipating his next words. He returned to the end of the table and continued in a calmer voice. "We don't have to be. The strategy of *Operation Swarm* is based on two concepts proposed by Sun Tzu, the great Chinese military strategist of old. The first is '*The supreme art of war is to subdue the enemy without fighting.*'

He studied the blank expressions around him. "We can't afford a war. We do not have the financial or military resources. Fighting would only deplete us further, and we will suffer and not be able to support our loved ones. It would be a war of attrition that we can't win. We must, indeed, subdue the enemy without a fight."

"Secondly, Sun Tzu advised, '*The opportunity to secure ourselves against defeat lies in our own hands, but the opportunity of defeating the enemy is provided by the enemy himself.*' In other words, by studying the enemy we can find the weaknesses that will enable us to be victorious."

Jamal scanned the faces around the table.

"This is why we had to come up with a strategy where we play our own game. Not theirs. On this basis, Nasir and I created a plan with the following objectives…"

"First, to satisfy Nura's constraint, let's be clear. No one is to be harmed, if at all possible. We will show that we are greater than an enemy who kills women and children."

"Second, we cannot compete head-on. We had to find a way to deal with the lopsided military capability Israel holds over us."

"Third, the strike must be brief but decisive. Another philosophy of Sun Tzu is that no one is ever the victor of a long, drawn-out war."

"And fourth, we must use their own strength against them."

"Excuse me," Hassan interrupted, his demeanor uneasy, "but how is all that possible?"

"Patience, patience, my friend. We're getting to that," Jamal replied, the corners of his mouth forming a small grin. "Since we cannot match their sheer force, nor break through the physical barriers that ensnare us, we must strike where they cannot defend against us. Where they are big, we must become small. Where they have a finite number of huge, devastatingly powerful weapons, we must deliver a storm of *unseeable* soldiers, each packing a sting greater than a million hornets."

"What we propose is a swarm of very small drones that will overpower their cumbersome, lumbering weapons…their artillery, their tanks, and yes, even their jets. That is their weakness—the inability of those weapons to fight the tiny enemy."

"They know all about drones," Hassan insisted. "And are developing ways to combat large numbers of them. We know that they are working with American defense contractors who just developed a vehicle that uses a number of communications technologies, and a vehicle-mounted laser, to track and eliminate groups of drones."

"But that vehicle itself is large, and the tactic is born from the same overkill thinking." Jamal countered. "You cannot swat a fly you cannot see. And if there are clouds of unseeable flies…then what?"

Jamal paced in front of the table, then continued. "There are groups, and then there are *swarms*. We propose multiple smaller clouds of drones—clusters that make up the swarm. The clusters will be assigned targets according to their capabilities and mission. There will be tens to hundreds, per task. Tens of thousands of little, but powerful pests all together."

Jamal turned to Nasir. "Help me lead them through the implementation of the strategy."

Nasir backed his seat out and joined Jamal at the end of the table.

"Yes, Jamal is right. They will not be able to take down these drones. Maybe a very small number perhaps…but only with some luck. And not with their technology. Here's why."

Nasir took the drone from Jamal and held it up. "*Stealth* material is built into the carbon composite structure and coated onto the propellers. I don't mean to steal Jamal's thunder, but rather give him credit. He has modified the stealthy material retrieved from parts of a downed American plane and created his own. The original material itself provides a seventy to eighty percent *mask,* if you will, reducing what is called the *radar signature* of an aircraft. Jamal found a way in the lab to increase the effectiveness of an additional 10 to 20 percent, especially on the smaller object we are talking about here."

Jamal jumped back in. "At a distance of a few miles, the defense companies claim the signature of a small fighter jet can sometimes be reduced to look more like a hummingbird instead of a plane. And if you keep in mind that we are starting out with something that is only twice as big as a hummingbird, that makes the drone virtually invisible to radar. Even a cluster would likely be undetectable, since each drone would effectively be the size of a small coin. With a relatively vast distance between it and its neighbor, it may look like only a group of insects spaced widely apart. Even by human sight, they will not *appear* as a true swarm, since the number of members will be much smaller, and the distance between the drones much greater than a flock of birds."

Nasir began pacing. "The material scatters the visible light as well, eliminating the ability for humans or ground systems to visually *see* them. In addition, other ways of locating objects-would be based on ground positioning systems, GPS, that can use satellite communications and cellphone towers to zero in on the target. Yet, *we* are not using cell towers, radio signals, or satellites for communications or positioning. We are using mainly infrared light."

"Really?" his boss questioned. "I didn't realize that, Nasir. How will you be able to talk to the drones or receive messages? Or for that matter, how will the drones be able to communicate with each other? Isn't that a small antenna on top? What about GPS? And how will they know where they're going?"

"I'll address all of those more clearly during the next few days. I know Jamal has to get back to his job before they miss him. For now, suffice it to say, each drone will have a map of the area and specifics about its target. They will fly in groups of various numbers, which we'll refer to as clusters. Collectively, we will call these the *swarm.*"

Nasir stopped pacing and tweaked the stubby, flexible rod sticking up on the main body. "You are right in one respect, sir," he said, looking to the other end of the table. "This is indeed a radio transceiver. This one also helps analyze GPS. But these will only be used prior to flight, and only on rare occasions during the mission, to confuse the enemy or as a quick spot-check on the drone's actual position relative to its target. If the brief signal is sensed at all, it will be worthless since the drone will have already moved on. But the basic reasons for this are two-fold: the drones will not be returning, and it is critical that no one ever be able to trace their original source."

He continued. "This makes drone-to-drone communication even more critical. So, we have patterned their behavior after birds. By using short-distance communications, no more than five meters, there is no chance of them intercepting the signals. Each drone will know its position, relative to its nearest neighbors, the six or so closest to it. This is how birds fly together. And we will use infrared light to do so—the very same technology used by your tv remote, except, of course, enhanced a bit."

"All during their flight, the drones will use the powerful cameras on their underside and in front to receive visual data from their surroundings and compare it to the actual terrain mapping data and target information programmed into their memory. The flight controller will then keep them on the right path. It will also sense the earth's magnetic field at every point, as well as the positioning of the sun or moon, and the markers of several large objects, like buildings, lakes, etc. The entirety of this method is exactly how birds migrate and find their way home each year…except these birds will not be going home."

"Sorry gentlemen," Jamal broke in. "And Nura," he added, bowing ever so slightly to her, "but I really must be going. Nasir, please continue if you like. I'll see you all here tomorrow, at the same time. The plan is to meet over the next four days, with the last time being Sunday—Launch Day."

"No worries, Jamal," Nasir replied. "I think we've covered a lot for now. I'll walk you and Nura back out."

The CEO took Hassan up the stairs and out the front of the building. The others left through an obscure rear exit around the corner from the conference room.

Nasir unlocked the heavy metal door behind a small storage area and led Jamal and Nura back through the narrow, poorly lit tunnel he had brought them through before. While the tunnel was familiar to Jamal, having been working with Nasir on the project for some time, it was new to Nura. She had followed Nasir down it when she arrived earlier, then joined Jamal before Hassan and Sayf Yasin showed up.

They walked in silence for a while before it was broken by Jamal. "You've been quiet Nura, even more now than during the meeting. It's not exactly what I expected, given your reputation."

"It's the media," she replied. "They like a good story, don't you agree?"

Jamal laughed. "Yes, yes. I see your point."

"I was there to listen," she said, her nervousness increasing. "I don't have much else to offer this project other than what money I can give."

After a short distance, Nasir led them up a few stone steps and pushed open the double doors of a wooden bulkhead above. They stepped up and into the sunlight. A small stretch of beach that flanked the Mediterranean Sea was visible in the distance.

"We moved the factory here nine months ago, Nura," said Nasir, "to the southern edge of Gaza City, so that it would not draw attention when we test individual drones. Jamal parks his car near here." He pointed to the parking lot at the corner, one street down, toward the water. It's the same place I met you before the meeting. I'm sure he doesn't mind...Jamal?"

Jamal shook Nasir's hand. "No. Of course not. See you tomorrow."

Nasir watched them until their forms shimmered like a mirage, caught between the early afternoon sun and the sandy terrain.

Ten

LIYAH BLINKED HER eyes open. It was dark as night. She sensed a heavy weight crushing her spine. *Where am I?* She struggled to lift her head just enough to look to her other side. She felt something against her leg. *Someone's foot? Who is that? Am I dreaming?* She tried to get up, pressing her hands against the floor, craning her neck to face forward, striving desperately but unsuccessfully to see anything.

I know this dream, she thought. *I'm at home. There was an explosion, and now I'm trapped under the rubble.* She slid her hands as far forward as she could, until they bumped into a wooden object. *Am I in a box? A coffin?* She felt panic setting in. Her eyes began bouncing all over like a pinball. *Breathe, Liyah. Breathe. That's what she had learned, wasn't it? Who said that? Was it Kai Li? Morningstar? Oh, isn't Morningstar with me?*

She steadied her eyes. *Don't panic. Do it. Breathe!* She sucked in some air, then pushed it back out—then again—cautiously at first, progressing to deeper and longer breaths. Her pulse slowed. Her thoughts became clearer. *This is not like before, when all seemed lost. I have control. Thank you, Ooray. Thank you, my friends, for teaching me.*

She turned her head back to the side, her eyes adjusting a little. She could see the hijab on the head of the person next to her. She recognized it. It was the one she gave to Morningstar to wear when they were in town. They were headed to the Café Pasha. *Now I remember...*

"Oh, Allah!" she shouted. "Morningstar…Morningstar!"

The body next to her twitched. A voice groaned. "Liyah?"

"Can you move?"

Morningstar shifted, rolling onto her side, then bringing her head around. She stared at Liyah. "What happened?"

"No idea. I do recall an explosion. We have to get out of here, but I can't move. I'm pinned down. Do you see anything?"

Morningstar glanced down the length of Liyah's body. "We're in some sort of a frame, and the back is pressing down on you. I have some room to maneuver but not much."

"Frame?"

"Yeah, and there are some books packing us in."

"Café Pasha!"

"What?"

"We were getting a snack, remember?"

Morningstar looked down at her feet. "Aah, you're right. Believe it or not, the bag is still at my feet. How are we gonna get out of here?"

Liyah pushed her back against the weight. *Nothing.* "Can you see anything?"

Morningstar moved to her stomach, lifted her head, and surveyed the surroundings. "Just the bookcase frame. It seems to be in one piece, except for the corner of it near my right hand, which has pulled away. I'd say we're pretty lucky, though. It seems like the shelves broke and came down with the books. Otherwise, I think we could have been seriously hurt."

"Don't get too optimistic. We don't know what's above us, do we?"

"Maybe someone will come and dig us out."

"Before we run out of air? I think we'd better try ourselves, don't you?"

"Any ideas?"

"Well, there's only one thing that comes to mind, Star," Liyah said, grunting as she pushed uselessly against the weight pinning her down. "This might be a real good time to practice our powers."

Esty Blum hustled into the main foyer of the church in her white dress slacks and bright blue blazer, with the Israeli Tourism Ministry insignia stitched to her left breast pocket. Her dressy wedge sandals *tap, tap, tapped* against the marble floor, echoing throughout the great hall. A group of about thirty people stood behind a cordoned-off area, facing a small chapel that sat directly in the middle of the rotunda.

She made her way around the side of the group to the front. A middle-aged woman wearing a floor-length print gown unhitched the brass clasp of the red velvet rope to let her in.

"You're late again, Esty," she admonished, frowning her displeasure. "I would have thought you'd be here on time…at least this week, given that the schools are on vacation."

"Very sorry," Esty replied, timidly, catching her breath. "It's a mob scene out there. Not only in the Old City, but all over Jerusalem. I've never seen it this crowded."

"Well, you should have allowed for that, you know. Plan ahead, as they say. This is a Christian group from America. So, play that up, okay? It's good for tourism, as you are well aware."

"Yes, ma'am, certainly," Esty replied, as she headed to the middle of the chapel entrance area. "Understood."

Esty took her spot on the same marble tile where she began most of her tours. She tucked an unruly tuft of blond hair up under the side of her puffy dark blue newsboy cap, pulled the brim down a bit, and addressed the crowd.

"Hello everyone. Welcome to Israel, this holy Old City of Jerusalem, and the Church of the Holy Sepulcher. I'll be your guide this afternoon. My name is Etsy, and I'm in my second year of a three-year high school program. My father is a consultant for the Prime Minister of Israel. My mother used to design programs for the Ministry of Tourism. So it wasn't hard for me to get a job here." She tipped her visor and smiled.

A spatter of laughter spread through the crowd.

"Come now, Esty," her tourism boss injected. "She's way too modest, folks. At her young age, she already speaks three languages fluently: Hebrew, English, and Arabic."

"Yes, well…" Esty continued. "I appreciate the many languages and spiritualities of this region. I love it here in East Jerusalem, the spiritual center of the world and home of this ancient Christian church, as well as Islam's sacred Al-Aqsa Mosque and Dome of the Rock. It's only a five minute walk between each site."

Pausing, she canvassed the crowd, some still gaping at the huge dome above the archways, with paintings, and ornate gold trimming everywhere. She waited until all wide eyes were fully back on her before continuing.

"What say we get started?"

Esty tipped her brim once more, then held both hands out to the side in a welcoming pose. "Behind me is the entrance to the Chapel of the Angel, the home of the tomb of Jesus."

Moving forward several steps, she reached over and released the middle section of the velvet gate. As she backed up into the entryway of the chapel, she began to tell the story of Jesus' visit to the Old City two thousand years ago. The visitors followed, gently jostling each other, taking in the beauty of the scene and the words of their host as she recounted the last chapter of *the story of all stories,* about the final resting place of the young man from Nazareth.

The muffled sound of a phone ringing caught their attention. "That's my phone, Star…in my purse. I can't free my arms. Can you get to it?"

Morningstar inched her body to the left until she was close enough to blindly feel around the floor close to Liyah, eventually locating the purse down by her friend's knee. Shifting to her side, her shoulder now rubbing against the back of the bookcase, she slowly brought the purse up close to her neck. Tilting her head, she twisted the latch, separating it. She reached her hand in, her fingers fumbling until they found the phone. Gently slipping it out, she brought it up before her eyes just as it stopped ringing.

"Damn!" Morningstar grunted under her breath.

"Oh, Allah," Liyah echoed. "Who was it from?"

"Your baba."

"No idea why he's calling, but he might be able to get us some help. Just call him back. But you'll have to talk. I'll tell you what to say."

Morningstar pressed the callback icon and held the phone to her ear.

"Liyah?" came a testy male voice from the other end. "Your mother called me here at work. She was expecting you some time ago. You know how she is, so get your butt home. Where are you, anyway?"

Morningstar covered the phone against her neck. "He says your mom is pissed."

"Tell him we are at Café Pasha and we need him to come right away!"

Morningstar heard her dad's irritated but muffled voice vibrating against her neck. "Liyah. Liyah. What are you doing?" She returned the phone to her ear.

"Sorry, Mr. Rahim. It's me, Morningstar."

"Morningstar? Oh. Well, where is Liyah?"

"She's tied up."

"Tied up?"

"Uh…I mean she can't talk right now, but she wants me to tell you that we need you to come right away and get us."

"Why is that?" Mr. Rahim replied, sounding confused.

"Well, we're in some trouble."

"No, no." Liyah blurted in a loud whisper.

"What? What do you want me to say?" Morningstar replied, only half-covering the phone.

"What? Who's that? Is that Liyah? Put her on please, Morningstar."

"I can't. I mean I can't reach her."

"How come you have her phone?"

"Ah…well, we're really stuck, sir. Please forgive me. We're at Café Pasha in Gaza City and there was an accident inside. We're okay but trapped under some stuff. We just need you right away."

"What?" Liyah's dad exclaimed in horror. "What do you mean? Well, stay on the phone!"

"We can't. We have to get out of here before something else happens."

"Something else?"

"Sir, please. We've got to go now."

"I'll be there in twenty minutes. Stay right where you are."

"I don't think there'll be any problem with that, Mr. Rahim."

"Don't tell mom!" Liyah shouted, giving in to her situation.

"Liyah doesn't want you to…"

"I heard, I heard. I'm heading out the door now."

Morningstar ended the call then looked over apologetically at Liyah.

"Never mind, Star. Let's get to it before something else happens. We need to try to use our powers to create a space, so we can crawl out."

"How?"

"You're freer than me. Grab onto your bracelet with your other hand, hold it up and imagine a force pushing against the frame at that broken corner. It's what Ooray told us to do. I have been able to experiment a little with it since I've been home. It's how I called you, and how you must have found me. Just focus your mind so that the energy is channeled through your hand, okay? Remember how? I'd help but my bracelet is on my other wrist, and I can't reach it."

"Yes, okay. I'll try." Morningstar replied, twisting her body over to the other side as she banged against the back of the bookshelf.

Once situated, she held onto the bracelet and positioned her free hand close to the corner of the shelf. As she concentrated her thoughts, the bracelet started to vibrate, its dangling jewels lighting up. She could feel the vibration from the bracelet in her body and a warmth coursing through her veins. She heard the wooden frame creak, but whatever was on the other side wouldn't allow it to budge more than a few inches.

"I can see something happening," Liyah encouraged. "Concentrate more, Star."

Morningstar paused, took several deep breaths, then focused like a laser, willing whatever was in the way to be repelled from her hand. She could feel the force flowing through her arm and into her hand.

The end of the frame began to shake, then slide ever so slightly away from her. She doubled her effort, imagining the box that had entrapped her was giving in to her strength.

The frame scraped along the floor, forcing what was blocking it to move as well. A gap opened and dust and bits of plaster filled the void. Morningstar kept her hand steady, her thoughts strong. The entire end-board of the frame suddenly broke away, sweeping the debris out of the way before it like the blade of a snowplow.

Larger pieces of plaster, some wood, and bits of debris slid off the bookcase that had held them captive, tumbling into the spaces left by the frame-blade moving outward. Liyah felt the pressure ease from her back.

Morningstar could now see daylight between the large chunks of debris. The back of the bookcase, propped up by the three sides of the frame that remained, was the only thing keeping them safe.

"Can you move, Liyah?" Morningstar called over to her friend.

Liyah pushed her hands hard against the floor, her back against the bookcase. "Almost, but not quite."

"Okay. Let me see what I can do..."

Morningstar began to crawl her way through the narrow gap in front of her like a soldier under fire. She inched ahead, squeezing past large pieces of plaster, until she was free enough of the frame to push herself up on her knees, and eventually to her feet. Her eyes blinked at the sudden onrush of light. She breathed in the unsettled dust and began to cough. Covering her mouth with her hijab, she looked out over what was left of the café.

The floor was covered hip-deep in the carnage. Several mounds that were four to five feet high rose up above the rest, like distant mountains above a plain. The counter where she and Liyah had been standing before the last blast hit remained but was covered in debris from the ceiling and broken parts of furniture from the room above were scattered around. Two large copper ceiling fans sat atop the wreckage, looking like bent propellers at an airline crash site.

The upper stories of the building had held up. *At least for now,* she thought. But smaller pieces of debris still tumbled down around her every few seconds like loose rocks on a hillside. Nothing else moved.

A quiet voice startled her out of her daze. "Don't forget me, Star?"

Morningstar turned quickly around and began to slide the leftover large chunks of plaster from around the bookcase. She then grabbed hold of the back edge and started pulling up. "Try to stand, Liyah. Push up against the case with your back."

Liyah complied, and within a few minutes she was able to slip out from under it, as Morningstar held it at bay. Once she was clear, Morningstar let the bookcase fall with a c*rash!*

The girls brushed the dust from their clothes then hugged each other. "You okay?" Liyah asked. "By some incredible miracle, I seem to be fine."

"Well, except for the gash on the side of your head," Morningstar returned. "You might need to have that checked out."

Liyah brushed her fingers against her hijab where it met her face. Most of the blood had crusted, but her fingertips still came back red. Morningstar removed her hijab and helped wrap it more tightly around Liyah's head, forming a bandage like that of a wounded warrior.

"This isn't the first time you rescued me from a pile of debris," Liyah said, as Morningstar tied the ends of the hijab securely.

"No, but it's the third time you've been in one," she chuckled lightly. "You must like it."

"Third?" Liyah questioned.

"Yeah. There was the one you told me about when we first met—when someone threw a bomb into your home. Remember? And then the time in the cave during our crazy adventure that Ooray sent us on…and now this." She fixed on Liyah's eyes. "You didn't seem to blink during this one. We've all come a long way, haven't we?"

"Well, to be honest, I did start to get panicky, but yes, yes we have, Star," Liyah replied as she wrapped her arms around Morningstar again, squeezing her like a vice.

Surveying the remains of the café, they noticed a pair of legs jutting out from some plaster behind the service bar. They lifted the cement sheets off a young barista. He regained consciousness as they tended to him, then sat leaning against the base of the bar as the girls headed across the room looking for more people. Or bodies.

The sirens of emergency vehicles began filling the streets. A fire truck stopped directly in front of the building, and two men in heavy jackets and helmets, one carrying a medical kit, forced their way down the stairs and into the café. Liyah and Morningstar, bending over and trying to dig out another person, looked up at them as they neared.

"You girls, okay?" one of the men shouted, throwing aside sections of ceiling matter as he walked atop the mass of broken plaster, wood, and metal.

Liyah assured him they were fine, and that her father would soon be there. The man studied the side of Liyah's head. "Let's see what we have here."

"It's nothing," she said, as he pushed aside the knot in the hijab.

Opening his kit, the man removed a small sterile wipe along with a bandage. He applied them to the wound, then secured the hijab more firmly. "Okay. If you're certain he's coming. Promise me you'll have him take you to the hospital to get it checked out as soon as possible. Meantime, please go out and wait by the vehicle. We have some work to do here."

"Yes, sir. Thank you, sir," Liyah replied, as the two picked their way through the debris and to the street above.

ELEVEN

DARKNESS WAS SETTING in. The tires crunched over the gravel as Mr. Rahim pulled up next to the house. He and the girls exited the car and made their way up the concrete walk to the front door.

"Now, Liyah, like I said, not a word to your mother. Let me take care of this. I called her on my way to pick you girls up and told her that I'd explain more when we got back. She doesn't know we're coming from the hospital."

"Okay, Baba. We'll be careful," Liyah replied, her voice lacking its usual vibrant tone.

"We?" her dad asked, playfully. "I'm not worried about Morningstar. You and your mother on the other hand…"

The door swung open just as Liyah's dad reached for the handle. Liyah's mother stood there, fists resting on her hips. "Dinner is surely overcooked. Can't keep it hot forever. My, my! What am I going to do with the lot of you? And what happened to being home after lunch, Liyah?"

Liyah bolted up the stairs with Morningstar so they could wash their hands and change into cleaner clothes. Her dad followed her mother as she traipsed back into the kitchen. He took his seat at the table while his wife stood in silence in front of the stove, a potholder in one hand, and her back to him. Minutes passed. She stared at the clock above the stove.

"What's going on David?" she finally asked. "Seems like you're keeping something from me. Things have gotten a little strange ever since Morningstar appeared, don't you think?"

"No, dear," he reassured her. "Everything is quite alright. The girls went shopping and lost track of the time, that's all."

"Is that why you had to pick them up?" She stirred one of the pots and checked the oven. "I mean it's nighttime, for goodness sake! What were they doing that they couldn't call?"

"Well, that's my fault. They actually called me earlier. Apparently, they were out of money for a taxi. I had to finish some things up…and then you know how it is…one thing led to another."

"No I don't, actually." She turned toward the dining room, her tone elevated. "Everything seems to be suddenly off balance, you know. First, there was all that trouble in the square in Beit Lahia a week ago, the day Khalib disappeared, and Liyah was late for the party. Then there was the missile attack…and then another right in front of the Dawn. And now I hear that some artillery shells hit somewhere in downtown Gaza." She took a breath and sighed. "And where is my family? Everything is falling apart. No one is safe…I…I just don't know anymore."

Liyah's dad got up and entered the kitchen. He moved to her, wrapping her in his arms. Stroking the side of her face, he looked into her eyes. "I know, dear…I know."

"Caught you!" Liyah cried, as she and Morningstar entered the kitchen.

Her mother turned back to the stove, touching the corners of her eyes with her apron.

"Hi sweetie," her dad replied. "I guess you did. Why don't you and Morningstar grab a chair? I was telling your mom how things got all twisted up today. But everyone's back and safe…and dinner is about to be served. Things couldn't be better." He winked at the two of them.

The girls sat down across from each other. A small, fluted glass vase filled with a beautiful bouquet of fresh flowers caught Morningstar's attention. It was positioned in the middle of the table on top of a clean white linen tablecloth. A fine cloth napkin and full formal dinnerware setting were placed in front of each seat, framing an elegant blue plate with a floral design along its edge. Another smaller plate was positioned above it, and a full glass of water to the side of that. A full wooden salad bowl was placed to the side of Liyah's mom's setting.

"Wow, such a beautiful table, Mrs. Rahim," Morningstar noted.

"Why thank you, Morningstar," Liyah's mom replied, moving to the table and setting a casserole pot from the oven on the hot pad next to her husband. "During the month of Ramadan, we usually eat in the dining room because it's such a very special time."

Liyah's dad picked up the large serving spoon next to the pot. His wife took her seat opposite him. "If everyone will pass their plates," he announced, "I'll serve out this great dish."

He placed a generous spoonful on each plate, returning it to its respective owner. Morningstar positioned her face over the steaming food, breathing in deeply. "This smells so incredible," she beamed. "And I'm starving. What's in it?"

Mrs. Rahim smiled broadly. "All kinds of good things, dear. Lamb, rice, and vegetables like potatoes, carrots, onions, cauliflower, and eggplant. All cooked in olive oil. And many spices too, like garlic, cardamom, cloves, nutmeg, and allspice, that gives it that amazing aroma."

Morningstar brought a forkful to her mouth, cooled it with her breath, then chewed it hungrily. "Wow! Really, really delicious!"

Liyah's dad chuckled. "We should have more guests like you, Morningstar."

"This is one of our favorite meals during Ramadan," Liyah added, her voice perking up a bit. "We're all so hungry during the days from the fasting. This meal really sticks to you. Right, Dad?"

"Yes, indeed. Fills you right up. Do you have anything like this at home, Morningstar?"

"Well, my ancestors lived on the plains of America during the days of the buffalo, and we still eat some of the basic foods they did…what people might call *paleo* these days. We eat many types of nuts, berries, fruits, and a lot of things made from corn. But we also eat meat, potatoes, squash, rice, and onions, like some of the things in this dish. Just not as many spices…nothing so fancy. So, this is a treat for me."

"It's called *maqluba*, Star," Liyah said. "It means *upside down*, because it's cooked in a pan then flipped over."

"Like your day today?" her mom suggested. "Your dad said he picked you two up in Gaza City. What were you doing there?" Her eyes squinted. "Is that a bandage sticking out from your hijab?"

"I…I hit myself on the edge of a frame."

"Door frame?" She stared suspiciously at her husband.

With the undertone in her voice obvious, he intervened. "She received a call from a friend who said he might be able to help find Khalib."

"Well, that's at least something positive for the day," Mrs. Rahmin replied, still appearing wary. She caught Liyah's attention again. "But you shouldn't be meeting men in places by yourself. You know how I feel about that."

"Yes, mom. But Morningstar was there with me."

"Like…I…said," her mom volleyed back, slowly emphasizing each word.

Switching gears, she passed the salad bowl to Morningstar. "I think you'll like this too. I make it using bits of fried pita bread, orange peppers, sliced radishes, baby tomatoes, and *Baqleh*…in place of lettuce. The dark red spice is called sumac, and the dressing is a syrup made from pomegranates."

"It certainly is colorful," Morningstar agreed, trying a little. "And very light. Tasty."

Liyah's mother smiled. "Glad you like it. It's another favorite here in Palestine."

"I can see why," Morningstar replied. "My grandfather makes one like this. It has many of the same ingredients. We even use sumac as a spice. The *Baqleh*, I think that's what you called it, is a lot like dandelion greens to me. Sometimes he uses maple syrup or honey to flavor things, although that's definitely sweeter than this. This is much lighter."

"Have as much as you like, dear. It's too bad you'll be leaving us shortly. It's nice to have someone at the table who truly appreciates the food they are eating."

Liyah rolled her eyes.

As they finished the main course, Mrs. Rahim cleared the dishes and placed a pastry on each of the smaller plates. "During Ramadan, we often have this after a heavy meal. It's called *Qatayef*. It's filled with goat cheese, ground-up walnuts, and cinnamon. And guess what, Morningstar? We serve honey with it."

Morningstar laughed. "Bees are everywhere, aren't they? They are one of our relations."

"Relations?" Liyah's mom asked.

"Don't get her going on this, Mother," Liyah quipped, rolling her eyes again, so all could see.

Her mom frowned at her. "Go on," she encouraged Morningstar.

"Well, what I mean is, we are taught that all natural things in the universe have spirits…souls. Because they come from the source of everything—the Great Spirit."

Mrs. Rahim looked puzzled.

"In the case of bees," Morningstar continued, "my grandfather taught me that since they are small, they were sent here to remind us of our humility, to bring us meekness. I believe in this sense that it's like your fasting. To remember that we are not the center, and to think of those who are not as fortunate."

"I told you," Liyah said, chuckling, this time her eyes betraying the quiet pride she held inside for her friend.

"What a nice message, Morningstar," Liyah's dad noted. "I see what you're saying."

As they enjoyed their desserts, Morningstar provided a few added details of her home in South Dakota, her Lakota upbringing, and how she ended up living alone with her grandfather.

The girls helped clear the table and wash the dishes as Liyah's father retired to the den. Shortly after, Liyah took Morningstar up to her bedroom.

Mr. Rahim later ascended the stairs with his wife on their way to bed. Hearing muffled chatter behind Liyah's door, he paused and whispered to her. "I'll take care of this, dear. It's been a really long day for them. I'll be there in a few minutes."

Using the knuckle of his forefinger, he rapped gently on his daughter's door. "Liyah?" he said softly. "May I come in?"

The handle clicked and the door swung open. "Sure Baba, c'mon in. What's up?"

"It's time for bed, that's what," he replied, quietly, closing the door behind him. " You won't forget to be up before dawn this time, will you? We don't want to set your mother off again."

"Yeah, I know. Morningstar decided to sleep here tonight and I'll set the alarm on my phone."

"Okay, good. But there is something else I wanted to tell you. I got a call today from my contact in Israel. He said they are still checking to see if they can help with Khalib's disappearance, but in the meantime, he can get me a couple of passes to allow a few people in and out of Israel for a few days. I think you should use them so you can take Morningstar freely around Jerusalem."

"Oh. That's great!" Liyah replied, excitedly. "Thanks so much. Morningstar and I have been talking it over and we think, well…because things are really heating up here with the attacks, and all the people cramming into Jerusalem, there will be times when all of us will need passes."

"All of us?" He glanced over at Morningstar. "What do you mean?"

"I mean there are two others we need to call to help us. They are boys, so you should be glad about that. But what's more important is that they have powers like Morningstar and me."

"Powers?" he questioned, looking perplexed.

Liyah looked at Morningstar. "Yes. We've been talking it over and decided to tell you."

"Tell me? Tell me what? What's going on? Are you in some kind of trouble?"

"No, no. It's not that. Have a seat on the bed, and we'll tell you something. But you have to promise not to say a word to anyone."

"Well…we'll see. I have no idea what to expect from you two."

The girls told him of their journey the previous week. Of encountering some mystical being named Ooray. Of the trials they went through together. Of Zack and Kai Li. Of the powerful gifts they received. And how time seemed to have been suspended.

Her dad looked stunned. "That sounds pretty fantastical. You must be putting me on?"

"No. Really, Dad," Liyah insisted, her expression deadpan. "It's all very true. This is how Star came to be here. And now we need to bring the boys here."

He studied both of them. "I have no idea what to say, except that I am certainly not going to repeat that to anyone and risk being sent to an institution."

"C'mon Baba, we're serious," Liyah pleaded.

Morningstar tugged Liyah's sleeve, then pointed to her bracelet.

"Oh," Liyah hesitated. "I'm not sure."

"We have to," Morningstar replied. "We have to trust someone else."

Mr. Rahim studied his daughter's eyes. He took hold of her hand. "Trust? What does she mean, sweetie?"

"Let's bring him back to the time of the fire, Star. Okay?"

"Sure…we can try. Nothin' to lose."

Liyah began. "Dad, see these bracelets?"

"Yes."

"They're magical."

He frowned. "Sweetie, really…"

"That's right. Really," she replied. She glanced at Morningstar. "We've been practicing a little, haven't we, Star? I can actually do something without even holding on to it, as long as it is on my wrist. I simply direct my thoughts to my hand."

She walked over to the desk her dad had made for her. Holding her hand out, facing the picture of her with him and her mom when she was younger, she focused her attention on it. First imperceptibly, then slowly, the picture began to move toward her hand. She brought it to the edge, then caught it with her other hand as it fell.

"I can't believe it," her dad said, a stunned look across his face.

The girls approached him, each taking hold of a hand. As his own eyes met theirs, he felt his mind start to fade from his control. Suddenly he was in a sheltered area in a forest standing beside his daughter, looking out as smoke surrounded them and a fire raged in front of him. Out of the smoke appeared a small girl carrying wet blankets, choking and gasping. It was Morningstar. She took the hand of a young boy and led Liyah and another boy through the deadly smoke.

In the next instant, he was seeing it all through his daughter's eyes, exactly like she had at the time. He could feel the brutal heat against his face and smoke choking his lungs, as he watched Morningstar lead them, finally tripping and falling into a stream. He was bent over, trying unsuccessfully to save Morningstar as she lay face down in the water. The bigger boy with them interceded, lifting Morningstar up out of the water, and placing her on the bank.

The scene faded as the girls let go of his hands.

Liyah looked at him. Tears were trickling down his cheeks. The very same tears that came to her eyes that day when she realized that her friend had saved her life, at the risk of her own.

"There are two boys we will be in touch with, Baba. Can you get passes for them, too?"

She could see her father trying to collect himself.

"I'll need to get some pictures of you two and your other friends for your passes. It's possible I could get them this morning. Text me a headshot of at least you two and fill out a form with your names and home addresses. I'll text the form to you when I get to work. Make it up for the boys if you have to. We can get pictures of them later."

"Okay," Liyah replied with a nod. "Thanks, Baba. I love you."

He hugged both of them. "Thank you for my daughter, Morningstar," he said, clearly trying to fight back the tears again. "Now you two get some sleep."

Thursday

TWELVE

West Bank Border

A MAN APPROACHED the black car as it arrived at the small Bedouin encampment near the Israel and West Bank border. He wore the standard formal dress of a Saudi: a long white dress shirt, buttoned-up to the high collar. Its full length skimmed the top of the man's sandals, and a red and white scarf covered his head, topped off with a circular black cord. The car door opened, and another man stepped out.

"*As-Salaam-Alaikum*, Hassan," said the man in the white robe and trimmed white beard, his smile broadening, hand extended.

"*Wa-Alaikum-Salaam*, Yusuf," replied Hassan, shaking his hand.

The two men made their way past a series of small tents and simple lean-to shelters, entering a much roomier tent with a high, square roof. Several large, handwoven Iranian carpets covered the floor, with their geometric designs enhanced by the stunning gold, purple, black, and red colors of the fibers. Huge, puffy matching pillows were scattered around, and bright colored tapestries hung on the canvas walls of the tent. They took their seats, sitting cross-legged on several pillows with a low table separating them.

"Well, Yusuf, it's been quite a while since I visited. Almost a year in fact. We usually meet closer to Gaza City. I see your encampment here has grown."

"Yes, indeed. We're usually left alone here since it's so far out. We're less of a threat to Israel's expansion plans of scattering housing developments across your ancestral lands." He reached to the table for a pot of tea. "You must have seen some of the other Bedouin camps along the way, on the edges of Beersheba, where the city meets the Negev Desert, no? The camps have been bulldozed into oblivion. Some families try to reestablish themselves, even though the camps are what they call *illegal*, and will just be plowed under again. The people have nowhere to go. The children are starving."

Yusuf served the tea to Hassan from a large silver teapot, straining the tea through a camel hair filter, then smiled. "A few sips can be forgiven during the fast, eh?" He set the pot down. "But more seriously, these people are not as lucky as me. I have money. They have none. I have water trucked in for the people here and a generator for electricity. They live in the dark and cannot shower or feed their families…or even their sheep."

Hassan sipped his tea. "My heart cries for them, Yusuf. But let's talk about better things, shall we?"

"Yes, yes…of course. You said you wanted to test something, and that I could be of help. I would be happy to assist in any way I can."

"You have already done so much by donating generously over recent years to the Palestinian cause. As you know, Hamas is now using some of that money to fund a secret project."

"You recently mentioned that it should be completed soon," Yusuf replied. "As you know, I've earned a lot of money over the years. But although I am not from here, I felt my country was not doing enough to support the plight of the Palestinian people.

"Ten years ago, I moved my falconry training operations here. Unlike the Saudi desert there are high, isolated hills around us, with enough room to provide a safe location and local game to feed the falcons. I can train the falcons for competitions, while also breeding them, and letting many go free. Even the Israelis like this." He grinned. "They try to protect this amazing species of birds. In fact, they encourage me, not really knowing it is *me*, which is perhaps another reason why they have left me alone." Yusuf paused, then added, "...so far."

Hassan set his cup down on the table. "How can you make all this money from training a few birds?"

"Ha! Well, that's just it. Most falconers will buy a bird or two because they're so expensive on the world market…some up to a quarter million American dollars. By doing this, they are depleting the population of falcons, and if it weren't for me and a few others who breed them, they would be even more endangered. But the prize money in the competitions in Saudi, the Emirates, and other places is more than tempting. A single top prize can be over five million dollars. At a given time, I have over fifty falcons and many other birds here. And my birds have won the top prizes dozens of times. I can supply the best birds at a more reasonable price by sharing in the prize money. At twenty-five percent share." He smiled. "Well, you do the math."

Hassan nodded. "I see. That's quite something,"

"So, of course, I can help out more. What do you need?"

"It's actually not that," Hassan explained, lifting his cup and taking a sip. "We need a place to do some testing of devices. Someplace where it wouldn't draw attention."

"Uh-huh. Well, this would certainly qualify. What kind of device are you talking about?"

"I received approval yesterday from the team to fill you in on limited details, as long as you agree to keep it secret. Agreed?"

"Certainly. But the less I know, the happier we will all be."

"I understand," Hassan replied. "The specifics are in the final planning stage, and I am keeping them under wraps with a small group of others."

"Interesting. So, what kind of testing do you need to do here?"

"The devices are actually small drones. The first test is to send a number of them here, to see if they can fly undetected and follow the terrain map to this location, and land successfully."

"When will this be done?"

Hassan laughed. "I'm glad you asked. The answer is…today."

Yusuf raised his eyebrows. "Today?"

Hassan checked his watch. "I anticipated your generosity. As soon as I send a coded text, they'll be launched. That means they will arrive here about 75 minutes from now."

"So soon? How will they find a good place to land safely?"

"The drones are smart. They have a map that includes a picture of your tent and the open space in the distance behind it. They'll hover until the landing spot is clear or they will locate a better place nearby. Their accuracy is within inches, because of a combination of the terrain, special video, and magnetic information that they analyze."

"Very impressive!"

"So, is it a go?" Hassan asked, his eyes and expression anchored.

Yusuf nodded his agreement.

Hassan took out his phone, tapped out the coded acknowledgment, and sent the message on its way.

The two finished their tea while discussing the deteriorating, depressing situation in Palestine. Yusuf stood up, offering his hand to assist Hassan in bringing him to his feet. "Your *drones* will be here shortly. The field is next to the building where I house the birds. Come, I'll show you."

They exited the tent through the giant flap then walked up a small rise. At the top, the hill flattened into a large field that spread out into the distance, halting at a grove of trees at the base of another larger rise that marked the southernmost foothill of the Judaean Mountains. To the right of them, stood a long rectangular building with its sides covered with tar paper and topped with a thin, corrugated metal roof. Yusuf unlocked the door and led them inside.

On one side, was a series of ten horse-like stalls, each with a door and window. Their upper halves on the side of the door were open to the air, but sight into them was blocked by closely positioned vertical wood slats. The right side of the structure was free of stalls. In their place were rows of long wooden rails, varying in width from two to four inches in diameter. Small stump-like objects were interspersed with some covered in a greenish carpet-like material. Perched along the rails, and on many of the stumps, spaced about five feet apart with their legs tethered, were a number of birds of different sizes. Small hoods had been placed over their heads, blocking their vision.

Yusuf led Hassan to one of the stalls. "If you look at an angle through the slats, you can see inside. This one and several others are used for breeding. In that sense, it's more like a henhouse, except these birds require more distance between them. All falconry suppliers and participants are highly regulated across the world. It's even more so here in the Middle East, where the sport has been passed down for thousands of years and regarded as a royal and sometimes even a spiritual experience."

Hassan peered in. "Why the metal bars on the outside windows?"

"Theft. Simple as that. These birds are valuable and endangered."

Yusuf led Hassan down the middle of the building, pointing to the birds on their perches. "The two smaller ones up front here, with the bluish-gray upperparts and orange underparts, are sparrowhawks. The other larger ones are Harris hawks, red-tails, and goshawks. The red-tailed hawk is the light brown one…his front looks like he's wearing white and brown-striped pajamas. The slate gray one there with the white eyebrow is a goshawk, which is much rarer. And this one is a Harris hawk. It's very common and much loved by the British."

They moved on to the end of the line.

"All these raptors can be expensive," Yusuf continued, stopping in front of the last bird. "But nothing like this boy here. He's a Peregrine Falcon, the fastest animal of any kind in the world. They can dive at incredible speeds, surprising their prey from above and using their feet to *punch.*" He illustrated by snapping his fist into the palm of his other hand. "They can stun or even kill it with that single blow then circle down to catch it in midair."

Yusuf picked up a gigantic leather glove lying against the perch. Placing it on his left hand, he drew it up to cover his entire arm and shoulder. He unclipped the bird from its roost and reattached it to the ring on the wrist of his glove. Still holding onto the end of the line, he removed the hood that covered its head and eyes. The bird jumped up, perching on the glove, its eyes flicking nervously about.

"Come, Hassan," he said, heading back up the aisle to the door. "Let's get this guy some food before he tries to go after one of these hawks. We should have enough time before your guests arrive."

Making their way outside, Yusuf bent down alongside the barn and picked up a small cardboard box by its handle and headed out toward the middle of the field, stopping about a hundred yards out.

"Here," he said. "This should do."

Hassan studied the bird on Yusuf's arm, his eyes moving from the dark crest of the bird's head to its yellow beak, along its blue-gray back and white underside, to its beak-matching talons.

"Definitely beautiful," Hassan said. "Although he seems smaller than I would have thought."

"He's a little less than sixteen inches tall and weighs under a pound and a half. His mate is almost twice his size, like most female falcons. But he's powerful. And deadly. I breed for competitive flying and less so for hunting. But occasionally I let them hunt freely. This time I'll provide the prey. Keep your eyes on him. His name is Taliq."

Yusuf removed the clasp from his glove, lifted up his arm, and uttered something in a high-pitched tone. The falcon broke from his perch. Vigorously flapping his long, pointed wings, he jetted upward into the sky, until he appeared as a tiny object making wide circles high above.

"Aren't you afraid of losing the birds?" asked Hassan, still gazing at the dot above.

Yusuf bent down and picked up the cardboard box by his side. "Well, I do lose some. But not many. Just like us humans, they choose easy food, safety, and shelter above all else." He opened the top of the box and removed a pigeon from within. "The few that don't return will add to the wild population. So, while it might cost me, there is a balance…and that's the way it should be. Now, keep your eyes open!"

Yusuf threw the pigeon into the air then removed a whistle from his pocket. He blew into it twice, then shouted "Taliq!"

The pigeon fluttered up above them, trying to get its bearings. Hassan searched the sky for the black dot. Taliq made one wide circle and then started down toward them, getting bigger by the second. The dot doubled in size rapidly and doubled several times again as Taliq approached like a meteor, speeding downward, directly above the unsuspecting pigeon. Still flapping lazily, about a hundred feet overhead, the pigeon finally began to head off in its chosen direction, but it was already too late.

THWAP!!

Taliq rammed his claws into the back of the bird at nearly two hundred miles per hour. Feathers flew, and the pigeon spiraled downward. Making a tight circle, Taliq then sped after it, catching it with his talons in mid-air before it could hit the ground, and hauling it back up higher.

Yusuf took his whistle and blew a series of shrill notes. Circling again, Taliq flew back toward them, dropping the pigeon only ten feet to the side of them, before returning for a fresh meal.

As Taliq finished picking at his lunch, Yusuf called his name quietly. The bird perched back on his arm. Yusuf clipped the cord to the band on his leg, just as a whirring sound suddenly caught their attention; they turned simultaneously toward it. Five small helicopter-like objects hovered less than a hundred feet away.

Yusuf reached into his pocket. Pulling out another small hood, he placed it over Taliq's head. "He's not familiar with these drones. He might freak out over what's happening here. We don't need that."

The drones slowly descended, landing gently on the grassy field with their rotors then shutting down.

The two men walked over to the drones. Hassan squatted down to retrieve one and held it up before them. "Quite amazing, I'd say. Wouldn't you?"

"Indeed," agreed Yusuf.

"Yes. No one has been able to release one out of Gaza unseen, until today. It's hard enough just getting parts across the border."

"They're pretty small. That's got to help."

"Yes," agreed Hassan, "but there are other factors as well. Ones I can't divulge."

"As I said. Keep me in the dark. My involvement ends at providing financial support to you Palestinians through Hamas. I don't want to know any of the details of your plans."

"Don't worry," Hassan assured him. "But can you keep the drones in a safe place? They're only for testing, and I can't risk taking them with me."

"Sure. Follow me," replied Yusuf. With Taliq on his arm, he led them back to the other side of the barn where there were rows of large wooden bins with latched doors. "This is where we keep some live pigeons and other prey, all the training equipment, and other storage items. They'll be safe. No one will know what they're for, anyway. They just look like toys to me."

"Yes, well you keep thinking that, my friend. But we hope the day is coming…very soon…when things are going to finally change here in Palestine."

"I'll get Taliq situated in his stall then be back. I'll walk you out."

"No need," Hassan insisted. "I've got to get back into Gaza for a meeting. Praise be to Allah! I have a forged government pass to move freely between the borders, although I still have to sit and wait in that long line with everybody else."

The men kissed each other on their cheeks.

"*Ma'a salaam*, Yusuf," said Hassan,"

"*Salaam.*" Yusuf returned.

Hassan made his way to his car and sped off, sand kicking up behind his tires.

THIRTEEN

THE PHONE IN Liyah's purse buzzed. She fetched it out, lifting it to her ear. "It's my dad," she said to Morningstar.

"Hi, Baba."

Liyah listened intently as she and Morningstar rounded the corner and walked into a women's store in downtown Lahia, stopping at the end of the first aisle. "We're out shopping. Umi gave me some money to buy Morningstar her own hijab. Don't know what's gotten into her."

Her eyes bounced around the store searching for the hijabs. "Bethlehem? Now?"

She listened again while watching a wide-eyed Morningstar who was absorbed with the buzzing of the crowded store, the fine fabrics, and the great variety of unfamiliar clothing worn by those passing by her. "Okay. It kind of screws up our plans this morning. But, yes, we'll wait for him here. What's Ahmad's phone number? I'll text him the address."

"Okay. Got it. Thanks." She hung up, then typed their address into a text message for Ahmad.

"What did he want?" asked Morningstar.

"We have to hurry up, Ahmad will be here in about fifteen minutes."

"Where are we going?"

"Bethlehem…to meet the boys. My dad found a place for them to stay and already paid for it."

"Why so soon?"

"I don't know, Star. I guess Ahmad is going to explain it all to us on the way. The best part of it is that I got Ahmad's phone number." She winked as she grabbed Morningstar by the hand. Both laughing, they made their way to the hijab section where Morningstar decided on a light blue one to match her moccasins.

Liyah nervously tapped her foot as they waited in line to be checked out. The woman handed her a receipt. She yanked Morningstar's hand, dragging her away. "C'mon…Ahmad will be looking for us."

The two made it out to the sidewalk just as Ahmad pulled up to the curb. The girls hopped in the back and Ahmad inched slowly down the street, jam-packed with people, cars, and goods on display. He turned onto the main street, heading toward Beit Hanoun, the northernmost crossing point from Gaza into Israel.

Ahmad picked up a folder on the passenger seat next to him and passed it back to Liyah without turning around. "Here, Liyah. It will only take a few minutes to get to the border, and the line shouldn't be long getting into Israel from the Strip. They've pretty much sealed off all entry points into Israel for anyone from Gaza, except those with special passes. This folder has the passes for you and Morningstar. Your dad was able to arrange them quickly this morning. They carry the seal from the Ministry of the Interior and the *Press* mark, identifying you as associated with the *Filastin Dawn*. You should have no problem going anywhere. The passes are good for four days."

"What about Kai Li and Zack?"

"You still need to text your dad the pictures of them with the forms as soon as you can. The blank forms for them to complete are in the folder as well, in case you didn't print out extra ones. They will be able to cross any borders and stay out of trouble with the passes, to keep the authorities at bay. If they're picked up anywhere without a pass, they'll be on a one-way trip to jail."

"Well," Liyah replied, nodding at Morningstar. "I don't think they'll be crossing any borders. But unfortunately, staying out of trouble is not something I can guarantee…especially for Zack. Right, Star?"

Morningstar laughed. "Yes. That would be true."

"And by the way, Ahmad," Liyah said, a little stiffness creeping into her voice. "This is Morningstar. You haven't been introduced properly."

"Oh…uh…so sorry. I mean it." He tilted the mirror, making eye contact with Morningstar. "Hi. I'm Ahmad. I work for Liyah's dad…sort of…part-time that is."

"Liyah told me. Don't worry, I know things are a bit crazy here." She elbowed Liyah in her ribs, then whispered in her ear. "Pretty damn cute, I'd say."

"Hush you," Liyah whispered back before breaking into a giggle.

"Did I miss something?" Ahmad questioned, bringing his eyes back to the road.

"No, no. Nothing," Liyah insisted. "Nothing at all."

The car pulled up to the barricade at the border control station. Ahmad handed all the passes to the agent, as several uniformed police searched under the car with metal detectors. One officer beamed his flashlight into the windows. Ahmad opened the trunk for another by clicking the latch next to the steering wheel. The police completed their task and signaled to the agent who then embossed each pass with a seal and time-of-day stamp, and handed them back to Ahmad.

Once through the gate and onto the main road, Liyah started up the conversation. "So, tell us, Ahmad. What's the rush?"

Ahmad checked the rearview mirror again, catching her eyes briefly before focusing again on his driving. "A couple of things. It's going to be a hell of a weekend. Your father thinks it will get harder to get around, and that your safety is in jeopardy. Most importantly, though, he feels that whoever has Khalib may want to move him out of Gaza to another country, like Iran, or Syria, or even some dangerous place in Africa."

"I'm so scared for Khalib!" Liyah blurted out.

"Me too, Liyah," Ahmad replied. "But there's one other thing. One of my sources in the Strip thinks a group who might have him was about to cross the southern border near Rafah to get into Egypt. But the latest rocket from Gaza provoked the Israelis to send two missiles in that direction. Several tunnels were destroyed." He checked the mirror again.

Liyah's eyes met his. "We'll never get him back," Liyah fretted, her expression glum.

"And that's exactly why it's getting urgent. Your dad is doing everything he can. You know he has that connection with his friend at the Ministry who is providing the passes. He has also submitted inquiries to the Israeli Defense Force to help."

"What can the Israeli Defense Force do?

"It's simple. Liyah. It's the IDF who hunts down terrorists. So, if this is a new group, they want to find out about it."

"What's this about Bethlehem and the boys?" asked Morningstar. "How far is that?"

"It should take us about an hour to get there. We'll be swinging by Jerusalem on the way. I have to pick up something and then we'll head into Bethlehem."

"Why Bethlehem?" Liyah questioned.

"Well, your dad said you told him one of your friends is a Christian. That's probably the safest place for Christians this weekend. It's Easter, you know."

"Of course, I know," she countered, a bit sternly, then retreated. "But it's pretty far away. How will we be able to work together on this?"

"I'm going to be your driver," Ahmad replied, keeping his eyes straight ahead as he shifted lanes. "Your dad insisted. I'll help get you guys around, and work on my own leads when I'm not keeping my eye on you two…and *the boys*, as you refer to them. I assume they'll be waiting for us somewhere in the city. They're already there, right? That's the impression your dad gave me."

Liyah looked at Morningstar, who raised her eyebrows, her eyes wide. "Well, I might have said I could get a hold of them," she replied, still staring at her friend. "That is…maybe when the subject of Bethlehem first came up. I don't know. We'll contact them when we get there."

Ahmad checked the mirror again. "That seems a little half-baked to me…if you don't mind me saying."

"I don't mind you saying," Liyah replied.

Ahmad caught Morningstar elbowing her. His eyes narrowed. "Is there something you two should be telling me?"

"We just can't wait to see them," Morningstar assured him. "That's all."

"Hmm…" Ahmad replied. "Well anyway, first stop will be Jerusalem."

As the road turned north, Ahmad spoke again. "Morningstar, this town we're passing is Ashkelon. You can see the beautiful white sandy bank of the Mediterranean Sea beyond it to your left. Ashkelon is something like eight thousand years old, part of a group of cities of the ancient Philistine people. It was the largest seaport in Canaan, the land taken over by the Jewish people about four thousand years ago. The entire Palestinian region at one point included all of what you see as Israel, the East and West Banks of Jordan, and Gaza…and of course Jerusalem."

"I really don't know much about the history of this place," Morningstar admitted.

"Okay. Well, this was a major trade route of spices, clothing, and other goods over thousands of years. Groups of tribes and civilizations from Egypt to Syria, to Greece fought over the rights to rule, and subjugated the people they pushed out. Arabic, Hebrew, and Aramaic—Jesus's language, were all spoken back then. And they are still spoken here today."

"I thought Jesus was Jewish. Didn't he speak Hebrew?" Liyah asked.

"He was, but Aramaic is even older than the Hebrew or Arabic languages. Hebrew was spoken mostly by the rabbis. He wanted to reach out to the ordinary people."

Morningstar chuckled. "You sound like a tour guide, Ahmad."

"I feel like one with you two." He lifted his eyes to the mirror. "Kiryat Malakhi is next. It means *City of Angels*...named after Los Angeles in America. Seriously."

Liyah laughed. "I swear you could just entertain yourself forever, Ahmad."

Heading further north, Ahmad filled the girls in on his activities at the Dawn, how he planned to write up a piece on terrorism, and how Palestine was at a turning point and about to lose the chance at having its own country back. He spoke of the plight of the Bedouins, the violation of agreements, the Israeli's building on Palestinian land, the lopsided nature of the armed conflict, the unemployment and growing food insecurity in Gaza, and the overall hopelessness grabbing hold of the region.

FOURTEEN

THE DOOR TO the conference room opened. Sayf Yasin entered and made his way to the head of the table. "So sorry. Didn't mean to keep anyone waiting again. Let's get right down to business."

"Hassan, why don't you start? I received the coded text a little while ago. We have some good news to report."

"Yes, that's right," Hassan began, glancing at Nasir next to him and then nodding across the table to Jamal and Nura. "I visited one of my donors. He's doing some amazing things with his birds there. It's more lucrative than one might imagine. Moneywise," he paused briefly, catching Nura's eye, "he is more than willing…"

"What are you trying to say, Hassan? That you don't like to receive donations from me? Or that you are looking for an excuse to–"

Yasin cut her off. "Okay, that's enough, you two. Let's not go down that road. There is no time for squabbling. Please go on, Hassan."

"The important thing I wanted to convey," Hassan continued, "is that we had a successful flight test of drones. Five of them appeared in formation at the test field and landed successfully. Right, Nasir?"

Nasir cleared his throat. "Well, I didn't *see* anything but I received the coded message from Hassan and was quite pleased. In the open areas in the southern part of Gaza, we have been able to test the ability of the drones to fly at the speeds and distances needed and assess their navigation capabilities. But this was the first time we incorporated the stealth shielding, their vision and mapping system, and the inter-drone signaling with onboard infrared communications. So, the short answer is yes. It appears to be a total success."

"How much more testing is needed?" the CEO asked.

"We're pretty much set for the individual drones now, as far as flight navigation, power, and communications," Jamal answered. "We still need to practice with more drones to be fully secure about the stealth aspect and to test larger groups operating as one. And then test the payloads which will be inflicting the damage. Hassan, can you comment on the targets?"

Hassan removed the elastic band from a large paper cylinder, unrolling a map of Israel in the center of the table. "There are ten key areas on this map marked with a light blue pencil. I will erase the marks before I leave today. Each represents a key strategic location where there is either an airbase, an artillery fortification, a tank squadron, or any combination thereof. These here, denoted with a J, are the seven strategic bases where the military jets are housed, in the open airfields as well as the hangars." He looked around the table before continuing, pointing to several groups of A's and T's. "This is where most of the artillery and tanks are stationed. Because of the volatile situation brewing now through the weekend, most of these have been placed in their current locations ready to respond, and will remain there through next week. I'm anxious to see how the drones will be deployed to cancel this threat they have over us...once and for all!"

Hassan sat back in his chair as Nasir moved to the front, carrying a drone. He positioned a short metal pipe with its opening about four inches in diameter so that one end protruded slightly over the edge of the table. Bringing the drone close to the opening of the pipe, he addressed the others.

"The drones will be deployed in clusters. The goal is that even if some are destroyed by the enemy during the attack or don't make it to the target, there will be plenty that will make it through. And if some drones miss their initial target, they will be able to hit secondary targets. For instance, if it misses entering the barrel of the tank, it will quickly focus on delivering the payload to the next immediate target...the turret."

Nasir held the main arms of the propellers at the top of the drone. "By squeezing these together, the drone becomes a long, narrow object that can fit easily into the shaft of any artillery gun or tank barrel. The drone will automatically adjust to its form as it enters the end of the shaft." He slid the drone into the pipe. "For any barrels that are even narrower, the propellers will snap off, reducing the height of the drone. Momentum will carry the drone and its payload the length of the barrel, exploding on impact when it hits the end. There is also a timer initiated once the drone enters the barrel so that it will explode under any circumstances after five seconds."

Nasir took the drone out of the pipe and laid it on the table. "There is no problem getting the drones into the engines of jets, whether on the ground or in the air, as the engine openings are wide, and the suction caused by the engine's air intake will aid the process. The only potential issue we have is getting to the jets in the hangars. For that, we have a number of drones in each cluster programmed to fly into the windows and the sides of the hangars to detonate on impact, thereby opening huge holes for the others to fly through…Any questions?"

Nura reached over and retrieved the drone, holding it and studying it through the slit in her keffiyeh. "Very impressive, Nasir. But how will you be able to test these?"

"We have a great degree of confidence since there will be thousands deployed. You're right, though. We will have to do some testing to assure us of the accuracy and to test a small sample of the payloads. But we may have to wait on some of the tests until the day of the mission to avoid alerting the Israelis, or anyone favorable to them. It will be at that time that we will make the call on whether to continue with the mission or not."

"Any more questions, comments? I would like to keep these reviews as short as possible."

Hassan faced the CEO. "What's next?"

"Tomorrow we'll send out several larger groupings of drones with fake payloads to further test inter-drone communications, their ability to carry the payloads, and their stealth." He turned to Jamal. "I would like you to be with Hassan at the test site. Perhaps you and Nasir can reprogram and test them over the fields there? Some way to exercise their group communications?" He returned to Hassan. "Jamal can get in and out of Israel fairly easily with his pass. But I think we need someone who can assist Jamal. Someone we can trust."

"What kind of person do you need, Jamal?" asked Hassan. "Skill-wise?"

"Someone to help keep things under control during the test, and maybe help me to collect and retest the drones. Nothing too complex. I can do the software adjustments, but I may need to reassemble a few. So…some general help would be great…But if they have software or communication skills, all the better."

"I'll see what I can do," said Hassan.

The CEO stood up. "Okay then. Let's call it a day and regroup at the same time tomorrow. Hassan, I think you should leave at the rear entrance with Jamal and Nura. Nasir will show you where to park next time. There is a buzzer next to the bulkhead to signal your arrival. Meeting adjourned."

Hassan headed from the bulkhead toward his car in the side lot. Nasir led Jamal and Nura to the tunnel, closing the bulkhead behind them.

"The weather seems to be holding up nicely for the weekend," Jamal said, as they made their way down the sand-blown street toward his car. "I'm concerned that rain might interfere somewhat with communications between drones. And we haven't been able to properly test for that."

"It's a complicated plan," replied Nura. "At least to me. But maybe that's because I'm not a techy nerd like you."

"Ha! Yeah, maybe. Most of the technical complexity has been analyzed for some time now. The stealth signature, infrared comm, payload size, targeting, safety...all the critical strategic and operational considerations. Once we complete the rest of the testing over the next couple of days, I think we will have greater confidence in the mission."

"But then there is always secrecy and unplanned factors, don't you think?" Nura asked. "That's what I see all the time. Someone leaks information or a missile lands someplace unexpectedly. Even treachery. Don't count that out."

"Yes. There is always the unexpected. You can't predict everything. You have to plan the best you can. Then just pray…and go with the flow."

Nura grabbed Jamal's arm and they stopped. She turned to him, for the first time sensing something that was getting beyond her control…making her anxious. "I'm worried, Jamal. I've been doing this for over a year, and I feel things are getting worse, faster. I don't know…this weekend…I just don't know. There is static in the air. I don't dare show up in some places. Not dressed like this anyway. I'm drawing more attention. Not only from the Israelis. Some of our own people, and several extreme Islamic groups, are not pleased with any woman, especially someone as young as me, doing what I'm doing. I feel in some ways like I'm caught in the middle."

"Well, you are," Jamal replied. "We all are in a way…caught between extremes, caught in our time, trapped by those who have not learned from history." He opened the car door for her.

"Something has to change," she agreed, taking her seat. "Something has definitely got to change."

"That's exactly what we're planning," Jamal replied, closing her door.

He walked around the car, opened the driver's door, and settled into his seat. They sat there for an extended moment silently, looking straight ahead across the beach to the sea. Then Jamal started the engine.

FIFTEEN

Old Arafat Airport

THE GAS GENERATOR in the nearby room continued its incessant dull hum, providing an unsteady electrical current to the lightbulbs dangling off the cords draped overhead. A group of men and boys dressed in work shirts and jeans, and some in dusty white tunics, sat around as they scraped the last of their supper off metal plates.

Khalib watched as one of the men wearing a tunic and a red and white headdress tossed his empty plate to the side and stood up to speak.

"Alhamdulillah. Allah be praised!"

"Alhamdulillah," came the echo from the others.

He continued. "The Israelis must have traced the source of yesterday's rocket attack to somewhere close to here. It's likely that the Palestinians used mobile units in the desert to launch them. That's why the explosions from the counterattack shook the ground last night. I heard from our sources in that area about an hour ago. They told me the Israeli military is now planning another sweep of the area. We need to move out."

"How soon, Mabood?" asked an older boy next to Khalib.

"Right away. Before it gets dark. They think the Israelis could reach here by then. We've been lucky. They destroyed sixty miles of these tunnels last year used by Hamas to transport equipment and hide after launching attacks."

Mabood began to stroll among them. "We can no longer count on any tunnels to get out of Gaza. This will be our last operation, for a while at least."

"What about these captives?" asked one of the men in a tunic.

"Once we get past the border and out of Gaza, we'll take them farther north to the main camp near Tel Arad. It's a distance from here, near the foothills outside of Beersheba. But I've arranged for a couple of vans to pick us up close to this tunnel exit. We'll need to take everything. That means all the rifles and ammo too. We should collect them in one of these trolleys and drag it behind us." He pushed one into the middle. "Someone else can load what's left of the food and supplies into another one. A few of you check up top to make sure we don't leave anything behind that will give us away. Let's pack up!"

Khalib got to his feet and followed an older boy up a set of stone stairs to the base of a tall aluminum ladder that rose up through a hole in the ground above them.

"Join me up here," said the boy upon reaching the top of the ladder. "You can get some fresh air while I look around."

Khalib followed him to a small trap door directly above. They unlatched the lid, pushing it through the opening then sliding it to the side on the cement floor above. They crawled up through the hole, coming to a stand in a huge hallway.

"This used to be one of the concourses at the old Arafat International Airport," said the older boy, "before it was destroyed by the Israelis about twenty years ago." He removed a pack of cigarettes out of his shirt pocket. He tapped it until one cigarette popped up, offering it to Khalib with a nod of his head.

"No thanks," said Khalib, stone-faced. "Those things will kill you, you know."

The older boy pulled it out, placed it between his lips, flicked open his lighter, and lit it. He sucked in a deep breath of smoke then pushed it out slowly through his nose. "Wouldn't worry about that. I don't think we're goin' to make it that long. This life will take us before any cancer." He took in another long drag, then talked as the smoke floated out of his mouth with the words. "I've been working these tunnels for almost two years. Not sure if they're gonna send me to another country or keep me here to help bring others out. I'd rather be in on the real action."

"Where are you from?" asked Khalib.

"Gaza. Like most, I suspect. You?"

"Yeah, me too. I've been with a group in Gaza that took me about a week ago. Yesterday they brought me to this tunnel. You miss your family?"

The boy stared at Khalib. "We're not supposed to talk about that."

"I know," Khalib replied, his thick dark hair fluttering in the light wind. "It's just that there's no one up here."

"Doesn't matter. They'll find out. Best to be careful…not only for yourself but your family."

"So I've been told," said Khalib, trying to fight back a surge of memories and homesickness. "They threatened they'd harm them. I'm afraid I'll never see them again."

"Well, get used to it 'cause you won't. Me? Well, I don't care anyway. My parents are cowards. They're afraid to confront the Israelis. But I'm not. I'm here to fight them. That's why I don't wanna get shipped off to some other place to fight a battle that I don't give a crap about…like in Iran or Africa."

Khalib's expression turned hollow. "I just want to go home."

"Like I said, forget it."

"I think they took me by mistake. I was just in the middle of some trouble…headed home by myself. My friends were throwing stones and stuff."

"Maybe, but it seems to me they had other information about you. I mean it's clear you know your way around a computer. That's probably why they snatched you. They even asked you to help them, as long as they can look over your shoulder. I saw Mabood asking you to do something with his phone, too. Better play along." He nodded. "The alternative is worse."

Khalib looked puzzled. "Alternative?

"Exactly," replied the older boy, who began surveying the area. "You don't want to know."

Khalib stared out at the horizon. The sun was sinking low in the sky, its orange hue pouring in through the archways in front of him. Everything in sight was in ruins. Large chunks of broken cement formed small hills. Huge, jagged pieces stuck up like icebergs out of a frozen sea. *This must have at one time been the central building at the old airport*, he thought.

The breeze kicked up some of the fine dust lying about. Khalib covered his mouth briefly, then crossed his arms over his chest as a light chill in the air caught up to him. Suddenly a deep sadness crept up into his thoughts. *Liyah. How did I lose her? Is my family okay?...It's all my own fault.*

"Don't see anything here that would identify us," the older boy said, flicking the cigarette onto what was left of the original slab floor. "Might as well head back in."

Khalib followed him back down through the hole, pulling the heavy makeshift cement-like lid snug behind them, then latching it. They joined the others.

"Nothing up there," the older boy said to Mabood.

"Okay. Let's move out." Mabood opened a door to the room that housed the generator. Behind it was a narrow tunnel opening, only five feet high and three feet wide. He passed out several flashlights, then picked up two short man-made torches leaning against the wall. He lit the fuel-soaked rag ends. "The last two of you turn off the generator and put the stones back in place behind us to seal off the exit. The torches will provide the most light. One in the front. One in the back. The flashlights are for emergency use, in case the torches die. A little way up the tunnel splits. The right side goes to Egypt. But it's become too dangerous to use that one now. We'll go to the left to Israel and the Negev desert. We'll be picked up there."

One by one they made their way in, stooping down and slowly shuffling along. The light of the torches flickered off the rock walls.

Khalib could sense his chest tighten, his breaths shorten. He didn't like enclosed spaces. Much like his sister. His mind flashed to the bomb that destroyed their home when he was little, and then to the other tunnel that these people dragged him through. They must have walked for miles, all the time wondering if he was going to end up buried alive somewhere along it. All he could think of was home, that he had to survive somehow…that eventually he would make it back. But he also knew he could not run away or speak out because that would only place his family in danger. *This dark tunnel is like what my life has become,* he thought. *The way back sealed off, and the journey through it leading to nowhere. At least nowhere I want to be.*

SIXTEEN

Bethlehem

AS AHMAD, MORNINGSTAR, and Liyah reached the next town, Ahmad glanced back at Morningstar. "Awfully quiet back there. Everything okay?"

"Just thinking, Ahmad," Morningstar replied. "About broken agreements, poverty, and losing one's country."

"Wow. Well, sorry. Didn't mean to depress you."

"It's not that. It's just that it is a very familiar story."

"Do you live in a place like that?"

"Yes. America."

Ahmad jerked his head towards her. "Huh?"

"I mean that's what happened to my people only a few hundred years ago. Almost all the tribes of America. The people who were there first, like the ancestors of the Philistines, and others you speak about. We were killed and punished for being in the way of the onrush of arrogance and greed. *The Takers*, my Lakota ancestors called them."

"Lakota? Indian? Is that why you are dressed the way you are…except for the hijab? I certainly noticed…but I really like your tunic, by the way."

"Thanks. Yes, Native American." She paused briefly. "I'm not talking about everyone. Not everyone meant us harm…just enough of them. And of course, we had some people in our own tribe who were not helpful. But we had no chance against The Takers. Their cannons, rifles, and machine guns overwhelmed our bows and arrows, and the few rifles we could buy. We were kicked off our own lands to reservations, stripped of our rights, forced to comply, and be dependent on the white government. Some of our people were massacred."

"That's tragic, Morningstar. Obviously, I don't need to tell you more about what has been going on here for a very long time. And now…well…it's crushing us."

They passed the small town of Kiryat Malakhi, then Yad Binyamin. "This was one of the many settlements created by Jewish immigrants as they fled from their persecutors in Iraq, Syria, and Yemen, after Israel became a country. They continued to be attacked by Arab and Muslim communities."

"Why? What happened?" asked Morningstar.

"It was in 1948 after the Holocaust when millions had been killed by Hitler during WWII in death camps. Britain created a Jewish state by splitting Palestine and creating a safe homeland for Jews. Many Arab states got angry and passed laws against the Jews, who were then forced to leave to come here with those from Germany, Poland and other places. That only compounded the situation. But the odd part to me is that we Palestinians have received almost no help from any countries. They seem to have all abandoned us."

"It looks like the Jews have also had their share of trouble," Morningstar replied. "Wouldn't you say?"

"Yes. Yes, I would. There are forces out there beyond our control. Forces that were set in motion a long, long time ago."

Ahmad drove on, heading west past Tal Shahar and the hilltop town of Latrun. He passed along the edge of the Neve Forest, to Sho'eva, and finally Motsa, the West Jerusalem neighborhood at the base of the Judaean Hills.

Having reached the northernmost point of the trip, Ahmad followed the sweeping turn of the highway, heading now south, toward the city. "This town to the left is called Har Hotzvim," he said, as they passed a neatly planned modern cityscape of soaring blue-glass structures and green gardens. "It is a high-tech center…and where many government buildings are. Jerusalem is a short distance ahead."

"Tech center," Liyah whispered to Morningstar.

"Jamal?"

"Yeah. I think that's where he said he works."

"You're whispering again, girls," Ahmad called back. "Who's this Jamal?"

Liyah leaned forward. "Just someone who might be able to help us with a contact in Jerusalem. Speaking of which, I saw a sign that we're in the city now."

"Yup, city limits. In fact, I'll be turning off right up here."

Ahmad eased the car onto the access road and headed toward the government center. A few minutes later they arrived at Yig'al Shilo Square. He slowed the car to the curb, stopped, and texted something.

"Sign says that's the Prime Minister's office across the street," Morningstar noted, "where the road is blocked off and..." She turned her head to the sound of knuckles rapping on glass.

Ahmad lowered his window. A helmeted police officer peered in. "Move along. No stopping here."

Ahmad fumbled with something in his jacket pocket and flipped it open for the officer. "Just meeting someone." He checked his watch. "She should be here any moment."

"Ten minutes. No longer," the officer advised gruffly. "I don't care if you *are* from the press."

"Yes, sir." Ahmad acknowledged. "Of course, sir. We won't be long."

"Better not be."

Ahmad rolled the window up, then studied the street that led to the Prime Minister's office. *Nothing.*

"Who're we meeting?" Liyah asked.

"A connection of a connection of a connection." Ahmad turned around and grinned at Liyah. "Someone your dad knows in the Ministry of the Interior knows someone who works for the Prime Minister. And that person has a connection to the person we are meeting now." He pointed to a woman beginning to cross the street holding a manilla envelope in her hand. "This is probably her."

"Sounds like a spy thriller to me," Liyah replied.

Ahmad chuckled. "It kinda does. But then I get the feeling we're actually getting involved in one, don't you?" He lowered the front passenger window. A young blond woman in jeans and a blue jacket with her hair in a ponytail leaned in. "I was already headed to the square when I got your text. You must be Ahmad. I'm Esty." She handed him an envelope.

"Yes." He pointed his hand toward the rear seat. "And this is Liyah and Morningstar."

The young woman smiled, then nodded. "Hi girls. Someone here must have some pull. You'll find the special passes in the envelope. Even though the request was only for four, I got six of them, just in case. They are for a private tour Friday morning in the Old City. I'll be the guide. Just show up a little early. I need to get all the tours done well before dusk because that's when the madhouse will start...you know, the rush home for the Muslims during Ramadan. The city streets and restaurants will be packed, and I'd like to get home early.

Ahmad opened the envelope. "Sure thing, Esty," he said, checking the passes. "There aren't any names on them?"

"Not needed," Esty replied. "More flexible this way. I don't do these private tours often. The passes expire that day, so don't lose them."

Ahmad checked the rearview mirror and then started the engine. "We're gonna be kicked out of here. Thanks, Esty. See you then."

Esty slid her hands from the roof of the car. "Guess I'll see you then. Stay safe."

Ahmad made his way back onto the main road and headed back south. Within twenty minutes, their pace slowed as they joined the multitude of other cars headed to the birthplace of Jesus. Turning onto Hebron Road they inched their way into the outskirts of Bethlehem, where they were stopped briefly at a checkpoint to have their passes checked. They continued on, and ten blocks later Ahmad located a parking spot on a side street.

Ahmad led them into the Inn and paid for the room in advance, using a Filastin Dawn credit card, and signed in for Zack and Kai Li. The clerk handed him the keycards. "Thank you, sir. They should be here anytime. We'll wait for them in the room."

The latch made its electric whirring sound as Ahmad waved the card over the sensor. They entered. Ahmad set the folder on the bureau. "How long do you think they'll be?"

"Well, uh, it's all a surprise," Liyah replied. "So we're not sure. Can you find Morningstar a soda? We'll check."

As Ahmad left, Morningstar grabbed Liyah's arm. "What are we gonna do?"

Liyah sank down into the small couch in the sitting area. "Let's call them now. Then we'll have to stall Ahmad."

"Yeah, well we don't know if one, both, or neither of them will show up."

"We have to trust them, Star. Besides, we still don't know exactly how time works in all this. It seems that it slows down sometimes, and sometimes it stops altogether."

"I know what you mean. Alright."

Morningstar joined Liyah on the sofa. "Okay," Liyah began, "let's hold onto their symbols on our bracelets—the TrueHeart for Zack, and the Torch of Truth for Kai Li."

Morningstar complied.

Liyah continued. "Now let's think of them. With both of us doing this, the message should be stronger."

In seconds, Zack's stunning sapphire charm in the shape of a heart began to throb, pulsating its deep blue light from both bands. This was followed by the white light of Kai Li's torch. The girls squeezed their eyes closed, tight, hands brushing against each other. The bracelets began to buzz like the ring of a cell phone, vibrating against their wrists. They opened their eyes and sat back.

A minute later, two small fuzzy multicolored blobs of light appeared above the bed nearest them. They wavered like a flame, growing rapidly in size to form the outline of two bodies. The foggy lights became sharper, bringing the images of Zack and Kai Li into focus, solidifying, until there was a light *pop!* The boys dropped into a sitting position next to each other at the edge of the bed.

Zack looked over at Kai Li. "Jeez! I thought I got rid of you just the other day."

"Well," Kai Li replied. "Nice to see you, Mr. Grumpy. "I just got used to being home."

"You're not supposed to be *used* to anything," said Morningstar. "We're supposed to be out changing the world…remember?"

Zack rose, holding out his arms. "Only too well."

Liyah leapt up, embracing him and Kai Li, followed by Morningstar.

"You both look the same as when we left you," Liyah noted, stepping back.

"Well, it's only been a week," Zack answered, letting out a belly laugh. "What'd you expect?"

"I mean it looks like you're both still wearing the same clothes, except for Kai Li's coat."

Kai Li glanced down at his white shirt, black cuffed pants, and sneakers. "I got out of work a little while ago. It's evening in Hong Kong, you know. Can't be certain anymore, though, what time it is *anywhere* when we do this. Good that my mom was still asleep when I left. But, look…" He held onto the sleeve of his unzipped, gray casual jacket. "Somethin' new. Got it the other day."

Zack grinned. "Quite the fashionista, aren't you?"

"And you are your same wise-ass self, Zack?" Morningstar joked.

"So, I guess you are still in charge then, Miss Star?" he retorted, pulling the red hood of his sweatshirt down off his head and holding his breath until he blew it out in a burst, breaking out hysterically.

The others joined, filling the room with laughter.

"I was leaning against the porch railing," Zack continued, "getting ready to head off to school, when I got the call. I wasn't sure if I was using the bracelet right. But then here I am…or we are. And it's pretty amazing we arrived at the same time, isn't it?"

"Maybe not," Kai Li replied. "I mean *time and all,* as I say."

"Perhaps we had some help?" added Liyah. "Ooray? Maybe we'll never know."

Zack nodded. "But what is it we are doing here exactly?"

"There's no time to explain fully now. You're in Bethlehem. Palestine. My dad arranged this room for you two. And Ahmad, a sort-of friend of mine who works for him, brought us here. He'll be back any minute, so you have to play along, okay?"

Kai Li gave the okay sign with his thumb and forefinger, then turned to face the door as the lock buzzed. "Sure!"

Ahmad entered the room.

"Ahmad, this is, …Zack," Liyah informed him, her words tripping over her tongue. "And…uh, Kai Li. The ones I told you about."

Ahmad handed off the soda to Morningstar, then shook the boys' hands enthusiastically. "Welcome. Welcome. Yes, I have heard a bit about you." He turned to face Liyah and Morningstar, confusion suddenly imprinted on his face. "I didn't expect you so soon. How did you know where we were? "

The boys looked blankly at each other, then over to Liyah.

"Oh, well. We, uh, texted them when we checked in, so I guess they were nearby and got a quick taxi ride…right guys?"

"Yeah," Zack agreed, keeping his eyes on Liyah."

"I see," said Ahmad, glancing suspiciously at the girls. "Well okay. I just wanted to meet you and make sure you were settled here. Liyah's father asked me to take you around as needed, although I'll have to work it into the other things I have to do.

Zack nodded. "Sounds good."

Ahmad continued. "I think the best thing is to get your pictures and paperwork filled out so I can get you passes to allow you to move around freely." He opened the folder. "Here, hold onto these. They'll get you into the tour tomorrow in case we're not together. There are also two forms for the general passes from Liyah's dad, in case he didn't get the right details from Liyah. A couple of questions, like your full name and hometown…and signatures. I'll take them back with me tonight. Then tomorrow when I pick you up, I hope to have the passes ready." He handed them a pen.

Zack and Kai Li filled out the forms quickly and handed them back.

"So, let's see. Liyah, can you take their pictures?" Ahmad asked.

"Oh sure. Of course." She removed her phone from her purse. "Smile Zack." The camera flashed several times. "Now you, Kai Li."

"Sorry to run off so quickly," Ahmad apologized. "I have to get the girls back, then do a couple of things myself. We'll see you here tomorrow morning after breakfast. You can all make your plans then. The tour will be in the late afternoon…in Jerusalem. Liyah, Morningstar...let's go."

The girls followed Ahmad into the hall. He reached into his pocket, extracted a room key card and handed it to Zack. "There are two. The other one is on the bureau."

"Oh, I almost forgot," Liyah added. "We need SIMs."

Ahmad stared at her blankly. "SIMs?"

"Yes. SIMs…for the phones. We can't communicate with them, unless they get special SIMs for the network here in Palestine.

"How did you communicate with them a little while ago? Didn't you say you texted them?"

Liyah's eyes met Ahmad's. She looked like a deer caught in the headlights. "Oh, ah…well, I meant they called me from a phone booth."

Ahmad squinted his eyes. "Seriously?" He glanced over at the boys, their hands in their pockets, expressionless. "Hmm. Well, we'll talk more tomorrow. Does anyone know how to put SIMs in a phone, because I don't."

"I do," Kai Li replied.

"Okay, well give me your phones anyway, so I buy the right ones. You too, Morningstar."

Ahmad stepped inside to collect the phones, then returned to the hall. "See you tomorrow," he said, turning and making his way down the hall.

Liyah and Morningstar faced the boys. "Sorry it's so rushed today. We'll catch up more, don't worry." After a few hugs, Morningstar and Liyah turned and hurried down the hall, catching up to Ahmad.

Seventeen

Talbiya

THE LATE AFTERNOON sun cast its last strong rays through gaps between the trees in the backyard of the two-storied limestone home. It illuminated the white gravel pathway from the iron gate to the multicolored flagstone front steps of Esty's home in the Jerusalem suburb of Talbiya. Esty walked aside the high stone wall adjacent to the garage, stopping at the marble archway outside of the gate. She removed her key from the side pocket of her blue blazer, twisting it into the lock. The metal hinges creaked as she pushed the heavy gate inward and then closed it behind her.

The stones crunched under her feet as she started toward the house. Something caused her to slow her pace halfway up the path. She stopped, staring up at the orange-red terracotta roof. Her glance slid down the left side of the house to the second-story patio then jumped to the tops of the olive, almond, and eucalyptus trees evenly spaced throughout the yard. *She was lucky,* she thought, *growing up here. How many people in Israel, or the world for that matter, had this?* She concentrated. *But that's not it.*

Something else had made her slow to a stop. She breathed in deeply through her nostrils, then sighed as she let the air out. A symphony of delicious scents, a combination almost unrecognizable to her, overwhelmed her senses.

She glanced over the grassy yard to the rock garden by the front wall, taking in the bright red poppies and purple lupines, then the yellow tiger tulips up ahead along the walkway. Her eyes shifted again, leading her to the twisted, gnarled bases of the olive trees and their white blossoms that delivered the scent of the sea.

Her gaze shifted yet again to the middle of the yard where a sole eucalyptus tree grew, tall. Its fuzzy yellow flowers showered down their pungent, minty aroma. Her eyes then moved to the almond trees closer to the house—the trees that reminded her of the dogwoods she had seen in New England during her trip to America. Their brown bark and gentle curling branches exuded the sweet smell of their delicate white and pink blossoms. *It was odd,* she thought, *the blossoms on that tree are usually gone by now. They bloom in February.*

Esty bent down to smell the tulips at her feet, taking in their spicy tang. She moved slowly across the edge of the lawn to the rock garden, breathing in the fruity vanilla fragrance of the poppies, then the dense florid perfume of the host of upright tiny bundled, budlike blossoms of the purple lupine. She glanced back at the almond tree. She was familiar with the scents of each of the trees and flowers…but not all together.

That's what it is! The lupines and tulips would certainly have faded by now, she considered, *as well as the almond's flowers. This had never happened before. Not here in this yard. Not all these beautiful, sweet blossoms and scents at the same time. As a chorus. All in time for the rare gathering of all the people in the Old City this weekend.*

Making her way back to the walk, she stepped up onto the porch and into the front hall of the house. She hung her newsboy cap over the closest hook and her blazer on the next. Moving past the sprawling, shiny, modern kitchen on her left, she passed through the archway by the stairs and into the den on her right.

Esty paused, studying the man in the high-backed, cushy armchair next to the fireplace, buried in a book, two others on his lap.

"Hi, Pops."

He looked up. "Ah...Hamuda. My dear one." He smiled. "Sometimes I wish you'd stop using that word. You picked that up in America. Even though I don't think they really say it, do they? Sounds like it's out of the sixties."

"Okay, Abba. I'll try. Kinda got stuck in my head, you know."

"Uh-huh. Well, never mind. How was your day? Sorry I wasn't able to pick you up."

"It's fine," she replied, snuggling lengthwise onto the sofa and pulling a pillow behind her head. "I got out a bit late today anyway. What ya readin'?"

"A history book…several actually, about this region in which we live. So many troubled times over so many centuries."

"I know. So sad." She opened a magazine and started flipping through it.

"More than sad. And it seems to be getting worse. I didn't think that was possible."

Esty kept flipping. "Is it your homework or something?" She laughed, setting the magazine back on the coffee table.

"Sort of, actually. I think we're at a crossroads. These artillery and missile volleys have become more frequent this past year. The Prime Minister asked me to help figure out how to diffuse the tension. Calm things down."

"How will that happen? It always seems so lopsided to me. Every time there is a blowup, a hundred Palestinians get killed for every one of *us*."

He set the book in his lap and looked at her above the top of his glasses. "Whose fault is that?"

"Don't get so defensive, Dad. I'm not saying anything about you. I'm just saying that it must be hard for them. Their ancestors once owned the land here, too, you know. And now even the other Muslim countries don't seem to want to help them…except for maybe fueling the terrorists…but that's all about looking after their *own* interests."

"Everyone *shared* the land at some point," he replied. "This goes back before even the Bible—to the earliest humans who migrated in and out, forming tribes, who then made war on each other for thousands of years. There is no way of knowing who owned what, and when."

"Sorry. I didn't mean to get you upset," she returned. "I just think the situation is awful. And most times I think we're making it worse…by holding someone's face to the ground."

Her dad paused, gathering himself, a side he always showed her in moments of stress…that ability of his to change the speed and direction of a discussion at any time, even at the worst of times. She watched as his taut countenance softened and his eyes expressed his deepest concern for her. "Hmm. Maybe I shouldn't have gotten you that tourism job." His face broke into a broad smile. "You changing sides?"

"No, I'm serious." Rolling off the couch, she took a seat on the leather footrest, closer to, and directly across from him. She looked past him, studying a series of four framed maps of Israel on the wall. One depicted the land three thousand years before King David, the central figure of Judaism who united their region three thousand years ago. Next to that a drawing of the region at the time of Jesus Christ—under Roman rule. The third of the New Israel…in 1948 after the formation of the new Jewish state following WWII. The last showed modern Israel with its rule extending into the Palestinian areas of the West Bank and Gaza.

Esty glanced above the maps, to a picture of her grandfather, her father's father, who was largely known as the founder of a billion-dollar Israeli technology company, and founder of the tech center itself. Below the maps were two certificates—one of her father's engineering degree from a prestigious university near Boston, and the other one of his subsequent combined degree, also from America, in history and philosophy.

She brought her attention back to her father, and the small picture of her mother in a delicate silver frame, sitting by itself on the table beside him. *Always on his right,* she thought. *Close by, as if he were afraid to be apart from it…even for a minute.* She sensed the moisture forming behind her eyes, and the slowing, then reversing of time. For an instant, she was transported back to being a little girl holding onto the hem of her mother's skirt as they walked through the supermarket. Then suddenly, she was standing beside her simple, wooden casket.

"I miss her, too, Hamuda," he said, breaking the long pause.

"I know, Abba." She reached out and placed his hands into hers. "It's been several years since the cancer took her from us, but sometimes it feels like it was just yesterday. When I give tours, she is always with me. She loved our county, our people…us."

"Yes, she did. Her heart was bigger than the sea. Like yours."

She squeezed his hands, comforting him, absorbing his gentle way. She surveyed his graying eyebrows and hair.

"What does the Prime Minister think you can do?"

"It's not completely clear to me. Sometimes I think, like all politicians, he just wants to remain in the good graces of the big companies. Or it could be to stay close to the source of the money. Your grandfather was a force, one of the greatest industrialists and tech leaders in Israel. But I'm not as close to the corporations as he was."

"So what can you do for him?"

"Well, I know he sees me as a dreamer. The philosopher in that diploma. Perhaps he wants some of that for himself. But I do believe his intentions are good and that he really wants to change things…to be better for the Palestinians and safer for everyone."

"That would be nice. But look at what's happening. More attacks in the past few days by both sides, than all of last year. And there's something else. She searched his eyes."

"And what's that, sweetie?"

"Something's in the air, Abba. I can't quite place it. But in the last few days of giving the tours, I noticed how big the crowds have gotten. Not only in the Old City because of all three celebrations happening at the same time, but all over Jerusalem. I'm sure you noticed that in the afternoon the cars are moving slower than the pedestrians. It would have taken you longer to pick me up than it was for me to walk home."

"Yes, it does seem to be unusual. But I don't think the world is going to blow up if that's what you mean." He grinned.

"It's more than that. I don't know. Have you ever sensed something in the air but can't place it?"

He laughed. "All the time."

"No, I mean it. It's more than the electricity of this weekend. There's a different energy. And sometimes it feels very dark to me."

"Well, let's not dwell on that, huh?" He stood up, placing his hand on the top of her head and chuckling once more. "Come. I'm starving. It's time for you to make dinner again."

She followed him into the kitchen. "Oh, Pops. What am I going to do with you?"

"You can start by not using that expression."

EIGHTEEN

Tel Sheva

AHMAD PULLED INTO the parking lot behind the restaurant on the outskirts of the town of Tel Sheva, a city of 200,000 located south of Jerusalem and east of Gaza and recognized as the capital of the Negev Desert region. He shut off the car, leaving the headlights on per the instructions given to him. Shortly after, another car pulled up beside him. A man in black dress pants, a white shirt, and a light blue tie opened the driver's door and stepped out of the car. He approached Ahmad and knocked on the passenger window. Ahmad lowered the window, and the man, sporting a silver goatee and wearing a plain, small white turban, bent in.

"Ahmad?" the man asked.

"Y-Yes," Ahmad replied, his nervousness betraying him.

The man reached his hand forward, "*As-Salaam-Alaikum.*"

"*Wa-Alaikum-Salaam*," Ahmad returned, shaking his hand.

"You can call me, Fahzi," said the man. "Come. I'll take you there."

Ahmad opened his door and slid out. It was early evening. Strategically placed streetlamps provided ample light to see his way, but he was alone out here and a queasy feeling swelled in the pit of his stomach. He locked the car and walked with the man for several blocks, heading out of town toward the desert.

He vaguely remembered Beersheba, but it was only for a special trip there with his family when he was a child. He had never been here to Tel Sheva, its sister town directly east. It was almost impossible now to travel between Gaza and anywhere, but the press pass that Liyah's dad had given him allowed him some freedom. Beersheba had developed into a sizable city since the late twentieth century. Many of the traditional Bedouin had moved to Tel Sheva and combined with those in Rahat and other towns in the area, made up almost half of the Bedouin population of the Negev.

Ahmad followed him across the next street. They passed a number of open tents scattered about the base of a low, sandy hill before Fahzi entered one of the larger ones. Ahmad hesitated, his nerves getting the better of him. *What am I doing here?* he wondered. *Maybe not a good idea to start with.* He didn't know Fahzi, nor had he even heard his name mentioned. The contacts he had in Gaza only told him that someone who was willing to talk about the article would meet him in the parking lot. It was bad enough meeting him alone, Ahmad thought. *But now…now he was totally outnumbered.*

A hollow sensation seeped in behind Ahmad's eyes. He shifted his thoughts in order to beat back the onslaught of worry. *They will sense it, like wolves often sense the fear of their prey before they attack.*

Fahzi turned around. "Come. Come, my friend. It's fine."

Ahmad entered behind him. Several men were sitting around, most dressed in white robes with white head scarfs, crowned with black cords in the shape of a ring. A few wore jeans. One of the men wearing a robe stood up and greeted them.

"Fahzi," he said, kissing him on both cheeks. "*Salaam.*"

"*Salaam*, Yusuf," Fahzi replied. "Please meet Ahmad, the person I was telling you about."

"*As-Salaam-Alaikum*, Ahmad," said the man called Yusuf. "Come, sit," he said. We have reserved a place for you between me and Fahzi."

"*Wa-Alaikum-Salaam*," Ahmad returned. He bowed to the others in the room then took his seat on the pillow.

"Fahzi tells me you have a proposal for us," Yusuf began. "And that you will maintain strict confidence about those of us whom you'll speak with, not only today, but afterward as well."

Ahmad felt ambushed. He didn't know Fahzi and had only spoken to two other people and he wasn't even sure if they were directly a part of any terrorist group. He couldn't get his tongue to form any words.

Watching Ahmad appear to squirm a bit, Fahzi jumped in. "Yes, let's not get ahead of ourselves here. Let me clear a few things up." He scanned the room then pointed his hand toward Ahmad. "Ahmad and I have actually never met before today. This meeting was arranged by several *go-betweens*. Ahmad writes for the *Filastin Dawn*. I think you are all aware of that paper." He surveyed the group again, receiving affirming nods. "The paper is the only one in Gaza that has the ear of the Israelis. They claim to be impartial in their reporting but that is questionable." He paused and looked at Ahmad.

Ahmad could barely maintain his composure. He was beginning to feel like a wild animal caught in a trap. He wasn't a *writer* at all…not yet anyway. *Had they misunderstood me? I should say something. But this is certainly not the time.*

Fahzi continued. "You may recall that an article supporting the Israeli position against one of our activities came out some years ago. As a result, a few people took it into their own hands to throw a small bomb through a window of the home of the owner of the Dawn, David Al-Rahim. I do understand why the act of revenge occurred, although I may not agree with that particular course of action. Mr. Rahim tried to speak the truth, but he also has strong connections to some people in Israel due to the international nature of his paper. But these aren't the times to be trying to walk a narrow line to please both sides. After what has happened to us, that time has come and gone."

Ahmad felt beads of sweat forming at his temples. *If they don't like the paper, what's going to happen to me?* he wondered. He tried to keep his eyes to himself. He glanced at Fahzi, who was looking directly at him. A lump formed in his throat.

Fahzi turned again to the group. "But don't get me wrong. I have nothing against Mr. Rahim, or even the paper, which has for the most part been fair to us in my view. In fact, the reason why I agreed to this meeting is precisely because of those connections with Israel."

Ahmad felt confused. *Who is in charge here? Yusuf or Fahzi?*

"Yes," Yusuf added. "Agreed. No doubt we are at a breaking point. Either the Israelis let us breathe and understand our right to live as an independent state, and work with us toward it, or we will have to declare all-out war and bring in our Iranian friends…and others. It is out of control. Israel must now decide."

Ahmad noticed a hint of an Iranian accent in Yusuf's speech. *Is this guy really a Palestinian?* he wondered.

"So," Fahzi replied, "why don't we get to it." He faced Ahmad. "What do you propose? And what can you guarantee the paper can do?"

Ahmad hoped they didn't see his Adam's apple bob in his throat as he gulped some air. He tried to calm his mind before speaking. "Would you happen to have just a sip of water?" he asked Yusuf.

"Oh, yes. Please excuse me. How rude." Yusuf reached for a pitcher next to him as a man to his right grabbed a ceramic cup.

Ahmad took the opportunity to think quickly. *What should I say? I can't commit the paper to anything without approval. And what exactly is the proposal?* He hadn't really prepared for this type of meeting. *Maybe delay? Push back? The worst case scenario would certainly be to show weakness.*

"Here you go, Ahmad," said Yusuf. I should have offered earlier."

Ahmad took several sips, gathering his courage. He set the cup down next to him, then slowly looked around at the group of men before speaking. "I…uh, uh," he balked, then quickly regrouped. "I, um, think we need to figure that out together. The *proposal* as you put it." He studied their faces again.

"What do you mean?" asked Fahzi, seeming genuinely curious, rather than stern.

Ahmad sensed an opening to deflect the focus of the conversation away from himself. "What I guess…, well, what I mean is that I'm only the messenger. We…" he drew in a deep breath, thinking if he should use that word since this was all his idea. "We feel there is an opportunity…maybe a *last chance,* if you will, for everyone to state their case, especially us Palestinians. Before all is lost." He shifted his eyes sequentially to all the others in the tent. *These older men are actually listening intently,* he thought. *To me, Ahmad.* It was the first feeling of real power he had ever felt.

"Go on…please," insisted Yusuf.

Ahmad continued. "I can write an article pending the final blessing of Mr. Rahim, that highlights all the concerns of the Palestinian people, as well as the Israelis. But it must be based on direct quotes and participation from the leaders, specifically from Gaza for us—because in Gaza, we find the last sharp point of the spear. The *point* that irritates the Israelis the most, that provokes and polarizes both sides of the conflict. That brings attention to the unfairness of the situation."

Fahzi stood up and began to walk behind the circle of men. "Why would the Israelis, or the world, listen?"

Ahmad looked up, his eyes following Fahzi. "Because we will speak to all the issues and claims…even those of the Israelis, as I mentioned. We will lay out the *consequences* if they don't, and the opportunities if they do."

Fahzi continued his stroll around the circle. "And what might those be?"

"That is for us to figure out together. It cannot be my idea, Mr. Rahim's, or the Prime Minister of Israel, or even that of the Fatah party which leads our Palestinian brothers and sisters in the West Bank. It should be a set of ideas, a perspective that you all will help to create, and one that will give reason to a unified voice. That voice must speak out before all is lost."

"Maybe lost for us," agreed Yusuf. "But as Fahzi has asked, why would the Israelis listen?"

"Because even though we are at our wit's end we must remain strong. We will offer a carrot to them. But not in weakness. Because there will be a stick as well. And that is because our back is against the wall. And the world will hear that final voice."

Fahzi stopped pacing. "What carrot? What stick?"

Ahmad swallowed hard. He knew he was about to stretch the truth. "I have some ideas. But this has to be a cooperative effort."

"Okay," Yusuf replied. "What are your ideas?"

Ahmad felt like he was getting in way over his head. His mind spun. *I need to buy time.* Yes, that much he was certain of. "I cannot provide any more information until I have your agreement. I don't have that authority. I will need to take the message back first."

"Message?" asked Fahzi.

"Well, a formal note perhaps. Just something with one of your signatures on it that says you are willing to continue talking."

There was some grumbling by several of the men.

"I can't do that," Yusuf answered, his voice stiffening. "I don't know Mr. Rahim personally. And I certainly don't trust the Israelis."

"Hold on, Yusuf," Fahzi insisted. "Things are bad. You know that. We might get some small victories, but the noose is closing around our necks. Before we have no options left at all, let's see where this goes. I will talk with you more later about this. Let's at least have another meeting. I will sign the note. Mr. Rahim will have heard of me." He turned to Ahmad. "But you must bring a note back to us as well, from him, stating he will not let anything about this out unless he has our permission."

Ahmad nodded, unsure of how he was going to make this happen.

Fahzi turned to Yusuf again. "Well okay then. That's enough for today. Thank you for your time, gentlemen."

Yusuf stood up, followed by Ahmad, and then the other men. Yusuf then led him and Fahzi out of the tent.

"Be safe," he said to Ahmad. "These are dangerous times. Thank you for your time and your courage in coming here." He bowed. "*Salaam.*"

"*Wa-Alaikum-Salaam,*" Ahmad replied.

Fahzi led Ahmad back to their cars and retrieved a notepad and pen from his glove box. He wrote a few sentences on one piece of paper and signed it. Then he scratched something on another. He handed both to Ahmad. "You have a good heart, Ahmad. I hope it doesn't get you in trouble, young man."

After getting into his car, Fahzi opened his window. "The second piece of paper, Ahmad, is my phone number. Don't worry, I can always get yours. *Salaam*, my friend."

"*Salaam,*" Ahmad replied, slipping behind the wheel. As he drove off into the night, it suddenly hit him. *What did Fahzi mean by he can always get mine?*

NINETEEN

KAI LI CLOSED the door to their room and followed Zack down the hall, stopping at the front desk. An older male receptionist looked up from his computer. "May I help you?"

"Sure," Zack said. "We're in room 122. We were thinking of getting some dinner, but don't have any money...kinda left stranded here."

Kai Li elbowed him so the attendant couldn't see.

"I mean, is there a place to get something to eat here?

The man clicked on his keyboard and stared at the screen. "You must be Zack?" he said, peering over his reading glasses, and above the top of the screen.

"How'd you know that?"

The man smiled. "I'm looking at the registration list for your room. There are two names…and one sounds Asian. So, I'm assuming you'd be the other one. Yes?"

"Oh. Yup, that's me."

"Well, welcome to our inn, sir. Your room has been paid for in advance, up through Sunday."

"We don't have any cash to get something to eat," Zack replied.

"You can charge your expenses to your room, sir," said the receptionist. That will also be covered." He pointed past them. "If you go down that corridor and take a right, you'll find our restaurant."

The two turned and headed down the hall.

"What's got into you?" Zack whispered loudly.

"You are like a touris' in Hollywood."

"I suppose you know how to do this better than me?"

Kai Li chuckled. "Not be hard."

"Yeah, well…"

As they took the turn, the restaurant was off the hall to the left. It was a large open space, with booths on three sides and tables scattered around. A group of eight people sat in the middle where two of the tables had been pushed together. The others were empty. Linen cloths covered the tables. Kai Li slid into an empty high-backed booth in between the two that were occupied, the first by a family of four, and on the other side by three men. Zack took the seat across from him with his back against the seatback they shared with the men.

"Bit of a whirlwind, it seems," Zack said, looking about the room. "Here we go again. I can't believe I signed up for this."

"Sweet spot, Zack. You not fooling me."

"Uh-huh," Zack replied, an edge of playful sarcasm in his voice.

"At least you're not starting in a bad mood like last time."

Zack gave in with a laugh. "Do I have to take this from you yet again?"

A young waitress with dark hair arrived with two menus and glasses of water. "Here you go, gentlemen. I'll be right back for your orders."

Zack eyed her as she walked away.

"You all the time studyin' girls?" Kai Li asked him, mischievously. "I see you do same for Liyah."

Zack winked. "If you think of somethin' better to do, let me know."

The boys opened the black book-like menus with gold lettering and began studying them.

"You seem pretty comfortable here, Kai," Zack continued, his eyes perusing the offerings. "I can't tell you the last time I was at a fancy restaurant. Maybe that time I told you about, with my dad when I was little…in Niagara Falls.

Kai Li glanced up from his menu. "Nice but not fancy. More like cross between a motel and nice inn."

"How would you know?" asked Zack. "I thought you lived in a one-bedroom apartment in Hong Kong with your mom."

"Yeah, but I go on errands for factory, 'member? Meet many businesspeople to pick up and deliver documents at hotels. Hong Kong is very wealthy downtown, even if poor in some places like other cities. Maybe like Detroit?"

"I doubt it," Zack responded, still not looking up. "But then I wouldn't really know. See anything you like?"

"All look good. But think I jes' get some soup and sandwich. No heavy meal before bed."

Zack pointed to the menu. "This is great. You can have eggs here all day long. I'm in."

The waitress returned with a notepad and pencil. "So, what can I get you?"

"Chicken sandwich for me," said Kai Li, "with tomato soup. And glass of ginger ale."

"I'll have sausage, eggs, fried potatoes, and some toast. And a Coke. Do you have that, here?"

"Pepsi," said the waitress. "You must be American."

"Yup, but Kai Li here is from Hong Kong. How could you tell?"

"Well, that's an all-American breakfast, as they say. Or maybe the red sweatshirt gave you away?"

Kai Li laughed. "You a signpost, Zack,"

"We get a lot of Americans here in Bethlehem," the waitress added. "You can imagine."

"I guess so," Zack agreed. "I didn't know for sure that's where we were."

"What do you mean," she asked, appearing incredulous.

Caught in the headlights, Zack shot a nervous glance at Kai Li, then tried to backpedal. "Oh, I, uh…we just got here."

"You just flew in?"

"You might say that," Zack replied.

"Okay, well sit tight," she said, retrieving the menus. "I'll be back shortly with your drinks."

"Almos' give us away," said Kai Li.

Zack laughed. "She would never believe it. They'd lock us up."

"Pretty stuck here. What will we do 'til Ahmad arrive?"

"Yeah. I guess. He has the phones and we don't want to get caught without some sort of pass. This isn't like *wherever it was we were* a week ago. Although, I hope it's not going to be as dangerous. I'm still recovering."

"Ha. But we learn a lot, no? Grow up. A broad smile took over his face. "Become friends."

"Zack gave a thumbs up. "Yeah, buddy. Yes, we did. I wonder what's the deal here. How do you think we can help Liyah find her brother? I hope people speak English, otherwise, I don't know what we could possibly do."

"I think most everyone speak English…at leas' some. At home, we ship toys here from my factory. Ship all over the world. Most all business people speak it, I think."

"Hmm. Well, just wonderin'," Zack said as he played with his fork, twirling it and tapping the handle on the table. "I don't get out of my neighborhood much in Detroit. And I know I should be tryin' to use the powers to help people, but I haven't done anything big yet, except bend a basketball rim on the way home that day, and move little things around in my room, that is, until I had to use them to get here."

"I know, seem like dream sometime," replied Kai Li.

"This whole *thing* is still a bit weird to me, " Zack added. "I was thinking of Ooray the other day…well, actually a lot since I got back. "You can't even tell if he's a person, and sometimes the whole thing with us does seem like a dream, as you said. And when you wake up it fades away…except the powers.

"Or she?" Kai Li replied.

"She?"

"Yeah, not know if Ooray he or she?"

Zack chuckled. "Yeah, that too."

"I practice a bit. Use torch on necklace," Kai Li told him. "And also bracelet. Make light shoot from hand by concentrating thoughts. Almos' freak me out."

"Really?" Zack set his fork down and stared at it for a moment, then moved it to the middle of the table facing him. He reached into the neck of his sweatshirt and pulled out the TrueHeart sapphire pendant Ooray had given him. He took in its stunning blue crystal sheen briefly then squeezed it tightly in his palm. Pointing the fingers of his free hand at it, he closed his eyes and imagined it in his hand. Immediately, the fork began edging over the tablecloth toward him.

"Here are your sodas, boys," said the waitress.

Zack's eyes flew open. He let go of the pendant, which then dangled over his sweatshirt, the dark blue of the stone catching the light above the booth and shining brilliantly against the bright red of his sweatshirt. He and Kai Li simultaneously jerked their heads to the side, mouths gaping at her.

She glanced quickly at each. "Something wrong? That's some trick you're doing. Can you show that again? And wow, that is really a nice necklace. I don't think I've ever seen anything quite like that before."

"Optical illusion," Kai Li blurted out in recovery.

"Looked real to me," said the waitress. She studied the two again.

"He's right," added Zack. "Like you say. Just a trick. And this pendant is something a friend gave me. I was told it has many magical powers." He looked up at her with a grin. "So I keep it with me all the time."

Kai Li kicked him under the table. "Food ready soon?"

"Gee," she joked. "You guys need to be a little more patient I'd say…Not long." She turned and headed to the booth next to them where the three men sat, picked some things up off their table, and headed toward the kitchen.

Kai Li made a motion of wiping sweat from his brow. "Close one!" he whispered.

"I was just playin'. But good move to distract her."

Zack sat back, resting his head against the backrest of the booth. He could hear the men talking.

One of the men slid out of the booth and said goodbye to the others. As he walked past the boys' table, his eyes shifted slightly toward them. Kai Li was busy checking out a painting on the wall and didn't notice, but the man's eyes connected with Zack's. No words were spoken as he moved past.

"That was strange."

"What?" asked Kai Li, as he brought his attention back to Zack.

"That man with the mustache," Zack replied. "He looked like he was surprised to see us."

"What strange about that?"

"Not sure. But he was on the other side of the booth from me. When I leaned back I could hear him pretty clearly. He was saying something about having to go to a meeting in Gaza tomorrow…that he would have more information about the *Sunday surprise* after that."

"Su'prise?"

"Yeah. I don't know. Just a feeling I got as he looked at me."

"You spend too much time in city with those gangs," Kai Li suggested. "Not trust anyone. They prob'ly only talk about a plan for the weekend or somethin'. Sunday is Easter, isn't it?"

"Yeah. Maybe so. But there was still that *look*…like he wasn't sure how long I'd been listening."

"After we eat, what can we do? Not know when Ahmad come back."

"I wonder if the TV has programs in English. Otherwise, we're in for a boring time, locked in the room. And I hope we get some sleep tonight…It's still early for me."

Kai Li grinned. "Very late by my time."

Zack smiled at him. "You can always meditate anyway, right?"

"You too."

"Yes, Mr. Kai. And me, too. Thanks to you.

Friday

Twenty

Jerusalem

SITTING IN THE front seat of Ahmad's car, Morningstar stared at the entrance of the Inn, waiting for him to reappear with the boys. She played with the loose knot in her new hijab, tying it, untying it, and tying it again.

Liyah leaned forward into the gap between the front seats. "You've been quiet this morning. Hardly a word from you all the way here after Ahmad picked us up."

Morningstar turned her head. "Sorry. My mind has been wandering. I was thinking about how nice it has been with your mom and dad. I know you think your mom is a bit strict at times, but she's only looking out for you, from what her own experience has taught her. Your parents have been super kind to me, even if your mom may suspect something."

"Yes, they have," Liyah admitted. "I get that. But it doesn't help on a daily basis. I feel like my mom is suffocating me at times with her old ways."

Morningstar's mind drifted as she considered those last words—*old ways*. She had been living her short life in *recent* times, but her grandfather always tried to anchor her in the ways of the Lakota…their own *old ways*. "Everyone has their own fears," she said. "Isn't that what Ooray told us? I think your mom hasn't had the opportunity to see that in herself, nor felt empowered enough by her society here, to break out…to take charge of her life. She's afraid for you, but secretly she might even hope you have a different life than the girls of her generation had."

She watched as Liyah's face softened. "Leave it to you, Star, to ground everything. You are like a metal rod taking the sting out of a lightning bolt. Sometimes I think you are almost an older sister, even though you're younger than me." A broad smile broke out over her countenance. "Your grandfather has obviously taught you well. And like the boys, I feel it is a gift he has given us, through you."

As Morningstar smiled back, her mind took flight once more. This time to her parents. *Were their faces less clear this week than last week? Would she ever totally forget them.?* She tried to dig up that picture she had of them she had tucked up in a corner of her brain. A family of three during a happier time. *I barely knew them. But it would be so wrong of me to forget them. Wouldn't it? I need to keep that picture fresh.*

"Star?...Star!" Liyah said, reaching out to hold onto her friend's wrist. "Are you okay? I've never seen you drift off so much."

"Uh…yes. Yes, of course. Sorry, again. I was still thinking of how lucky you are. You have your parents, even if they seem to be a pain at times. They clearly love you in their own way. So, you probably should forgive them, especially your mom. Wasn't that what Ooray said…about forgiveness and love? That forgiveness is for *you*, not them. So that you can be free. And love being the greatest gift of all…the *highest state of being*. So, you already have that from them I'd say. That is what I got from my grandfather—love…with a lot of *useful lessons*, as he put it." She locked onto Liyah's eyes. "But it doesn't stop me from thinking about my parents. And when I do, I feel like more sand has slipped between my fingers." Her eyes turned down. She wiped the corners of them with her hijab. "And sometimes I feel ashamed."

Liyah tightened her grip around Morningstar's arm. "Ashamed? How can you ever feel ashamed? Look at who you have become. Who wouldn't be proud of that? I am proud of you, Star! So very proud to be called your friend. And so are Zack and Kai Li."

Morningstar placed her hand on top of Liyah's. "Thanks, Liyah. I didn't mean to get carried away. It seems ever since we were all together during our adventure, I've been getting sappier. I think you rubbed off on me." She chuckled lightly. "But we need to get serious, don't we? We have to find your brother…and soon. I hope seeing the contact that the imam gave you will get us going on the right track."

"Yeah, I hope so, too. Jamal is supposed to meet us there right after the tour. I–"

The car door across from Liyah opened, immediately followed by the driver's door. Ahmad slid into his seat and waited for the others to get settled.

"You first, Mr. Kai," Zack said. "I hate the middle. I get squished, and my legs are too long. You're the thinnest one here, except for maybe Star, who seems to have claimed the front." He gave her a frown then winked.

Liyah squeezed over towards her door, making room for them. "Sometimes I think you're reverting back to your irritating self, Zack," Liyah grunted.

Zack laughed. "Chill, girl. You know better than that. None of us will ever be the same since that strange adventure last week. Right?"

The corners of her mouth turned up slowly. "Yeah," she admitted. "You bet."

Ahmad started the car and pulled out onto the main street. Once onto the highway, he flipped the rearview mirror so he could see the faces in the back, then spoke to Morningstar. "The envelope in the side pocket next to you, Morningstar, contains your passes to the tour in the Old City. I have mine and will join you later. We'll go there directly. It also contains the general passes from your dad for the weekend, to allow the boys to get in and out of Israel and Palestine, like what you and Liyah already have."

Morningstar complied, taking one of the tour passes for herself, then handing the envelope to Liyah. Ahmad looked into the mirror again. "The general passes are like temporary visas but they are special because they carry the stamp from the highest level of the Ministry. No one will question them. But if you cause any trouble, it will be reported back. And we certainly don't want that."

He tapped Morningstar's knee. "And your phones are in the box at Morningstar's feet. The new SIMS are in them. You will be able to communicate with each other while you're here, but you'll have to swap out the old SIMS before you go home."

Morningstar picked up the box from the floor, found her phone, then passed the box back to Kai Li and Zack.

"The first stop is the Old City," Ahmad said, as they settled in. "We should be there about 10:30. That will give us plenty of time for the tour. You guys can have lunch, then I understand, Liyah, you and Morningstar will be meeting someone there. I'll take Kai Li and Zack with me and come back to get you later in the afternoon." He glanced at Morningstar. "Do you think you two girls can stay out of trouble?"

"Doubtful," replied Zack. "That doesn't seem to be something they do well."

Ahmad caught Kai Li in the mirror, elbowing Zack. "Well, let's go then," Ahmad said, "I have a subtle feeling that things are about to start to get more interesting."

Ahmad pulled into a car park off the main road, a few blocks from the entrance to the Old City. They exited the car, crossed the main road, and began walking up the wide stone path to the main gate. As they neared the archway of the gate, they passed alongside the ancient hand-hewn blocks of crystalline limestone, part of the remaining walls that marked the border between Jerusalem itself and the Old City.

Ahmad caught a glimpse of a young woman waiting under the arch as they neared. She was dressed in a blazer and white slacks. A puffy blue newsboy cap adorned her head. *Esty?* Ahmad wondered.

She waved to them in the midst of a throng of people moving past her in both directions and waited for them to join her.

"Hello, Esty," said Ahmad, reaching to shake her hand. "I was sort of hoping you might be here. I rarely come to the Old City. In fact, I rarely get out of Gaza. So, I wasn't sure how to find you, although it says the tour starts at the Church of the Holy Sepulchre."

"I finished the last tour a few minutes ago and figured you would probably be coming through this gate." She turned to the others. "Hi everyone! Glad you all could make it. I see we have a few additions."

"Yes, we do," echoed Ahmad. He held his hand out toward the girls. "You might remember Liyah and Morningstar. And this is Zack" he said, turning to the boys, "and Kai Li."

Esty nodded. "Welcome, guys. Yes, I do remember our brief meeting. How could I forget the native clothing of yours, Morningstar? And now I see those handsome beaded moccasins. How lovely you look." She turned to Liyah. "Not to ignore you, Liyah. You are quite lovely as well. I'm sure everyone tells you that. Are you from Palestine like Ahmad?"

"Thank you. Yes, Gaza." Liyah replied. I only visited here once or twice a long time ago with my father. It's been so crazy the past few years that it's been impossible to get out of Gaza, or feel safe to travel by myself. We're really excited to have this private tour."

Zack nudged Kai Li, who then pushed back at him as Esty turned to face the great archway.

"Stop it, you two," Liyah said, in a sharp, disapproving whisper. "Jeez, you're like two children sometimes."

Esty raised her arms, waving her palms. "This archway is part of the Jaffa Gate, the main entrance to the Old City. It was built in the year 1538 by Suleyman, who was viewed by Muslims and Europeans as one of the greatest leaders of his time. The entrance was destroyed and then rebuilt in the late 1800s. You can see how much smoother the stone blocks are for this entrance compared to the old stones of the wall."

She turned back around. "Suleyman expanded the territory of the great Ottoman empire, instituted great laws and architectural projects like this, was a military and political leader, and also a poet. He believed in justice above all, one of the key pillars of the Quran…the Muslim religious text. Right Liyah, Ahmad?"

Liyah nodded in agreement.

"Well, I'm not up on the history," Ahmad replied, "but, yeah, justice is an important part of the Quran, as well as morality."

"And love for all God's creatures," Esty added, then continued. "Just as a side note, this gate is one of the eight to the city, and is called the Jaffa Gate because it was the primary way people reached the city from the port of Jaffa. It also goes by the name Bab-el-Halil which means *the beloved* in Arabic, and refers to Abraham, who is regarded as the father of Christianity, Islam, and Judaism, my religion. All the gates are open except one, and that is the Golden Gate, also called the Gate of Mercy, where they say the Messiah will enter on the day of judgment and the dead will be brought back to life."

Ahmad couldn't help admiring Esty. She stood proud in her matching cap and blazer. Her face beamed as she spoke, her smile stretching ear to ear, and her light eyes sparkled in the morning light. *She is truly captivating,* he thought. *And she so loves her job. I could listen to her talk about history like this until the earth is swallowed up by the sun.*

"Ahmad, Ahmad!" said Liyah, impatiently snapping her fingers in front of his face. "Esty's asking you something. Boy, where did you go?"

"Sorry."

"Ahmad, I was just asking if I could collect the passes for today's tour? I gave them to you yesterday just to make sure you had them if something happened to me. But we must give them back to the head of the programs after we're done today. Now that you're with me you won't need them."

"Oh, sure," Ahmad replied, turning to the others. "Hey guys, how about it?"

Esty collected the passes and put them in the small pocketbook slung over her shoulder. "Follow me," she said, as she spun around and made her way under the archway, turned left, and entered the Old City.

The five stayed together as she walked backwards and talked. "The city is divided into four parts. Over there is the Armenian Quarter. Some of the stones in all these quarters date back to before the time of Christ. Jerusalem was first settled by humans almost 6,000 years ago, and King David conquered it about 3,000 years ago making it the center of the Jewish kingdom."

She pointed further to her left in front of them. "The Jewish Quarter is over there. And beyond that the Muslim Quarter. To my right is the Christian Quarter, where we will be visiting the holiest church of that religion next. Many armies and nations took their turn at pillaging and rebuilding this city since its inception. In that sense, it is perhaps the oldest living relic of the ebb and flow of human history…as vibrant today as it was during the world wars, the Crusades of the middle-ages, the Ottoman Empire, and the Roman Empire."

Esty was jostled repeatedly by the dense crowd pouring into the city. "See what I mean?" she said, leading them along the wide stone walkways then through the narrower isles that formed the core of the market, sheltered from the sun by the many billowing canvas tarps, tapestries, and flags.

They moved past fine leather bags of all colors and sizes, draped on hooks along the walls between sellers' booths, past bright gold jewelry displays and magazine stands…all the while shuffling and bouncing through the sea of humanity.

Ahmad kept up the rear, making sure no one got lost. He watched the others as their heads swiveled back and forth, absorbing everything they could, not wanting to miss anything. Liyah and Morningstar walked arm in arm. The boys joked with each other while still trying to take in the astounding sights and sounds around them. People from all corners of the earth, dressed in every imaginable way and speaking many languages passed by. Ahmad was surprised by how many wore jeans and other casual wear, but some, like the Hasidic Jews, sported long black dress coats and odd hats. There were people in business clothes. Many women wore hijabs, their bodies covered up, while other women wore skirts and other western clothing.

Escaping the throng for a moment, they made their way back into the sunlight at the courtyard of the church. Esty stopped and turned to face them. "Sorry we had to hustle through all that, but after all, this is a tour…no time for shopping." She smiled. "Any questions before we enter the Church of the Holy Sepulcher?"

"What's this church famous for?" Morningstar asked.

"Several things actually, Morningstar. Inside are two of the holiest sites in Christianity - the place where Jesus was crucified, and Calvary."

"The place where he was buried," Zack added, before she could finish.

"Correct. How did you know that? *Zack* it is, right?"

"He know lot about Jesus," Kai Li said, grinning. "But he won't let on."

"I see," Esty replied. "So, you are a Christian?"

Zack paused. "Well, you might say that. But I'm not really into the church, if you know what I mean."

"Actually, I do," Esty said, keeping her eyes on his for a moment. "I grew up Jewish but I don't attend synagogue as much as my father thinks I should. I may attend tonight, since tomorrow is Shabbat, our holy day, and I may have to give some tours during synagogue hours."

Esty glanced at the others. "Okay, so if we have no more questions, let's get to it. Behind me is the entrance to the church."

She led them past a huge, heavy wooden door and into the dimly lit cathedral. "Your eyes will adjust to the candlelight, and it will become much brighter as the sunlight streams through the stained glass in the great dome, illuminating one of the most spectacular places you may ever see."

Just a few feet in was a large stone slab, lit up with the soft glow from several beautiful ornate candles. Esty stopped. "This is the place where it is told that Jesus' body was laid and anointed with oil, after his crucifixion."

She moved on to her left, leading them down a great white limestone hall, past gigantic marble pillars, and into the large rotunda. The stunning architecture and elegance of the old building rained down on them. High above, unfiltered light poured through the windows at the top of the dome, while dimmer, multi-colored streams flowed in from the stained-glass windows in the archways encircling the rotunda. Ornate bronze fixtures hung down everywhere, adding their own light to the scene.

In the center of the rotunda, was an entire small building. Ahmad watched as people milled about the front of it. Esty stood to its side facing them near a beautiful altar. Her eyes darted about the rotunda.

"Something wrong?" Ahmad whispered.

"Yes," she said, her words unsteady. "Where is Zack?"

Ahmad glanced quickly at the others, then around the room again. *No sign of him.* He suddenly felt nauseous. *How could I not have noticed? I need to pay better attention.*

"You stay here, Esty," Ahmad said, continuing to whisper so he wouldn't alarm the others. "Keep them occupied. I'll find him."

"Sure," Esty replied, "Thanks. He shouldn't be hard to find in that red sweatshirt of his."

"I hope not," Ahmad agreed, slipping away and moving back through the hall, toward their last stop.

He stepped up his pace, glancing anxiously side to side. Once out of the rotunda he found his way back to the Stone of the Anointing. There he was, still standing in front of the stone.

"Zack," Ahmad called out as he approached him. "What are you doing? My God. You nearly gave me a heart attack."

"I could feel the vibration here," Zack said, matter-of-factly.

"Vibration?"

"Yeah, from the stone."

"Stone?" Ahmad brought his eyes from Zack and stared down at it. "What are you talking about?"

"I can feel its energy," Zack insisted.

"I'm not getting it, Zack."

Zack stood for a moment without answering, facing Ahmad.

Ahmad began to feel uncomfortable. "Is everything okay with you?" he asked. "We need to get back with the others."

"Yeah, I know. Sorry. I just wanted to take in the magic of this…the energy of the stone…and the rays."

"Rays?"

"Yup. Can't you see them?"

Ahmad scanned the room, then dropped his eyebrows and frowned at Zack. "No."

Zack went silent again.

"Are you sure you're alright?" Ahmad asked again, studying him.

"Ah, well I guess you should know. It's probably gonna come out sometime anyway."

"What's that? I have no idea what you're talking about."

"You're trying to help Liyah find her brother, like us, right? At least that's what I was told."

"Yes, of course. So?"

"I forget sometimes that not everyone can see and feel what I do. But we need you so it's time you know."

"Know what?" Ahmad prodded, a tinge of impatience rising in his throat. He watched as Zack pulled out something from under the neck of his sweatshirt and held it for him to see. It was a stunning deep blue stone in the shape of a heart. He could see the flame of the candle next to Zack reflected thousands of times in its facets. He gasped then heard Zack laugh.

"It's a magic stone, too, Ahmad…just like the slab here. I can feel the pull between them. It's called the TrueHeart. It connects all hearts there are, or ever were. It transcends space and time, and channels energy. It always finds the light."

Ahmad could feel himself getting anxious and concerned for Zack.

"Let me show you," said Zack. He removed the necklace and handed it to Ahmad. "This is what I see now, even without wearing it. Hold it tightly in the palm of your hand."

Ahmad complied.

"Now, watch me as I hold my fingertips above Jesus' stone."

Zack made sure no one else was near, then moved his hand above the slab, tilting his fingers towards it.

Ahmad watched Zack briefly close his eyes, then reopen them, still clearly focused. He could hear a crinkling, as if someone was making a ball out of tinfoil. A narrow band of white light connected the stone slab to Zack's fingertips. Zack then brought his hand back, and the light faded away.

"What the hell!" Ahmad exclaimed, looking aghast at Zack.

Zack smiled. "Your turn."

"What?"

"Keep hold of the necklace. And bring it over the slab."

Ahmad moved his visibly trembling hand above it.

"Now," Zack added, "take a few slow, deep breaths as if you were going to meditate, then concentrate on trying to make energy flow between the two."

"I have no idea how to do that," Ahmad replied.

"Yes, you do. Just think of those objects as having their own energy…their own *vibration.* And make them *one.* At least that's what I do." Zack nodded at him. "Go ahead."

Ahmad, trying to mimic Zack, closed his eyes and did as he was told. Feeling nothing, he opened them to see everything unchanged.

"Try again," Zack insisted.

Ahmad followed the instructions once more. But this time he felt a slight humming in his palm. He opened his eyes. To his astonishment, a dull red beam of light wavered between the jewel and the stone.

"You're doin' great," said Zack. "Now, keep your eyes open and concentrate harder. Imagine the energy flowing between them getting stronger."

Ahmad obliged, focusing more on the slab than the jewel. As he did, he could feel the vibration in his palm grow. Slowly but steadily the band of red light grew brighter, and shifted in color to yellow, then green, then blue…the color of the jewel.

"Hold that," Zack said. "And now, I'm going to imagine all the colors of light as one…sharing a common bond…talking together." He focused his attention on Ahmad's hand.

Ahmad watched as the bands of light changed in color again, then instantaneously merged in one solid beam of white light.

"Look around you," Zack whispered.

Ahmad shifted his gaze to the large painting on the wall behind the stone slab. His eyes grew large as colors in the painting jumped off the canvas and skirted about the room, swirling and blinking, merging and separating.

Zack tapped Ahmad's arm lightly, holding out his hand.

Ahmad released the TrueHeart from his grip and gave it back. As he did so, the colored images and bits of light faded until they disappeared completely. His jaw dropped.

Zack chuckled. "Amazing, huh?"

"I don't even know what to say," Ahmad admitted.

"I'm still playing with it to understand its full power. Just keep it under your hat, okay?" Zack cautioned. "No use causing Esty any concern. We have no idea how she would take it. Maybe she'd get the Israelis to lock us up."

"So, you mean the others know about this?

"Oh yeah. How do you think we all know each other? And how we all got here? Especially Kai Li and me getting to the hotel?"

Ahmad thought back to their arrival. It hit him. *I just knew it,* he said to himself. "I did have a suspicion that something wasn't entirely right." He grinned. "But I don't think I want to know much more. This is quite enough for the moment."

Zack returned the grin. "I'm sure it is."

Twenty-One

A MAN DRESSED in a light blue shirt and dark suit jacket stepped quickly past the Inn's front desk and made his way into the restaurant, stopping at the second to the last booth.

"Sorry I'm late, gentlemen," the man said, as he hung his jacket on a hook at the side of the booth. He removed his white collar and stuck it in the pocket of the jacket, then slid in next to one of the two men facing each other.

"It's quite alright, Pastor," said the man with the dark mustache and olive complexion sitting across from him. "Better late than never." He tilted his head. "Especially this weekend. I've ordered a pot of coffee and some pastries. This won't take long."

"What's up, Billy?" asked the man next to the pastor.

The man with the mustache unlatched the briefcase on the seat next to him, removed a rolled-up piece of paper, slipped off the rubber band, and unfurled a map of the Old City in the center of the table. He took a pen from his shirt pocket, clicked it a couple of times to make sure it was retracted, then used it as a pointer.

"Here," he said, moving the pen along the wall at the edge of the Muslim Quarter, "is the Western Wall, or Wailing Wall as some call it." He glanced up at the two. "We all know this is one of the holiest sites in Judaism. Due to the safeguards in place for Jerusalem, it's been protected from attack for many years. It has been feared that any destruction of the wall would be met with swift retaliation by Israelis to the holy Muslim and Christian sites in the city located in the same Temple Mount area."

"Isn't that basically what we would want?" asked the man sitting next to the pastor. "I–."

The waitress appeared at the table with a pot, along with a tray of pastries and coffee cups. She set the pot at the end with the sweets and placed a cup and saucer in front of each of the men. "Will that be all?" she said, her eyes drifting down to the map.

"Yes, yes," Billy replied somewhat abruptly. "Thank you." He stared at her until she nervously shifted her eyes then turned and walked away.

"Exactly, John," Billy continued. "It's something we have been hoping would happen to speed the arrival of the Apocalypse...the End of Days of the world." The corners of his mouth curled up slightly as he ran his thumb and forefinger through his mustache. "It's when the Messiah will return and all those who are not *true believers* will be gobbled up by the fires of hell. It's closer than you think."

"What do you mean?" the pastor questioned, his brow furrowing as he took a pastry from the plate, then bit into it.

"I mean that there is a way to finally make it happen now. That is why I asked you to come here so soon after our meeting yesterday. We no longer have to wait for promises made over thousands of yesterdays. *Soon, soon, soon,* it has been said over all the generations, God would send his messenger back to rescue us." He touched the fingers of both hands to his chest, then held them out to the others, palms up. "*Us,* and our evangelical Christian brethren. The only real chosen ones...not the Jews, not the Muslims, but us—his last remaining true followers."

"Why have things changed?" John asked. "Why is it so different now? Today?"

"During my meeting yesterday in Gaza, with a Hamas leader, I learned a couple of things. First, this *person*...I still cannot share his name yet... has been working with a man with ties to Hezbollah in Iran, and they have been providing new technology to make the Palestinian rockets more accurate. And second, there is something else secret going on that would disable the Israeli ability to defend themselves for a short period of time; during which we can put a plan in place to cause Jerusalem, and then the world, to go up in flames."

"How so?" the pastor asked.

"Well, I was thinking, if the defenses are down, we might be able to cause destruction to the Muslim holy site...the Dome of the Rock, and blame it on the Jews. And also destroy the Church of the Holy Sepulcher...and blame that on the Palestinians and Iran."

The pastor leaned forward. "When is this all supposed to happen?"

"This weekend...Sunday. Easter Sunday."

"Are you kidding?" John, asked, wide-eyed.

"Sounds pretty ambitious," the pastor added, tapping his finger on the table next to the map. "What are you proposing?"

Billy sipped his coffee and then set down the cup. He reached across the table and flipped the map over. On the reverse side was another map of Israel, including the Palestinian territories. He pointed to the Gaza Strip. "This is where all the rockets are fired when Hamas builds up enough of them. But we all know that they are notoriously inaccurate, and the Israeli defenses pick them out of the sky as if they were swatting mosquitoes. However, a situation has developed where the combination of the new parts from Iran that makes the rockets smarter, and the shutting down of the Israeli defenses that could allow the hundreds of last remaining rockets to hit their marks this time."

"That's if they can even launch them first," John interjected sarcastically.

Billy laughed. "Yes, I know. But Hamas has been working on this for quite a while. My contact told me on several occasions he's planning a diversionary tactic to take the Israelis' eyes off Gaza briefly…by causing a commotion in the Old City. During the last few meetings with me, he has become confident that they will not be able to stop an attack on Tel Aviv and the government buildings, or the Old City itself. Rockets aimed at the Western Wall."

The pastor and John both looked aghast. "The Wall?" they both blurted out, stunned.

"Yeah. Indeed," said Billy. "He plans to have them aim some of the rockets directly at the Western Wall. And destroy it."

The pastor stared at Billy. "Holy crap!... Excuse my French. How can you be sure the defenses will be down?"

"I don't have the details on that yet. It's being kept secret. But I'll know on Sunday when it all begins."

"What are you planning to do to the church? And the Dome of the Rock?" John asked.

"Like I said, all the plans are just coming together over the next two days. I have another meeting later this afternoon out at the edge of the Negev. It will bring us another step closer. My connection wants me to help him with something."

"He's been incredibly helpful to us the last few years, Billy," John added.

"Keep in mind it's not *us*," Billy cautioned. "He has no idea who you guys are, or that I am involved with Evangelicals at all."

"You've convinced him you're a Muslim?" the pastor asked. "That's a fine line you're treading. If Hamas finds out, I have a feeling we'll never see you again."

"I know," said Billy. "But the end is near, as they say. Just a few days now…and *everything* will change."

"How do they think you're getting the money to help them?" John asked.

"They think it's from my successful business operations in America. They ran a security check on me several years ago before deciding to get in bed with me on the political front. Fortunately, I did make some money, although much of my wealth at the time came from my father, upon his death."

John probed further. "So, they don't know that you got the money from us, through our evangelical Christian friends in the States who also believe that supporting the Jews in Jerusalem will bring the Messiah here, as prophesied?"

"Not at all. And by the way, John, I really appreciate your coordination with them and with our pastor here. There is now a way for us, on behalf of all true Christians, to speed up the Rapture this Sunday. To hasten the end of times. And to bring forth the *second coming* of Christ."

"Amen!" said the pastor. "Is there more you need from us?"

"Actually, yes. I need another injection of funds. A bigger one this time. Things are happening fast, and we'll need to do everything possible to capture this opportunity and secure my position with Hamas. This may be the only chance anyone has in our lifetime, or many lifetimes to come. We don't want anything to blow up at this late stage."

John chuckled. "*Blow up*. Ironic choice of phrase you chose there, Billy. Yes, of course. How much do you need?"

"I think we should plan on a quarter of a million US dollars. Deposited into the special account through the church. I can access it as needed. As you know, my contact has made arrangements with the bank in Gaza using his influence with Hamas. No one will question it."

The pastor nodded. "Done."

Billy rolled the map back up, secured the rubber band around it. He placed it back in his case, snapped the latches shut, and rose from the table. "Will you cover me on this one?"

"Sure," said John, signaling a thumbs up. "The tab's on me. We'll keep this quiet on our side, but please remember to do the same, Billy. After all, Pastor's congregation here is not fully in alignment with us. They are closer to the Palestinian people than you may understand. Evangelicals, by and large, here in Palestine, generally support their neighboring Muslims. They aren't looking for any trouble, and don't share the same beliefs as us three, or some of the more radical Evangelicals in America…that the Rapture can be accelerated by pretending to support the Israelis then turning the tables."

Billy reached out and shook their hands. "Yes. I understand. You can count on me. Thanks. Let's keep it on the down low 'til Sunday, for sure. I'll be in touch."

Twenty-Two

The Old City

ESTY HAD TO stall for time. She recounted to Kai Li, Liyah, and Morningstar how she got to be a tour guide and found out they were all similar ages, all the while keeping a nervous eye on the hallway, hoping for a quick return of Ahmad with Zack.

"S'cuse, me," Kai Li said, raising his hand somewhat timidly, interrupting the discussion. "We lose Zack."

Liyah turned around and scanned the area around them. "And Ahmad."

"I noticed that," Esty agreed. "But I was thinking maybe they stepped out to the restroom." Then she saw Zack following Ahmad who waved his arm above the crowd as he entered the edge of the rotunda. "Never mind. Here they are now."

The two hustled along to rejoin the others. Ahmad addressed Esty as they approached. "So sorry. Zack got a bit distracted by the Anointing Stone."

"Like I said before," Zack added, "I think Kai Li has rubbed off on me."

Morningstar and Liyah let out a laugh, but the joke was lost on Esty. She wanted to move on quickly. "No worries. But we've got lots to get to before lunch."

She pointed to the altar in front of them. "This is the altar of Mary Magdalene, one of the true followers of Jesus and his rumored companion," she said, ending with a wink and a grin. "Mary is also said to have witnessed his death on the cross."

Esty paused briefly. "And right over there," she said, pointing to the doorway to the small building, "is the entrance to the Chapel of the Angel…and the chamber of Jesus' tomb. It is closed to the public today because it's Good Friday for the Christians, the day of the crucifixion. But I think I can get us in. Follow me."

She unhooked the velvet cord that separated the small chapel building from the crowd of onlookers, then led her group in between several giant candles standing over ten feet high and set in ornate bronze footings, to the entrance. Stopping at the very small marble arch entryway, she bent down and stuck her head in, then stepped back out.

A man in clerical robes appeared, his bent form easing past the marble archway as he exited the chapel. He smiled at Esty and then tipped his head gently several times toward the others. "Good morning, Esty. I hear you have some special guests today. They're of course welcome here, on this precious day of the Lord."

The cleric faced the others. "Tight quarters in there, but just enough room to fit the small group of you. Mind your head, now. I guess when they built this structure, they meant it to really feel like a tomb."

Esty ducked into the darkness of the chapel and the others followed. The six of them barely fit into the tiny room. They encircled a stand that was lit up by only two small, white candles and one large one sitting atop the glass enclosure.

"This is the first chamber," Esty informed them. "Under the glass is a piece of flat stone which is believed to be part of the stone that was used to seal Jesus' tomb."

She watched as the group studied the glass enclosure from a few feet away. Zack moved closer, his head hovering over it. When he brought his palms within a few inches of the glass surface, the flames of all three candles wavered and then grew stronger. As he moved his hands back to his side, the candlelight flickered before returning to normal.

Am I seeing things, Esty wondered. *What was that?* She glanced around, but no one else seemed to have noticed, except maybe Ahmad, who may have had a bit of a concerned look on his face.

"Okay, let's move into the other chamber," Esty instructed. "Be careful, this entranceway is even smaller." She waited as the others went in first, bending down low and squeezing their way into the room. She joined them.

Again, only three white candles provided the light. In front of them was what appeared to be a plain stone bench, surrounded high on either side by white stone and polished marble. At the back were several large, stamped metal plates depicting Jesus, along with a painting of him bathed in the glow of orange-yellow light.

Complete silence settled in around them. Esty waited briefly then began speaking.

"This is the place where it is said Jesus was laid to rest. The tomb, where, according to Christian belief, he spent three days before rising from the dead."

"It does feel like a tomb in here, for sure," Liyah said, softly, peering around, looking somber.

"Doin' good, Liyah," Kai Li noted, chuckling lightly. "I remember story about when you were 'fraid of small space, but then rescued Star in that cave."

"Well, I practice your breathing exercises to get me through." Liyah replied, seeming to force a smile. "But I can still feel an urge to panic sometimes. Her voice shook. "Like right now."

"This is quite something," said Ahmad. "I mean, like a big deal in human history…no matter who or what you believe in."

"And a bit creepy too, if you ask me," added Morningstar. "We don't have anything like this in our Lakota ancestry, even though we descended over ten thousand years ago from ancient peoples too…just like Liyah was telling me about her people."

"And us Jews as well," said Esty. "Before Moses, who was like Jesus to my faith, and Muhammad to the Muslims, all ancient peoples here were like tribes. Jerusalem is five thousand years old, but there were also people here before then, about ten thousand years ago. They were hunters and gatherers."

"Yeah," replied Morningstar. "Hunters and gatherers. No real tribes then. That's what we were too when we first came to the American continent."

"No Palestinians, no Jews, no Christians," added Ahmad.

Esty studied Ahmad in the dimness, his handsome face awash in the soft candlelight. *Not your typical Palestinian boy from here,* she thought. *No hint of hating the Jews. Maybe more spiritual like me, perhaps?*

Morningstar gently fanned the flame of the candle next to her with her hand, wafting the smoke toward her nose. "The smell of the smoke from the candles in this old space reminds me of *hanté blaska*, a sacred herb we use during times of prayer." She fanned some of the smoke toward Zack who was standing next to her.

Esty observed Zack as he breathed in the air and then slowly exhaled. He had taken down the hood of his sweatshirt, revealing tight braids that dangled down, brushing lightly against the dark skin of his face. He appeared to be in a sort of calm trance. *Perhaps he is meditating? He's definitely striking in the strength of his features and the way he bows his head to this bench…as if it were an altar.* She noticed the candles flicker like the others, almost as if the flames were attracted to him. *Some sort of energy?* she wondered.

"Time to go," Esty said, her voice almost a whisper, as she thought would befit the sacred space.

Zack came to, his brown eyes linking with Esty's lighter ones as he brought his attention back. Esty felt a brief, silent communication between the two of them.

They began filing out of the Chapel of the Angel. Zack lingered until Liyah grabbed him by the hand. "Allah. You're beginning to worry me. Try to stay with us, okay?"

Zack shot her a playful grin. "Sure thing, Momma."

"That's more like it! We need to see the old you sometimes…just not all the time."

They both laughed.

Esty brought them back out of the church the way they came in. She headed toward the Muslim Quarter, crossing back through parts of the crowded market area. Ten minutes later, they entered an open square. Hordes of people scurried about, most crowding in along the ancient, rough-hewn limestone Western Wall stretching out before them.

"Hold tight to each other!' Esty yelled out. "This is no time to get lost." She reached out for Morningstar's hand as they all formed a chain, and she guided them to a small section of the wall that was clear of visitors. Backing up against it, she addressed them again.

"This wall that you see is called the Kotel, or Western Wall, and is about fifty feet high and three times that in length. But it goes much deeper below the ground and its full length extends over a quarter mile. It was originally a retaining wall built by King Herod a few decades before the birth of Jesus, and it supported the Temple Mount where the early Jewish temple was built."

Esty paused, distracted by several men near them dressed in dark shawls and Jewish skull caps. They were yelling at a group of women.

She continued. "Many Muslims believe that this wall is part of their holy Al-Aqsa Mosque. That mosque and the Dome of the Rock, which is a sacred site for Muslims, are right behind me," she said matter-of-factly. "On the other side of the wall. We will be going there next."

Esty stopped speaking again, glancing to her left at the crowd in front of the wall right next to them. She noticed the group was made up mostly of women waving signs and yelling about women's rights. She had seen them here before but had never seen the square this crowded. Things seemed to be heating up between those women and others gathered by the wall.

Ahmad called out to her from behind his small group, his voice just strong enough to carry above the loud chatter of the crowd. "What's happening?"

"There's a demonstration going on," she called back. She looked again to her side. "Technically, women don't have the same rights as men to pray at the wall. The men there are extremely orthodox in their beliefs. We, and those women, are actually standing in the men's area. The women's area is farther over. But I have never had much trouble from anyone about standing on this side for the tours. Of course, I have never seen the courtyard and entire marketplace this packed either."

Esty returned to her tour mode. "The term *Wailing Wall* is used mostly by Christians who witnessed Jews being brought to tears in front of it. To us Jews, it is the Western Wall that is the single gateway to all communications to, and from, God."

She pointed to some of the men leaning against it, adding their own prayer on pieces of paper by sticking them in the cracks between giant stones while sobbing. "But I don't mind the name *Wailing,*" she said. 'I think of it as weeping in remembrance of the difficult journey our Jewish ancestors faced over so many years…yet also crying with happiness for the founding of the new Israel almost seventy-five years ago."

A few more men joined in on the disturbance next to them, yelling, "Reform is forbidden. Go home." Several objects flew in the direction of the women, causing them to duck.

Esty looked nervously about. *This is not good at all,* she thought. *Better to get them out of here.* "Okay, let's go everybody," she called out. "Things are getting a bit out of control. The women are being pushed and threatened by some radical men who don't think they should be able to pray here."

"Seriously?" Zack said loudly. "That's freakin' crazy. Aren't they Jews too?"

"Yeah," Esty replied. "I completely agree. But we can talk about that another time. I'm getting a bad feeling."

One of the men next to them suddenly caught a glimpse of Esty and shouted at her. "Hey, you! You in the blue suit with the seal of the Ministry. You can't be a real Jew! What are you doing in this section? You and your other female heretics?"

Several of the other men also took notice. One threw a stone. Esty heard the brush of air as it whizzed past her ear.

Ahmad rushed up, standing in front of her, holding his palm up to the crowd to stop. Next to him, another man had pushed one of the protesters off her chair, then lifted the chair high over his head, ready to strike her.

Suddenly Esty heard a powerful crackling sound, that sounded like a severed power line dancing about on a paved road. A beam of light had struck the chair like a lightning bolt but remained connected. The chair quickly became red hot, and the man dropped it instantaneously. While he screamed and tended to his hands, the people around him stood stunned.

Esty had seen it all happen, but she wasn't sure exactly what it was that really *did happen.* She witnessed the light strike the chair and followed it back to Kai Li's outstretched hand. Once he let go of the chair, the light vanished. The crowd nearby reacted at first in confusion, then several people began pointing at Kai Li.

"Damn!" Zack shouted. "Nice shot, Mr. Kai. But I think we aren't acting quite like the nice guests the Ministry expected us to be."

Esty grabbed Morningstar and shouted at the others. "This way! Stay together!"

Before the other men could react, Esty snaked her way toward the southernmost end of the wall, pushing and bumping her way through the mass of humanity. She took the corner and then began descending a set of stone stairs. Down, down to the inner base of the structure they went…to the tunnel that ran underneath the length of the entire wall. At the bottom stair, she stopped to make sure she had everyone, then turned her head to see if anyone was still following. *No one there.* She felt her heart race. Her ears pounded from the rush of blood being pumped by her heart. Then the sound of heavy, rapid footsteps echoed through the stairwell from above.

"Ahmad! Bring up the rear. This way," exclaimed Esty. "Let's go!"

They flew through the narrow limestone passageway, Esty in the lead, the others toe to heel, at times brushing up against the sides of the tunnel, barely three feet wide in places. They ran without looking back, squeezing past a few worshippers in the middle where the tunnel widened, and past others gathered inside the long archways until Esty's strength began to fade. She slowed but kept moving with her lungs burning, until they eventually arrived at the opposite stairwell.

"This is the end of the tunnel," Esty breathlessly announced. "We're going back up now…to the plaza above." She had been this way before, but never at a run.

Up they went. Her legs ached. At each step, a searing pain coursed through her thighs. Her mind raced. *I don't remember there being so many steps.*

Finally reaching the top, they stood a moment to catch their breath. Near them, atop the Temple Mount and rising tall above the plaza, stood the Dome of the Rock, its giant arching gold roof glittering in the noonday sun.

Esty led them across the busy stone courtyard, zigzagging through the throng, bringing them within fifty feet of the holy Muslim shrine. She stopped and rested briefly, finally collecting enough breath to speak.

"I think we're clear. No one will find us now, if they are even still looking." She turned to face the dome then back again. "Sorry to have to speed things up with the tour info, but the craziness of Jerusalem this weekend appears to be even more than I anticipated. I have a feeling it's going to get even worse, so you might think twice about coming back in here. This may be your only chance to get an appreciation of what you are seeing here, and a feeling for why this *Old City* is not only an ancient religious jewel, but a melting pot of today's hopes and frustrations of those religions. As well as a warning sign to the world."

"Warning sign?" asked Kai Li.

"Yes. What I mean is that people seem to have lost their way. As I mentioned, Judaism, Christianity, and Islam share a common father in Abraham, and although the time span from Moses to Jesus to Muhammad is over two thousand years, each of those men was considered a prophet of the one we call Yahweh…God…Allah. We have turned from that. Look at the hatred, the extremism, how we block our ears to our own brothers and sisters and turn away. We don't understand the gifts that these *founders* of the religions have given us. We don't seem to learn. And I'm afraid the chance is slipping from our grasp."

Zack thrust his fist above his head. "You go, girl! You're one of us!"

Kai Li burst out laughing. "Yeah, she need to meet Ooray."

"Ooray?" Esty questioned, feeling a little embarrassed that she may have gotten carried away and stepped up on her soapbox again without an invitation. "Ooray who? Ahmad, do you know what they're talking about?"

Ahmad shrugged. "Well, no…but I'm beginning to think I'm in the middle of some dream."

"Not to worry, Esty," Liyah counseled. "If we have time, we'll fill you in. Go ahead."

Esty searched their faces then reverted to her tour persona again.

"The *rock*, protected by the dome," she continued, "is the highest place in the Old City, the place from which it is said that the Prophet Muhammad ascended into heaven to meet Moses and Jesus. Brass plates form the gold dome that symbolizes that ascent. The circle of the structure, and messages of the purple-blue and other mosaics represent the wholeness and balance that is the beauty of the Muslim faith. No humans or animals are depicted on the mosaics, just artistic representations of the bounty of Allah, and the essence of the Quran.

"Not being a Muslim, I cannot get close to the sacred stone. I was able to step into the building only once, during a special ceremony. You will have to take my word that it is as astounding in its beauty on the inside as it is from the outside. Light streams in through the stunning, arched, stained glass windows to illuminate the multicolored porcelain mosaics covering the pillars, walls, and archways. In the center of the building is an open section of the floor where the rock rests."

Esty paused, taking a deep breath. "And just to finish…it is important to note that the Dome of the Rock is also sacred to Jews and Christians and is known as the *Holy of Holies*. It is the spot where Abraham showed his willingness to sacrifice his son to God as a symbol of his belief, although he never had to go through with it."

Esty chuckled, sensing the weight of some of her tension washing off her. She loved this job! How it made her feel, how it helped connect all the stories together for others. She went on. "The Ark of the Covenant, the golden chest that housed the tablets of the Ten Commandments given to Moses, is also believed to have rested underneath the stone of Muhammad. And deep within is the Well of Souls, believed by Christianity and Judaism to be the cavern where the spirits of the dead mourn, waiting for the Judgment Day."

Esty pointed to her left to another large limestone building. "Over there, across the courtyard is the Al-Aqsa Mosque. It is a functioning, sacred mosque that can hold up to five thousand people." She looked at her watch. "And it's almost noon, so soon you will hear the *call to prayer* by the muezzin from the minaret—the open cupola sitting above the mosque."

She stopped and glanced around at her companions. "We should go now. I'll take you to a place where we can get some lunch. Any questions?"

"Many but maybe we can chat while we eat?" asked Liyah.

"Sure. Good idea, Liyah. Follow me, everyone."

Esty led them back through the crowd and down the wide stone steps. As she took the corner heading to Via Dolorosa, the main street that would take them out of the Old City on the eastern side, a man began shouting.

"That's her! She's the one!"

The man and a compatriot blocked their way. Esty froze. *And how am I going to get us past this, now?*

Zack quickly stepped between Esty and the men. "Go you, guys! Get out of here! Have Liyah call me on my cell. We all have each other's numbers now. I'll find you."

"But…" Esty protested.

"No buts!" Zack ordered. "Go! All of you…now!"

Ahmad grabbed Esty by the hand and fled toward the main street with the others close behind.

The men tried to follow, but Zack stopped them, grabbing each by an arm. One of the men began pushing him and yelling at him. A small crowd began to gather. The men were saying something in a language foreign to Zack. When he didn't respond, the man got angry. He was pointing in the direction that Esty and the others had gone, but they were no longer anywhere in sight.

The crowd had now grown larger, and Zack knew he needed to do something drastic. If he didn't, they might overwhelm him.

Zack let go of the two men and took a step back. He raised his hands and turned in a circle. The night before, he and Kai Li had secretly been testing how to create a force field as Ooray had shown them. Everyone within thirty feet slowly froze, becoming live statues. Pushing his way through to the back of the crowd, he broke free and began to run, disappearing into the packed, narrow alleyways of the market.

TWENTY-THREE

THE CLICKING AND sandpaper-like grinding sounds from the waiter's shoes echoed off the walls as he made his way down the curving stone steps. Carrying a tray with three china cups and a pot of hot tea over his head, he passed under two white brick archways, through a cavernous room of empty tables, and into the small, sheltered side room off to the right. He set the tray down on the end of the heavy wooden table.

"Will there be anything else, Hassan?"

"No, I think that will do it, Rafiq. Just add it to my tab. We'll just leave when we're finished. We won't be long...*Shukran.*"

The waiter nodded as he backed away. "You're very welcome...as always. *Salaam.*"

Hassan handed out the cups, pouring the tea into each. He then held his cup up to the other two gentlemen. "Here's to a successful operation."

The men gently tapped the rims of the cups together.

"Delicious," said Hassan. He set down his cup and smiled. "A few sips won't kill us. We can make it up at the end of the fast." He shifted his body to directly address the man next to him sporting a thick black mustache with the ends turned up just slightly. "Although you, Murtaza, were Christian once. So maybe this is not so important."

"Quite the opposite, I assure you," replied the man. "You know how it is. The new ones in the game always take it more seriously. Like a converted smoker."

"Yes," Hassan admitted. "Perhaps so. Well, it's good to have you on our side as a Muslim, as well as a financial supporter...and a key leader in this effort."

Hassan gazed off to his side and into the large empty room, then back to his companions. "This is one of my favorite places. I come here a lot to talk business or to just take in the quiet strength of this ancient building. You can feel the history here and smell the same food that was served thousands of years ago. I think those pungent odors have been baked into these walls."

After taking another sip of his tea, he continued. "The reason for this meeting is to give you both an update on plans. I also wanted the two of you to meet, since I've been working with each of you separately, and the operation will be executed on Sunday...only two days from now."

He turned to the other man. "Fahzi, I wanted you to meet Murtaza. He is from America. He came here to Palestine a number of years ago and set up new business roots."

"Is that so?" asked Fahzi. "What was your business in the States?"

"Security software," Murtaza replied. "It's critical these days for everyone's computers, but especially the big companies...what with Russia and China stealing secrets and disrupting operations. Even independent tech thieves out there are getting large ransom payments from them by threatening them with computer viruses that can not only shut down a business but permanently corrupt all their data."

"Why come here to Palestine, then?" asked Fahzi.

"I sold the business a couple of years after going public...when it had optimum value for me. I had time on my hands, plenty of money, and wanted to do something even more important."

"He was a Christian at the time," Hassan added, turning to Murtaza, "but he felt his evangelical friends were ...*over the top*...with their Christian beliefs and support for Israel. I don't mean to speak for you, Murtaza, but isn't that right?"

"Yes, my friend. Exactly that. I felt that the Palestinians were getting a raw deal and I wanted to level the field. So, I spent the last few years donating funds and getting involved in *supporting the cause,* as many refer to it. That's when I met Hassan. Hamas had recently come into power in Gaza, where most of the trouble with Israel seemed to be focused. And Hassan was already a well-respected leader with them. We have been working on various projects together ever since."

"But why convert to Islam?"

"Well, as you know, Islam, Christianity, and Judaism have all come from the same father...Abraham...four thousand years ago. The core beliefs are not so different. Everyone knows this. But sometimes, when you see your own faith mistreating others, you can begin to turn away. It's not so different from when many of the Protestant faith...also Christians...were persecuted by the Catholics in places like Italy. A number of those Catholics who witnessed that persecution turned against their own church—they became Protestants themselves...changing sides, you might say. That's how I felt."

"Interesting," said Fahzi, holding his cup up to Murtaza. "Well, it's very good indeed, then, to have you on *our side* as you put it."

Hassan clicked his pen several times. "Well, my friends, let's talk business, shall we? I wanted to steal a few minutes of your time to give you an important update on recent plans." He took a plain, large, notepad from his briefcase and set it in front of the other two. Using the pen, he drew a crude map of the Israel-Palestine region. He placed a small rectangle in the bottom left part and labeled it *Gaza*, a much larger one to the upper right, which he labeled *West Bank*, and a square near the top left marked *Old City*.

"I cannot tell you all the details at this time. I'm working on a separate plan with others in Gaza that is top secret. But what I *can* tell you is this." He circled the Gaza area. "Here in Gaza, is where the Israelis are giving us the most trouble. Mostly because it's us who trust them the least and fight them the hardest. But it has had devastating results. They are destroying our ability to stand up for all Palestinians. Their attacks on us have crippled our communications and businesses, leaving many people without work, and companies failing. There is great unemployment and poverty. More than ever before."

Hassan placed an 'X' in the middle of the page. "Here, their new rules against our Bedouin brothers, our ancestral nomadic tribesmen, allow the Israelis to steal the land, leaving them homeless and on the brink of starvation."

He pointed to the West Bank. "And here, unfortunately, our own brothers do not want to risk being treated like us, so they don't stand up for themselves. They hope there will eventually be two countries—one for the Jewish state and one for us Palestinians." He paused, tapping the point of the pen on the table. "But that is not going to happen. They just keep on *taking* from all of us. We cannot count on our brothers there to help fix the problem." He stopped tapping. "We are running out of time. We must go it alone."

"And are you proposing something new?" asked Fahzi. "I thought we were pretty set on plans for this weekend."

"What I'm going to tell you is simply this—Sunday will still be the day of reckoning, but I want to make it more *explosive,* since the word seems to fit, and time is running out." He took his pen, pointing again to Gaza on his crudely drawn map.

"The original plan, which will still be executed, is to send the rest of our rockets from Gaza to Israel on Sunday afternoon." He turned to Murtaza. "Fahzi is part of Hezbollah with ties to Iran. He is the one who has been secretly supplying us with new parts for the last of the rockets we have left, ones that will have better accuracy than the older ones. I have told him of our plan to incorporate that technology into this effort on Sunday...when we will focus all those rockets on one single target." Hassan set the point of his pen on the edge of the box that represented the Old City. "Here," he said, "is the Western Wall, the most sacred of Jewish sites."

"That will break a tradition of not going after holy sites," Murtaza cautioned.

"So be it," Hassan replied, his brows furrowed and his voice stern. "As I said…we are out of options." His glance shifted back to Fahzi.

"Murtaza has been helping me with funding for recent retaliations toward Israel. And he is one of the biggest supporters, although a silent one, for this special event on Sunday."

Hassan then paused, his eyes now moving slowly back and forth between them. "But what I have not told either of you, is that I am part of another team. One that will help us cripple our enemies so that they cannot retaliate from this attack. I can't tell you anything about this right now. It will have to wait until Sunday after those plans have been initiated."

Hassan took the notepad from the table and put it back in his briefcase. "Today is Friday. I will continue with my plans with the other group. I think the three of us can operate in silence until Sunday morning. I will call you at that time, and we will set up the last meeting to see if we can give the final go-ahead to all of the plans. Until then, go with Allah."

Murtaza and Fahzi followed a short distance behind Hassan as he made his way back out through the archways, the sound of their shoes clattering and reverberating through the hall until he disappeared at the top of the white stone stairs.

Twenty-Four

As Esty led the others down a narrow cobblestone side street, the call to prayer blasted out over loudspeakers. She stopped and looked back in the direction of the Muslim Quarter. The intermittently tinny electronic sound of the loudspeakers couldn't dull the deep melodic resonance of the tone of the Muezzin, as he reached out to all believers to drop their worldly concerns and come to Allah.

"It's sort of haunting, isn't it?" Morningstar said. "It reminds me of the Lakota chanting for the dead. On the anniversary of the death of my parents, and the death of my grandmother, my grandfather—I call him Lala—will listen to the music of a drum and wooden flute. He holds a rattle with beads in it, then shakes it while chanting in a low tone. It is more like speaking than singing, similar to what we are hearing now. He said it would honor their spirits and the spirits of all the dead—our ancestors…and all our relations. By that, we mean all things living and all that *once* lived."

Liyah bowed her head to the sound and grabbed hold of Morningstar's hand. "It is very much like that, Star. Leave it to you to put it that way. The muezzin calls everyone to pray, as Allah calls to all souls. And it is meant to be talking, not singing, but in a beautiful way. A way that echoes the elegance and depth of the Quran."

"It is probably the voice of the muezzin of the Al-Aqsa Mosque," added Esty. "The place we just left. Come, let's find something for lunch."

They moved along the street and Esty stopped in at a small Palestinian café. The chatter inside was a mix of many languages. She picked out a loaf of bread, three apples cut into slices, several figs, some cheese, a couple of bottles of water, six paper cups and plates, napkins, and a small knife. The owner placed everything into two plastic bags.

"I'll take those," Ahmad said in Arabic, handing the man a credit card. "No need for you to pay, Esty. This card is from the Dawn. Liyah's dad, Mr. Al-Rahim, runs the paper and I'm working there."

"Doing what?" she asked.

"I'm on assignment," Ahmad replied. "Well, sort of. Actually, I'm doing errands for her dad over the next few days and looking after Liyah and her friends. But really, I'm trying to write an article on the situation here…one that maybe would get published. My first one as a real journalist."

"What's the article about?"

Ahmad suddenly felt unsure of himself. He wondered why sometimes he had confidence, especially when he had to look out for others, but then at other times he simply thought he would not be taken seriously, and that he might fall apart at any moment. This was one of *those* times.

The man handed the slip to him. He signed it and stuck it back into his pocket with the card. "*Shukran*," said Ahmad.

"*Afwan*," replied the man, nodding to them. "You're very welcome, sir…and miss."

The two left the crowded little boutique café and joined Liyah, Morningstar, and Kai Li who were waiting around the corner from the entrance. Liyah was on her phone standing close to the front of the building, trying to block out the buzzing sounds of all the people hustling around her.

"What is the article about?" Esty repeated.

"Oh, sorry. Well, it will be about the different perspectives on this conflict. You know, like why has the situation here gotten so far out of hand?"

"Situation?"

"I mean how awful it has gotten here in recent years…for Palestinians for sure. Not that it wasn't already bad. But also for others. It's not safe here anymore." He paused. "For anyone. People don't seem to have any idea of the real reason why things have spun so out of control on all sides. And I have to say that for some of it, the Jews are at fault for ramping things up, even though they may feel threatened too. Everyone shares the guilt…or should I say more aptly *has blood on their hands*." Ahmad finished the last phrase just as the hum of chatter around them trailed off suddenly, creating an eerie pocket of silence for an instant into which Ahmad's loud voice had rushed.

A few people glanced at him as they passed by. Ahmad felt his face flush. He looked over at Kai Li and Morningstar, who seemed to be listening intently. *Maybe they didn't notice the reactions*, he wondered. *I should probably be more careful of what I say, especially here. Especially now.*

"I do hear what you're saying, Ahmad," Esty replied. "I feel bad about things. But I'm also Jewish. There have been some reforms allowing Palestinians more freedoms. And don't forget we have fears as well…and that bombs blow up in Jerusalem from time to time, set off by your people that kill innocent Jewish residents. There is plenty of distrust to spread around."

"I didn't mean to sound that way. But there have clearly been more restrictions than what you might be calling *benefits.* At least that's the way I see that part of it." Ahmad looked past Esty, feeling a bit uncomfortable and avoiding direct eye contact that might spark some sort of argument. *Keep a level head and don't air your personal opinions,* he told himself. *Be a real journalist.* "But this probably isn't a good time to get into this," he added. "Shouldn't we be worried about Zack?"

"Yes, absolutely," Esty replied, handing him a reprieve. "I didn't–"

Liyah suddenly appeared and handed Esty the phone. "It's Jamal. I'm supposed to meet him here today. Can you please talk to him and get directions for me? I'm not sure what to do."

Esty held the phone to her ear. "Hello? This is Esty. I can help get Liyah there. Where will you be? Uh, huh…yes. And what time?...Can you make it a bit later? We're having lunch soon and we also have to track down a friend in the city. Okay. Yes…Certainly."

Esty hung up the phone and handed it back to Liyah. "You've got until two. We can take our time and have lunch. Then I'll lead you back into the Old City. He wants to meet you by the Al-Aqsa Mosque. It's the place I pointed out…next to the Dome of the Rock."

Ahmad raised his eyebrows. "You're saying we have to go back there?"

"Yeah, but I doubt anyone will be still looking for us then."

"That's what you said the last time," Ahmad teased.

Esty changed the subject. "We need to locate Zack. Does anyone have his number?"

"I do," Kai Li replied. "We all do. We exchange when we got SIMs."

"SIMs?" asked Esty.

"We had to have chips put in the phones," said Morningstar. "Otherwise, our phones don't work here."

Kai Li clicked on Zack's name and waited until he heard his voice. "Zack? Esty for you," he said, handing her the phone.

"Hi Zack. We were worried about you…Uh-huh…Good. Put Lion's Gate in the Map app. If you get lost, just ask someone how to get to that gate by way of Dolorosa Street. When you exit the gate, take a right and walk a very short distance until you come to the light at Al-Akma Street. We'll be waiting for you across the street on a stone wall overlooking the Garden of Gethsemane...Yeah, the place where Judas betrayed Jesus...Uh-huh. See you then. Oh, and text Kai Li if you have any trouble...Bye."

"Is he okay?" Liyah asked.

"He's fine but he said he has no idea where he is. He's been trying to get to the street he thought he saw us go down. He was just about to call us."

After following Esty down two congested cobblestone alleyways then out onto Via Dolorosa, Ahmad felt his phone buzz. It was a text from one of his contacts stating that there was a chance that Liyah's brother had been with one of the groups that may have tried to flee out of Gaza near the southern border with Egypt, but was cut off when the Israelis bombed the tunnels.

Ahmad checked his watch. *How am I going to take the girls back home, the boys to the inn, and get all the way to the airport before dark?* He shoved the phone back in his pocket as they passed through the Lion's Gate and out of the Old City.

Esty took them across the street to the Al-Akma. On the corner was a stone wall with plenty of room for them to sit and eat...and wait.

With barely more than a couple of minutes to rest up, they heard the muffled ring of a phone. Esty extracted her phone from her purse and began speaking with someone. At the same time, a loud voice called out from across the street.

"Hey, you guys!"

Zack crossed at the light and joined them. "Man, am I relieved," he said, short of breath. "I was beginning to get worried." He pulled at his sweatshirt. "Not the right thing to be wearing I'd say, even in this crowded place. I stick out like a red cape to a bull."

"How'd you get here so fast," Liyah asked.

"Turned out I must have been going in circles, then ended up closer to Dolorosa than I would have expected. After I got your call, I hit it in just two blocks."

"How'd you get away?" asked Ahmad.

"Let's just say I blew out a' there and left them cemented in their shoes. They're probably still wondering if it was real?"

Esty returned the phone to her purse. "What do you mean *real?"*

"Oh, just an expression," Zack replied, not wanting to get into things.

Ahmad didn't understand what was going on either. His mind drifted back to Zack at the Church of the Holy Sepulcher. *What was it Zack already showed him? Talk about reality!*

"You should all eat your lunch so we can get going," Ahmad said "I have things to do this afternoon. And Esty needs to get back to do the next tour, I'm sure."

"Actually, no." Esty replied. "That was the tour center. They've canceled tours the rest of the day…maybe for the weekend. They told me the level of tension is building throughout the city. They even commented on the trouble we had at the wall."

"It shouldn't be a surprise," added Liyah. "Remember two years ago around this time? Several people were killed in the Old City by an explosive device. The police came in firing rubber bullets on Easter Sunday. Today is only Friday. And already they say the crowds are bigger than any year in memory."

"This is nothin'. People are nuts all over the world," Zack replied. And there are things like that happening in Detroit and other places every day in America."

"Breathe, Zack," Kai Li suggested, exaggerating his own breathing, then grinning.

Zack paused, took in a long breath, and let it out slowly, then smiled. "Okay, bro'. How's that?"

Morningstar tried unsuccessfully to smother her laugh. "You may have changed permanently, Zack."

"We all did, didn't we?" Zack replied, his voice edging more somber. "Sometimes it doesn't feel real, but on days like today, I am totally reminded. Ooray taught us well."

"Ooray?" Esty interjected.

Zack's face paled and his eyes shifted up for an instant. "Inside joke," he finally replied.

Ahmad took a deep breath himself. Maybe out of sympathy. But he did feel his shoulders relax. "This is all good, but I can't let the afternoon fade away, even if you guys can."

Esty pulled the items out of the plastic bag and set them along the top of the wall beside her. She cut up the cheese, apples, and figs, placing them on top of the bag with the bread. "Help yourselves to a plate and some water."

Thanks, Esty," Liyah replied, "but it's fasting time for me. I already cheated once this week."

"Likewise," said Ahmad.

"Oh. Sorry. So sorry," Esty apologized profusely. "I forgot for a moment. And today is your holy day of the week on top of that. How stupid of me… especially *me* being a tour guide."

Ahmad felt her pain. Things were happening fast, and she was doing them all a giant favor. He nodded to her. "No worries, Esty. Isn't that the American expression? We really appreciate your efforts."

Zack and Kai Li had already piled the snacks on their plates and grabbed a cup of water. Esty turned to Morningstar. "How about you?"

Morningstar caught Liyah's eye. "Thanks, but I'll pass...sticking with Liyah."

"Don't be ridiculous, Star," Liyah replied. "I think I can hear your stomach growling from here."

"No, no. It's okay. This weekend I am a Muslim. That's what I would like to be today. That's how I would like to feel."

Liyah smiled. "Thanks for the support," she said, then turned to Esty. "Star is not fifteen. She's actually forty-five...in case you hadn't noticed."

The six sat along the wall, facing out toward the hill and gardens while enjoying the warm sun and finishing their snack.

"So...," drawled Zack, looking down at the nearby stand of trees and gardens. "That is actually Gethsemane? Surreal."

"And up beyond it to the left is the Mount of Olives," said Esty, "where Jesus gave his speech before entering the Old City...before he was crucified."

"I know," Zack replied. "How far is it to the top of the hill?"

"Not far at all. Less than a mile the way I go. All uphill, though not too steep. Probably take about twenty or thirty minutes. Interested? I have the time. We could–"

"Well, I don't," Ahmad broke in, speaking a bit gruffly. "And I'm responsible for them. I have to get the girls home to Gaza, and Zack and Kai Li back to the inn in Bethlehem. And on top of that, I have a lead on Khalib that I have to track down."

Liyah leapt from her seat on the wall. "Really? Let's go! I'll help you."

"I can't bring you along, Liyah. You know that."

"Besides," said Esty, "You're supposed to meet someone in the Old City. If we all want to go up on the Mount, you'll have just enough time to do that and get back with a little time to spare."

"Kai Li and I can go with you, Ahmad," Zack offered. "That way you can drop us off afterward. Maybe Esty can bring Star and Liyah back instead."

"I'd be happy to, "Esty replied. "I can borrow my dad's car at the Ministry. And we all have passes...so no problem."

Ahmad was about to throw the option out, not wanting to get them involved in such a risky mission, but he considered it some more. *After all, what are the boys here for anyway?* he thought. *Obviously not to sightsee, now that it's evident something else is afoot...like Kai Li with that thing with the chair and magic man, Zack. He's stronger than I am. Obviously able to get himself out of jams. And I'd be taking an even greater chance going by myself. Maybe it's not such a bad idea after all?*

"Okay, Esty. I guess I can join you on the walk. But let's not linger."

Esty collected the leftover trash, dumping it in the bin as they made their way past the tour buses parked along the street. One of the buses pulled out of its spot, blowing billows of diesel smoke and fumes in their faces.

"Holy Crap, man!" shouted Zack, gasping, then turning his back to take in some cleaner air. "If they're trying to make me feel at home, they succeeded."

"Over there, across the street," Esty announced, pointing through the gap left by the departing bus. "A little ways down…See that big archway in the side of the city wall, all boarded up? That's the Golden Gate, also called the Eastern Gate or Gate of Mercy. I mentioned it before. It's the only gate to the Old City that's closed. It's said that the Messiah will re-enter Jerusalem through this gate and begin a new kingdom on earth. The gate was sealed by Muslims to prevent that and has not been reopened for almost five hundred years."

Zack stood silent, staring. He turned his palms away from him and closed his eyes. The air between him and the gate began to wave, radiating beams of energy.

Ahmad shook his head. *Who is this boy?* When Zack came back to earth, Ahmad locked eyes with him, feeling stunned beyond amazement.

"Sorry," said Zack. "I got carried away. The energy in that wall is amazing. It's actually scary. I had to let go."

"You need to explain this to me," Ahmad insisted, as they pivoted to follow Esty. But she was staring at them, standing with the others, her mouth agape.

"What was that?" Esty mumbled. "It looked like the whole gate was melting or something."

"I think we're going to have to talk about it soon," said Liyah. "But let's get this done. I'm dying to get up there."

"Me too," added Kai Li.

"Me three," said Ahmad as he caught up to Esty.

She whispered in his ear. "Any idea what's happening here, Ahmad?"

"Something strange," he replied under his breath. "For sure."

TWENTY-FIVE

Mount of Olives

THEY FOLLOWED ESTY through a small iron gate and into the gardens, carving their way along the cement path laden with tourists and past the tomb of the Virgin Mary. They merged onto a stone path, then an earth-packed trail, meandering between scattered bushes and small olive trees. Up they climbed, arriving at the base of a stone wall.

Esty stepped up over the wall and onto a raised section of the hill, set off from the earthen path, and motioned to the others. Zack joined her first, then gave the others a hand up. From there, Esty took them up a short, steeper incline and into a small open area sheltered by trees. At the top of the gently sloping glen, she turned and looked out over the Old City a short distance away.

"There you have it," she said. "The best view in all of Jerusalem! The one Jesus must have had when he came here to preach to his followers and potential converts."

They all gazed out over the Mount, past the olive trees with their gnarly, fat trunks and twisted limbs. A gentle breeze crept up, blowing through the branches, filling their noses with the fragrance from the fragile, pale-yellow blossoms.

"The scent of the sea," Esty gushed. "Don't you just love it?"

"And the piney smell of fir trees," said Morningstar.

"That's right, Morningstar," Esty acknowledged. "Let's sit and take it all in for a minute before we return to the chaos of the busy city below."

The ground was covered in a thin, packed layer of grass, more faded-yellow than green. Unaccustomed to sitting cross-legged, Ahmad found the ground hard against his butt, with his legs extended stiffly and awkwardly. But he couldn't deny the view; it was all worth it. He studied the others.

Kai Li, with his jet-black hair, pushed his glasses up on his nose and zipped up his jacket. Ahmad could tell he was clearly more relaxed with his yoga position than he was…as was Morningstar, her blue-sequined moccasins crisscrossing one another over the legs of her jeans that jutted out below her stunning, beaded tunic. But *Magic Man* seemed as uncomfortable as he was, his eyes fixated on the hill below them, the red hood of his sweatshirt flipped up over his head.

Ahmad glanced over at Liyah, the *dark beauty* as he thought of her—the one with the flowing dark brown hair, deep brown eyes with their thick black lashes…and that Mediterranean skin like his. On his other side was Esty, who had just removed the blue newsboy cap, allowing her long blond hair to spill over her shoulders. *What could be said about her? Liyah's opposite*, he thought. *But just as stunning in her own way….and equally as poised.*

His eyes followed a path back down the hill to Gethsemane, to the road with the buses, then across the street to the great wall of the Old City, to the Eastern Gate, and finally to the spectacular blue and gold domes of the Church of the Holy Sepulcher and Dome of the Rock. It was a place like no other. Ahmad knew it belonged to all of them regardless of religion. Who better to share it with than those with him at this very moment?

"It's so magnificent," Zack noted, his tone understated, his mind shifting back into reality. "All of it."

"It must be very special to you, Zack," Ahmad replied. "You're the one who seems to be so connected in a special way to Jesus, or at least Christian beliefs."

Zack glanced at him then back to the hill and the city. "Well, it's not that I'm super religious. Not at all. It's a feeling I get sometimes…like static in the air. I got it at the church, while looking at the Golden Gate, and then in the garden. Now as I stand on this hill where Jesus likely spoke many times, especially the last few days of his life, I feel it here too. Very strongly!"

Breaking his stare, Zack turned and studied their faces as they sat in silence, caught up in rapt attention to the view and to his words. "I grew up as a Catholic, but we stopped going to church when my dad left me, I mean us…a number of years ago. It's hard for me to remember how long. I guess I tried to put it out of my mind. But even though I couldn't stand the formal rituals of church back then, the messages got through. They helped me. I believe in them."

Zack held the palm of his hand up and swept it in the direction of Liyah, Kai Li, and Morningstar. "Then just a week ago I met my friends here. And I came to realize they were stronger than me. They are filled with messages too. The very same messages that come through other ancient sources such as Buddha, Muhammad, and the Great Spirit. Morningstar showed us that we are forever connected to all things. I learned we are bound by the compassion that Liyah somehow innately understands, and as Kai Li taught us, that we must share this…knowledge, this light, with the universe…And I think that here, in this very spot, a young man delivered those very same messages…two thousand years ago."

Moisture welled up under Ahmad's eyes. He had never heard a boy, so close to his own age, speak like that. His own beliefs were not dissimilar. He was raised by strict Muslims in the faith of Islam. He tried to follow their lead but still could not adhere to many of the rituals, despite how hard he tried. When a man befriended him and introduced him to Sufism—a more spiritual facet of Islam, it seemed to be in alignment with his own feelings… to connect with Allah through expressing love, not through blindly following rituals. That the source of the universe is one with all people, and that we are its children, mystically bound together through love and compassion.

Ahmad tried to speak, but the words tripped as they fell out of his mouth, his newly found confidence spilling out onto the ground. He was back at his foster home, mocked by his peers for being so small when he was a young boy, and he and his younger brother were unsupported by his new parents…convincing him by their words, and expressions, that he would never amount to anything. But in this young boy from America—one so different from himself—he saw a good path. *If not the only one, certainly a true one.*

Esty, as if reading his thoughts, reached out and pressed her finger to his lips. "Shh…there are no words for it anyway." Tears trickled down her cheeks.

Ahmad had never felt anything so powerful in his life.

"Sorry," Zack said, addressing them both. "I didn't mean to upset you."

Ahmad struggled to collect himself. "It's okay, Zack," he assured him, finally. "It's been an overwhelming day. And it's not even over yet." He managed a forced chuckle, followed by a broad grin. "I call you Magic Man."

"What magic?" asked Esty, wiping her eyes with the sleeve of her jacket.

"Nothing really," Zack replied.

"We can talk another time," Liyah interjected.

"Look like you and Ahmad will be part of mission," added Kai Li.

Ahmad could sense his head spinning again. "Huh?"

"We are on a mission," said Morningstar. "That's how we met last week. We have been concentrating so much on how to adjust at home, and now how to help Liyah find Khalib that we haven't had time to recruit others…to begin to pass the light on."

"What light?" asked Esty.

"The light we each have," Zack replied. "What Ooray taught us about overcoming fear and suffering. The light of our own true selves."

"There we go again with that name," Esty said, throwing up her hands. "I–"

She was interrupted by the sudden vibration of the ground under them.

"Are you doing that, Zack?" asked Ahmad, a touch of panic in his voice.

"How could he do that?" replied Esty. "This is getting weird."

A low, repeating sound, like the revving up of propellers, surrounded them. As the intensity grew, they covered their ears. Then an eerie silence engulfed them. Directly ahead, about fifty feet down the slope, sheltered on either side by two tall poplar trees, a shimmering, multicolored light appeared. The background created by the fir and olive trees gave the scene a kind of framed stage-like appearance.

Ahmad looked around at the others, thinking he was surely losing his mind. But they had noticed it too.

A translucent egg-shaped form slowly precipitated into view. Its surface began to glow, first like a kind of purple-blue haze then in all the colors of the rainbow. They began to sparkle and swirl inward, leaving a space for only the purest white light that radiated from the center. The object then emitted a barely audible buzzing sound.

"Holy Crap!" exclaimed Ahmad.

Esty grabbed hold of his hand, gripping it like a vice, as a scratchy, high-pitched tone began to grow, then resonate, modulating like the sound of a voice…colors mixing and pulsating.

"Ooray!" shouted Kai Li. They all rose to their feet.

Ahmad's eyes remained glued to the object. Then it spoke. *Not in, like, a real voice,* Ahmad noticed. *But better than a computer voice,* he thought, *with some crackling and buzzing thrown in along with the colored lights. The radiant light in the middle pulsated in intensity with the words.*

"Hello my friends."

To Ahmad, the voice was indecipherable as to whether it was male or female. *Perhaps mixing them or shifting between them.* He looked over at Esty, her mouth slightly open, as if trying to speak. She gripped his hand even tighter. But he shifted his attention back to *it.*

"Hi Ooray," Zack and Morningstar shouted, almost in concert.

"Why have you come?" added Liyah.

"Because you called."

Liyah glanced at the others, who held out their hands as if to say, *not me.*

"The energy," said the orb. "Together you have a lot of it, as you know. And this is a special place, isn't it?"

Ooray paused, then continued. "You have all been thinking of me. I felt it. Something is happening here, but I am not certain of what. I can sense the high negative energy of this region of your world as well as the positive energy right here on this hill, with you."

The white light flared briefly then settled. "When so much bad energy mixes with good energy there is only one result; an explosion…the result of which can never be certain."

There was another pause as Ooray's form took a vaguely human shape.

"I will always sense your danger, but I cannot be with you all the time. There is so much to do everywhere. But in spirit, we are all one. Have faith in that. I have told you that your job is not to save the world by yourselves because no one can do that…not even I. We can only do our part. And your part is to find others, who will then find others…and so on.

"You will all grow into the powers of the gifts I have given you, each in different ways. I have told you that, as well. They will help. But it starts with the passing of the light…your light. Soon you will be able to feel some of that power provided by your gifts, even without them, or your friends at your side. That is when you will know your fear has been conquered and will never return. When you have become whole.

"I welcome these new friends joining you here today. For you are already passing the light to them. And they are ready. They have been ready longer than they realize, and you will need them in the days ahead…for a battle will likely occur here in Jerusalem. And I fear it will be a dangerous time for everyone."

The voice stopped. The orb ceased pulsating. The six gathered on the hill looked around at each other briefly. Then Ooray's voice returned with lights flashing and swirling in synchrony.

"On this hill, long, long before your time, a young man spoke about the light that must be returned to the world…the light that is the essence of you, me, and everyone. On the day before he died, he reminded those gathered of what was good—the blessings would be received by anyone who followed in the path of the light, and those who showed that light to others."

As Ooray moved closer to them, the voice softened. Its tone became more female and spoke slowly and deliberately.

"Close your eyes and imagine his voice as he looked out over the crowd gathered here that day, telling them that the poor in spirit would become the strong in spirit...and be one with the light. That love will flow to all who suffer and mourn. That the kindness of the meek will overwhelm the greed of the few. That those who hunger for the light will have it given to them. That mercy and compassion will be given to those who provide it to others. That the peacemakers are the true children of the light as they pass the light to others. And that those who are persecuted today will together become the flashpoint—when the light is finally restored to all."

Ooray rose higher, hovering above them. "This young man's heart was filled with compassion for everyone, for the world, for all things that came from the source. His face radiated love...and his words, truth."

The multicolored lights reached out farther, engulfing them.

"His path is the path you are now on, the path that focuses on others, so that the light may be returned to them. It is the one true path, the only one that will bring eternal joy and happiness out of the darkness that could be shared by everyone."

There was a long silence.

"What will happen here?" Liyah called out beseechingly. "Will my brother be found?"

"I cannot predict the world," Ooray replied. "I don't know the future. I can only tell you what you already know...that the light is the way in as well as the way out. It is that small voice within you that you must let guide you - the one that always knows what is right and true. And by uncovering that voice in others, you free their light and yours grows ever stronger."

"And here...this weekend. What of the danger?" asked Liyah. "How can we avoid it?"

"Danger is only a warning. It is fear causing you not to act. There is no point in putting yourself in the path of danger for no reason. But should danger fall in the path of others then your voice must be heard. Your fear will melt away and you will rise to the moment, regardless of harm to your physical body or even your life."

Ooray drifted even higher.

"Jerusalem is as ancient and steeped in history as any civilization on your planet. There is magic in this Earthly city. It is tangible. It can be felt. Three passers of the light are honored here. And, like you, each had a special yet different gift to give. But they all brought the light, through their attempts to save the many."

The aura around Ooray began to sparkle.

"Moses, the eldest of the three, led his people—the Jews, out of slavery in Egypt. Though he died before getting here, this was the *Promised Land* of which he spoke. His gift was the law…common rules from which to form the foundation of a united society. The Western Wall you visited once supported the Temples of Jerusalem and would not have existed if Moses had not saved his people and put them on the journey that led to this place.

"The youngest in age, Jesus, came next…arriving in the Old City through the Eastern Gate. His gift was compassion and the forgiveness that comes with it. As in the Zah-re that you learned about, he embodied the highest state of being—*Love.*

"Muhammad was middle-aged and the most recent to arrive here and he brought the gift of a warrior's strength. Surrounded by many who wished to harm his followers, he defeated them, saved his people, brought forth the messages of the Quran, and founded Islam.

"Moses, Jesus, and Muhammad all brought their unique gifts to bear, to better the lives of their people…to give them hope. But since all beings are connected to the same source, the message from these prophets was also the same:

The Oneness of the Light.

That we are not separate from the source of the Light.

Although presently lost, we will inevitably return to the Light.

To keep the Light present and strong, we must commune with the Light frequently, through mindful meditation.

Bearing false witness…lying…dims your Light and harms the Other.

That fasting cleanses both the body and the mind. We give up what we have as a reminder and ease the suffering of others.

That it is always about the Other…and the Light within them."

A great silence returned. Ahmad looked over at the others as they sat on this hill, gazing beyond Ooray, to the hill across the way, to the Temple Mount and the two domes.

The light formed an orb again and began flashing and pulsating. Ooray's voice returned.

"I will leave you now. Go with the Light."

A whining sound came from within the orb. It grew louder and higher in frequency until they all covered their ears in pain.

There was a piercing *POP!* And Ooray was gone.

A deep silence surrounded them once more. Ahmad slowly brought his mind back to the tasks at hand.

"What was all that?" Esty exclaimed under her breath.

"Maybe they can tell us on the way out," Ahmad replied. "We've got to get out of here. I'll try to find Khalib before the sun sets and then get to Gaza. Esty, you have to take Liyah and Morningstar back into the Old City to make their connection."

"Before we leave," said Zack. "I just have one question, Esty."

"What's that?" she asked, visibly trying to gather herself together.

"Is there something funny about that road…the Via Dolorosa?"

"Why?"

"When I started jogging along it, I suddenly felt a heavy weight pulling me down. I had to walk, and even that was hard. I was exhausted when I arrived at the Lion's Gate. But maybe I'm out of shape?"

"Dolorosa means *Way of Suffering,*" she replied. "It was the path Jesus took while carrying the cross to his crucifixion."

Zack stood quietly, then looked back at the trees where Ooray had been.

Esty picked her newsboy hat up off the ground and twisted her long blond hair up under it as she stared blankly at Ahmad.

"Right now, I really don't think I know a lot," she said. She turned, taking the lead once more down from the Mount and back toward an *overheating* Jerusalem.

Twenty-Six

AHMAD AND THE boys split with the girls at the entrance of the Garden of Gethsemane and returned to his car. Ninety minutes later, they arrived at the checkpoint at the northern end of Gaza. A long line of vehicles waiting to be checked halted their progress. Concerned about the time, Ahmad got out and made his way half up the line, signaling one of the uniformed soldiers. Kai Li and Zack watched as he spoke briefly to the soldier.

Ahmad returned and slid back behind the wheel. "This press pass works wonders sometimes. They'll take us now, but we still have to get screened." He pulled out of line and followed the directions of the guard, stopping at the side of the checkpoint. Another man approached their car. Ahmad handed him Zack's and Kai Li's passes.

The man signaled another officer who slid a large, flat rolling device under the car and moved it about like a vacuum cleaner. When finished, he nodded to the guard. who returned the papers as he leaned through the window and searched the interior with a flashlight. He pulled his head back out and nodded. "*Wasal.* You're clear."

"*Shukran,*" Ahmad replied, always relieved to get past the border guards.

They quickly passed through Beit Lahia, with Ahmad pointing out the general location of Liyah's home. They skirted Jubalia, the home of the Dawn then merged onto Salah Al-Deen, the main road south. He pulled the car off to the side of the road as they neared the city of Khan Yunis, about ten miles from their destination—the old airport.

"What's up?" Zack questioned.

"Just texting my contact. He was going to try to make it here."

They waited silently for a moment before hearing the ding of Ahmad's phone. Ahmad texted something then stuck the phone back in his pocket. "We'll have to go it alone. He said it got too late for him. He's already on his way to an appointment outside of the Strip."

Ahmad started the car back up and headed onto the highway, not knowing what to expect at the remains of what used to be a bustling airport and the pride of Palestine. Turning off the main road he followed his GPS to a dirt road filled with potholes and scattered with debris. He slowed to a crawl and stopped in a weed filled desert area that used to be the main parking lot. Not a soul could be seen in the area.

"C'mon," said Ahmad as he opened the car door. "This doesn't look hopeful, but we might as well check it out. I just wish it didn't take so long to get here. The sun will be going down in a few hours."

They snaked through the mounds of dirt and debris until they got to what used to be the main terminal. All that was left were the once beautiful arches and the partial walls that connected them. Huge slabs of cement hung down with their metal rebar rods protruding out in all directions.

"Where we goin'?" asked Kai Li. "No one here. Look bad."

"Yeah. Doesn't look great, does it?" replied Ahmad. "But this is where I was told to come…to look for a tunnel where some people might be hiding."

"Needle in a haystack as they say," said Zack. "Looks like no one's been here in a dog's age."

Ahmad started walking along what was left of the main concourse, crunching through the plaster and sand and between the few scattered scrubs. Zack and Kai Li followed him into what looked something like a wide central hallway with just a shell of the old building above it.

"Must be around here somewhere."

"What are you looking for?" Zack asked.

"Maybe an entrance," replied Ahmad. To the tunnel."

"Like I said," added Zack. "Needle…"

"Yeah, just look around, will ya? Any sign at all."

The three walked slowly in concentric circles, expanding outward from each other until they were near the edges of the hall.

"Nothin' from my side," Zack shouted.

"Me either," Ahmad yelled over.

After a pause, Zack called out again. "Mr. Kai?"

"Ah…have somethin' maybe."

The other two walked over to join him. "What you got?" asked Zack, as they approached.

Kai Li held up a half-smoked cigarette butt. "This…"

Ahmad studied it. "Can't say that's much of a clue."

"Been used recently," Kai Li countered. "Nothing else anywhere near here."

Zack began combing the area close to them, using his sneakers to scrape the wind-blown sand off the cement tiles that remained visible.

"There…there!" said Ahmad, pointing to a crack between the large tiles. "What's that?"

Zack bent down and used his hands to clear away the rest of the sand from a small area, uncovering the top of a tunnel entrance. He groaned as he tried to lift it up, using the inset groove on one side that acted like a handle, but it wouldn't budge.

Ahmad tried with the same result. "It must be bolted shut or something."

"Step back," said Zack, holding his hands out palms down above the lid. Once Ahmad was clear, he pressed down on it. A creaking sound emanated from it until it began vibrating, then shattered suddenly into a thousand pieces, sending concrete raining down into the tunnel below.

Once the dust cleared, Zack caught a glimpse of a long ladder, resting up against the wall. As he followed the rungs with his eyes, the ladder disappeared into the darkness. He tested it with his foot, then turned and slid over the edge until he had solid footing for both feet. He began descending.

Ahmad called down to him. "Where are you going, Zack? This doesn't seem like a good idea. I'm thinking we should go home."

Zack looked up, briefly catching sight of Ahmad's concerned face in the fading sunlight before he disappeared from view.

There was a brief silence as Kai Li and Ahmad stared blankly at the hole.

"Down!" Zack's echoey, muffled voice rose from below. "Really dark here, man!"

"Turn on your cell light!" Kai Li yelled back, then laughed.

After a minute a blast of light came up through the hole then went out. Peering down Ahmad and Kai Li could see a narrow beam flickering, like someone searching at night with a flashlight. Suddenly the hole lit up as if a switch was flipped on. Kai Li's head jerked back, away from a surge of black smoke and smell of gas fumes, and hit Ahmad's.

"Sorry," said Kai Li.

"It's okay," Ahmad replied, pressing the side of his head and waving him off. He stood up. "Brutal on the eyes." He then bent back down and called out to Zack.

"What's happening? Smells like a torch."

"It is. Come join the fun. This must be the tunnel. I doubt we'll find another one."

"I don't know," Ahmad yelled back. "They must be long gone."

"Yeah, but maybe there's a clue."

Ahmad stared nervously at Kai Li.

"No worry," said Kai Li. "I go first…help you."

They descended the ladder, Kai Li reaching up and guiding Ahmad's feet onto the rungs. At the bottom both turned to face Zack. He was holding the torch to the side. He swung around and began surveying the cave-like room, his eyes dancing up and down, his head swiveling as he studied his surroundings.

Above them was a string of insulated wire with a few bulbs dangling off. Zack followed it to the back wall where the light from the torch illuminated a plaster door. As Ahmad opened it, Zack stuck the torch through the hole and into a small room. The only thing they could see was a large metal box at the back.

"Clever," said Kai Li. "Generator."

"Dead end?" Zack wondered out loud, pulling the torch back.

"What's this here?" asked Ahmad, pointing at the wall to their right.

Zack studied it. "No idea. Maybe a gang?"

"Maybe," Kai Li agreed, tracing the scraped markings in the stone with his finger. "I see marks at home too. This one almost look Chinese. Like symbol Shui…mean water."

"I've never seen a symbol like that used by anyone around here," Ahmad noted. "Certainly, no water around here, but it could belong to the terrorists I suppose."

Zack entered the room, ducking his head, yet still scraping it against a protruding ridge of stone.

"F'-all!" he snarled, rubbing his head. "Well, there's nothing else around. Maybe the tunnel starts somewhere in here?"

The other two followed. "Nothing here," Ahmad proclaimed. "Except the generator. And a few more torches. I guess we can go."

"What's the hurry?" Zack questioned, as he lit two of the torches and gave one each to Kai Li and Ahmad.

The room lit up.

Kai Li moved over to the generator and tried to figure out how to start it but quickly gave up. As he began to step away, the light from the flame of his torch caught a gap in the stones nearby. He got closer. "Somethin' here," he said, using the bottom of the torch to poke between several of the larger rocks in the wall.

Zack and Ahmad joined Kai Li in removing the loose rocks, setting them down behind the generator. A large hole opened up. Zack leaned inside with his torch out in front of him.

"This is it, guys," said Zack. "Let's go."

Ahmad felt his neck muscles tighten. "Go where? We should go back," he urged. "Like I said, they're probably long gone."

"Check out a little," Kai Li coaxed.

"We're safe with the three of us here," assured Zack.

"I don't know," Ahmad said, trying not to let his nervousness show.

"Oh, c'mon," Zack insisted.

They removed a few more stones and Ahmad followed the other two in. "Feels like the walls are closing in," he said, as they stood up, hunched slightly to avoid hitting their heads on the ceiling.

They walked along in single file until they came to a fork. Zack bent down, picked up a sharp-edged rock, and scratched a "Z" onto the face of the largest stone in front of them. "Something Star taught us," he said, chuckling. "I can't remember if I called her an idiot at the time."

"Prob-ly," replied Kai Li, sarcastically playing along.

"The point is," Zack continued, "that if we go down one of these paths and get turned around, as soon as we see this mark we'll know where we are."

Zack set out into the tunnel on the right. After about ten minutes, it ended in a pile of sand and rocks that cut off any further movement.

"Looks like a recent cave-in," said Ahmad. "I've seen enough bombed-out areas to tell. Maybe this is what my contact meant when he told me the Israelis were trying to make sure they sealed off the last of any tunnels."

Zack poked at the blockade with his toe. "If Khalib was with a group, they might have been trapped or killed."

"Not much we can do about it, Zack," Ahmad replied. "We can go check the other tunnel but that's about it." He felt sweat dripping down his back. "But I'd rather get back."

"You look pale," Kai Li said. "Okay?"

Ahmad felt his chest constricting. "I'll be alright," he replied, his breathing noticeably labored.

"Breathe," Kai Li offered, using his hands to show him how to take in deep breaths and then slowly exhale. "Focus mind on something else. Control breath and you control fear."

Ahmad listened to Kai Li but became distracted as Zack began retracing their steps. His anxiety still bubbling, he brushed by Kai Li to follow Zack hoping to get to some real air outside as soon as possible.

A grin crept over Kai Li's face. "No worry, Ahmad. You be okay…need you 'round."

They made their way back to the fork with Zack stopping to let the others catch up. Kai Li turned past him and started down the other tunnel.

"That isn't the way out, is it?" Ahmad asked Zack.

"It's probably one way out," Zack joked, as if trying to make light of the situation. "Might as well check it out. We can always come back this way to get to the car."

"I don't know," Ahmad replied, nervously. "Let's just get back."

Zack ignored him and headed after Kai Li.

Not wanting to be left behind, Ahmad followed right on his heels with his eyes glued to Zack's back, refusing to look at the rock and dirt walls closing in on him. He gripped his torch tightly while hoping that they would reach the end soon.

They walked hunched over for a short time before the tunnel narrowed even more. Ahmad felt beads of sweat collecting on his forehead. He stopped abruptly and called ahead.

"Wait!"

Both of the others stopped and turned around.

"I don't think I can do this, guys," Ahmad complained, his voice quivering slightly again. "Sorry. I feel like the walls are going to squeeze the life out of me…like we'll run out of air. I don't want to be buried down here."

"How about just a little more?" Zack asked. "If nothing, we can turn back."

Ahmad hesitated, then caught up to them. "Just a bit, Zack. And that's it."

"I promise," Zack replied.

Ahmad began moving again, passing by both Zack and Kai Li. *Maybe if I lead, I won't feel like I'm being left behind,* he thought, trying desperately not to show the fear that was consuming him.

Kai Li grabbed hold of Zack's arm as Zack began to follow Ahmad.

"Hold on…minute," Kai Li said, handing Zack his torch. "Stones in shoe."

Kai Li undid his laces. Holding onto Zack's pant leg for balance with one hand, he untied his laces, shook the dirt and pebbles out of each sneaker, then tied them back up.

As they began to catch back up to Ahmad, they heard a loud rumbling sound above them. The sides of the tunnel began shaking. Sprinkles of loose dirt fell on top of them.

Zack shouted out to Ahmad. "Hold up!"

Ahmad stopped, turning around a short distance ahead. As he took a few steps back toward his comrades the rumble got louder. The rock walls looked like small waves were passing through them. Ahmad halted again, looking around. Just then, an avalanche of earth and stones rained down next to him, filling the tunnel from top to bottom. Clouds of brown dust blew back through the tunnel on both sides.

Ahmad fell to his knees, coughing and gasping for air. As the dust settled, he regained his breathing. He stared at the blocked passageway. His shouts to Kai Li and Zack went unheard. Only a deathly quiet remained. Fear gripped his throat.

I'm cut off. Trapped!

TWENTY-SEVEN

LIYAH AND MORNINGSTAR stuck close to Esty as she led them through the jostling holiday crowd back through Lion's Gate. They went up the Via Dolorosa and to the compound of the Dome of the Rock. She was able to answer the many questions they posed along the way. But her mind was elsewhere. From the time they left the Mount of Olives, everything that had just happened buzzed in her head like background noise.

They mounted the wide stone stairs and entered the plaza of the mosque. Liyah checked her watch. "Five minutes to spare," she said.

Nearing the pillars of the entrance, Esty halted. "We can't go any further than this. Only Muslims are allowed inside. Young women are also prohibited during this holy prayer day."

Not too far from them, a group of middle-aged Palestinian women wearing white hijabs were yelling at a handful of Jewish men, telling them the mosque would never fall into Jewish hands. Israeli police dressed in bullet-proof vests and carrying batons, tried to keep order.

Esty looked at Liyah. "It's really getting tense around here. Where are you supposed to meet him?"

"Right here in front of the mosque. I had no idea it would be this crowded." Liyah stood on her tiptoes trying to see above the crowd.

"Let's stand on the wall…near the fountain over there where people wash before prayer," Esty said. "Maybe he'll see you then. It's about as high as we can get above the crowd. Why don't you and Morningstar stand together? I might draw the attention of the wrong people…especially in this blue and white outfit."

The girls had a good view of the plaza from standing on the wall. Liyah waved her hands back and forth above her head. She waited a minute then did it again and again, until she finally saw a man wave his hand in return. He was with another man who was wearing a long dark robe and colored skullcap. People nodded, some bowing to the other man as they walked toward her.

Liyah hopped down while Morningstar still stood on the wall. The men approached. The man with Jamal looked up at Morningstar in her Lakota clothes and hijab, then over to Esty in her dark blue jacket and bright blue newsboy cap. Esty, feeling a bit off-center and unsure of what else to do, bowed her head. She'd been in a mosque only once. But this mosque, the Al-Aqsa Mosque, had been totally off limits to her. She didn't even really know if this man was an imam, or the muezzin Liyah had mentioned.

"Safir," Jamal said to the man, "this is Liyah, the girl I was telling you about."

Safir nodded to her, then to Esty and Morningstar. "It seems like we have an international convention here."

Jamal cleared his throat. "Yes…well sorry…I didn't mean to complicate things. I–"

"No worries, Jamal. I'm just the muezzin here, the servant of the mosque. I'm not judging anyone." He smiled.

Esty believed she could see Jamal's shoulders relax, as did her own. *I should have stood away*, she thought, *let them do their business*. She caught Jamal's eye and motioned that she would leave. Jamal shook his head lightly, indicating with his hand for her to stay.

Esty studied the man as he began to speak to Liyah. His robe was dark purple and had gold embroidery covering the lapels and cuffs. His skullcap was mauve with yellow, green, and red intertwined in a kind of helix surrounding the upper portion. *He looks kind*, Etsy thought.

"Jamal knows the imam quite well," Safir said to Liyah. "So, he comes to me quite well-recommended. I am told you are trying to locate your brother."

"Yes. He has been missing over a week."

"And you think he has been abducted?"

"There's no other explanation."

The muezzin turned to Jamal. "Are these the people charged with finding him?"

"Morningstar…up on the wall there, and Liyah are the ones. I'm not sure about…" He faced Esty.

"Esty. I'm Esty. Just a tour guide. Jewish, if you hadn't guessed."

"Yes," Safir replied. "I see. You wear the colors well." He grinned then bowed his head.

Esty felt more relaxed. "Morningstar is here from America. There are two boys as well trying to help out. One from Hong Kong and the other also from America."

"So, I was right. It is indeed an international gathering." He smiled again.

"What can you tell us?" Liyah asked, anxiety evident in her tone. "Where can we find Khalib?"

"Sorry to say, but as I was telling Jamal, I don't know for sure."

"But you know something?"

"There was a time when I knew much more. You can imagine how many Muslims come through this very famous place of worship." He held a hand up toward the mosque. "I see and hear a lot. But I am no longer connected to any of the, what you may be calling, terrorist groups." He paused. "However, I do know of one such group which could be involved."

"And…" Liyah beseeched.

"And, although I cannot disclose this information to you here, I have given Jamal the name of a man and where you might find him. I just wanted to come out here and meet you before I approved him to release it." He nodded to Jamal.

Jamal reached in his pocket, removed a piece of paper, and handed it to Liyah.

"I must go now. But it was a pleasure meeting such nice young ladies. These are troubled times, my friends, so be careful." His eyes shifted toward Esty. "And by no means allow the Israelis to get hold of this information."

Esty sensed her face flush. She pulled her eyes away as if they were the recipients of daggers. Then they returned to his face.

"I will not look at what's on the paper. Nor will I ask Liyah." She gathered up her courage to look him in the eye. "I will not say a word," she assured him."

"Yes," replied the muezzin. "I'm sure you won't. After all, you are Dr. Blum's daughter."

Esty was dumbfounded. *How would he know that?* She nodded.

"Then go. And may Allah, peace be upon him, go with all of you. *As-Salaam-Alaikum.*"

"*Wa-Alaikum-Salaam,*" replied Jamal.

Safir turned and headed back to the mosque.

"I have to get going," Jamal said to Liyah. I have a meeting to attend.

"I can't thank you enough, Jamal," Liyah replied. "I hope we will get the chance to see you again soon."

Jamal smiled at her. "I'm sure of it."

He then turned to Morningstar and Esty. "*Salaam.*"

"*Salaam*, Jamal," said Morningstar, smiling.

"*Salaam,*" Esty repeated.

Liyah took the piece of paper and clutched it tightly in her hand before placing it in her purse.

As Jamal disappeared into the crowd at the plaza, Esty led the girls back through the Muslim quarter, out the Jaffa Gate, and to her father's car—parked at the government offices garage.

TWENTY-EIGHT

AHMAD SCRAMBLED AHEAD in the tunnel, getting as far away as he could from the swirling dust. He slowed to a walk and listened for sounds. Sounds of falling rocks. Sounds of sand leaking from above. Vibrations of any kind.

Nothing. *I'm safe,* he thought, *for now.*

He could feel his heart thumping against his rib cage, but the shot of adrenaline through his system had propelled him to action and he forgot to be afraid, at least for a moment.

As the threat of imminent danger began to subside, other thoughts started to creep into his mind. Thoughts of being cut off…alone, of never getting out, of dying by starvation. Or worse…suffocation. *What if the torch goes out? What if the torch uses up all the oxygen? What if the tunnel ends? What if…*

His stomach knotted up. He felt nauseous. It seemed he might puke at any time. He set the torch upright against the wall as he sank to his hands and knees. His body heaved and retched but nothing came up. He turned and sat cross-legged in the dirt of the tunnel, breathing hard, trying to get control of himself.

What was it Kai Li had said? Breathe? How? On the verge of crying, he hung his head in his hands. *Concentrate,* he said to himself. *Concentrate! What was it?*

His feeling of panic eased slightly as he sat there, enough for him to think more clearly. *Deep breaths…but slowly. That was it. That's what Kai Li had said. And focus your thoughts.*

Ahmad lifted his head from his hands. The wall of the tunnel, not even two feet from his face, stared at him., His heart began to race even faster. His throat tightened. He blocked the sight of the wall by cupping his hands lightly over his nose and eyes. He started to breathe. Short, quick breaths at first. Then longer ones, until he felt the muscles in his neck and shoulders relax. He remembered what Kai Li had told him when they were in the car on the way to the airport, that this was what Liyah had to do to save Morningstar…and that you can calm your mind and your body by simply concentrating and breathing.

He tried harder, breathing deeper and slowly exhaling. He could feel his sense of panic, his fears, begin to fade. He brought his hands down to his lap and stared back at the wall. He could still sense the talons of fear trying to claw at him. But he could breathe. *At least I can do that…and I can think.*

Getting back to his feet, he grabbed the torch. He knew he had to move forward. There was no sense in going back the way they came in. He started down the tunnel, head bent, torch still burning.

The boys, he thought, after a few steps. *Yes. What about them? What about Zack and Kai Li? They could be buried.*

Ahmad focused his mind on that…of getting out to help them. He stepped up his pace, his head now and again bumping into the low-hanging rocks of the tunnel, his mouth dry, his legs weary. But he moved on.

Back at the airport, Kai Li popped his head out of the entrance to the tunnel. He climbed out and signaled to Zack, giving him a hand up from the last rung of the tall ladder.

"What ya think?" Kai Li asked.

"I think we need to get help."

The two jogged their way back to Ahmad's car. As they got closer, they could see a vehicle in the near distance driving away from them. They slowed their pace.

Kai Li turned to Zack. "Look like army truck."

"Yeah, camo painted. But not a truck." He squinted. More like a…a…*tank*."

"Tank?"

"Yup. I'd say we should be glad they didn't see us. Remember what Ahmad said about the Israelis searching for more tunnels? That must be them."

Arriving at the car, Kai Li opened the driver's door and slid in. He checked the ignition, opened the glovebox and console then scrounged through their contents. Next, he pushed the seat back and felt under it, then around the floor mat.

"No key, Zack," he said, climbing back out. "What can we do now?"

Zack knelt down next to the door and leaned in. He removed his knife from the pocket of his pants, flipped it open, and started working on something on the other side of the steering column.

Kai Li leaned in above him. "What's up?"

"One minute," Zack grunted. "Just need to connect these two wires now."

Suddenly the car started. Kai Li backed away, allowing Zack to extricate himself from his awkward position.

Zack closed the knife and held it in front of Kai Li. "Tool of the trade," he said, grinning. "Most of the things I learned from the gangs in my neighborhood in Detroit I'd like to forget. But a few are useful." He stuck the knife back in his pocket. "Survival in the city is one…and how they steal cars is another. You want to drive?"

"You forget. No license and no car. No need in Hong Kong."

"Well, I'm supposed to get my license this year, but I didn't see the need either and my mom's too busy most of the time to help. But I've taken her car around the block a few times." He snickered. "So, no problem, Mr. Kai…Jump in."

Once behind the wheel, Zack headed up the potholed dirt road in the direction of where the tank had come from.

"Can't go through a checkpoint," Kai Li advised.

"Yeah. I know. But I've got an idea. I think that cave-in may have been caused by the tank. If we follow its tracks back, they probably crossed the path of the tunnel. We'll see."

In a couple of minutes, they came to the tread tracks of the tank. Zack steered the car to the right, the opposite direction of where they saw the tank heading then followed them through the sandy terrain.

"Watch out for dip," Kai Li warned in an urgent voice.

Zack stopped the car at the edge of a shallow indentation in the land where the tracks vanished. They got out and walked closer. Zack looked around, finally locating the tracks again on the other side of the depression. "This is it," he said.

"Is what?"

"It's the tunnel…below. The tank must have forced the collapse of the tunnel just by driving over it. The tracks continue there on the other side. They probably didn't even know it happened."

"Enough to fill tunnel in this spot," Kai Li added.

"Yeah, so maybe Ahmad is still alive? But we can't dig him out by hand. It's too deep."

"Tunnel must have its end somewhere."

"I don't know Kai. How would we ever find it?"

"Use powers somehow?"

"But how? Crap. I think we're really stuck." Zack's eyes flashed. "He'll suffocate in there."

Kai Li moved to the side of the depression. Holding his hands above the ground, he moved them up and down. He then stepped close to the edge of the depression and did the same.

"What are you doin'"? asked Zack

"Minute." He crossed to the other side of the depression, repeating the exercise, then looked back at Zack. "Time to practice."

"Practice? C'mon. Quit playing games, man."

"No game. Can feel difference in force if I try to push energy down. Depression resist more."

"So?"

"So, I think we have a gap underground, where tunnel is. But depression feels solid."

Zack scratched his chin. "Hmm."

Kai Li took his cell phone from his pocket and held it up. "Can you sense this?"

"Of course." Zack pointed the fingers of his right hand at it, immediately drawing it from Kai Li's hand. Kai Li grabbed onto it tighter. Zack backed off.

"You getting good at that," said Kai Li, winking. He buried the phone a half foot deep in the sand. "Now try."

As Zack concentrated on the phone, it inched its way to the surface.

"Just checkin'," Kai Li said. "All cell phones have many tiny magnets. Use for voice coil—for speakers, and a motor for vibrating. Magnetometer, too…compass uses it. New ones even have magnetic charger–"

"Okay, okay," Zack interrupted. "Don't get carried away."

"It's what you connect with by pointing…using own magnetic field."

"Like I said, I get it," Zack added, impatiently. "And your point is?"

"Point is even if phone is off, or no signal, you can sense magnet underground…like a compass." He chuckled. "You are a living compass, Zack!"

Zack stared wide-eyed at Kai Li. "Christ!" He grabbed onto Kai Li's shoulders. "That means we can locate Ahmad."

"Maybe," Kai Li replied.

"Maybe?"

"Well, you could get signal from iron and other metal too."

"And what does that mean? Jeez, do I have to pull all this stuff out of you?"

"It's why I test hollowness of tunnel. Together we can follow where it goes. Try to locate him. At least get to end of tunnel."

"You're a genius! We all know it." He laughed.

"Test here first," Kai Li said. "See if he is buried in tunnel."

Zack's face dropped. "Ah…"

"Go ahead," Kai Li encouraged. "Have to do."

Zack pointed both hands toward the depression, focusing his mind. He moved his hands in small circles, then stopped and held both thumbs up.

"Nothing!" he said. "Thank God!"

Kai Li used his technique to check the area to see the exact direction the tunnel was headed. Zack retrieved the car every now and then, keeping it close. Each time, he got out and surveyed all directions for a possible clue of where Ahmad could be.

After two miles of returning to the car again, Zack let out his frustrations.

"I don't know, Kai," he said. "Look." He pointed toward the horizon. "It's a freakin' desert out there. We're not even on a road anymore. And we have no idea how far this goes." He slumped behind the wheel. "On top of it, I probably missed him somehow. He can't survive for long in there."

"No worry. Must end soon," Kai Li assured him. "No point to make tunnel go very far into desert."

"Yeah. *No point.* Well, that's what I'm afraid of."

They agreed to keep going but to stop once the sun started to go down, then see if they could find the closest town on the GPS. But after just two more search sessions, Kai Li called Zack over to where he was marking the end of that search with a rock.

"What ya got?" asked Zack.

"Feel solid on other side of rock. Maybe tunnel end…or cave-in again."

"It doesn't dip here. Probably not a cave-in. Let me see." Zack began moving his hands over the area. Suddenly, he was drawn forcefully to a section a little beyond where Kai Li had placed the stone.

Kai Li noticed the strong pull on Zack. "Something there? You look like a divinin' rod…you know…bend toward water."

"That's what it feels like. Yeah, definitely something here. But you said the tunnel might end here, right?"

"Think so."

Zack repeated the exercise, with the same result. He began to kick the sand away from over the spot of the strongest signal. "Well, this is much stronger than the cell phone signal. So can't be that."

Kai Li knelt down. Using his hands, he scooped away more sand as Zack extended the circle.

"Something here, Zack," Kai Li said.

Zack used the edge of his sneaker sole to clear away some sand, then tapped down with his heel. "Something metal, I think." He kicked away more sand until his foot bumped into an object sticking up.

Kai Li cleared the rest of the area by hand, uncovering a handle, protruding from a flat plate. He grabbed hold and yanked on it.

"Too heavy."

Zack helped him. Together they pried it loose, then began to lift it from its position. Suddenly the plate became light, causing both to fall backward as they pulled the object onto the ground next to them.

Scrambling back to their feet, they looked down at the hole where the metal plate had been. Ahmad's head poked up.

"Jesus!" Zack cried. "You scared the crap out of me."

"You okay?" asked Kai Li.

"Yeah. Help me out of here."

On their knees, Zack and Kai Li each took an arm and lifted him from the ladder he was standing on, to safety.

Ahmad sat on the ground with the two. He could feel his body trembling inside but managed high-fives all around. "I thought I was done. How the hell did you guys ever find me?"

"It's a long story," Zack replied. "We'll tell you on our way home."

"Home," echoed Ahmad. "Yes. Let me see."

He reached into his shirt pocket for his phone. "I can get a GPS signal here, so we're good for a map." They waited while he checked their location. "It looks like we're two hours from Bethlehem. But it's less than fifty minutes to Beersheba. I was supposed to meet someone there anyway after I dropped you guys off. Maybe he's still there. We could get a bite when the sun goes down, after the fast is over. It's sort of on the way."

Ahmad held the phone to his ear. "Hassan? It's Ahmad. Sorry, I'm running late. I could meet you at a restaurant around eight if that still works for you?...Uh-huh…Yeah. Asian is good…Ganbei? Sure. Okay, see you then."

He stood up. "Let's get to the car. We can get some dinner in Beersheba and then get gas. I'm sure Hassan won't mind you guys coming along. He's late too…finishing up with a meeting somewhere near here. I'm working on some ideas for an article in the Dawn and he's one of my contacts. It'd be different if you guys were Israelis."

They placed the lid back on the hole, covered it with sand, then began walking back to the car.

Zack glanced at Kai Li. "The plate must have blocked any signal from Ahmad, huh?"

"Yup. Good thing we dig it up."

Zack turned to Ahmad. "What did you do with the torch?"

"I set it against the rock wall at the bottom of the ladder, still burning. I never want to see one again. But it gave me hope, even if it was using up the oxygen. That and your breathing exercise, Kai Li. I was freaking out!"

"It's helped all of us, Ahmad...Kai Li's gift from home. And now, if I heard correctly, it seems like we're gonna eat his food as well."

Twenty-Nine

Beersheba

THE BOYS ENTERED Ganbei restaurant in Beersheba as the last rays of the sun disappeared below the horizon. Ahmad approached the receptionist.

"May I help you, sir?" asked the Asian attendant, disapprovingly scanning him slowly from head to toe.

Ahmad looked down at his clothes covered in dust then over at Zack and Kai Li, as if caught off guard, forgetting where they had just been.

Kai Li stepped forward and spoke briefly in Chinese to her.

She nodded, answering back in his native language.

He pointed to Zack and Ahmad then switched to English, the common language between all of them. "Quiet table?"

The hostess studied the table plan in front of her, glanced into the dining area, then back at the boys. "You can see how it is here tonight. The busy weekend has started and now that Passover has begun and the day's fast for the Muslims is over, we are expecting a large crowd. We're fully booked."

"Maybe Hassan called it in?" Ahmad asked.

"Hassan?" asked the woman.

"Yes," replied Ahmad. "Do you have a reservation under that man's name?"

She scanned the list.

"It would have been for two," Zack reminded Ahmad.

"Two?" asked the hostess. "Oh, yes. Here it is. I do have a table for two."

"Can we add chairs? There are four of us."

Kai Li watched as she studied their clothes again then tapped her pen on the list. "I'm so sorry. We just don't have anything for you. Perhaps you could find another place to eat."

Kai Li looked over at a number of empty tables at the far end of the restaurant, suddenly feeling embarrassed. *This is not what I expect from someone of my own culture.*

"Must have extra chairs…we can squeeze in?" he countered sharply, interrupting her.

"I'm sorry boys."

"Boys?" Kai Li said, raising his voice a bit.

Zack tugged inconspicuously at his shirt sleeve.

Kai Li snapped his arm free. Keeping his eyes on the woman's, he returned to Chinese and launched into a steely but controlled monologue."

"Just a minute," the hostess replied, her voice quieter and tone more deferential. She pushed a button on the house phone and spoke briefly to someone on the other end. After a pause, she set the phone back down.

"There is one table for six…in the corner. We had a cancellation. Would that be acceptable?"

"Yes, thank you," said Ahmad. "That would be fine. Sorry to put you out."

"Quite alright," she replied, turning back to Kai Li. "The extra towels are being brought to the men's room now. You can clean up there. Just place them in the metal basket below the sink."

Zack and Ahmad stared at each other.

Kai Li said something else in Chinese and then bowed from his waist. She returned the gesture.

They took turns washing their hands and faces, as well as wiping the dirt off their hair and clothes. They gathered again at the reception area. A waiter collected four menus and nodded to them.

"Follow me, please."

Arriving at a large, circular table in the far corner of the restaurant, Kai Li and Zack eased onto the plush, horseshoe-shaped bench seat. Ahmad sat at the server's end next to Zack.

"I'll be right back with your water," the waiter said, setting the menu on the heavily lacquered rosewood table.

Zack looked over at Kai Li and smothered a laugh with his hand. "Christ, Kai!" he blurted out. "What the hell was that all about?"

"Yeah," Ahmad joined in, grinning. "Good job. What'd you say to her?"

Kai Li was somber. "Say I shamed on behalf of all Chinese. And mean it." A grin then washed slowly over his face. "So I tell her we on international mission. Zack from America, his dad is famous architect, me from Hong Kong with family to talk about funds for project with businessman from Palestine. Together we help rebuild airport. And Ahmad…I say you journalist for cover story."

Zack chuckled again. "Wow. Quite the storyteller, aren't you? And the towels?"

"I tell her truth. We get caught in cave-in at old airport…tie in with story. She felt bad."

"Ha!" exclaimed Ahmad. "You should be a politician."

"There were enough lies in there to choke a cow," Zack added. "Never seen you talk like that…so bold! And making all that crap up at the same time. What happened to the truthful, shy, Buddha boy?" He pointed to the Torch of Truth pendant hanging out over Kai Li's shirt. "After all, you did get that for a reason, didn't you?"

Kai Li winked. "Not bear false witness, Zack…jes' little white lie, maybe. But not hurt anyone."

Ahmad smiled. "Maybe there is a *gray* area in there somewhere," he joked, providing some cover for Kai Li. "And just what *is* on that chain?"

Kai Li slipped it over his head, handing it to Ahmad. "Called Torch of Truth, as Zack say. Ooray gave each of us a special present…and this." He unbuttoned the cuff of his shirt and showed his bracelet to Ahmad.

Zack did the same, sliding up the sleeve of his sweatshirt. "It's because our mission is to pass the light, and to understand that we are all from the same source. Ooray told us that knowledge leads to truth, and that truth will help us all rebuild the human family. Kai Li seeks the truth in everything. He understands the truths that bind all spiritualities. Ooray saw that and brought him to us…me, Liyah, and Morningstar. That's what I believe."

Kai Li sensed his emotions rising, creating pressure behind his eyes. His mind drifted back to their short journey together and the first time Zack's rough exterior had cracked. He had seen that same honor in the expression on Zack's face when he spoke similar words. *I guess that's what brothers do when you least expect it.*

Ahmad held the pendant above the flame of the red candle resting in a flowered crystal glass cup in the center of the table, emitting its sandalwood floral bouquet. The facets of the clear jewel, shaped like a flame, scattered red and white fractals of light everywhere. Kai Li watched them bounce around in Ahmad's mesmerized eyes.

"What's that, Ahmad?" boomed a voice. A man was standing right at the end of the table. "You boys look like you're examining stolen merchandise. I don't believe I've had the pleasure."

Ahmad jerked his head away from the flame, still holding the pendant by its chain. "Oh…uh, Hassan," he said, standing and holding out his hand. "*As-Salaam-Alaikum.*"

"*Wa-Alaikum-Salaam,*" replied Hassan. "What do you have there?"

Ahmad handed the necklace back to Kai Li. "Just a gift Kai Li was showing me…uh, excuse me. This is Kai Li and Zack. They are friends visiting Jerusalem. Sorry, I didn't have a chance to tell you they were with me."

"Not a problem, Ahmad. Sit back down. I'll sit across from you, next to…Zack it is, right?" Hassan asked, sliding in next to him, shaking Zack's hand as he did so.

"Yes," Zack replied. "Nice to meet you."

"And nice to meet you too, Kai…ah–"

"Li," Kai Li said, shaking his hand across the table.

"They're actually here to help Liyah find her brother. I mentioned you to them. I hope you don't mind. I felt we all are concerned about the same thing…locating Khalib, that is."

"Sure, just a reminder, though, not to give out any secrets of those others I have put you in touch with, unless they don't mind. They are important contacts."

"Absolutely," Ahmad agreed.

Hassan nodded. "Good then. Unfortunately, I've got limited time." He picked up the menus and passed them out. "This is on me."

Kai Li glanced briefly at the featured items then gazed around at the room. He had never been in a place so elegant. He breathed in the woody scent from the candle, taking him back to the incense his mother burned the few days a year when she was able to relax in the bathtub. His thoughts shifted to the woods they had made their way through while seeking the pages of the Zah-re during their quest the previous week. *Still kind of a dream,* he thought. *And now here. How quickly my life has turned.*

He turned his attention to the long oval bar in the center of the room with its buffed, thick rosewood top matching their table. High-back chairs made of bamboo lined the brass rail underneath. The restaurant was nearly full, with only a smattering of bodies seated at the bar—Passover forbade the mixing of grains and water which meant limited consumption of beer and many alcoholic drinks by the local Jews. Most Muslims avoided alcohol in general.

His eyes continued roaming, noting the glossy, black-framed shoji screens separating the tables in the room, several others jutting up around them. Tiny spotlights along the top of each folded section lit up the translucent rice paper panels, and red plum blossoms glimmered softly along twisted, fragile branches within each panel. His mind drifted back to Hong Kong. *Oh, how I wish mom could be here to see something like this…just once.*

"Kai…Kai." Zack snapped his fingers in front of him, yanking him out of his fantasy.

"Huh?"

"We need to order, Kai. I figure you're the expert here."

"Oh, sure." He scanned the menu again. "Anyone got favorite?"

"I wouldn't know what to order," Ahmad admitted.

"Me neither," said Zack.

"Spring rolls for me. You boys order anything you like," said Hassan.

The waiter returned with a pitcher of water and poured a glass for each of them. Kai Li ordered the spring rolls first, in English, receiving a smile from Hassan, then ordered the rest in his native tongue of Cantonese ordering wonton soups all around, Kung Pao Chicken—his favorite—some sticky rice and chow mein…and dumplings.

He then nodded to thank the waiter. "M goi."

The waiter bowed his head slightly, collected the menus and disappeared towards the kitchen.

"Well…," said Hassan, facing Ahmad, "What brings you here instead of our original meeting place in Gaza?"

"I followed up on the suggestion you gave me about that group that might be involved with Khalib's disappearance, and the possibility they may be trying to get out of the country via the tunnels. Most have been pretty much destroyed the last few years by Israeli tanks, bombs, and artillery."

"And did you find anything?"

"We found a tunnel was still partially in use at the airport. Kai Li and Zack dragged me through part of it. Some of it was already caved in. But one part led out a mile or two into the Negev…to nowhere. They pulled me out there."

"Pulled you out?" questioned Hassen, looking quizzical.

"Yeah. It had caved in on me and I got lost trying to get out. If they hadn't located me using the car and their wits, I wouldn't be meeting you today…or ever."

"Wits, you say?"

"Long story. I'll just say that the tunnels are not of much use any longer, like you mentioned. But someone was in there recently. I found some torches near the exit."

Hassan scratched his chin. "Maybe…"

"Well, what have we here?" a man approaching the table called out.

"Hassan stood and greeted him."

"Sit. Sit," said the man with the Iranian accent. "Hello, Ahmad."

Ahmad reached his hand out. "Hello, Mr. Fahzi," he replied hesitantly.

"Just Fahzi is fine, Ahmad."

"Ah, yes," said Hassan. "Of course. You two have met, haven't you. Care to join us? This is Kai Li and Zack."

"Hi boys. Unfortunately, I'm on my way out. Were you able to get a reply from Mr. Rahim, Ahmad?"

Ahmad gulped. "Ah, no. I actually haven't seen him yet. But I was just thinking about that...and you, strangely."

Kai Li noticed Ahmad's nervousness. "Sync'onicity," he said.

Ahmad stared at him. "Huh?"

"Mean you think of him and he show up. Like magic...but maybe not."

"Don't mind him, Mr. Fahzi," said Zack. "Sometimes we never know what he's talking about. But he's smart anyway...at least we think so." He winked at Kai Li. "He figured out how to save Ahmad today, and how to save me a week ago. And he knows technical stuff about things like cell phones, computer programming...you know...the stuff none of the rest of us have a clue about."

Fahzi laughed. "Really?"

"What kind of programming?" asked Hassan.

Kai Li's rescue of Ahmad had just turned into his own embarrassment. He felt his heart begin to race. "Software for toys. I work in toy factory in Hong Kong."

Hassan persisted. "What kind of toys?"

"All kinds. Animals that talk, games, robots...so much these days, no? Everything computers."

"Hmm," Hassan continued, "and these robots. What do you do with them?"

"Program behavior. And remote control."

"Are you familiar with infrared signaling?"

Kai Li looked around the table, wondering why he had suddenly become the center of attention. It was not a place he liked to be. "Sure. Use it to move robot, and for robot to see what he might bump into."

Hassan smiled. "Interesting."

Kai Li, feeling uneasy under Hassan's attention, broke away from his stare, shifting his eyes to his glass of water. He reached for it.

"Sorry but I must be going," said Fahzi. "Nice to meet you, Kai Li and Zack."

He turned to Ahmad. "You know how to reach me."

"Ah, yes of course, sir."

"Fahzi," he corrected.

"Yes, sorry. Fahzi."

"*Salaam*, all. Enjoy your dinner after fasting. You must be hungry. Allah be with you." He turned and walked away.

Ahmad looked at Hassan. "Thanks for the contact, Hassan. I'll get back to him as soon as I can."

"I'm sure you will," Hassan replied. "How are things going with your article?"

"Working on it. Had a bit of a delay today."

"Well, I like what you're doing anyway. But be careful. A lot of people, including me, don't think it's possible to resurrect peace and equality, and raise our country from the ashes. I'm afraid it is all going to get much worse. As you know, we, Hamas, are at the end of our rope. We feel it's time to cut the leash, once and for all. I don't think anyone will negotiate seriously with us unless we give something to *wake them up*."

"I understand," replied Ahmad, his serious tone unable to camouflage the sudden sadness in his eyes. "But what do you mean by that?"

"For another time," Hassan replied. He reached across the table and subtly handed Ahmad a folded piece of paper he had taken from his shirt pocket. "More names I promised you," he whispered. "They are Hamas but could still be useful for your article. You didn't get it from me."

Ahmad nodded, sticking the note in his pants pocket.

The waiter arrived with the plates of food, alleviating the tension introduced by Hassan. They dove in, hungrily devouring everything. Hassan stayed long enough to take care of the check and said his good-byes.

The boys stayed for a short while and then made their way back to the car. Ahmad looked over at Zack. "It's going to be late by the time we get to the inn. Mind if I stay on your couch there tonight?"

"Sure. No prob." Zack assured him.

Kai Li sat in the back seat, oblivious, daydreaming. His mind wandered home, to his mom, alone again in Hong Kong. *I will surely lose my job this time,* he thought. *Or are we once again trapped in time?* The engine started, jerking him back to the moment. He looked out the window. *This is looking like another dangerous mission,* he mused. *I hope not.*

He closed his eyes as they got back onto the highway, headed to Bethlehem. In no time he was fast asleep.

Thirty

JAMAL PULLED INTO the packed parking lot of Marin on the Sea. He switched his casual shoes for a pair of tan leather dress loafers. Donning his neatly folded, tweed sports jacket from the rear seat, he headed up the cobblestone path to the entrance. He made his way through the throng of people in the waiting area to the hostess at the podium.

"Sir, how may I assist you?"

"Table for two," Jamal stated in the most gentlemanly manner he could muster.

"I'm so sorry but we are completely booked. Do you have a reservation?"

"No. Perhaps my companion made one?"

The hostess glanced down at the list. "Name?"

"Ah..." Jamal said, pausing. *What was Nura's last name, anyway? I don't think I ever asked.*

The hostess looked up. "Sir?"

"I guess I'll wait for her, thanks."

Jamal looked for her in the waiting area again without success. He stepped into the large, open dining room, and scanned the tables and booths as he made his way to the far end of the room. *Surely, she was here already.* But he found no sign of her. *Why would she even show up here?* he wondered. *Why suggest this place? Break her trademark secrecy.*

As he reversed direction and started his return to the front desk, Nura entered the room through a side door of a patio that faced the sea. He noticed she wore the same outfit she always did—the long black double-breasted trench coat with the collar up, and traditional black and white Palestinian keffiyeh.

As he moved toward her, Jamal watched the heads around him turn. Not for him. He was quite certain of that. People were taking notice of *Nura.*

He met her in the middle of the room and held out his hand. "Nice to see you."

"Jamal." Nura shook his hand and then cupped her other on top of his. *An extremely unusual thing for a Muslim woman to do, especially in public,* he thought. *And so unlike her.*

A dull but audible murmur began to replace the normal ambient sound of table talk, rattling glasses, and scraping forks. Their voices carried more easily. Jamal didn't notice.

"This place is busy," he said. "Did you make a reservation?"

"I forgot it might be so crowded with people eating after fasting. Especially this weekend."

Jamal found that odd. *She does live here, doesn't she? She must. How could she ever live anywhere else…dressed like that?*

"So, I failed to make one," she added.

As the hostess joined them, the murmur subsided, and silence descended upon the entire room.

"I'm sorry," Jamal said, turning to her, his deep voice traveling unimpeded. "Apparently we don't have a reservation."

Instantly, the scraping sound of a host of chairs sliding across the hardwood floor filled the room. The voices of those now standing flooded his ears. "Here, Nura…For you Nura…Please Nura…Take ours…Allah bless you, Nura."

"You should have said Nura was your companion," said the hostess. She faced her. "I'm sure we can find something for you."

"No, no. That's fine. I couldn't do that. There is no privilege here. I wouldn't have it. But it is nice out on that small patio, and no one is there. Do you–"

"Absolutely. I'll have someone set up a table for two." She signaled one of the waitresses who had stopped to witness the scene.

"Thank you," Nura replied. "That would be nice."

The waitress brought two menus with her, passing by the hostess who was returning to her podium. She nodded to Jamal and Nura. "Follow me, please."

As Jamal trailed behind her, Nura turned to the people who were standing by their chairs, the ones who had offered her their table. She bowed deeply, then held out her arms and bowed again.

Turning once more, Nura headed towards the patio. The room remained stone silent, the only sound the *squeak, squeak, squeak* of her black running shoes against the polished wood floor.

The two sat across from each other with the Mediterranean Sea to their side. Night was descending but the sky still held stubbornly on to the dusk, its ashen hue slowly giving way to the light of the rising moon. A spattering of fishing boats moored a short distance from the sandy shore, bobbed gently, kissed by the low, slow-moving waves. Jamal secured the top button of his jacket against the evening chill then peered over his menu.

"It turns out we got a quiet place to talk after all. Maybe the quietest?"

Nura looked over at him, her keffiyeh covering her eyebrows, but pulled down even with her chin. What Jamal could actually see of her, he found attractive. Her light eyes, long lashes, and smooth complexion. But it was the mystery of her that attracted him the most.

"Yes. Sorry again for any confusion, Jamal. It's probably better this way. We can talk without worrying about who may be listening."

She always seemed so serious to him when they were at the meetings, even with the last conversation they had, when he dropped her off in Gaza City afterward. *So young to be like that*, he thought. He was older. He felt he had earned his seriousness and occasional moments of anger by losing part of his family to *them*, after all.

"You said something about another explosion?" asked Jamal. "And a hospital?"

"Something has been going on south of here. I think the Israeli IDF has stepped up surveillance over the past weeks in anticipation of this holiday weekend. They probably fear another attack, with rockets coming from Gaza toward them, like last year."

"They said they already shot a few rockets down. That's why they attacked here with artillery the other day," Jamal replied.

"And today," added Nura.

"Well, Hassan hasn't said anything about sending rockets in their direction. And he would know. But everyone is certain that the rockets are fired from mobile platforms in various Gaza locations, especially in the south. Not a real secret."

The waitress arrived and took their order of hummus, falafel, molded rice, pomegranate molasses, vegetables, and traditional seabream fish.

"The fish is a bit expensive, Nura," Jamal noted, as the waitress left.

"Ocean fish are getting rarer here due to the increased restrictions placed on Palestinian fishing," Nura replied. "My treat."

"Are you sure? I have a good job in the tech area near Tel Aviv."

"I'm sure. You're doing a lot for this project for free. I have access to money. In fact, I have to drop a check off for the hospital where my car is parked, not far from here."

He studied her, thinking about questioning her about the source of funds but she left no room.

"It's awful what has happened to the fishermen, don't you think?" she continued. "I mean if it weren't for some of the new fish farms, no one could afford fish here at all."

She gazed out at the sea. "The best fish, like the ones at this restaurant, can only be found farther out."

Jamal watched her eyes. He could almost feel the sadness radiating from them. "I know what you mean, Nura. The attacks by Israel damaged the infrastructure along the coast, especially here, by contaminating the water closer to shore with untreated sewage. Most people now avoid fish, not only because of the cost, but for fear of the safety of the food…from the sewage and from the remnants of the artillery shells, leaching chemicals and metals into the soil. Cancer rates have gone up, they say."

"Yes," replied Nura. "So I've been told at the hospitals I visit."

"You have quite a reputation of generosity. I'm sure you know that. People here at the restaurant are giving you some space, but pictures in the paper show lots of people surrounding you and wanting to be near you. You're like a saint."

He noticed her cheeks flush.

"You exaggerate."

"No, I don't think so. Not at all. You are generous in spirit and in contributions. It's quite clear. I honor your dedication to peaceful solutions, especially given the oppression we are all certainly experiencing as Palestinians, and Muslims. I just don't fully share that opinion."

"About the solution?" Nura asked, surprised.

"Yes, exactly."

"But you defended my position at the meeting against Hassan…that we must avoid injuring anyone on this mission."

"Yes, I did," agreed Jamal. "I don't hate the Israelis. But it's hard to avoid some amount of collateral damage if you're retaliating using weapons…even very small drones."

Jamal's eyes narrowed, his voice now adopting a perceptible tinge of anger. "And we absolutely *must* retaliate."

Nura didn't reply immediately, but he could sense her calmly studying him. The tense muscles in his face began to relax.

"Do you carry some scars?" Nura asked.

Jamal became silent. *Who is this person,* he wondered. *I probably have four years on her, yet I feel like I'm talking to a therapist.* "Don't we all?" he answered.

"I guess," she replied. "It certainly seems to be how most Palestinians feel. But I was asking about you, personally."

Most Palestinians? Seems? He felt his body become more rigid again. Jamal picked up his glass and drank a large sip of water. He took in a deep breath as he set it down. "My parents died a few years ago. They were blown to pieces in one of those artillery attacks. The shell missed the so-called target and was a direct hit on our home. My brother and sisters who were much younger than me, had just left for school. I was at college." He paused, his voice cracking. "Our parents were at home, my father was just about to go to work…" he trailed off.

"Oh, so sorry Jamal. Really. It's my fault. I shouldn't have pried."

"No. It's okay. I try to suppress the anger but it goes deep. The wound is still raw. And when I'm not working to feed part of my family, or implementing this project we are doing, I seem to vacillate wildly between despair and anger. May Allah forgive me."

Nura sighed softly. "I understand. We humans are not very good at living together or caring for each other, are we?"

"No," Ahmad said, simply.

"I get the anger," Nura continued. "My father taught me about the Holocaust when I was old enough to understand. So many lives lost, and people tortured during the second world war. So Jews feel that anger too, you know. As must many other groups…like the Native Americans, some tribes in Africa, as well as other persecuted minority groups around the world. And all the political prisoners everywhere."

Jamal listened but didn't respond.

"It's the hate that is bad," Nura added. "It just perpetuates the cycles of destruction and pain."

Jamal sat back in his chair. "It's certainly pretty hard to *love your enemy*. If that's your message?"

"It's the word *enemy* that is the problem. Not the people. The hate had already been passed on, don't you think? It was already in their bones. We all shared this valley here, didn't we? Palestine was for everyone once…especially Jerusalem."

"I hear you. Really. And I applaud you. But we're living in this mess at this very minute. It's not like it happened a long time ago." He leaned forward. "It's happening every damn day."

"Someone has to stop it!" Nura said, her tone forceful. "If not us…then who? The Israelis are not all bad. Isn't the new leadership trying to open things up? Provide more liberties?"

Jamal's pulse quickened. He knew that feeling, the first sign of losing his control. He fought it, but without much success. "How can you say that?" he asked sternly. "You make it sound like they deserve to be our masters. We were here just as early as them. Who knows, maybe before. I don't think anyone really was *first*. How could anyone prove it? That seems to be the problem I'd say. And they are always violating their own agreements…building settlements on land they promised not to. Pushing us around. Pushing us out. Doesn't that sound familiar? Speaking of tribes and Native Americans."

"Jews feel threatened," Nura countered. "They deserve to be here too. But they are afraid that Muslims want them eradicated like the Germans tried to do to them. They are holding on for fear of losing their way of life…and their very lives."

"You call their treatment of us *holding on?* Excuse me, but if I didn't know what you have done for all of us here in Gaza, I'd say you sound like you're one of *them.*"

"We are all one, Jamal. My father preaches it. Somehow, we have to help change the path of things or we will just be consumed by it, like so many generations before us."

Jamal looked deeply into her eyes. He knew what she was saying was true but he couldn't seem to let go of the anger. Pictures of his parents spun around in his head like a Ferris wheel.

"Then why are you working on this project with us? And even supplying money to the cause? We intend to use the drones to cripple them. Don't you get that?"

"I am not trying to cripple *them,* as you put it. I am trying to cripple the machinery of war…the instruments of hate, so that we may talk without fear."

Jamal settled himself. "Very admirable of you…"

Nura averted his stare.

"No, I'm dead serious. But it's also a bit naïve, don't you think? Do you really believe that will bring them to the table?"

"They will have to," she insisted. "The world will notice. It's the only chance we have."

"Sometimes I think that too, Nura. At least I like to. But a part of me wants to get some sort of revenge. I even see Hassan's point of view at times."

"Yes, but that's his job. He's part of Hamas. They sadly expect him to be that way. I don't think he even knows why he says some of the things he does."

"Generous of you to say that," Jamal replied, feeling his pulse rate calming a bit. "I may agree with him sometimes, but I don't trust him."

"Nor *should* you. I don't think he would care if people got hurt."

Jamal nodded. "I *know* he wouldn't."

They sat in a brief, awkward silence before the waitress arrived back at the table with the large tray of food. "Anything else you need?" she said as she set the last plate on the table.

"We're fine," said Jamal. "*Shukran.*"

The waitress bowed and returned to the kitchen. After finishing their dinner, Nura paid the bill using a bank card.

"Thanks, Nura," said Jamal, feeling a little guilty for the downward turn in the conversation. "I apologize if I appeared upset at times today. Nice of you to pick up the tab."

The waitress returned with the receipt and card.

"No worries, Jamal," Nura replied, signing one copy and returning only the card to her clutch before sticking it in her coat pocket.

"Let me make it up to you and drop you off at the hospital."

"No need," she replied. "It's only a few blocks."

"Indulge me," he pleaded, in a more playful tone.

"Well, okay," Nura replied, smiling. "Thanks, Jamal."

It was the first smile he had ever seen appear on her face. *A very pretty one at that,* he mused, what he could see of it.

Jamal pulled up in front of the hospital. Nura shook his hand. "I'll see you tomorrow. Text me when you have a time for the meeting."

"Sure. And thanks again."

"*Salaam,*" she said, tipping her head.

He watched as she walked to a silver BMW a few cars down on the street, opened the passenger door, and retrieved an envelope. Making her way up the sidewalk to the main entrance, she raised her keffiyeh to just below her nose, then disappeared through the large glass doors.

Pretty fancy car, he thought. *My favorite. Someday…*

Jamal swung back around and parked the car at the only open spot across the street, a short distance away. He slid from behind the wheel and went over to check it out.

The BMW had a fancy dashboard and a black leather interior. He grinned. *It couldn't be more than a year or two old. Lucky girl. Nobody has a car like this around here. Her dad must be somebody important,* he thought…*or well connected.*

As he walked around the front of the car, he noticed an emblem affixed to the inside of the driver's window—a white, seven-candle menorah against a blue background with a bar code at the bottom. He'd seen that once before, on the car of his boss at the tech center. But the person who owned it was one of the Prime Minister of Israel's cabinet members.

Jamal checked out the black leather interior and clean dashboard, lit up under the light of a nearby streetlamp. He lingered for a moment then walked back to his car. Opening the door, he turned around and glanced again at the BMW, then to the entrance of the hospital. He paused, then sat down behind the wheel of his car and waited.

Fifteen minutes later Nura exited the hospital. Approaching her car, she clicked her key fob. The trunk popped open. She removed her keffiyeh and placed it in a bag along with her trench coat. She replaced the coat with what looked like a blazer and exchanged her shoes.

Jamal squinted to catch as many details as he could. He noticed that she wore light slacks. The jacket was also somewhat light in color as far as he could tell…*maybe bluish?* She pulled another hat from the trunk and gathered her long hair up under it.

The silver BMW pulled away from the curb, heading towards him. He ducked into the passenger seat, catching only a glimpse of the driver. But it was enough to know that *this* person was not the same person he had dined with.

Thirty-One

Talbiya

THE DOOR LATCH clicked open. Esty entered the front hall of her home. Slipping the strap of a small duffel off her shoulder, she set the bag on the floor next to the bureau, hung her blue jacket in the closet, and placed her newsboy cap on a hook. Picking the bag back up, she headed up the stairs to her room.

"Welcome home, Esty."

She cringed. His voice seemed shorter than she had heard it in quite some time…since her mom died.

"I'll be right back, Dad. Just headed up to the bathroom."

She dropped the bag on the floor of her bedroom closet, waited a few minutes, flushed the toilet, then descended the stairs. As she passed by the dining room, she glanced at the unlit, seven candle silver menorah sitting in the middle of the table. She then entered the den. He was waiting for her with a book in his lap, and reading glasses fixed at the tip of his nose.

"Well, young lady. Nice of you to show up for the first night of Passover."

"Sorry but I did tell you I'd be late," she said in her defense. "I had to drop my friends off in Gaza."

"Yes, but that was hours ago. I expected you home for dinner, you know, and lighting of the candles. We were supposed to do that at 6:30. You seem to be losing your Jewish customs each day…ever since your mom passed."

Esty moved next to him and kissed the top of his head.

"You think that's going to make up for it?" he said, his voice softening with each word. "What am I going to do with you? Come. Let's sit at the table and light the candles. I'll get you something."

Esty sat at one end of the table as her father entered the kitchen. She heard the refrigerator door open. "I'm not really hungry," she called to him. "I had a late lunch. Just a snack would be fine, thanks."

He returned with a tray of matzo, bitter herbs, orange slices, and mixed nuts and set it in front of her. He selected two candles in silver bases from the tall mahogany cabinet and a small gold vessel. He placed them at the end of the table between them and took the seat across from her.

"So, sweetie, tell me how it went with your friends from the tour."

"It was quite...*eventful,* you might say. They're very nice, Dad. Amazing, actually."

"How so?" he asked, reaching for a square of the unleavened bread and slice of orange.

"After the tour, we had lunch by the gardens. Gethsemane. Then I took them all up to the top of the Mount."

"How many is *all*? I thought you said there were just the two others, one from America."

A nervous feeling crept over her. She took her eyes off her dad, plucking a few nuts from the bowl. "Uh, well yeah. Sort of."

He cocked his head. "Sort of?"

"Yes. I mentioned Morningstar to you on the phone because she stood out so much to me. She's the Native American from the States. And the other was Liyah. She lives here, in Gaza...Beit Lahia to be exact. Morningstar is visiting her. That's why I needed the car...to get them home before dark."

"I see," he said. "What made you so late?"

"Traffic." She turned and retrieved a piece of fruit. "You know how crowded it's getting. I've never seen anything like this."

"Neither have I, but you still should have made it home a bit earlier."

"You know us girls, Dad."

"No, I don't. I don't think I ever will." He chuckled. "But never mind that. Tell me more. What about the other girls?"

"Uh, well, there were three. But not girls."

She watched her dad as he rubbed his hands slowly together. *Am I getting myself in too deep here?* she wondered.

"By *not girls* I'm thinking they might be boys," he said with a touch of sarcasm then smiled. "Just guessing, though."

She grinned. "Oh, Dad."

"Well?"

"Well, yes. Two of the boys were also friends of Liyah. One named Zack, also from America...Detroit I think he said. And Kai Li, who is visiting from Hong Kong."

"You were right. That is indeed quite amazing. From all around the world."

"And where are the boys staying?"

"Bethlehem."

"Hmm. Must have been fun…And the third?"

"Third?"

"You said there were three."

"Oh. Yes, I did. Ahmad."

"Sounds like a local."

"He is. And quite cute."

Esty looked up at the ceiling. *How stupid was that? Could I please take that back?*

"I see." He winked at her.

She rolled her eyes.

He laughed. "Does he live in Israel?"

"Gaza."

"Well, that's a problem I would imagine. Getting in and out of there, unless you had my car."

Her nervousness began to return.

"Why would I want to do that?" She paused. "Oh, I see. C'mon, Dad. I just met him. He works for the *Filastin Dawn*. Liyah's dad runs the paper."

"Ah, I know of him. David Al-Rahim. Always thought that was an odd name. Sort of a mix between Jewish and Arabic. But I guess that's good for the paper." He smiled at her. "Just kidding, you know. But you should have a boyfriend. It's your time. A nice Jewish boy from school would fit the bill."

She blushed. "Jeez, Dad. I've got stuff to do…school, the tours…"

"Just saying," he replied. "Isn't that the expression I hear?" He laughed again. "So, tell me then. What did you do on the Mount?"

"We talked about spiritual stuff and how similar the religions really are. That Judaism, Christianity, and Islam are all built from the same foundation. From Abraham, Moses, Muhammad, and Jesus."

"I like what I'm hearing," her dad said.

"Yah, and Ooray said…" she stopped herself abruptly, realizing she had gotten carried away.

"Ooray? Who is Ooray?"

"Uh…well…um…"

Her dad stared at her in anticipation. She almost panicked from the pressure she felt.

"It's, uh…someone that they know…words from him. You know that the spiritual base is the same—love and compassion, that we are all brothers and sisters."

"My…I'm liking your friends already. Maybe we can have them over."

"They have to leave in a few days. Although, since the tours are closed to avoid more violence from our latest artillery attack on Gaza, maybe there will be time. Do you have to go in at all to see the Prime Minister?"

"I'm not sure. Normally no, since it's such a big religious weekend. But if things heat up more, then maybe."

He removed a box of matches from his shirt pocket. "Let's light the candles for Sabbat, in remembrance of the Seder…Passover…and of course your mom."

He struck the match and lit the first candle. "I light this candle in remembrance of Sabbat, our holy day." He handed the matches to Esty.

She lit the second one. "I light this candle in prayer for domestic peace."

Her dad continued. "May the flickering of their flames remind us of how fragile our lives are. How fragile freedom is. And our need to keep these flames alive."

He turned to her. "Light the vessel, sweetie."

Esty scratched another match along the side of the box. The sulfur set the end on fire and the pungent smell filled her nostrils. She held it to the wick, fed by the oil below. As the flame caught, she blew out the match.

She reached for her father's hand, gripping it tightly. Love and sadness welled up within her. Tears poured down her cheeks. "This is for you, Mom. We are here. Can you see us? We miss you so."

Saturday

THIRTY-TWO

Bedouin Encampment

FLIPPING THE CANVAS flap to the side, Khalib stepped out into the cool morning air. He took in a deep breath and gazed into the distance. The rising sun appeared as a red ball, perched atop the opposite hill, ready to break from the grasp of the earth and rise through the orange-layered sky. A guard wearing jeans, a blue work shirt, and hiking boots lifted the machine gun from his lap and shifted in his chair to eye the prisoner.

Khalib glanced over at him, then quickly diverted his eyes back toward the horizon. He noted a few black tarps nearby, stretched across crude wooden frames, creating the rudimentary roofs for the make-shift homes of the Bedouins living a hardscrabble existence.

He poked his head back into the tent. The dull light from the sun passed through the open flap, partially illuminating the inside. His eyes passed over the others lying about, still asleep in one big room with the seven other bodies scattered about. Khalib knew of three tents close by were similar, where the other captives and guards stayed, including several from his group as well as from other groups he had seen the other evening.

Scanning the room, he noticed trays on the ground to one side which held the dirty plates and remnants of food from the previous dinner. A large metal bin for boiling water rested in the center, along with two ceramic teapots and a host of cups. Shisha water pipes, which he liked to call *hookahs*, stood upright and formed an almost perfect ring in that part of the tent. Khalib jerked his head back out and walked to the end of the tent canopy.

"Hey!" the guard grumbled. "Where you headed?"

"Just here," Khalib replied. "Stretching my legs."

"Well, be sure to *stretch* them where I can see you."

"Uh-huh." Khalib assured him, trying to keep his cool while taking a few more steps from the tent.

Free from the overhang of the canopy, he could see clearly all around him. Some homes were in densely packed groups, only a few feet apart with some even sharing cloth walls. In other places, homes sat isolated in the harsh, dry, desert-like environment. Near the closer ones, he could see small, slatted wooden pallets—the kind used in storehouses to raise goods off the ground that were stitched together with nails to form cubes. He had seen these cubes used as seats, tables, and even places to keep chickens, or just to tether the odd sheep. Laundry was strung along cords connected to posts, fences, and frames of the homes near each other. Additional tarps were extended from the buildings to create canopies, like the one next to him. They provided some shelter—usually from the hot summer sun as well as the occasional rain at this time of year.

Khalib liked to stand there outdoors, away from the feeling of the closed-in space where he was forced to spend too much of his time. Away from the odor of animals, the smell of smoke from the fire, cooked food, and the unbathed inhabitants - those who neglected to use the sand as an abrasive cleanser to remove dirt from their bodies and to kill the stench.

It was a large camp. Many homes were strewn about the near landscape, some having corrugated aluminum siding and roofs in place of those with cloth sheets tacked to wooden studs. The odd tree and scrub bush dotted the landscape, with a few porta-potties sprinkled along the edges of the camp.

Khalib could tell his camp was on the side of a small hill, the top of which was man-made. It was composed of bulldozed dirt and trash, including twisted metal, broken plastic objects, cinched garbage bags, bits of clothing, fragments of the wooden and aluminum frames of a previous camp, dented teapots, and mangled books. All were remnants of a settlement that was once an existing community on these very grounds.

How many levels of settlements might be in the layers of this trash? Khalib wondered. *Maybe someday archeologists will dig it up, like they do in search of ancient civilizations. Or maybe some future alien species from somewhere in the universe, trying to piece together what life was like for people long ago on Earth. How surprised they would be to see that humans once lived in such squalor, starving, with no future ahead for them…or their children.* He let out a small sigh, realizing for an instant, how lucky he had actually been there in Beit Lahia, with his mom and dad, food on his plate and protected by his older sister.

Her name flooded his thoughts. *Liyah. She is out there somewhere. But I can't escape. Can't do anything that would put her in danger.* His heart sank. A sudden sense of fear crept into his throat. *What is going to become of me?*

Khalib looked back out over the littered terrain, thinking that the Israelis would be back again at some point. He knew it. Everyone knew it. They would do this again. They would bulldoze the lives of these generations of Bedouins into oblivion…to *keep the land free,* as they put it…for the building of new Jewish housing developments. It would be the expansion project they promised they wouldn't do. One more broken agreement.

Another of the men, this one dressed in a full-length black *thawb* and white headdress, appeared at the flap opening and stood there.

Khalib kept one ear to the conversation as he squatted down and pretended to dig for something in the dirt. He knew the man in the *thawb* to be one of the leaders of the entire camp but had never seen him until the man arrived late the previous evening.

"When are we leaving?" grunted the man with the gun.

"Hopefully tomorrow," replied the other. "We're short on supplies and we'll need two more vehicles to transport the additional captives we picked up over the past few days."

"Where will we get them?"

"There's a town only about ten miles away—Tel Shiva. They'll have everything we need. Tomorrow we'll steal a couple of trucks from a dealership on the outskirts of the town and head up the main road to the Yatir Forest. Once we get there, we'll stay on this side of the West Bank and follow the desert along the border to the Dead Sea into Jordan."

The guard looked up at him. "Jordan? They're an ally of America."

"I know. But we have friends at the border. And once we get through, it's a straight shot north to Syria, where we'll cross that border through a desert again. From there they can send boys to Iran or Africa…or even Russia." He paused. "That kid over there, for one," he continued, nodding in the direction of Khalib, "could bring some added value due to his tech skills. And within a short time, we'll have already been paid."

The man in the *thawb* turned to look out at Khalib. "Hey, you!" he called out.

Khalib stood up and faced him.

"Get me some tea."

"Yes, sir," Khalib replied, acting aloof while feigning a smile. "My pleasure, sir," he added, as he passed by the man and ducked into the tent.

Thirty-Three

Jabalia

AHMAD LEFT KAI LI and Zack without making a sound and headed for Gaza for a meeting with his boss. He parked the car on a side street two blocks from the Dawn and scurried his way to the building, checking his watch nervously several times. Finally passing the boarded-up broken window, he pushed open the door to the main entrance.

The receptionist smiled. "He's waiting for you in his office."

Ahmad looked up at the clock behind her.

"You're fine," she laughed. "Only five minutes late this time."

He forced a grin and made his way down the hall, checking the folder in his hand to make sure he had the note. He rapped the knuckle of his forefinger gently against the door.

"Come in."

Ahmad turned the handle. The heavy wood door creaked as he pushed it open and stepped into the room.

"Hello, Ahmad. I was beginning to wonder if I'd ever hear from you again."

"Sorry, Mr. Rahim. The last few days were long ones."

"Really? Take a seat."

Ahmad took the chair across the desk from his boss. A perceptible tremor crept into his hand as he set the folder down, hoping it hadn't been noticed.

Liyah's dad wasted no time. "So, Ahmad," he said directly, obviously anxious to hear some good news about his son. "Tell me about the progress you've made."

"Well, uh, sir. I'm not sure how *good* the news is. Only that we're still trying to locate Khalib."

"And?"

"We traced a lead to the old airport yesterday and…"

"We?"

"Ah, yes. I mean me and Liyah's friends, Zack and Kai Li…the ones you got the passes for."

"Okay. So, what'd you find?"

"Nothing."

"Nothing?"

"Yeah, well the group we think that may have something to do with his disappearance may have been transporting captives into Egypt, but the Israelis pummeled most of the tunnels they found there with artillery, closing them off."

"So, are you saying Khalib could have been killed in the process?"

A lump grew in Ahmad's throat. "No, sir. I mean I don't know. Anything is possible, I suppose. But we did find a couple of open tunnels at the airport. One that headed toward Egypt. It must have been still open recently but looks like an explosion closed it off in the last few days. If he had been taken through that one, they could have made it safely to Egypt. We don't know."

His boss's voice dropped an octave and lost its energy. "Or he could be dead in the tunnel."

"I have to be honest, sir. It's a possibility. But we don't think so. He may not even be with that group. Or…there was another tunnel connected to that one, and it seems that a group did pass through it recently."

"And where did that one lead to?" Liyah's dad asked, the wheels on the feet of his chair clicking as he pushed himself free of his desk. He stood up and began pacing. "Did you follow it?"

"Yes, of course. But it led to a spot in the middle of nowhere, in the Negev." He paused as he watched his boss stride back and forth, wearing a look of deep concern. "The closest place was Beersheba, about fifty miles away."

Liyah's dad stopped pacing when he reached the desk on the return trip. He turned and faced Ahmad. His voice was quiet and serious. "Are we at a dead end?"

Ahmad glanced up at him. "Not yet, sir. I don't think so. I still have some other contacts." He blinked nervously. "I'm working on it," he lied.

"Okay. Fine. Please do. We're running out of options." He sat back down in his chair. Silence engulfed them, as he watched Ahmad's fingers drumming on the folder in front of him.

"Is that all?"

Ahmad followed his boss's eyes to the folder. "Oh," he said, snapping out of his momentary lapse. "There's one more thing." He opened the folder, removed a piece of notepaper with scribbling on it, then handed it to his boss.

"Here."

Liyah's dad studied it. "Hmm."

"It's just a few lines," Ahmad continued. "Looks like he's reaching out for your agreement to maintain silence. He signed it, but there's a line under it...for yours."

"I see that." He locked eyes with Ahmad. "And what is this actually about?"

Ahmad looked nervously at the notepaper. "Sorry, again. I forgot to mention. It's about the article I am putting together for the Dawn. I'm sure I mentioned it before. I'm trying to get the views of all the warring parties and do a piece to link them together."

"And who is this...this, Fahzel?"

"Fahzi...with an *I*," Ahmad corrected. 'He's connected with Hezbollah somehow, in Iran. I got his name from Hassan, one of the main guys in Hamas, he..." Ahmad stopped suddenly, his eyes widened.

"Don't worry, Ahmad. I'm a journalist. We don't give out our sources, remember. Except to each other." He glanced back down at the paper. "I'm not familiar with him anyway."

"There was another man. I think he was the actual leader. Fahzi took me to him outside of Tel Sheva, on the way to the hills."

His boss studied him again. "And who is the *head guy* you mentioned?

"Yusuf. Don't know his last name."

"Yusuf Al-Najafi?"

"Could be," Ahmad replied. "It was never mentioned."

"I do know of Najafi. But I'm surprised he would actually be here again. Especially hiding near the hills of Israel. Hezbollah and the Iranians are sworn enemies of Israel."

His boss scratched his chin, looked down at the paper then at Ahmad. He took his pen from his shirt pocket, clicked the end and signed his name above the line Fahzi had drawn. He clipped the pen back in the pocket and then reached for a business card from the holder on his desk. He handed the card and the paper back to Ahmad.

"There you go. You said this Hassan is keyed in as well?"

"Yes."

"And what exactly did you say to get all these people to talk to you?"

"There is no time left anymore. That no one group can solve this situation here in Palestine, Israel, and the Middle East. Not by themselves. We will all lose big time. Maybe this is the last chance. But

I might be able to get their views aired honestly, and some common words or thoughts. That is if everyone agrees to let us put them together with the others on a safe page. A page of the Dawn."

"That's what you said?" Liyah's dad questioned again. "That's it? And they are willing to talk? Seriously?"

Ahmad's face took on a slight pallor. "Uh, well maybe not those exact words. B-but the idea." He waited nervously.

"And what do you mean by *common words*?"

"Just that. Words they might agree on like safety, fear, honesty."

"That you just might suggest, so to speak." Liyah's dad said, eyeing him as if Ahmad was secretly manipulating these characters.

"Well. Not exactly." Ahmad defended himself. "But maybe a little." He cringed, expecting judgment—a self-critique on how utterly naïve he knew he was.

His boss simply smiled and held out his hand. "Good job, Ahmad. Damn good."

A wave of relief spread over Ahmad's face as they shook hands. "Really, sir?"

"Yes really, Ahmad. I'm impressed." He handed the folder from the desk to Ahmad and escorted him to the hallway.

"Who do you have on the Jewish side? Anyone lined up?"

"I'm working on it," Ahmad replied, knowing that he'd lied…again.

THIRTY-FOUR

Bethlehem

KAI LI AND ZACK slid into their usual booth at the Inn. The waitress handed them menus and then disappeared. Zack ran his finger down the page of the breakfast offerings while speaking. "What's up today, Kai?"

Kai Li scanned his menu. "No idea. Ahmad s'posed to call after meeting with Liyah's dad. He texted me on way to the paper. Not hear again yet. You?"

"No."

"How can we find Khalib? I worry a lot for Liyah."

"Things look bad."

"Ahmad also said Hassan wants to talk with us. Might show up at Inn. So I said we keep eyes open."

The waitress returned with two glasses and a pitcher of water. She removed the pencil from behind her ear and flipped the page on her order pad. "What can I get you, boys?"

"A couple of scrambled eggs for me," Zack responded. "With bacon and potatoes." He smiled up at her. "Feels like America here."

"Lots of people like you come to Bethlehem," she replied, jotting his order on her pad. "Tourists all over the place. From around the world."

"We're not tourists," Zack corrected her. "And I almost forgot…I'd like some pancakes too, with butter and syrup, and some toast. Oh, and a glass of orange juice."

Kai Li stared at him over the top of his menu, the black frame of his glasses resting on the tip of his nose.

"What?" Zack objected defensively, sensing the daggers. "Ahmad said get anything we like. It's all covered by Liyah's dad."

"Yeah…anything.' Not everythin'."

"I don't know about you, Mr. Kai, but I never get a chance to stay in a place like this and eat great food. I'm takin' advantage of every bit of it."

"I can see."

"C'mon, man," Zack countered. "Loosen up. We're gettin' compensated for helping out." He grinned. "We're on *important business.*"

"We *failing* at business," Kai Li countered. "Hardly do anything yet." He handed his menu back to the waitress. "Bowl of oatmeal, please. And cup of hot chocolate."

The waitress collected Zack's menu and stepped back. "Well, I have to say, it's been entertaining with you two the past few days. I hope you stay a bit longer." She laughed and moved to the booth next to them.

Zack felt an uneasiness creep over him. He knew Kai Li was right…he shouldn't take advantage of the situation. Was it just frustration? *Crap*, he thought. *We just got done with that last adventure, and I was tryin' to do better at home. Now we're already on another one. And God knows how, or when, this will end. I might be losin' my mind.*

A voice from behind him, addressing the waitress, interrupted his daydreaming.

"What ya thinking 'bout?" Kai Li asked. "You stare into space."

"That voice," Zack answered, pointing with his thumb to the back of his booth.

Kai Li listened, then shrugged his shoulders.

"It sounds like Hassan, doesn't it?" Zack whispered.

Kai Li listened again. "Maybe."

"We should find out, shouldn't we? You said he might be lookin' for us."

Kai Li slid out of his seat and took a few steps to the next booth.

"Why, Kai Li," said Hassan, surprised. "I was going to try to reach you after I finished this meeting. Wasn't sure when you boys would be up. But I'm glad you came over."

"We're pretty much done, anyway," said the man with a mustache seated across from Hassan. "Please join us. Hassan told me of your meeting last night, and that he has been trying to help you on your quest to find someone by providing some possible contacts to your friend, Ahmad?"

Zack appeared next to Kai Li.

"Yes. By all means. Do sit," said Hassan. "This is Murtaza. Murtaza, meet Zack and Kai Li."

Kai Li took a seat next to Murtaza.

"Okay, I guess that's what we're doing," replied Zack, nodding to Kai Li, then sliding in next to Hassan. Once seated, facing Murtaza, he recognized him as the man who had stared at him when he passed their booth after dinner at the Inn on Thursday. A funny feeling came over him, like a warning of some kind. An intuition. *Was this guy not to be trusted? Hmm, maybe nothing more than a ridiculous notion. He'd certainly been wrong before.*

He avoided direct eye contact at first, but Murtaza didn't give any indication he remembered the previous encounter the same way he did. His increased level of anxiety faded.

"I don't have as many connections as Hassan," Murtaza admitted, "but I'd be glad to help out if I can."

Zack looked directly at him. "Our friend, Liyah…We think her brother was abducted by some terrorists."

"Doubt from Palestine," added Kai Li. "Maybe some other place."

"I'll keep my ears open," Murtaza replied.

"Murtaza is helping me with some things in Gaza," said Hassan. "And he's originally from America, like you Zack."

"So, you're living here now?" Zack asked.

"Yes. I came to Jerusalem some years ago and love it. It's a holy place."

Zack nodded in agreement. "So do you live there in the States or here?"

"Neither place. I live in Gaza. That's where I met Hassan. I'm just here to visit a friend of mine, a pastor in a local church here in Bethlehem."

"Is he from the States too? I'm from Detroit."

"No," replied Murtaza, "he's lived here his whole life. Many Christians live here as well, so he formed an Evangelical church a few years ago. I used to be Christian. That's actually how we first met. But I'm a Muslim now."

"Hmm," Kai Li replied. "Big switch."

Zack frowned. "Sorry, Kai's always curious. About everything. He doesn't mean to pry."

"No apology needed," Murtaza assured them. "I guess I adopted the Palestinian cause in more ways than one. I was Evangelical, but the Evangelical community in Israel is not the same as in the States."

"Muslim and Evangelical 'bout opposite," Kai Li said, returning to his theme.

Zack kicked him under the table.

"I guess you could call me a Christian too," Zack replied. "But I don't go to a church. I just believe in the messages of Jesus."

"Well, maybe you'll get a chance to meet my pastor friend. Sounds like you'd get along. His church is very informal."

"Born again," Kai Li interjected. "I think too extreme for Zack."

Zack swallowed hard. Sometimes he didn't know what to do with Kai Li. He pursed his lips and squinted at him, trying to give him a sign to not go down that road.

"Oh, it's not that rigid, Kai Li," Murtaza assured him. "We…I mean they…feel a very close connection with Christ, as it appears your friend does as well."

"Yes," agreed Kai Li, "Zack identify with founder, Jesus. But not rejec' views of others."

Zack could feel a sinking sensation begin to take over his body. "Kai…"

Murtaza held up his hand. "No, it's alright. I don't mind." He turned back to Kai Li. "You're right. There are many people in all religions who are not tolerant of the views of others. But I think I should make the point that there are differences in beliefs even within each religion. For instance, there are many types of Protestants, and although the church service of, say the Episcopalians, is almost identical to the Catholics, they are often at bitter odds…especially in places like Ireland. Wouldn't you agree?"

There was an uneasy silence. Zack watched as Kai Li studied Murtaza. *Jeez, here we go,* he thought. *It seems Kai Li knows more than is good for him. I need to get him off this. We just met this guy!*

Kai Li glanced at Zack's face, then smiled at Murtaza. "Yes. True. I jes' hear many Evangelicals in America believe in Rapture…that all will die in the apoc-lypse at the end of times. They support Jews only cuz they think Jesus will enter Jerusalem again. Then only true believers will be saved. They not really care for Jews or anyone who not believe like they do. Support Jerusalem only because believe it's place where Rapture will happen."

Zack threw his hands up, looking wide-eyed at Hassan then over at Murtaza.

Murtaza acknowledged Zack but continued to respond to Kai Li. "You seem to know a lot about religions, my friend. But I can tell you that the Evangelicals are not of just one single mind. For instance, here in Palestine and Israel, they and other Christians are close neighbors with Jews, and don't want anyone to, how you may suggest, *blow up* Jerusalem. Let me just leave it with you that they do, at their core, however…and like Zack…have a strong affinity for Jesus."

Kai Li nodded without smiling, letting any more debate on the subject slide. Murtaza appeared to accept it as a kind of truce.

Zack was relieved to see the end of their debate, one that he was certain was only heading downhill. But the exchange had pulled up a memory of when Murtaza had been with two others for dinner in this very same booth next to him and Kai Li…when his and Murtaza's eyes first met. He recalled pieces of the conversation Murtaza was having with those men—words about the Rapture, about a surprise, about Sunday and Jerusalem. The seeds of suspicion entered his mind again. *Perhaps I shouldn't let go of my first impression after all.*

The waitress arrived with two trays after finally locating the boys in the next booth. She set the plates in front of Zack and Kia Li.

"Excuse me, Kai Li," said Murtaza. "I should be going. And I know that Hassan would like to talk with you two."

Kai Li stood up to let him out while the waitress retrieved the settings from the other booth.

Murtaza shook hands with Kai Li then Zack. "I hope to see you boys again. Nice to meet you." He bowed slightly. "*Salaam.*"

"*Salaam*, Murtaza," Hassan replied.

The waitress re-set the silverware and napkins in front of Kai Li and Zack. "Anything else?"

"We're good, finally," said Zack, directing a disapproving glance toward Kai Li.

"Finally?" asked the waitress, surprised. "Sorry, we're doing our best."

"Pay no attention," replied Hassan, chuckling. "He's referring to our conversation. Nothing about you."

As the waitress retreated and the boys dug into their breakfasts, Hassan spoke directly to Kai Li.

"Last evening you mentioned you have some understanding of programming various devices, like robots, and the use of infrared technology. Correct?"

Kai Li nodded as he swallowed a mouthful of oatmeal.

"Then I would like to ask you to help me with a project. It has to do with drones."

"Drones? Sound interesting," Kai Li replied, "but suppose' to be looking for Liyah's brother."

"Yes, I understand. But what I need help with would only take a few hours. And I could drive you anywhere you like to meet Ahmad afterwards."

Zack stopped shoveling the food down for a moment. "Okay with me. I'll tag along. We can check with Ahmad to make sure before we leave…Kai?"

"Sure."

"We're testing some small drones for a demonstration on Sunday. We need to adjust a group of them before we feel fully confident in using them. So, we could use all the help we can get." He paused briefly. "It's a surprise, however, so you'll have to keep anything you see or do to yourself until after Sunday."

"Sound good. Hope I can help." He turned to his friend.

"How far is it?" asked Zack.

"There's a place about an hour or so from here. It's sort of on the way to Gaza, so we can catch up easily with Ahmad shortly after lunch."

"Fine," agreed Zack, holding up his hand to signal the waitress.

She finished setting the table where she was and made her way to them. "Ready for the check?"

"Yeah," replied Zack. "And can you bring me another order of pancakes with it?"

THIRTY-FIVE

Tel Sheva

AHMAD PARKED HIS car in the same spot on the outskirts of Tel Sheva where he first met Fahzi. He followed the exact sequence of steps they traveled to the camp—several blocks east, to the first rows of tents near the base of a sandy hill. He spotted the largest one that was white with a big canopy. Pacing in front was a man in a long white robe and red headscarf, secured by a double-ringed black cord resting atop. He had a full but trimmed, beard and mustache. The moment Ahmad recognized him, he felt his pulse rate take off, the flow of blood throbbing in his ears.

"Mr. Yusuf," he said, fighting off his nerves. "*Salaam*."

"*Wa-Alaikum-Salaam*, Ahmad. Don't worry. You can just call me Yusuf."

They shook hands.

"Come. We have this big tent to ourselves today." He showed Ahmad in.

The inside was as Ahmad remembered it, except cleaner, and more organized, or it simply seemed that way because no one else was there. He sensed some of the tension slipping off him. *One on one. I might be able to get through this,* he told himself.

They sat cross-legged on two embroidered blue pillows set across from each other on a fine carpet, colored in swirls of deep purple, gold, black, and red. Ahmad withdrew the folded, simple document signed by Fahzi and his boss from his sports coat pocket. He handed it to Yusuf with his boss's business card clipped to the top of it. Yusuf scanned it briefly then set it down next to him.

"So, Ahmad. Welcome back. I apologize, but there is no water for us. Ramadan, you know."

"Yes. Understood." He did, but the dry air and his nerves made his mouth feel like the desert that surrounded them. "I was expecting the others might be here too. Your friends from before."

Yusuf's dark eyes penetrated Ahmad's. He had a stern look about him but his eyes suddenly softened. "I'm glad you're here." he said, breaking a brief, painful silence for Ahmad. "You have some courage for a young man. I like that. More of us *older* men should show the same. But I guess that's not part of our times yet."

"No, sir. Yes, sir. I mean I agree with you, sir."

Yusuf grinned. "How should we start? I guess it is really, how they say in America…*your nickel.*"

Ahmad took in a healthy breath of the still cool morning air as he removed the small pad and pen from his shirt pocket. He flipped the cover, glanced at his notes then brought his eyes back up to meet Yusuf's.

"Do you mind if I just ask a few questions to help kick off the discussion?"

"By all means, Ahmad. Go ahead."

Ahmad looked down, tapping the pad with his pen, reading. "Do you represent Hezbollah?" He glanced back up, unsure of what to expect.

"Well, I guess you can say I am known by that organization and know a lot about it, but I am not formally a part of it. In my younger years, when I lived in Iran, I consulted with the government there, as an interface to Hezbollah. Now I have my own small organization in Saudi that works with both parties, as well as other organizations. Some are more hardcore, like Hezbollah, but many less so."

Ahmad looked down again at his notes. "Do you share the views of Hezbollah and Iran that only Palestine has the right to exist, but not Israel?"

Yusuf tilted his head. "Quite a loaded question there, Ahmad. Almost feels like one a television anchor would pose to create a sensational story."

Ahmad studied his subject, swallowing hard. "I didn't mean it to come out like that."

"I'll tell you what," Yusuf replied. "Let's simply have a discussion, like we did the other day. You were good…passionate but fair, I'd say. Okay?"

"Okay, sir."

"Yusuf."

Ahmad swallowed again. "Yusuf."

"With that out of the way, I'll answer your second question anyway. We can go from there." He paused, studying the tent canopy above him before continuing. "Everyone deserves a homeland. I am not a Palestinian. I have been a Saudi for some time. An Arab. And many of my relatives and friends are from Iran, where I grew up. As a group, Iran supports a separate Palestinian state. But not necessarily because they feel it was the Palestinian homeland before all this trouble began.

"For over fifteen hundred years, Jews and Muslims had lived in the region harmoniously...before the creation of the state of Israel in 1948, after World War II. Jews had already been emigrating from Europe and Africa before that, but the partitioning of Palestine and Jerusalem after the war, supported by America, Russia, Jordan, and other countries was the seal that left the fates of all the Palestinians up in the air."

Yusuf gently massaged the worry beads he had in his right hand.

"So, to get back to your question about...how did you put it—*the right to exist?* In my view, perhaps we should ask: *Who doesn't have the right to exist? To have a country, a homeland?* Jews and Muslims have lived side by side for longer than most people understand. No one will ever prove what tribe or what people were *first*...before that. And does it really matter at this point, anyway?

"I am here to support Hamas, to support all Palestinians, not because I hate Jews or like Hamas. I don't, and neither do most Muslims. But there is a lot of anger here due to the treatment of the Palestinians ever since Israel became an independent state. And anger, left unaddressed, often turns to hate.

"Didn't the Native Americans in America deserve a home as well? One where they could grow crops, raise animals, have a decent life, keep their own beliefs, and their own language. Not to be forced onto reservations of rocks and dust, like the Bedouins here in the Negev. It is a simple question of fairness, and treating others with respect, as Allah would want, wouldn't you agree?"

"I don't know," Ahmad replied, jotting cryptic notes on his pad.

Yusuf's eyes grew narrow. "You don't know what? That the Native American's plight was not much different than the Palestinian's...or whether everyone deserves a homeland, and to be treated with respect?"

Ahmad was frozen in Yusuf's stare. He suddenly felt powerless again. *Why? Why do I so often give up my power to someone else? I was doing better...finding my legs...my strength.* He began to stammer, then caught himself, remembering the tunnel and the words of Kai Li. He breathed in, then slowly out, relaxing his shoulders, and calming the muscles in his face.

Yusuf's eyes kept their piercing focus. "I thought maybe you were different, Ahmad. Not the regular journalist just looking for a sensational story, or to twist a simple phrase out of context, like a vulture picking at a carcass."

Ahmad kept his poise, even though he felt Yusuf's words digging into him. He maintained eye contact, not giving an inch. Finally, the words came.

"Who you describe is not who I am. I may not be a real journalist. Perhaps I exaggerated my position at the Dawn. But it was with good intentions. I do not aim to expose the weaknesses that we all have or bear false witness against others through lies and deception. I only seek to bind the common good within all people, so that the walls are torn down, and we all can feel safe, and prosper. Everyone.

"This is why I am here. Why you are here, from what I am now understanding. So, yes, I do believe everyone has the right to a good life, a homeland, and their beliefs, as long as they don't harm anyone, but rather put others first. That is my intent here. To open up all eyes and ears, and to break the cycle of hate. We need everyone to help overcome the darkness that has set in."

Ahmad paused very briefly, then added. "I simply didn't *know* about the Native Americans." He pulled his eyes away, moving them to the notepad in his lap. He scribbled a few quick notes. When he looked back up, Yusuf was smiling.

"That is the person I met the other day," he said. "The brave one. The honest one. I was only afraid you deserted me, my young friend."

Ahmad again sensed the strength of this man, like when they first met. His directness. His sincerity. It was clear and almost palpable. He could be hard, maybe even impulsive, but there was no hatred spewing from his words, or in his heart. Yet he also knew Yusuf was categorized by some as a dangerous terrorist. The question entered his mind. *Why?*

He continued. "Hamas and Hezbollah are considered by many to be terrorist organizations. What do you feel about that?"

"I don't feel anything about it," Yusuf replied. "I see injustices being done to the Palestinian people. The choice of that term often depends on whose eyes one is looking. Were Indian warriors savages? Were the Romans the *terrorists*, or those they conquered? Is any country or group of people totally guiltless?"

He snaked his beads between his fingers.

"I do not actually condone many of the tactics of Hamas or Hezbollah. I am not part of either organization. I condemn the taking of innocent lives. Yet I am hiding here, with my life in jeopardy at times. It is because I give them support to fight for a new Palestine, a homeland, and the respect that has been stolen. If I could see a better way to reverse this catastrophe that is happening every day before our eyes, I would choose it."

"How can you not hate the Israelis, if you feel they are the ones responsible?" Ahmad asked.

"Many others are also responsible," Yusuf replied. "The Egyptians likely treated Jews like slaves thousands of years ago. The Nazis, under Hitler, slaughtered millions of Jewish men, women, and children during the Holocaust of World War II, ultimately forcing many survivors to leave Germany for their old homeland. During the same period, and after, the Russian and Polish governments treated Jews harshly too, and as unequal citizens, even though the Russians supported the new Israeli state in 1948. All those countries either enslaved, murdered or cast out the Jews. This is the only place they felt they could regroup and establish their own homeland. If not for the historical mistreatments, this could have remained one homeland, shared peaceably by both Jews and Palestinians, as it had been for thousands of years.

"Once the Jews returned and created a state, supported by the big powers, the real struggle began for the Palestinians and other Muslims. Political boundaries then split the world, polarizing Jews and Muslims, and even many Christians. It was the creation of the Israeli state, without concern for the Palestinians, that ultimately became the fuel for the troubles we now have…not the Israelis…not the people. The Palestinians felt left out, and now the Jews feel threatened by angry Muslim states surrounding them, and by suicide attacks and the like. I believe that many feel their actual existence is at risk…but the Palestinians feel their own existence is also at risk, and in fact is being slowly suffocated. The situation has gotten even more polarized over recent years. This is what I believe."

Yusuf took a deep breath and stared blankly through the opening of the tent. "The *new state* of Israel has now broken many agreements with the Palestinian people, inflicting unwarranted suffering." He looked across at Ahmad. "The Palestinians, even with the help of my country and others, are still fighting with one arm tied behind their backs. I disapprove of the actions of the Israeli state and its leaders. I don't hate the people of Israel. I even blame my own people for not helping to resolve all this sooner."

Ahmad returned to his notepad, writing furiously, trying to capture as many of Yusuf's words as he could. He rested the pen for a moment on the pad and looked across at Yusuf, who sat quietly, expressionless.

"And these groups that are fighting the Israelis *on behalf of my Palestinian brothers and sisters,* as you suggest," Ahmad pressed, "what about their influence on Muslim values? Most Palestinians I am friends with don't share some of their extreme views, even if they applaud retaliating against Israel. Do you see that as a step back in human rights?"

"You are a tough questioner, my friend. I see you favor the truth over revenge. It is another good quality in a journalist, even if it seems to be a rare commodity these days. Mr. Rahim would be proud of you at this moment. But I believe you have answered your own question. The pool of extreme views is overflowing…everywhere it would seem. Islam has a great history of science and literature through the ages, of treating others fairly. The vast majority of Muslims want to live in peace with their brethren of different political and religious philosophies, wouldn't you say?"

"I would hope so," Ahmad replied, without hesitation.

"And it *is* so. But there are extremists, as you suggested in your question. And some have more power than they would in other circumstances. Their voices most often distort the voice of the population they claim to serve. And they are louder."

Ahmad watched as Yusuf stared down at his beads then back up at him. "There are extremists all over the world. Look what is happening in the United States, in Indonesia, in Asia, in South America. It is not unique in any way to Muslims. There are cruel, hateful people who gain power—like Hitler, Stalin, Genghis Khan, and others, who killed tens of millions of people. They were true terrorists. They define the term."

He continued. "And then there are others who actually fight against abusive power in their own way, intending good for their people, not power for themselves, but have been labeled as terrorists of sorts. American leaders labeled the great Chief, Sitting Bull, a savage, a kind of allusion to being a terrorist of a different kind. Yet he was anything but that. The Jews viewed Jesus as a radical and crucified him, yet even Muslims recognize him as the prophet of compassion. And Muhammad…what about him? We, his followers, see him as a prophet of peace, the messenger of God, yet Muslim extremists tout his military skills and kill in his name. Perhaps it is the term itself that should be scrutinized at times."

Yusuf stood up. "Come, Ahmad. Let's talk while we stretch our legs. I am beginning to get older and my body screams at me for sitting too long."

They passed through the flap of the tent and walked side by side through the camp, with Yusuf doing most of the talking, and Ahmad the writing, flipping the pages of his notebook, scribbling, and occasionally falling back a few steps.

Yusuf accompanied Ahmad back to his car in the remote section of the parking lot, at the edge of Tel Sheva. Along the way, they talked about how Yusuf had become involved with helping Hezbollah provide technology assistance to Hamas, Ahmad's experience with Liyah's dad at *Filastin Dawn*, and Ahmad's plan to create a series of articles to break down the barriers between the Palestinians and the Israelis—to try to get everyone to see that helping out the Palestinians would be in the best interest of all parties, and a potential example for the world.

Ahmad opened the car door and shook hands with Yusuf. "It was good of you to see me, and to speak your mind, Yusuf. I will not betray your words. I will treat them honestly."

"As I said, it was brave of you to come here, Ahmad, by yourself, and to set out on this mission you have created. It is an important one…a worthy one. I believe your day as a leader will arrive before you know."

"How long will you remain in the area?" asked Ahmad.

"Not long. I feel the net around me is tightening. I plan to head back home very shortly. To my roots this time, in Iran. As I get older, my family becomes more important. You should know that not all the leaders there hate Israel, or America. But they are not so different as many leaders in the world, having big egos and engaging in power plays that have nothing to do with Palestine. Unfortunately, at times, they use the grievances of Palestinians as a political sword, to the detriment of the long-term interests of the Palestinians…and the following generations. They just can't seem to see that."

Ahmad slipped into his seat and rolled down the window.

Yusuf leaned down toward him. "My job now will be to try to influence them, based on my experience here. I'm certain we will be in touch. And you are always welcome to visit me…that is, if you can get a visa." He winked.

Ahmad ripped a page out of his notebook and wrote on it. "Here's my cell number. Thank you, Yusuf."

Yusuf took the paper, then with his own pen wrote his phone number down in Ahmad's notebook. "*Salaam*, my young friend. Go in peace. And may Allah go with you. Praised be his name."

Thirty-Six

Talbiya

LIYAH PRESSED THE button set into the stone pillar next to the iron gate. A voice crackled through the small speaker. "Yes?"

She brought her face close. "It's Liyah and Star."

A buzzer sounded and the latch clicked. Liyah pushed on the iron gate. Its hinges squeaked as it swung open. Closing the gate behind them, Morningstar and Liyah started up the gravel walk toward the house. It was not yet midmorning, but the rays from the sun already warmed the air, breaking through the branches of the olive, almond, and eucalyptus trees around them, illuminating their delicate white and yellow blossoms. Morningstar tugged at the sleeve of Liyah's jacket as she halted, taking in the view of the large, carved wood door at the front of the house.

"Yeah…I know," said Liyah. "Intimidating, isn't it?"

"It's unbelievable," replied Morningstar. "It's even bigger than *your* home."

"Esty's dad is well connected, remember? She told us he advises the Prime Minister of Israel."

Morningstar gazed off to her side, to the red poppies, purple lupine, and yellow and white tulips. She breathed in all the scents of perfume, of mint, vanilla, and the sea permeating from the garden.

She turned to Liyah. "There is natural beauty everywhere in the world, Liyah." Her eyes took it all in one more time. "Here, it all seems to have gathered in one front yard."

"No one appreciates it more than you," Liyah replied. She grabbed hold of her hand and headed up the steps.

The rapping sound from a heavy knocker filled the hall. Esty turned the knob and opened the door. She felt more excited than she had in a long time.

"Hi, you guys. Welcome to my house."

Esty steered them into the den, where her father was waiting.

"Pops…oops." She glanced playfully at Liyah and Morningstar. "I mean Dad. This is Liyah and Morningstar, my new friends I told you about."

He placed his book on the side table and stood up. "Nice of you to visit. I've heard nothing but good things. It must have been quite a day you had, what with the tour, the crowds, and the craziness in the city. Esty was pretty overwhelmed herself, and she goes in there quite a bit. Some trouble at the Temple Mount I guess, although she seemed to leave out a few details, and didn't tell me a lot about your trip to the Mount of Olives." He smiled. "Only that I *wouldn't believe it,* as she put it."

Esty's cell phone buzzed in her jeans pocket. She took it out.

"Yes?"

She held up her index finger to the others. "Hi…Fine, thanks…Uh, huh…Sure."

Esty handed the phone to her dad. "It's Ahmad. He's the boy I was telling you about. He was with us yesterday, in Jerusalem. He wants to talk. Something to do with the interview I mentioned to you."

Her dad accepted the phone and pressed it against his chest. "I'll take this in the office. Make yourself comfortable, girls."

"Sit," said Esty, as she sat down in her dad's chair.

Morningstar and Liyah took the loveseat by the coffee table.

"It's nice to see you before you have to leave," said Esty. "When is that again?"

"Probably tomorrow night," Morningstar replied.

Liyah gave her the eye. "Maybe a bit longer."

"Probably? Maybe?" asked Esty.

Liyah looked again at Morningstar. "I mean, I don't want to keep Star, but we have to find my brother. We're running out of time. Maybe it's already run out."

Esty noticed Liyah lightly wringing her hands, her beaming eyes adopting a kind of sadness. She felt deeply for her. *It must be difficult,* she thought. *I know what it's like to lose someone you love, even though I have no brothers or sisters.*

"I'll stay as long as it takes," Morningstar assured Liyah. "Don't worry about that." She winked. "After all, what is *time,* anyway?"

Esty noticed it. She wondered if it was an inside joke, or just Morningstar's way of trying to make things a little lighter. She felt a bit jealous of how they seemed to be so close, and after knowing each other, what? Not much more than a week? At least that's what they said. Her mind drifted to her own situation—now almost seventeen with no real friends to speak of. *I do have some friends after all,* she thought. *It's just that they don't visit me here in this big empty house. And Dad is always working, although it's not his fault, is it? I think he works because he's lonely and worries about me…which is why I work—so that he won't worry. Sort of weird. But even my best friends at school are not friends like these two are.* She studied Liyah and Morningstar. *Maybe I just haven't thought about it much until now. I–*

"Esty?"

"Oh, sorry Liyah. I guess my brain flew out the window for a moment." She laughed.

Morningstar laughed along with her.

Esty observed the corners of Liyah's mouth turn up, but she couldn't bring herself to join them wholeheartedly. She felt sad for her again.

"What's on your mind, Esty?" asked Morningstar. "Liyah said something about helping out. Maybe contacts from your dad?"

"Yeah. I wanted you to meet him. He's well connected, as you probably figured out. But I thought if he saw Liyah, and listened to her, he might come up with some ideas."

She paused, taking in a breath, shifting her eyes between the two several times, gathering her courage. "But I really wanted to find out more about Ooray…and the other strange things I saw yesterday. I think Ahmad knows something more. Well, at least more than me." Her eyes settled on the bracelet, half hidden by the sleeve of Morningstar's tunic.

Liyah nestled herself in the corner of the sofa against a pillow. A broad smile finally lit up her face. She glanced over at Morningstar.

Morningstar grinned back. "Okay. Anything we can tell you won't come close to Ooray yesterday…for sure. You want to know about the bracelet?"

Esty sensed her excitement return. "Great! I see you both have identical ones. I thought I saw one on Kai Li as well."

"Yup," Morningstar replied. "All four of us have one. Although Zack tends to hide his most of the time in his pants pocket. You know, some sort of guy thing or something." She chuckled. "I don't think he's fully in touch with his feminine side yet."

Liyah laughed. "Whereas Kai Li is oblivious to all of that, since his brain is constantly in overdrive."

Esty joined them in a round of laughter. She felt more comfortable with them. They had talked about some things on their way back from the Mount of Olives. Some serious at times, and some not so. Yet there had always seemed to be a guard, something preventing them from being totally free. *Maybe the newness of their relationship?* she thought. *After all, it's only been a day or two.* She now laughed at herself as much as with them, sensing that hard shell cracking.

Morningstar removed her bracelet and set it on the table. Liyah did the same, placing hers right next to it. Esty moved to the table, sitting cross-legged on the floor facing her friends. Liyah sat forward, while Morningstar knelt down, moving her right hand back and forth above the bracelets. As her hand passed over each charm, it lit up—the white light of Kai Li's torch, Liyah's blood red teardrop, and Zack's deep blue TrueHeart. Waving her hand above both bracelets, Morningstar created a concert of flashing light.

Esty gawked. "Which one is yours, Morningstar?"

"Star," Morningstar corrected her with a smile. "It's the band itself. The strange silvery metal that binds the jewels together. The Web of Life, Ooray called it. It is a symbol of the connectedness of all things."

Esty picked up one of the bracelets as Morningstar sat back on her heels, bringing her hands to her lap. The blinking stopped. She stared across the table, her mouth open. A giant grin lit up her face.

"I have so many questions!"

Sometimes laughing, sometimes serious, and sometimes emotional, Liyah and Morningstar recounted their journey of the previous week; the strange circumstances of their meeting, the scavenger hunt concerning the spiritual letters, the dangerous encounters, the arrival of Ooray, the mission, and the returning home.

Esty was mesmerized. It was a story like none she had ever read or heard. Her own emotions flowed with the storytelling—the wonder, the struggle, and the bonding they described during their journey.

Morningstar ended with her description of finding her grandfather, who all the time she thought had perished in the tornado, and then the flashing of her bracelet, telling her that Liyah needed her.

"No wonder you are such good friends after so little time." Esty uttered, quietly, astounded, unable to think of what to say next. *What a stupid comment after all that*, she told herself.

Her mind suddenly became overwhelmed with it all. She felt her heart pounding even more, anticipating something. *But what? My world is now upside down. Nothing seems real.* It was as if her thoughts were swirling like the tornado Morningstar described, and that she too, was frozen, unable to speak, or think of what to say next. It was all simply *too much.*

"You look a bit stunned," said Morningstar.

Liyah reached out to her, touching her hand. "So sorry, Esty," she said softly. "It's a lot. We had a whole week to get used to the craziness of it all. And I still wake up thinking it was just a dream. That it couldn't be real."

"But it is," added Morningstar.

Liyah grinned, pointing to Morningstar with her thumb while maintaining eye contact with Esty. "Miss matter-of-fact next to me always brings things back to the ground level. But at the end of our journey in that place…wherever it was, she fell apart too."

She turned to Morningstar. "Just sayin', Ms. Star."

Morningstar burst out laughing. Esty joined in, then Liyah.

Esty could feel her tension ease, her muscles relax, her mind begin to recover. "Thanks for telling me all that," she said, finally. "For opening up. You really don't know me. And it's a secret bigger than anything I can imagine. I won't tell anyone…for sure."

"It was inevitable," Liyah replied. "I mean, jeez, you already saw Ooray. What could top that?" She chuckled again. "Besides, we all have secrets, don't we? And they seem to come out eventually, no matter how hard we try to hide them."

Esty's mind was triggered again. The word *secrets* pushed out everything else. *Liyah doesn't know how right she is.* In a flash she thought of her own secrets—the ones she couldn't even tell her adoring father, her thoughts about the polarized and worsening situation in Palestine, her own spiritual beliefs, her simultaneous love and disappointment with her country, her attraction to Ahmad (which she noticed Liyah appeared to share), and the biggest secret of all…the one she could never tell anyone…*not ever.*

She collected herself. "I want to help in this mission of yours."

Morningstar glanced at Liyah before replying. "Of course," she nodded. "That's exactly the mission…to get everyone involved. To build from the bottom up. As Ooray says, everyone must follow, and everyone must also lead."

"What about all the, uh…uh…*magic?"*

"It's not really magic," Liyah told her. "Actually, we don't fully know the extent of the gifts that Ooray gave us. We're learning as we go, so to speak." She smiled. "There's definitely that strange power though. It exists at a higher level than we can understand. Star and I often talk about it. But we're also seeing that we can bring it up at times, even without holding onto the gifts or wearing the bracelets. I mean a little of it…not the full force of it. But Ooray taught us that we can change the world with the power from within, especially when combined with others. Like how single rays of light can all act together to become the sun."

"How wonderful," Esty effused. "It is just, well...*wonderful!*"

"What's wonderful?" boomed Esty's dad, as he entered the room.

Esty looked up. "Oh, nothing Pops. Just chatting."

"I see. And there you go again." He forced a frown. Esty watched as it slowly morphed into a sly smile.

"How was your call with Ahmad?" Esty questioned.

"Yes," Liyah jumped in, moving right into what was always foremost on her mind. "Did he ask you about finding my brother, Khalib?" she asked, her eyes clearly begging for the right answer.

"Actually, no. We talked about an article he is writing."

Liyah's countenance sank immediately, betraying her dismay to the others, and elevating her desperation again.

"Esty mentioned the situation with your brother," her dad said. "Unfortunately, most of my contacts are on the Israeli side. But you never know. I'll keep my ears open and inquire when I can. I dare say, though, that your own father probably is a better bet than I am. I'm sure he is working every avenue he can."

"Yes, he is," replied Liyah. 'Sorry to be so...well, pushy. I don't know how much time we have left, if any, to find him."

"No apologies necessary, Liyah. Keep me posted. If you need any introductions to others, I think I might at least be able to help there."

"Thank you, sir."

"My pleasure. Now, what's next for you girls?"

"Liyah said she has to get the car back home before lunch to pick up her dad," Esty replied. "He's busy at the paper even though it's not a workday there."

"Speaking of which," Esty's dad added, tilting his wrist with the watch, "I have a meeting this afternoon in Tel Aviv. I'll be needing the car."

Esty gulped. "It's the Sabbath, Dad. I was thinking of borrowing it."

"Sorry, sweetie. Something has come up. The Prime Minister has asked me to attend a meeting on his behalf. He said it's of international importance. He needed someone associated with his Office to be there."

"Does it always have to be you?" Esty complained.

He touched her shoulder. "For a while, dear. Comes with the territory. I'll back off at some point. Until then..."

"Yeah. I know Dad. Sorry."

"Why don't you ask Ahmad to take you where you need to go? He is shuttling the two boys around. Said he's headed for a meeting out near Beersheba. Maybe after that?"

"It's a lot to ask, Dad. I hardly know him."

"Maybe it's time to get to know him then. We only have one car…and you seem to use it more than I do."

Esty sighed heavily and rolled her eyes at Liyah.

"I saw that young lady," her dad grumbled, then smiled at her as he made his way past her and into the kitchen.

Thirty-Seven

"How far is it?" Zack asked Hassan, as he tried unsuccessfully to tune the car radio to a strong signal.

"Don't think you're going to find any FM channels out here," Hassan replied. The one we lost was a station out of Beersheba."

Kai Li popped his head in between the two front seats. "Boonies."

Boonies?" questioned Hassan.

"Yeah. Mean no one out here. American expression. Right, Zack?" He poked Zack's arm from the back seat as Zack continued his struggle with the radio.

"Huh?...Yup. Right."

"Mostly Bedouins here," Hassan said, "except for the city of Beersheba and a few towns. It's only a little way ahead, at the foothills. We'll be there in a few minutes, so it's probably a waste of time with the radio."

Zack sat back in his seat.

"Same mountains as Mount of Olive, right? suggested Kai Li. "I saw on map."

"That's right. These hills are part of a chain, beginning here and heading north towards Jerusalem. I'll drop you guys off with Jamal, he's the one working on the drones.

"Any news on Khalib?" Kai Li asked Zack.

"No. Ahmad didn't say anything about that when I spoke to him. We should probably call the girls and get the plan for the rest of the day."

Zack removed his phone from the pocket of the hoodie and pressed Liyah's name in his contacts list. He held it up to his ear, looking back at Kai Li. "That SIM card works like a champ, doesn't it? Very cool."

"Morning, Zack."

"Mornin', Liyah. Hold on. Let me put you on speaker so Kai can join." He propped the phone up against the dash. "Can you hear me?

"Yeah."

"What is plan for today?" asked Kai Li."

"We're at Esty's, still trying to figure out what to do for transportation. Her dad needs the car and I'm supposed to drop this one off for *my* dad. Where are you?"

"We're in a car with Hassan," Zack replied, jumping back in, "someone Ahmad knows. He said he'd pick us up later. I'm just along for the ride this morning. Kai Li got invited to help out with some project around here." He chuckled. "He's probably the only one of us who could get a decent job here."

No response.

Zack brought his mouth closer to the phone. "Liyah?"

"Yeah," Liyah acknowledged, her voice sounding a bit despondent. "I'm here. Just wondering why you guys are taking the morning off?"

"Jeez, Liyah," Zack replied, exhibiting some irritation. "Cut us a break. This is a favor, and Hassan happens to be well connected around here. We can meet you somewhere later."

"Well, let me see if Esty wants to join us. She's trying to get out today. Call us when you're finished."

Zack took the phone from the dash. "Okay. Sounds good. Oh, hold on…Before I forget, whatever happened to your lead from when you were in Jerusalem with that guy Jamal?"

"Jamal?" Liyah asked.

"Yeah. The handsome guy I heard you were drooling over."

"Zack!"

"Ha, sorry…Not!" He let out a loud laugh. "I think he's the one Kai Li will be working with."

"I need to get the name out of my purse, which is on the bureau. I'll text it to you, but it's very confidential. No one else should know, okay? Promise me!"

"Got it. No worries."

Hassan brought them into a small Bedouin encampment at the end of a dirt road. A man stood waiting as they stepped out of the car.

"*As-Salaam-Alaikum*," the man said to Hassan.

"*Wa-Alaikum-Salaam*," Hassan replied. "This is Kai Li and Zack. Your helpers for the morning."

"Well, him anyway," said Zack, pointing to Kai Li.

"Yes," replied Jamal, nodding to them. "Welcome. I'm Jamal. Glad you're here."

"Go ahead, boys," Hassan assured them. "Jamal won't kidnap you. I need to get to my meeting. If you're done early, call me. Or perhaps Jamal can bring you back."

Kai Li and Zack waved, then turned as the tires of Hassan's car kicked up a spattering of dirt and pebbles on its way out.

Jamal led the boys into the barn-like structure. Sitting at a table inside were two people, one working on something and the other chatting with him. They both stood up when they saw Jamal enter with Zack and Kai Li.

"This is Kai Li and Zack," said Jamal.

"I'm Akeem," said the one who had been working at the table. "And this is Dawoud."

While the four shook hands, Jamal flipped open his testing kit on the table. He grabbed a drone that Akeem had been reassembling and motioned to Kai Li.

"Take the extra chair, Kai Li. It's good to have more hands today."

"I'm just baggage," Zack joked. "Not a tech nerd like you guys."

"Sorry, Zack," Jamal said. "Dawoud, you mentioned you could use some help with the falcons. Why don't you show him around and then take him to the upper field with you for a while?"

"Falcons?" Zack asked.

Dawoud pointed to several rows of birds on perches a short distance from them along the inside wall of the barn. "Most of those birds over there are hawks, but you can see a couple of falcons at the far end. This year, as part of Ramadan, and since there will be a big crowd with Easter and Passover happening this weekend as well, we were requested to do something special. So, we'll be putting on a show tomorrow in the Old City."

"Wow," Kai Li acknowledged. "Those birds are somethin'!"

"Sure are," Zack agreed. "I can't believe I didn't notice them right away. Must be slippin'."

"Jamal distracted you," Dawoud replied. "Those, and others here, are competition birds. Some of the best. We train them for various competitions all over the world. But tomorrow will just be a fun thing."

"Feel like doing a little work with me?" Dawoud asked.

"I'm in."

"We'll be up there in a while for a quick test of these drones," Jamal noted. "See you then."

Dawoud motioned to Zack and escorted him toward the back of the barn. He opened one of the stalls and brought out two of the hooded falcons. He selected an arm protector and a whistle for Zack then led him back out of the barn and up to the field.

Jamal turned to Kai Li and handed him one of the drones. "How much do you know about these?"

"I see a lot of them. Program a couple, but mostly work with robots. Very similar in some ways."

"They can be," agreed Jamal. "Hassan mentioned you're familiar with infrared signaling applications."

"Yeah."

"Great," replied Jamal. "Let me explain how we're using them in groups."

Kai Li and Akeem peered over Jamal's shoulder as he reprogrammed the last of the drones that was unsuccessful in the previous test. As he explained how the drones share information with one another, Akeem collected all of them and began placing them in three boxes, to be transported to the test site.

Jamal passed the last drone to Akeem, then picked up his notes and turned to Kai Li. "The problem we had on the last test, Kai Li, was that some of the drones at the back of the pack crashed as they reconfigured for the landing. I tuned the algorithm for the communications to allow more location information to be shared by only the neighboring drones, the six closest to each in a three-dimensional space. If we include too many drones as active neighbors, the messaging and analysis gets complicated."

"Why only rear ones crash?" Kai Li asked.

"Well, that's just it. I don't know. I'm hoping that this might fix it. We'll see. But we're running out of time. We might have to abort the mission, for now at least."

"Mission?"

"Oh. I didn't mean to use that word. Maybe I should say *exercise*. It's not important for you to know, anyway. In fact, best for you not to worry about it."

Kai Li felt confused, but let it drop for the moment. He was impressed by Jamal's mathematical algorithms, something he hoped to study more when he goes to college in America someday. He understood the underlying communications using infrared light, because that was what some of the robots in the factory used to sense things and communicate. But he also knew there was a lot more to advanced computer communications than simple messaging and downloading stuff.

"Don't know about all adjustments you make, Jamal. Above my head."

"It's okay. I'm tweaking the algorithms. And it helps me to have you ask questions and then explain it to you. You know how that is…with creative types, right? Problem-solving."

Kai Li laughed. "Yeah. Funny thing. Like magic."

"Exactly," Jamal replied, nodding his head. "But the important part is that you seem to understand enough about how the drones use infrared signaling."

"What's drawing for?" Kai Li asked, pointing to the piece of paper on the table.

"It shows how the drones were organized for the landing. Each is numbered, and since we're trying to find out why only the rear ones collided, I want to run the exact configuration again. Otherwise, I don't think we'll know what happened if different drones collide this time."

"I see. But you put new software into all drones, correct?"

"Yes. All the drones will use the same update. We need to eliminate any differences in software levels to avoid even more confusion as we figure out what went wrong."

Jamal folded the paper and stuffed it in his jacket pocket. "Okay, guys. Everybody grab a box and let's go see how we've done."

Akeem and Kai Li followed Jamal out of the barn and up to the field. Arriving at the testing spot, they arranged the drones in the configuration that Jamal drew. He motioned them to stand back with him, about ten feet from the drones.

"I've programmed them just to rise up fifty feet, so we can still see them. As they reach that height, they will configure into a three-dimensional group, each drone about ten feet from its neighbors, as they would for normal travel to their target. They will then fly in a small circle before returning."

"Target?" asked Kai Li. He began to wonder about the use of the word, along with the small packets attached to the underside of the main body of the drones.

"Uh…location," Jamal replied. "As they come back down, they'll form into the landing arrangement—closer together in a flat grid, like they are now. That's where we had the trouble yesterday, Kai Li. So please keep an eye on them, especially the ones in the back."

Kai Li stuck his right thumb up. "Got it."

Jamal took his cell phone and typed in the commands to initiate the program then hit *send.* In a few seconds the propellers of all the drones spun up, their combined whirring sound clearly audible, even though each made very little noise on its own. Jamal sent one more command and the drones were on their own, rising together, straight up, separating from one another, then forming into a three-dimensional diamond shape as they reached the prescribed height.

Kai Li moved further away to get a good angle on the drones. "So far so good," Kai Li called over to Akeem and Jamal, now standing together a short distance from him.

The drones completed a large circle, flying out over the field to the far side, where Kai Li could see two human forms; one was clearly Zack in his unmistakable red sweatshirt. As the drones neared Zack, he raised his arm and waved in Kai Li's direction.

As Kai Li waved back, he could vaguely make out something resting on Zack's other arm. *That couldn't be a falcon, could it,* he wondered*?* He brought his attention to the drones once more as they traced the edge of the field and began their return.

"Still good," Kai Li shouted.

The drones slowed as they arrived overhead and broke out of the diamond formation, flattening slowly into a grid as they descended and moved closer together. Then Kai Li noticed something odd; several drones at the far end appeared to wobble slightly. Then a few more.

Suddenly, one drone clipped another. Then two more. A total of five fell out of formation and crashed to the ground. The others landed successfully a short distance away at their appointed location.

"Damn!" shouted Jamal. "Damn, damn…damn!"

He rushed over to the ones on the ground, collected them and returned to Akeem and Kai Li. He handed one to Kai Li. "What do you think? I hate to call this whole thing off, but I just don't know how many will survive in bigger groups, over larger distances, and hit targets that require even more complex clues."

Kai Li let the *target* word ride again, but an uneasiness was planting itself in his brain. Turning one of the drones upside down, he removed his glasses and used the edges of the lenses as a magnifying glass to examine the underside. He turned to Akeem.

"Hold one in each hand…above head…okay, Akeem?"

Akeem selected two from Jamal and did as asked.

Kai Li held his drone so it was underneath, and between the two held by Akeem. He moved his back and forth, and up and down, studying the relative positions of all three. Taking his phone from his pants pocket, he turned on its flashlight, then squatted down as he raised his drone up over his head. He moved it around under the other two, all the while directing the light from his phone at different angles between all the drones.

"Okay for now, Akeem," said Kai Li.

Akeem brought his arms down.

Kai Li turned to Jamal, exposing the underside of the drone. "What is this?" he questioned, resting his forefinger on the black rectangular package.

"It's something each drone needs to carry as part of the, uh, exercise."

"So, they are *delivery* drones? Like to homes?"

"I guess you could say that. We're working on something special."

Kai Li's brow knitted in concern. Something was beginning to seem clearly *off* to him. *Probably better to not keep asking too many questions in that direction*, he thought.

"You see something?" asked Jamal.

"One time at factory, we try to get many small bots to work together…to build a toy house. Work okay at first, then bots start acting funny. I figure out that communication breaking down…"

Kai Li's mind drifted, as it often did, not due to technology or mathematical intrusions or puzzles this time, but to thoughts of the toy factory, and home. *What were his fellow workers doing at the factory? Had time stopped this time, too? What time was it there? Was his mother sleeping?*

"And…," Jamal broke in, his voice anxious, bordering on impatient.

Kai Li blinked several times. "I think maybe same here. Look like some signals getting blocked by the package. When I shine phone light, sometimes package cast a shadow on receiver of next drone, so must be same for infrared signals, since the LEDs operate like flashlight."

"But why would that cause a problem just on landing?"

"Can't tell. At factory same thing happen with arms and bodies of bots…and part of house block their messages. Bot have hard time adjusting because some signals not received. It cause bot to thrash then stop."

"You mean it's not the communications code I corrected?" Jamal asked in dismay.

Your code still have a part in it…so good you fix it. But signal need to be clean."

"Why wouldn't all drones have the problem then? Why just the rear ones?"

Kai Li waved his hand back and forth underneath the drone. "They have issue too. Signal blocked like if my hand doing this. When fly far apart, signal not blocked. If closer together, begin to have problem."

"Very clever, Kai Li. But it still doesn't explain why just some of the drones crash."

"Feedback," Kai Li replied.

"Feedback?"

"When drones close, package block beam more often. All get location and info from neighbors, and drones in front send map coordinates. It act like wave, starting with drone in front and moving back. Since all drones are closer now and not get good signal, by time info get to last drones, it is bad. Drone try to correct by sending bad info back to neighbors, so then get even worse. Like feedback loop of microphone and speakers…get worse and worse until it hurt your ears." He smiled.

Jamal had a stricken look. "You might not know how to write the complex algorithms, Kai Li. But that is one piece of detective work!"

Kai Li turned to Akeem. "Can I have the Swiss knife you use to fix the drones?"

Akeem dug in his pocket and passed it to him.

Kai Li swung the small blade out and cut very small wedge shapes into the package of the drone in his hand, near where the LEDs were set on the body of the drone. He looked up at Jamal. "Should do it…easy fix. Signal get through now. But have to do for all drones."

"Well, let's do it now, and run another test!" Jamal urged, his face beaming.

Akeem repaired the minimal damage done to the arms and propellers of the drones that crashed, while Kai Li carved small openings on the plastic packages to allow the signals to be transmitted and received better. After about thirty minutes, they were ready to test.

Akeem placed the drones in the same positions as before, using Jamal's drawing as the guide. Jamal studied them for a moment, holding his chin between his thumb and forefinger. Bending down, he moved the ones that crashed to the front, switching them with the others.

"I thought we should be testing the broken ones, no?" Akeem asked.

"This time we need to make sure that it is neither a problem with those drones nor any of them. This will solve that. If any fail, we'll cancel the plans. If they all work…well, then I think we're good to go."

They moved back to give the drones some space then Jamal reset the test sequence. The propellers whirred again. The drones rose. They circled the field and returned a few minutes later, hanging in the air above them. Then they began to descend, slowly regrouping as they came closer and closer to each other, and to the ground.

Simultaneously they all touched down in the grass. Their propellers stopped spinning, and the engine modules shut down.

Jamal let out a gigantic sigh, which Kai Li thought was probably heard across the field. He grinned at Jamal, who held up his hand for high-fives by him and Akeem.

"Let's get it all packed up, guys," Jamal ordered. "It's a red-letter day!"

As they packed the last drones in the boxes, Zack and Dawoud approached from behind.

"Having fun with your toys?" Zack kidded

Jamal turned his head and stood up. "Yes, in fact. And I see you have a new friend with you."

Kai Li, still on his haunches, looked up. A large, hooded falcon came into view, perched on Zack's shoulder, its talons clutching the leather sleeve.

"Hey, Kaibo. How'd it go? Looked from over there like you may have been having some trouble."

"Yes, we did," replied Jamal. "But your friend here solved the problem. Amazing!"

"Oh, I don't doubt that he fixed it. But nothin' amazin' about it. That much I know. Routine for him." He smiled at Kai Li.

"Zack didn't do so bad either," Dawoud announced. In fact, he's a natural with the falcons. Taliq looks quite comfortable perched there, doesn't he?"

"Probably sweatshirt," Kai Li joked. "Birds like color red."

"Interesting you know that," replied Dawoud.

"No it's not," complained Zack. "It's more like *irritating* that he knows it."

"Like most all birds, falcons do actually like red," Dawoud added. "So Kai Li's right, but that's not to take anything away from Zack. There's something else. I mean it's incredible. I've never seen these birds react to someone like that. It's as if they just want to be close. Like he has some energy about him or something."

Zack grinned at Kai Li.

Jamal's phone rang. He stepped aside to answer it. There was a brief exchange, then he brought the phone from his ear, covering the speaker with his hand. "Zack, Kai Li. You guys have a ride back? I called Hassan a little while ago since it was taking us longer to complete this than we expected, and I wasn't sure how things would go. So he scheduled another meeting and asked me to take you. But now my meeting was moved up to a few hours from now. I'll have to go straight to Gaza."

"We can wait for Ahmad," Zack replied.

Jamal pressed the phone back against his ear. "They're good!...Uh-huh...No, don't worry."

"Sorry, everyone. Things seem to be changing fast." He signaled to Akeem. "I've got a tight schedule and still have to double-check things. Let's get all these boxed up again and back to the barn, if you would."

All six walked down the hill together, Dawoud recounting the training runs with the falcons. He told of how Zack's nervousness initially put Taliq off, but then how the great bird slowly became like Zack's best friend as if they were connected in a previous life.

Kai Li's attention was fixed on Taliq the whole way back, except for a few moments when he stared up at the sky and then down at the drones in the box he was carrying, rechecking his assumptions.

Once in the barn, Dawoud made sure the falcons were returned properly to their roosts while Jamal studied his notes and retested a few of the drones using his analyzer.

Zack's phone buzzed.

"Hi, Ahmad. When will you be here?...Seriously? We don't have a ride. We got delayed and Hassan is now tied up. And so is Jamal…Uh-huh. Well, while you try to figure it out, I was meaning to send you this contact information I received from Liyah. She texted it to me earlier. It's from that imam. Confidential she said…Hold on."

Zack copied the message from Liyah and texted it to Ahmad:

Yusuf Al-Najafi
Tel Sheva (Bedouin camp)

"Did you get it okay? The name is Yusuf…Hello, Ahmad? Ahmad?...Oh good, you're still there…Uh-huh. So you already know this Yusuf Al-Najafi?"

Dawoud was returning when he heard Zack say the name. "Al-Najafi? Yusuf?" he said to Zack. "Can I speak to your friend?"

"Hold on, Ahmad. Talk to Dawoud, here."

"Hello, yes, Ahmad? This is Dawoud. Yusuf is my boss. Jamal and the others are using the field here…Yes…Alright, we'll wait for your call."

Zack hung up. A few minutes passed before the phone rang again.

"Hi Ahmad. Any luck?...yeah…okay. You better tell Morningstar and Liyah. They might be pissed, and I don't want to be the messenger they shoot…sure…see you then."

"What's up?" Kai Li asked.

"Ahmad said he was able to reach Yusuf, and Yusuf said to have Dawoud bring us over to his place and we would spend the night there. Ahmad will pick us up tomorrow."

"Maybe girls calm down by then," suggested Kai Li.

"I wouldn't bank on that, Mr. Kai."

Thirty-Eight

Gaza City – To the South

CEO SAYF YASIN and Nasir arrived at the testing area which was a flat roofed metal building four miles south of Aleab Ltd.'s toy factory. It was not far from the eastern border between Israel and Gaza—a sandy, deserted no-man's-land. They parked on a hard-packed patch of gravel and exited their vehicle. Nasir opened the trunk, removing an aluminum alloy demo case. They headed toward the building with Nasir dragging the wheeled case. He knocked heavily on the hollow metal door. A man in baggy camo pants and jacket showed them in.

"*As-Salaam-Alaikum*," Sayf Yasin said to the man. "This is Nasir. He'll be helping us with the test. Is Hassan here?"

"*Wa-Alaikum-Salaam*, Mr. Yasin, Nasir. Welcome to both of you. Hassan is tied up. He asked me to let you know that he *will* be attending your meeting later this afternoon."

"*Shukran*," replied the CEO. "Let's get right to it, if you don't mind. I need to be back at the factory in an hour."

"Certainly, sir. Follow me."

They tailed the man through the middle aisle of the building that was disguised as an operating warehouse for security reasons. Rows of shelves were stacked to the ceiling with bins and boxes of all sizes. The man led them through an emergency exit doorway at the far end and they descended a circular set of metal stairs. He unlocked a heavy door at the bottom that led them into a hallway. Each door off the hall was marked in sequence: *S1, S2, S3*...

The man stopped in front of the door marked *S6*. "These are different *stockrooms*, as we refer to them. But they are actually large rooms for testing of signal emissions of electronic devices, explosives, radiation, etc. This one is for smaller explosives." He pushed down the bar, opened the door, and flipped on the lights.

The room was completely sealed. All four walls, the floor, and the ceiling were constructed of thick concrete blocks. A large object was positioned on top of a six-inch high metal platform that rested in the middle of the concrete floor. A few similar platforms were positioned even distances from each other in the sizable area.

"This room is protected from collapse or serious damage by the incorporation of alternating layers of steel and cement in all directions," the man noted. He made his way to the first platform, then stopped. "I believe you have the devices your team wishes to test. Hassan has provided the test objects for you, as requested. This one is the engine of a small military jet."

He pointed to the platform at the far end. "And that one over there is a section of artillery gun housing—the piece of the shaft attached to the part in which the live shells are placed before firing. Hassan asked me to send you the picture of it yesterday. Did you receive it?"

"Yes," replied Nasir.

"How did you get the engine and the gun section?" asked Yasin.

The man smiled. "Well, I guess I'm not at liberty to give out that information, even to friends of Hassan. Let's just say that over the years, some Israeli weapons like these have been destroyed or captured, here and in other countries. It's rare, but it happens."

"I see," replied Yasin.

"Okay then," said the man." Ready when you are."

Nasir lifted the aluminum case, set it down on the end of the testing platform then snapped open the clasps. He lifted the lid, removed a section of foam rubber lining, retrieved a small rectangular box and placed it on the platform. He then closed the top of the case, secured it, and turned to the others.

"Better stand clear, you just can't be too careful. These are designed to be quite safe before detonation. But there's no sense in taking a chance. I'd say at least fifty feet."

They began backing away.

"Wait, sir," Nasir added. "Take this with you." He wheeled the case over to him.

They watched from a distance as Nasir opened the small box and retrieved the contents: a rectangular packet four inches long, one inch wide, and one inch deep, and secured in a thin layer of foil. He unwrapped it to expose a black plastic device. He rested it gently between two of the propeller blades in the intake of the jet engine, then joined the others.

The man then led them to a steel door at the side of the room. They stepped inside, taking seats on a bench behind a large, thick, bulletproof window. Nasir opened the case again and removed an electronic tablet with three LEDs custom-built into the top front. He closed the case and slid it under the bench.

"What kind of explosive are you testing?" asked Hassan's representative.

"It's an adapted form of TNT. Quite similar in fact, except smaller and more stable. The detonator and electronics are built into the package, so it's sort of like a solid-state device surrounding the modified TNT."

"It's pretty small," the man observed. "I don't think you'll be blowing up any big stuff with it."

"No." Nasir agreed. "And we're not trying to. We just want to incapacitate them."

"How much explosiveness are we talking about?" asked Yasin. "It looks small."

"All the drones can effectively carry…enough to do the job, and no more."

Yasin nodded. "Got it."

"Much smaller than a stick of dynamite," Hassan's man added. "How powerful is it?"

"I guess we'll see soon enough, won't we? But this explosive device is also modified to have almost twice the power of one stick of dynamite, and we have also been able to form it into different shapes, so a small packet can be made into whatever we need. We can get fifty percent more explosive power than a stick in two-thirds the volume. Only about six ounces total weight, including the electronics."

"Pretty impressive, indeed." said the man. "Let's see what it can do." He reached into the drawer of the bench, brought out three sets of safety goggles and headphones, and handed them out. "Unlikely you'll need these but it's a good idea. Our *small* explosives are much larger than what you have here. And the walls and safety glass keep us protected even in those circumstances."

When the safety gear was in place, the man nodded. "Give it a go."

Nasir pulled up two screens on the tablet. Three small square boxes in the application mimicked the LEDs. He began typing in the *Module 1* portion of the screen.

After a minute the first box began blinking red, as did the LED at the top of the tablet. He typed some more. The second box began blinking, followed by the corresponding LED on the tablet. Once the third box was programmed, all tablet LEDs matched the boxes in the application.

Nasir turned to the other two. "Ready?"

They shook their heads and stared out the window at the test platform.

Nasir typed another command, then looked up. A high frequency, beeping sound emanated from the tablet, the time between sounds shortening with each beep until they blurred into a steady ear-piercing stream.

Nasir pressed the *return* on the keyboard. "Here we go."

The blinking LEDs began cycling. Then…

BANG!

The thick security glass bowed perceptibly inward and vibrated like an old bass speaker. The noise, even though dampened by the glass, caused Yasin to press his palms against his headset automatically. They all ducked, reacting instinctively, as fragments of flying metal scattered throughout the main room and smashed up against the window.

An eerie silence captured the room.

The Hamas agent looked at Nasir. "That was quite an explosion for such a small device," he conceded. "Caught me a little by surprise."

Yasin returned his jaw to its normal position, still staring out through the glass. "I'd say!"

Nasir grabbed the aluminum case from under the bench and they walked back to the testing platform. The partially warped body of the engine lay on its side a few feet away. A small portion of the turbine section that housed the blades was still attached, although badly damaged. The rest of the blades were scattered about.

Hassan's man glanced around the room at the scattered pieces, then at the smokey cloud hanging above. "I don't think this jet will be flying anywhere after that. Don't worry about the mess. I'll have someone clean up the room after the next test. Routine procedure here."

He led them next to the far platform where an artillery housing was placed.

Nasir opened the case and retrieved the second explosive device along with a small drone. He secured the package to the drone, slid it along tiny inset ridges along its bottom, and close to the infrared signaling lights. He then pushed the drone into the narrow end of the artillery housing and tested the fit, forcing the propeller armatures of the drone to collapse into a linear formation. He pulled it back out and snapped the armatures back into their operating state.

He took his phone out of his pocket and snapped several pictures, from multiple angles, of the platform with the artillery piece resting on it. Moving closer to the opening in the narrower gun section of the housing, he did the same.

"All set," he said, as he picked up the case.

Their host nodded. "Okay. Let's do round two, then."

All three returned to the observation room and assumed the same testing positions, donning their headgear and goggles.

Nasir placed the drone on the bench, selected the pictures from his phone, and sent them to the tablet. From the tablet, he fed them into an application, ran a simulation, then radioed the assembled program to the drone. He picked up the drone and set it on the floor just inside the main room, then flipped the power on. With the drone stationary, he closed the door and returned to his seat.

Shifting his attention again to the tablet, he brought up the Module 2 screen and started typing. The drone rose up in front of the window, circled as if getting its bearings, then headed toward the far platform.

"What's it supposed to do?" asked Yasin.

Nasir stared through the window with his eyes locked on the drone. "In a moment it will be completely on its own, using the pictures I sent to locate the gun and the pre-embedded instructions to complete the task. Do you remember the metal pipe I showed you at the last meeting, and the wings of the drone collapsing as it entered the end?"

"Definitely."

"Well, this is the same thing, except this is a real target, and once the drone enters the gun the explosion sequence is initiated, somewhat similar to the last one…but for just this test. We'll see it on the LEDs of the tablet." He pointed. "Here at the top."

They watched as the drone slowly approached the gun from behind, moved past, swung around in a wide arc, then picked up speed. Nearing the open end of the gun section, the LEDs on the tablet lit up. As the drone entered the nozzle, the propeller arms folded into a single line. The LEDs began cycling red with the tablet emitting a high-pitched, whining sound.

Just before the drone crashed against the loading mechanism at the other end of the gun shaft, an explosion ripped through the housing. Percussion waves from the blast pounded against the window glass, yet only a few metal parts flew about the room. Other than that, the explosion appeared quite contained by the solid, thick metal artillery housing.

Yasin shot a questioning look at Nasir.

"Let's go see," said Nasir.

A grin swept over Nasir's face as they approached the testing platform. Part of the thick steel alloy shaft had been turned inside out, and the loading area for the shells was permanently damaged.

"Now that is *truly* impressive," the Hamas agent announced, clapping Nasir on his back. "That is one tough gun. And now it's useless. I don't know what you folks have planned…well maybe only a few details Hassan said I needed to know for this, but I wish I was around to see the fireworks."

"No one will see everything," Nasir replied, "But I'm sure many will see something…and *everyone* will hear about it."

Thirty-Nine

AHMAD PARKED AND waited across the street from the iron gate in front of Esty's home, his fingers tapping rapid fire on the keyboard of his laptop. Two knocks on the passenger side window broke his focus. He pushed the button on the dash, unlocking the doors.

Esty swung open the door. She tossed her backpack through the opening between her and Ahmad onto the floor behind her. Sliding into her seat, she pulled the seatbelt over her shoulder and clipped it across her lap.

"All set," Esty said, a bit breathless.

Ahmad laughed. "And good afternoon to you, too."

"Oh, so sorry Ahmad. I had a few last-minute things to do. Yes, good morning. I mean afternoon…It's flying, isn't it?"

He laughed. "You or the day?"

"Both I guess," she replied, sitting back and managing a smile. "It really is very nice of you, Ahmad…I mean helping me out like this. I hate not having a car and being trapped at home."

"My pleasure, Esty. It was a short trip up here anyway. I was near Tel Sheva." He shifted the car into drive and headed up the street.

Esty let out a long sigh. "I don't know. Is it my imagination or are things super crazy or what?"

"Super crazy, I'd say. You can feel the streets vibrating where I live. And with the artillery shells flying at times, and the pressure around finding Khalib, who needs more things to stress out about?"

"Did you know that they canceled the tours for this weekend?" Esty asked. "Due to the trouble in Jerusalem. And the weekend has only started. I may be late for my meeting."

"Chill," said Ahmad. "I've got you covered. We'll be in Gaza before you know it. What happened to Morningstar and Liyah? They were headed home you said, right? To Beit Lahia."

"Yeah, but my dad said he needed to talk to me about a few things and I didn't want to make them late getting Liyah's car back to her dad."

"Everything okay with him?" asked Ahmad, as he turned onto the main road, heading south. "I had a good conversation with him about my article for the paper."

"He is disappointed in me."

Ahmad kept his eyes straight ahead, adjusting to the heavier than normal traffic for a Saturday. "Seriously? Anything you care to share?"

"Well, you know parents. My dad thinks he has to worry twice as much, since my mom is no longer with us."

"So sorry, again. You mentioned that yesterday when we were walking through the garden at Gethsemane."

"It's okay. It's been a little while, but my dad's having a much harder time than me getting over it."

Ahmad looked over at her. "I can understand that. It must be hard losing someone after so many years together."

"And what about you? Big plans for this busy weekend with your family? I know it's not Easter or Passover for you, but you'll be celebrating the end of Ramadan in a few days, right?"

"Yup. Well, I'm actually still living with my adopted family until I graduate. They have plans, although nothing that involves me directly. But it's okay. I need to focus on looking for a job, in case Liyah's dad doesn't hire me full-time to work at the paper. So, I'm mostly focused on figuring that out." He paused, letting out a sigh. "I can't afford college and the end of the school year is coming up fast."

"I should be saying sorry to *you*, Ahmad." She turned to him. "Here I am complaining. Where are your parents?"

"I never had any as far as I'm concerned," he replied. "Well, that's not technically true. Of course, everyone has to have parents." He struggled with a chuckle. "Mine abandoned me and my brother when we were very little. I burned their pictures and wouldn't recognize them if they ever crossed my path. I spent most of my growing up in an orphanage and a couple of foster homes. A family finally did adopt us. Liyah's dad knows them. But it's been a struggle"

Esty noticed his facial features harden, his mouth sinking at the edges. "Oh, Ahmad." Esty managed, caught by surprise.

"Not worth talking about. Was a long time ago. So, back to your dad," said Ahmad, catching her stare as he turned his head. "What did you do that pissed him off?"

"Financial stuff."

"Like what? If I'm not prying too much."

"I hate to say it. I feel embarrassed now that I know your situation."

"I don't care," Ahmad said, quieting his voice. "Money is just money."

"Okay. But don't laugh at me, promise?"

"Sure. Whatever."

"I have…well…a rather large trust fund. And he saw how much I spent the past six months."

Ahmad almost choked laughing.

"You promised!" Esty protested.

"Sorry," he said, failing to cover up a snicker. "Go on."

Esty shot him a sideways look. "I spent *a lot more* than I care to say…maybe a third of the total."

"Of the entire fund? In six months? Holy Crap!"

"Yeah. I really can't tell you how much. But it's *definitely* a lot. Some of it was actually spent over the last year. I'll get more though when I turn twenty-one, so I don't know why he's so mad."

"I do. And I'm not feeling particularly sorry for you at the moment. How do you get to spend money from a trust fund when you're only sixteen anyway? Isn't it supposed to be for school and other important stuff?"

"I have my own bank account. My father set it up when my mother died and gave me full access to it this year, on my birthday. He was afraid if something happened to him somebody would take advantage of me. So, he sat me down, and over a month taught me about budgeting, keeping a balance, basics of investing…you know, the regular stuff."

"No, I don't know," Ahmad replied.

"Anyway, it's really not that big a deal. When I turn twenty-one, I will get a whole lot more added to the trust. And then, of course when my father dies, which I can't even think about, I'll inherit the remainder…like the house and other stuff."

She glanced at Ahmad, who looked like someone had shot him with a stun gun.

He collected himself. "And what are you spending *all this money* on that he is so concerned about? Too many shoes?"

"Stop it, Ahmad. I'm serious. No. I don't spend it on me. I donate it."

"To whom?"

"To people who need it more than me."

"That's generous of you, for sure. But who is that?"

"I can't say. Even my dad doesn't know. He just knows it's going out of my account. He gets the balances from the bank but not the full statement. That was the arrangement."

"You should tell him, so he doesn't think you're blowing it all on yourself. Maybe that would help. Along with swearing that you won't spend any more."

Esty's voice quieted. "I can't do that."

"Why not?"

"Because I'm not sure I've finished yet. And…well, he wouldn't approve of where it was going. He might even get in serious trouble if the Prime Minister should find out."

Ahmad gripped the wheel tighter, keeping his eyes on the heavily trafficked road ahead. "I think it's time for me to stop asking questions. It's not my place anyway."

"Don't you be mad at me too, Ahmad," Esty pleaded.

He glanced over at her. "I'm really not, Esty. Like I said, it's not my place. I was just thinking I could help, but clearly, I can't."

Esty slumped back in her seat as an awkward silence surrounded them.

After about fifteen minutes, the traffic ahead began to slow. "We'll be at the border in a minute. I can usually get into the lane where they do a less intense check and move you along. I flash my press pass. They'll still check our papers but won't necessarily search the car."

"I know," said Esty.

"You do?"

"Yeah, I have a special pass too. But I called ahead, and they are on the lookout."

"Really?"

"It's a political thing. Sorry I didn't mention it."

"No need to apologize," Ahmad replied, smiling. "I should have known."

"I'm also sorry for all that back there. I want us to be friends. I like you."

"I like you, too, Esty. Why would you think a discussion like that would ruin anything?"

"I don't know. I'm not good at it, I guess. And you probably disapprove of me because you're working hard for whatever money you can earn, while in your eyes I just squander what I am lucky enough to be given."

The depth of Esty's sadness suddenly hit Ahmad. He paused before addressing her, shifting off the track they seemed to be on, his eyes briefly catching hers. "It's interesting that you can see through *my* eyes," he replied, "That's quite a trick."

Esty noticed his grin. The corners of her mouth turned up. "I admire you, Ahmad. You are smart, you care for others, and you're trying to make a difference in this madness here."

Ahmad turned to her and winked. "Look who's talking."

The traffic had slowed to a crawl. A guard walked toward them in their lane, and moved from one car to the next, asking for papers from each driver. A few he waved ahead. Most remained in line.

Ahmad brought his window down as the armed guard approached their car. He handed him his press pass. The man studied it for a few seconds then waved him out of line, pointing to the booth to the far left side of the border crossing, where there was only a small number of cars.

After a short wait, they finally pulled up to the booth. Another guard asked Ahmad to step out of the car while yet another guard approached Esty's side.

As Ahmad got out of the car, he turned to Esty. "Don't worry. It's getting more difficult every day to get through here. They've recently banned almost all Palestinians from crossing between Israel and Palestine, even with a valid passport." He shook his head." Supposedly due to the escalation in hostilities. They may call the Dawn to check, but it won't be a long delay." Ahmad stepped out and showed his press pass.

The second guard rapped on Esty's window. She rolled it down.

"Documents!" the guard growled.

Esty reached behind her and retrieved her Israeli passport from the backpack, along with her bright blue newsboy hat with the Ministry emblem. She placed her hat on her head, removed the sunglasses she had been wearing, and handed him her passport.

"How old are you?"

"Sixteen," Esty replied, calmly.

The guard unclipped his walkie-talkie from his belt, and called the booth. He began reading Esty's passport information into the phone but suddenly stopped. "Yes…that's right." He checked her picture against her face. "Affirmative," he said into the phone.

There was a short pause. The guard gave a half salute to Esty. "Sorry ma'am, I hope we didn't inconvenience you."

"Not at all," replied Esty, putting her sunglasses back on.

The guard shouted across the roof of the car. "Never mind, Eli…Prime Minister's pass."

The guard stopped in the middle of asking Ahmad another question and looked over at the other guard, who was now waving him off. He handed Ahmad's papers back to him. "Looks like you're good to go."

Ahmad appeared confused as he slid into his seat behind the wheel. Esty had returned her hat and passport to the pack and was already pulling her head back through the gap above the console.

"What was that all about?" asked Ahmad

Esty smiled. "Connections. Isn't it always about that?"

"Too much so," Ahmad agreed.

They left the checkpoint behind to enter Gaza, then Gaza City.

"That's a fair-sized pack you have, Esty. Looks like you're going on a trip instead of to a meeting. Who are you seeing on the Strip?"

"A few people I've been working with on a project."

Ahmad cast her a glance. "It's not exactly in your backyard, or even a place anyone would expect to see someone like you."

Esty met his gaze. "It's another thing I can't tell you. Sorry, Ahmad. Sometime."

Ahmad smiled. "So many 'sorries' today…Forget about it. I have a meeting here, too. And I can't say anything about who I'm seeing either."

Esty pointed ahead. "Take a right up at the next light. The hospital is a block up from there."

Ahmad made the right and then pulled up to the curb by the emergency entrance to the hospital. He reached behind her seat, grabbed the pack, and handed it to her. "Is your meeting at the hospital?"

"No. Someone will be meeting here shortly to take me there. We made good time. I'm actually a bit early."

"I could drop you there," Ahmad offered. "My meeting is quite close to here."

"This is fine," Esty insisted, climbing out of the car. "I also hate to have you take me all the way home." She leaned back in before closing the door. "Maybe we could meet my father halfway?"

"We can figure it out later. See you here in about an hour and a half?"

"Yes. See you then," Esty replied. "I'll text if there's any problem."

As Ahmad drove to his meeting with Hassan, Esty entered the hospital.

Forty

Gaza City

AHMAD FOLLOWED THE waiter down the spiraling stone steps, through the white brick arches, and into a small room off to the side of the main dining area. Hassan was sitting at the end of the table, facing him. Another man, whom he didn't recognize, sat at the corner.

Hassan stood up. "Ahmad!" he boomed. "Welcome. *Salaam.* So good to see you again." He walked over and warmly shook Ahmad's hand.

"*Salaam,*" returned Ahmad.

Hassan turned to the other man, who remained seated. "This is Murtaza. I think I may have mentioned him."

"Yes, perhaps," Ahmad replied, deferring to Hassan's boldness, although he was certain the name had never come up. He nodded to the man. "*As-Salaam-Alaikum*, Murtaza."

He extended his hand.

"*Wa-Alaikum-Salaam*, Ahmad. I've heard good things about you."

"Sit. Sit," said Hassan.

Ahmad took the chair across from Murtaza as the waiter handed out the menus. He was uncertain of quite what to say. He thought it was great that Hassan was giving him time for an interview. After all, he really didn't know him that well. Hassan was his *high-level contact* with Hamas, but he had barely spoken with him at any length. He'd been introduced to him through an acquaintance in Gaza when he began first thinking about a story for the paper, and then had a brief call with him when he was looking for leads into Khalib's disappearance. *Why did Hassan invite another person,* he wondered. *This needs to be kept under wraps until the article is released. He must know that?* But more troubling at this moment was he simply didn't know what to say about ordering food during the fast. It was still early afternoon, and wouldn't be dusk for another four hours.

"You seem a little preoccupied, Ahmad," said Hassan, laughing lightly. He collected the menus and handed them back to the waiter. "Just some fruit and water if you would, Rafiq...*Shukran*"

"Sure, sir. No problem. I'll be back in a few minutes."

As the waiter walked away, Hassan brought his eyes back to Ahmad. "Don't worry. We've all been working hard, so we deserve a little something. Wouldn't you agree? The fast for today will end soon, anyway. And regardless, it's not much. We can make it up another time."

Ahmad forced a smile. He felt his old nervousness knocking on the door. *What is it with some of these people I've been meeting lately?* he wondered. *It seems half the time I spend with them I'm avoiding the truth, and the other half I'm outright lying... Or maybe it's me? Maybe I'm simply not cut out for all this...this compromising. This intrigue.*

Ahmad's mind suddenly shifted. He wished he was someone else, something he remembered doing when he was little. He'd pull the covers over his head in his bunk bed at the orphanage. It was dark under there—not the tiniest ray of light entered. He'd imagine he was invisible to all the evil lurking about. He'd dream of rescuing people, becoming a hero. But more often he'd cry himself to sleep, scared, hoping that when he awoke, he would be in his real home...the one he was supposed to have. *I fight so hard to be brave, to be honest,* he told himself. *Why is this little thing about the fast triggering me and making me crazy?*

"It's just a matter of time before we pay for burying the truth," Ahmad mumbled under his breath, his words barely disguised. "Facing it is the only way out."

"Sorry, what was that, Ahmad?" asked Hassan.

Ahmad blinked his way out of his stupor.

"Umm, sorry. Thinking about something."

Hassan looked curiously at him. "Anything I can help with?"

"Not really. I was thinking about hunger."

"Well, food is coming soon," replied Murtaza.

Ahmad chose not to belabor the issue.

"Let's get to it then, shall we?" Hassan said, before pausing briefly to check his watch. "I have to be at another meeting within the hour. Perhaps you are wondering why I invited Murtaza here? Well, I just thought that he might be able to add something to your article. Not only is he contributing to the Palestinian cause, but he also has friends in the Christian community. He might be able to give you an angle there. I mean, if you are truly writing on behalf of all parties, it would be wise to include them as well...not that any of this is going to make a difference. But I do admire your effort, Ahmad."

Ahmad nodded. "Thank you, sir. I appreciate it, sir."

"Please. Call me Hassan. What would you like to ask us?"

Ahmad pulled his notepad and pen from his pocket. He flipped a few pages until he found a clear one, clicked the end of the pen, then looked over at both of them.

"With regard to the Palestinians, what do you see as the main objective of your group?"

"It's simple," replied Hassan. "To liberate all of Palestine from any Jewish control, and create a new state."

"And how would that be accomplished?"

"By pushing the Jews out of our land, once and for all…from the Jordan River to the Mediterranean Sea…out of the entire area. Completely."

Ahmad looked up at him. He thought he could actually feel Hassan's piercing stare.

"You asked," Hassan said matter-of-factly.

"I don't get the sense that all of us Palestinians support that, especially those in the West Bank."

"Things have changed over the last handful of years," Hassan replied. "You must know that. When we…Hamas, that is…took over Gaza in 2007, many thought our tactics and our goal of becoming an Islamic state were too extreme. But Israel has continued to bully us, more so than ever before…and here in Gaza in particular, where we are mostly dependent on their communications, electricity infrastructure, and water supply. They tighten the band around our throats every day. Our people are hungry. Our people are thirsty. We are trapped, without a way to fight back. Because of this, the momentum is swinging away from people in favor of two independent states, one for us and one for Israel. More and more are now in favor of regaining all the land we once owned."

Ahmad tapped his pen against the notebook. "The majority of people, on both sides, still feel that a two-state solution would be best. And that a single state would work, neither Palestinian nor Israeli, but one with equal rights for all inhabitants, where people can live together…as they did for so many years in the past."

"Impossible!" Hassan replied, raising his voice and banging his fist on the table, startling both Ahmad and Murtaza. "It has gone too far! They continue to break promises and push us out of our homes. When the Americans declared Jerusalem to be the location of their new embassy, they sent the message to the world that all of Jerusalem belonged only to Israel. I think it broke the back of any joint solution to our situation, at least in my eyes. Through the centuries everyone has known that the magic of Jerusalem was that it was a great *shared* city. The people of all the faiths here shared its wonder, together, in harmony."

Hassan hit his fist lightly on the table. "And now these new Israeli settlements on our land are claimed to be legal, turning the threads of the screw to their last possible rotation."

Ahmad scribbled as fast as he could, then looked up again at Hassan, noting the fire in his eyes. He straightened his spine, keeping his own eyes steady, then spoke slowly and softly. "Why should we push them into the sea? Don't they have a right to be here as well?" He glanced over at Murtaza and then back to Hassan.

"You surprise me, Ahmad," Hassan said, calming his voice. "For someone who lives in Gaza, you appear to be an apologist for the Israelis."

"Not at all. I am a journalist. This is my job. I'm only suggesting that perhaps there is not much difference between what we call Israeli defensiveness and arrogance, and what they call Palestinian defensiveness and hostility."

"You make it sound like we both have reasons to feel defensive."

"Isn't that possible? Maybe even likely?"

"Allah is on our side, Ahmad. We will win."

"Many Israelis might claim God is on theirs."

"Blasphemy," Hassan returned, his voice harsh. "Allah is the only true one."

"I thought all three religions believe in the God of Abraham," Ahmad replied, "no matter what he is called. Is that not right?"

Hassan frowned but did not answer. Murtaza rubbed his hands together slowly, studying Ahmad. "You're a smart young man, Ahmad. But suppose it really doesn't matter? What if, soon, nothing will matter?"

"What do you mean?" asked Ahmad.

"The Christians claim their God to be the right one." Murtaza replied. "What I mean is that many Christians I know believe in the Rapture…the end times. Do you know what that is?"

"Yes, generally," Ahmad answered. "It's when the world will end, and true believers will be sent to heaven. Allah will send a savior, and that will occur the day before Judgment Day, when the Guided One, the Imam Mahdi, appears. But what does that have to do with this?"

"The Jews also believe in the end time." Murtaza replied. "Or apocalypse…whatever you want to call it. They call it the *end of times*. And along with us, they believe the Messiah has not yet come but is soon to appear. The Christians believe that Jesus is that Messiah and that he will come again, through the Eastern Gate of Jerusalem, signaling the end is near. I'm just saying, if all three faiths believe, in their own way, that the Messiah is coming soon and bringing the end of humanity with him, then one has to be right."

"What do you mean by *us*?" asked Ahmad. "I thought you were Christian."

"No. I should have been clearer. I was once a Christian but converted. I'm a Muslim now."

"So, what are you telling me? That all this conflict here…this death, pain, and misery, doesn't matter?" Ahmad sat back, stunned. "I can't believe that," he replied, grimacing.

"Christians here don't hate us Muslims," Murtaza continued. "They want to get along, like before. But many see Jerusalem as their salvation. It is why they support Israel, because of Jerusalem. They are helping to guard it—protecting it for the return of Jesus, whom they believe to be the real Messiah. Many Evangelical Christians believe they should hasten the end times. And why not…if that is the end anyway? And if all faiths believe something will happen soon, then there are only two questions left: When? And who is right?"

Ahmad locked onto Murtaza's eyes. Something about this man made his skin crawl, but he couldn't place it. "So, you have chosen our, shall I say, *team*?"

Murtaza was silent.

Ahmad, not knowing what more to say, turned his head to Hassan, silently questioning him.

"I have to admit, Ahmad," the Hamas leader said, "that Murtaza has surprised me too. But I can't disagree that Allah is the only one. However, since I don't know if the end is near or not, in the meantime I'll continue to fight for the survival and ultimate victory of the Palestinian cause. By any means possible."

Rafiq entered the room and set a large tray down at the end of the table. He placed two bowls of fruit, a basket of bread, and three small plates from the tray between them. He then poured a glass of water for each.

"Will that be all?"

"Yes," replied Hassan. "Please put it on my tab."

The waiter bowed slightly and left.

Hassan passed a plate to Murtaza, and then to Ahmad.

While the other two buttered the bread, ate the strawberries and pieces of melon, and sipped from their water glasses, Ahmad watched them with his mind wandering. *Was Murtaza hiding something? Was he suggesting the end time is closer than we know? Why did he convert, yet still maintain strong contacts with his old Christian friends? How was he supporting Hassan?*

"You're not eating, Ahmad." Hassan encouraged. "Have some. Enjoy. I thought you said you were hungry?"

Ahmad placed his hands on his lap. "I said I was *thinking about hunger*. But also about fasting…about honoring others who have nothing to eat today."

"And so should we all," replied Murtaza. "But this will just go to waste."

"No. I'm good, thanks," Ahmad insisted, feeling the tension leaving his body, his mind becoming more at peace. *No more lies.*

FORTY-ONE

MORNINGSTAR WALKED ALONGSIDE Liyah in the late afternoon, scouting the small shops and stands in the Beit Lahia market that offered women's articles for sale, like gold pendants, silver bracelets, fine silk scarfs, leather sandals, and colorful clothing of all kinds. They stopped in front of a table stacked with t-shirts. Morningstar watched as Liyah selected one with an eagle displayed against the background of the Palestinian flag. She checked out the size label and rubbed the material between her fingers.

"I don't think your mom would approve of seeing you in that," Morningstar chided, jokingly.

Liyah held the shirt against her cheek. "It wouldn't be for me, Star."

Morningstar noticed Liyah's eyes misting up. "You okay?"

"I fear there's no time left," Liyah replied. "What are we doing here, stuck without a car, and clues of Khalib slipping through our fingers? And you have to leave soon."

"I'll stay as long as it takes, Liyah. I told you that."

Liyah folded the t-shirt and set it back on the pile. "Khalib would like this. He loves his country."

"Well, get it for him then."

"What if he never comes home? It would only remind me of my failure."

"You're doing everything you can. If you buy it, maybe it will be like the *law of attraction*...help us get what we're seeking."

"I don't know, Star." She sighed. "I just don't know."

Morningstar could sense the pain weighing Liyah down. Her own heart sank with her friend's. She knew it was something she might have never felt if it weren't for meeting Liyah. Liyah's bottomless compassion helped her feel things she had buried since she was a little girl.

"What if we join the boys?"

"It's getting late," Liyah responded with sadness still evident in her voice. "Besides, they found nothing in the tunnel. And they're stuck somewhere near the West Bank now. Nothing is going to happen."

"You know better than to give up, Liyah. We have to be strong. We are the seed of hope for everyone. Isn't that what Ooray told us?"

"Yes, but it doesn't mean that we'll find Khalib. And while we look for him, we're actually *not* looking after others...only my own selfish needs."

"Enough with the self-pity. Who knows? Maybe Khalib will be one of our strongest warriors."

Liyah showed a hint of a smile and hugged her. "You're, well...just *you,* aren't you? Always a rock. *Our* warrior."

"Clearly not always," Morningstar protested. "But I will be one for you, here."

Liyah sighed again. She picked the t-shirt back up and took some cash from her purse.

Kai Li and Zack sat cross-legged on cushions in the large tent, amusing Yusuf and several local Bedouins, who hung on every word they said about America and Hong Kong. As the only who spoke both Arabic and English, Yusuf provided the translations.

"We famous travelers," Kai Li whispered under his breath to Zack before grinning ear to ear.

Zack held his finger to his lips. "Shhh!"

An outdated boombox in the center of the floor was playing a CD of an Arabic band from Dubai, when Zack's phone rang. It was Ahmad.

Zack turned to the side cupping his free hand over the phone. "Hello...Yeah, Kai Li and I are with Yusuf, at his home...Uh-huh...Just a minute." Zack handed the phone over. "Our friend, Ahmad, would like to speak with you."

Yusuf stood up and moved away to get clear of the music from the boombox. "Hello, Ahmad. What can I do for you?. . .Okay. One moment."

Yusuf took a pen from a small table, bent over, and wrote on a piece of paper. "Got it." He passed the phone back to Zack.

"Thanks, Ahmad. Will you be joining us?. . . Fine, I guess we'll see you sometime tomorrow...*Salaam.*"

"Important?" asked Kai Li, looking up.

"Could be. We're supposed to follow Yusuf to somewhere close by."

Yusuf nodded to Zack and then addressed the others in Arabic to excuse the emergency. He then led Kai Li and Zack from the tent to his car.

"How far is it," Zack asked, as they pulled onto the dirt road."

"Not far. Only about twenty minutes.

Zack and Kai Li explained how Liyah's brother may have gotten kidnapped, and the unsuccessful attempts so far to locate him. "Thanks for helping out," Zack added.

"Glad to do it. I'll be leaving the area soon, so you caught me just in time. I know some of these people, but many come and go. So, no guarantees."

"No guarantees," parroted Zack. "Understood."

"It might be a long shot," he said, "but I know this area. And I have a lot of eyes and ears around here that look out for me, to let me know if the Israelis are snooping about, or if anything unusual is happening that I should know about. I guess Ahmad heard from someone that Khalib may be in the area somewhere...perhaps at this camp. He sounded desperate. I also heard there has been some new activity there...plenty of new people arriving the other day. So, we'll see."

Yusuf parked the car near the entrance of the camp. Zack and Kai Li walked alongside Yusuf as he strolled up the dirt road, past some tents.

"So, Khalib here, then?" asked Kai Li

"Let's not get ahead of ourselves," Yusuf warned. "It's a good size camp, and it's not unusual that people come in and out. There are many different people and groups hiding in these parts, especially here, near the foothills, the West Bank, and Jordan... especially since Egypt is pretty closed off now."

"It doesn't sound very promising?" Zack noted.

Yusuf nodded in agreement.

"How will we ever find one person, particularly one who might *blend in*?" Zack asked.

"It's not that bad," Yusuf replied. "We'll do what we can. The good news is that my source tells me that the escape route to Egypt from the old airport has been closed off, so anyone looking to get out of the area within the last few days would likely come in this direction."

"Not sure if Khalib even escape tunnel near airport," Kai Li added.

"You might be right. Maybe he's not here at all. I've been to this camp before, but it was quite a while ago. Let's head up this way…where many newcomers stay."

Yusuf took them to the base of a small knoll. As they walked along, Kai Li and Zack scanned their surroundings, focusing now and then on various groupings of tents, looking for a sign…any sign.

For the most part, the people appeared disinterested in them, going about their business wearing battered expressions on their faces, trying to scratch out a living, survive the destruction of their homes and the lack of food and water. Only the children, as children can be, had any trace of real happiness in their eyes. The adults paid little attention to the three of them meandering through the camp. It was the children who ran up to Zack, reaching out to touch his red sweatshirt, attracted like young moths to a flame.

A handful of boys and girls gathered around him, twittering in Arabic and giggling. Kai Li snickered. "You a rock star! They not see anything like you before."

Zack's face transformed into one enormous grin. He held out his arm so the kids could play with his sleeve, then crouched down and lowered his hood, exposing his long, braided hair.

Kai Li laughed, watching them rub his head and pull gently on the braids that dangled over his ears. "Too bad we have to come here to feel good, instead of feeling it at home, huh?"

"It's a Jesus thing," Zack replied, holding his hand out to each of them, then standing up and pretending to dance.

"Jesus?"

"Yeah, you know…when he said *only in one's home and hometown is a prophet without honor*. It means people see you as they think they know you…especially those who have known you when you grew up. The image that they had of you remains. It's the only one they are comfortable with. They don't want you to change, or maybe don't believe you can, because they feel stuck themselves."

"You mean like false story you tell yourself of who you are, before you can become whole again. Like in letter from Ooray."

"Exactly. If you go home as a new person, people turn away. I think they are afraid they have lost you, or maybe you remind them of someone they would really like to be, but feel stuck in their own lives. Instead of changing, they deny you, so they don't have to face themselves."

"Maybe why they say sometimes you cannot go home?"

Zack broke free of the kids. "Yeah, something like that." He looked to his left, seeing Yusuf already heading up the hill. "We're going to lose him. Better hurry."

They waved to the children, finally catching up to Yusuf who was now standing in front of a large tent near the top of the hill, talking to a man in a black *thawb* and red bandanna. Yusuf was asking the man something. The only word recognizable to Kai Li and Zack was Khalib's name. The man shook his head and said something back in Arabic.

Yusuf turned to Kai Li and Zack. "He isn't aware of anyone with Khalib's description, or any new activity in the area. Come, let's move on."

They followed him to the next set of tents and stopped in front of one with a large tarp shading a chair placed near the entrance flap. Yusuf stepped inside. A few minutes later, he popped his head out and waved them in. In the tent, a man in jeans and tan tunic faced them. At the back of the tent stood two others, dressed similarly, both with white head wraps covering most of their faces.

The conversation between Yusuf and the man was brief. The man, his voice stern, called over to the others. One stepped forward, offering Yusuf some water in a metal cup. Yusuf declined, mentioning Ramadan, one of the few other words familiar to Kai Li. The young man turned to Zack, offering him the glass instead, but suddenly faltered and spilled the water down the front of his sweatshirt, dropping the cup. As they both bent down to retrieve it, they bumped into each other. Kai Li helped steady Zack. The water carrier, his young face wide-eyed, apologized profusely in Arabic, brushing the water vigorously from Zack's sweatshirt. The man with Yusuf yelled at him, apparently for his clumsiness, then said something else to Yusuf.

Yusuf paused for a moment, then bowed. "*Shukran…Salaam.*" He turned and exited the tent. The boys followed. Yusuf then led them to several other tents, with no success in locating Khalib, or even hearing of his possible whereabouts. Without another plan, Yusuf took them back to the car, and turned to them.

"I don't fully trust those men up there, especially that young one who spilled the water. He was told to bring it to you and Kai Li, since you were foreign guests, yet he offered it to me, knowing I'm Muslim and we should be fasting. Are you sure you didn't see anyone that looked like Khalib anywhere?"

"Well, it's hard to say," Zack replied. "Liyah only showed us one picture of him, with some friends. And with the headgear on some of these guys around here, who could say? How about you, Kai?"

"Same here. Did feel something strange like Yusuf say, but not look like a bunch of kidnappers."

Yusuf nodded. “No, they didn’t. I’m afraid we’re at a dead end, my friends.”

Forty-Two

SAYF YASIN TAPPED his finger on the table. "Go ahead, Jamal."

Jamal rose and stepped to the front, carrying a drone in one hand and a dummy explosive pack in the other.

"Sorry for the delay. We had to figure out what was going wrong when multiple drones tried to land or change formation. We got some last-minute assistance which helped a lot."

He turned the drone over, touching his pen to the underside. "We were having trouble because LEDs on the sides and underneath were not operating properly, especially the ones close to the explosive device. We found they could get blocked at times during maneuvering, depending on the proximity of each drone to its closest neighbors, causing some to spiral out of control and crash into the others."

Jamal placed the revised dummy packet in position under the drone, then moved it as one unit as he spoke, pointing so all could see.

"The newly beveled edges on the explosive packet allow for uninterrupted signal flow. We did a second test with the multiple drone configuration earlier today, and I'm happy to report that everything went very well. Well enough to give the drones the green light for tomorrow."

Yasin spoke as Jamal sat down and passed the drone and packet to the others.

"We ran two tests on the explosives at the testing facility. Nasir, could you please update everyone?"

"Yes, certainly," said Nasir. "We modified the packet by hand before the retest, but it will not compromise the explosives, or make them any less safe to attach to the drones. I checked with manufacturing, and they have put together a plan to rework all of the existing packets before affixing them to the drones tomorrow morning. In order to do that, a small team will be working through the night.

"As far as the actual explosive test…it couldn't have gone better. The test drone was able to enter the artillery gun barrel as designed, and explode near or at the shell housing, making the gun inoperable. When tested on a jet engine, the explosive not only destroyed most of the turbine blades, but it also completely blew apart the engine itself."

Nura handed the drone back to Jamal and turned to the CEO. "Is there any additional funding needed?"

"Well, we have it covered for now. But when we do a final accounting next week, I'd be happy to come to you, hat in hand, to cover the difference."

Nura nodded, her light eyes peering through the opening in her keffiyeh.

"What's the schedule look like now for the mission tomorrow?" asked Hassan.

Sayf Yasin leaned on the table. "After all the drones and explosive devices have gone through their final inspection, we will begin assembling them in groups by mid-morning. Each group will have a different mission as originally planned. The majority will be sent out in different sized clusters to the airfields, gunnery and tank locations throughout Israel. Most of the others will be sent on other special missions to knock out radar defenses and communication towers. The remainder will be given to Hassan, for special use by Hamas.

"There will be waves of attacks on all these targets, only a few hours apart. Not only to make sure we eliminate those targets, but also to take out the replacements they will bring in from airport hangars, buildings, and other sheltered areas which are currently hidden from our view."

"How many drones in all will be deployed?" asked Hassan

"Not counting yours," Jamal replied, "over seven thousand. We are holding back about twenty-five percent of the total arsenal to cover replacement and deployment at another time."

"They will lift off about five miles from here," added Nasir. "That will be led by Hassan's team. At that point, total secrecy will of course be difficult to guarantee. Jamal will be here for the first wave but return to the tech center, even though it is Sunday so that he is not directly implicated should something happen. We will need his expertise in any future missions."

"We have people stationed in the cities, especially Jerusalem, and near the bases, to report back as things unfold." added Hassan. "That way, we can ascertain the level of success for each wave, the highest hit rate, and how best to follow up."

"And to address what we all agreed on earlier," Nura added, glancing around the table, her eyes flashing, "all of the missions and use of explosives is for defensive purposes only...to attack their *machinery* so it can't hurt us anymore. Not to kill anyone. Correct?"

Everyone nodded, except Hassan. She glared at him.

"Yeah, yeah," he finally agreed. "Of course."

Nura let her stare linger. "Better be," she replied.

Hassan slapped the edge of the table with his palm, his ire taking over. "Or what?...Just what?" he challenged, his voice sharp.

Nura continued staring at him until he turned away.

"Okay, okay," admonished Yasin. "Things are tense, but we can't afford to be fighting each other. There is no need for another meeting. We don't want to risk compromising anything at this point. We can communicate via coded text messages tomorrow. But keep them to a minimum. Like I said before...we all have a lot to lose. I'm already deeper in this than I planned to be."

Jamal was the first to rise. "Thank you, everyone. It's been a pleasure. Tomorrow is a big day for Palestine. May Allah go with you all."

They all shook hands. Hassan stayed to talk with Yasin and Nasir. Jamal walked Nura through the underground passageway, out the bulkhead door, and toward the parking lot.

"What's with you and Hassan?" Jamal asked.

"You mean besides the fact that his ego is larger than the moon and he mistreats women?"

Jamal laughed. "You should be used to that, being a Muslim woman, and knowing men in general." He laughed again.

"I don't trust him."

"Because he belittles women?"

"No," Nura replied. "Because of his eyes."

"His eyes?"

Nura stopped walking. "Yes. The windows to his soul...How all of us can be read."

"Some people will likely get hurt, maybe even die tomorrow." Jamal cautioned. "Nothing can be assured. Maybe that's why he doesn't answer you at times."

"That's not it, either," Nura replied. "I simply don't trust him. You can't act like those who harm you. It just gives them fodder for more oppression. We must have the strength to be bigger than that. We cannot compromise with evil doers. Ever."

As their eyes remained fixed on each other, Jamal's smile melted away. "I have to ask you something."

"What's that?"

"I checked your car out yesterday. I like BMWs so I took a look." He hesitated briefly. "I...I saw an Israeli sticker on your window."

Nura waited for a moment before replying. "Oh, well I can see your concern. I have connections. It's a way I get in and out of Gaza. No one there knows my real identity…Let's just leave it at that, okay?"

Jamal studied her. "You're a tough one, Nura," he said, finally prying his stare away. "Whatever you say. This project will be over tomorrow, anyway."

FORTY-THREE

Talbiya

AHMAD PULLED INTO the guest parking lot across from the hospital entrance, shut the engine off, and checked the time. He reached down, lifted the seat lever, and eased himself to a comfortable position as he waited to hear from Esty. *Probably fifteen or twenty minutes,* he figured. He clicked a playlist on his phone, turned the car speakers up, and nestled in, occasionally glancing toward the walkway near the main entrance.

Twelve minutes later, a dark form approaching the entrance caught his eye. The sun was almost down, and was blocked by the hospital building. Enough light remained for him to clearly make out a small dark form carrying a package, and wearing the traditional white Palestinian keffiyeh. He knew who it was. She was *unmistakable.* Her picture had been all over the papers in Palestine the last year, and especially lately.

He sat back again and listened to a couple more tunes. As the last one ended, he turned down the volume on the car speaker and picked up his phone. He texted Esty.

ETA?

The response came quickly.

Five min

Ahmad turned the volume back up and reset the seat to his driving position. He gazed out to the intersection near the hospital. Traffic had been picking up rapidly over the last few hours. *Almost dusk,* he reminded himself. *People are anxious to end the fast for the day.* His stomach let out an audible grumble as he thought about not having anything to eat or drink since early morning. And now he had to drive Esty home, and then come all the way back to Gaza.

His mind wandered, first recounting the busy day he had already had, then skipping back to being with Esty and the others at the Mount the previous day…*what was that about anyway?* Things were happening so fast that he had almost put Ooray completely out of his head. He drifted some more. *And what about the article? I've got to get that done! And then there's Khalib…so many pieces to keep moving.*

There was a tap on his window. It was Esty.

Ahmad unlocked the passenger door. She opened it and slid in, tossing her backpack into the rear seat.

"You looked like you were in a trance."

Ahmad started the engine. "Sorry, thinking about things."

"Like what?"

"Oh…just stuff. How'd you know where I was parked?"

"There aren't too many cars here. I didn't see you at the curb when I came out of the hospital…and I know your car, of course."

"I was checking over there, thinking the wind was picking up and making it a bit nippy…that maybe you went in to warm up. But since I didn't see you, I figured you hadn't come back from your meeting yet, so I chilled out here."

Esty balked. "Uh, well, yeah. I did go in…for a couple of minutes…that's when I got your text."

Ahmad was perplexed. He pulled the car out of the lot and onto the main street. "Did you see Nura in there?"

"Nura? Who's that?"

"She's the one in the black trench coat outfit and white keffiyeh."

"No idea. Why would I know her?"

"Just because her picture is in the papers a lot."

"Well, probably *your* papers, Ahmad. Don't forget I don't live here."

"Perhaps. But I seem to recall seeing her picture in at least one of the Israeli papers. We get all the papers delivered to the Dawn…competition, you know."

"Well, I don't know anything about her. What makes her so special to you?"

"Not to me," Ahmad protested. "She's someone who apparently donates money to the hospitals and helps out many Palestinians who are caught up in the violence these days. But it's the mystery that surrounds her that everyone comments on. She seems to just *pop up*, and then disappear. And there's the clothes she wears…the ones I was describing. She must have walked right by you."

"Hmm," Esty replied. "No, I must have been in the ladies' room."

Ahmad glanced at her curiously but became suddenly distracted as the driver in the next lane cut him off, trying to make a turn.

After passing through the border check and nearing Talbiya, Ahmad exited the main road and swung the car onto Esty's street, pulling up by the gate.

"Here you go."

Esty grabbed her pack and opened the car door. "Come in for a snack?"

"Oh, I don't think so. I should be getting back."

"You were complaining the whole time about how hungry you are. It's getting dark, so you can eat now, right? Maybe my dad has dinner already on the table. He enjoys cooking and loves to have guests."

"Well…I don't know," Ahmad replied, his resistance breaking down.

"Don't be silly. I insist. Park the car over there by the garage. I'll wait here." She climbed out and stood by the gate.

Ahmad hesitated briefly before fully caving in. He returned a few minutes later and they made their way to the front door. Esty unlocked it, showing him in.

Sweet scents wafting through the hall caught Ahmad's attention.

"Pops?" Esty called out.

"In the den. Be right there…And *stop that!*"

"Sorry, dad. Still in my head."

"This place is even more impressive on the inside," Ahmad observed, scanning his surroundings, and noting the archways into the rooms off the hall, the vaulted ceilings, and the elegant wood rails of the stairway. "Smells good, too."

"He's definitely been working on dinner."

"Well, I can't stay for that. I thought you said *snack*."

Esty ignored him, opening her pack and removing her blue puffy cap. She hung it on the hook near the door and then headed up the stairs. "Make yourself at home. I'll be right down."

Ahmad stayed put, afraid to venture even a few steps away from the hall bureau. A few minutes later Esty's dad appeared from the den, heading for the kitchen. He noticed Ahmad standing near the front door and walked toward him.

"My apologies, Esty didn't tell me she was having a guest for dinner. Just like her." He held out his hand. "I'm her dad, obviously."

Ahmad reached out and shook his hand. "Hello, Dr. Blum. I'm Ahmad…from the Dawn. We spoke earlier today."

Esty's dad paused for a moment, then smiled broadly. "Yes. Yes. Welcome, Ahmad. Nice to have you visit. Esty can be a bit scattered at times. She didn't tell me. Did you bring her here all the way from Gaza?"

"Yes, sir. She needed a ride to get to a meeting there."

"In Gaza? How interesting."

Suddenly Ahmad wished he could take it back. *'Interesting' is a word parents use when something doesn't quite sit well with them*, he thought.

"Well, thank you," Esty's dad continued. "Come. Join me in the kitchen. I just have to check on something. I'm sure she'll be right down, after she finishes whatever it is that they do when they keep you waiting." He grinned.

Ahmad smiled and followed him.

"We're having what we call second Seder tonight," her dad said, as he removed the lid from a pot and stirred its contents with a wooden spoon. "It's the second meal of Passover. I understand you are Muslim, so you may not be familiar with Jewish traditions."

"A little bit…but not much," Ahmad confessed.

Her dad chuckled. "I probably know about as much of your customs. Passover is the celebration of the Israelites being led out of slavery in Egypt by Moses. It signifies the *passing over* of the forces of harm…the sparing of the children…and Moses leading our people to the land promised to them by God. Here in the Levant."

"Esty says you're a great cook. What are you making?"

Her dad smiled. "Not sure about that. I cook on special occasions but try to get Esty to cook most of the time. My wife is not here to cook for me anymore, so I had to learn to survive when Esty is not available. I've found it's relaxing, and better for Esty than the fast food and packaged junk kids eat these days. Take a whiff."

Ahmad leaned over the pot. "Cinnamon?"

"And right you are. It's called *haroset*, a mixture of apples, nuts, cinnamon, and wine. You have a good nose. We men were not gifted with the sense of smell like women. I think their sensitivity is something like ten times ours. I always wondered a little about that…since they have to live with us men."

Ahmad laughed.

"I heard that," said Esty, entering the kitchen. "Gosh, dad. I mean really. I'm away for a minute and you're already saying gross things to Ahmad. Totally embarrassing."

"Well it's not *gross*, as you put it…simply a fact." He chuckled.

Esty shook her head at both of them.

"It's almost ready," her dad added. "Why don't you set the dining room table, sweetie? There's plenty for the three of us, even though you like to keep me in the dark."

Ahmad watched Esty roll her eyes as she headed to the cupboard to get some plates. "Don't worry about me, sir. I was only going to steal a snack."

"Nonsense," her dad retorted. "You will be our honored guest. It's the least I can do, considering you've been looking after her. And one thing I do know about Islam is that Ramadan is happening now, and you must be famished from fasting. Besides, how many chances will you have to share Passover with a Jewish family?"

"Oh, Dad," Esty complained from the dining room, as she removed the fine silver settings from the drawer in the tall bureau and placed them on the table.

"Take a seat in there, Ahmad. I'll bring this out in a minute."

Ahmad joined Esty in the dining room and sat down where she directed him. As she continued to set the table, he glanced around the room, noting the brass chandelier with its crystal glass pendants dangling down, and the fine embroidered white tablecloth. Two crystal wine glasses were positioned above the plates, one across from him, and one at the head at her father's seat. *It's a beautiful home,* he thought. *And her dad's obviously a nice man. They may kid each other…but there is love here. Yes. Love resides in this house.*

"You've gone silent, Ahmad," said Esty as she took her chair across from him.

"Just thinking."

"Not again," she joked.

The journey his mind had begun to take—to a darker place of loneliness and of sadness, was halted by the beauty of her smile, and the caring that seemed to always be present in her eyes. The corners of his mouth turned up. "You're a lucky lady."

Her dad entered the room carrying a serving bowl filled with the *haroset.* "Did you say something about being lucky, Ahmad? We are the ones who are lucky to share a meal with you." He set it on the table and returned to the kitchen.

A moment later, he was back with a large plate of the traditional matzah flatbread. After setting it next to the *haroset,* he selected a bottle of wine from the rack next to the bureau and pulled the cork. Noticing Ahmad had no wine glass, he retrieved one from the cabinet and set it down in front of him. He began pouring the wine, starting with his guest.

Ahmad began to protest, holding up his hand, but then thought the better of it and let her dad continue. *Now is not the time,* he considered. *Besides, I'm really not what my Muslim friends would call a strict adherent to the rules of Islam, anyway…not at times of certain celebrations at least.*

Esty's dad brought the two unlit candles at the center of the table closer, then slid the oil vessel with its flame already strong, in between them. Taking his chair at the head, he raised his glass. "Welcome to our home, Ahmad. We are pleased to share this very special time with you. I know most Muslims do not drink alcohol, so please do not feel obligated. I just didn't want to make assumptions and leave you out. I look at this as a spiritual offering, not as a casual affair. Neither Esty nor I drink alcohol, other than at these times…to show appreciation for life, home, and the blessings we have been afforded."

Esty clinked her glass gently against her dad's, followed by Ahmad.

Her dad took a match from a small box next to his plate and handed it to his daughter. "Okay, dear. Can you please light the first candle?"

Esty held the end of the match above the flame of the vessel. After catching fire, she transferred the flame to the wick of the candle then blew out the match.

"I light this candle in remembrance of Passover, in gratefulness for the delivery of the Jewish people from slavery to safety."

Her father turned to Ahmad, handing him another match. "The second candle signifies the hope of peace. Will you do the honors?"

"Okay. Is there a special thing about the vessel? I noticed it was already lit."

"Yes," Esty replied. "It represents my mother. We try to keep it lit all through Passover. Since we both may be away from the house, the candles need to be put out, for safety. The flame of the vessel can then be used to relight the two candles. My mother sort of becomes the firekeeper, so to speak." She smiled at Ahmad, the flame of the vessel reflected in her eyes. "When you light the candle using the flame from the vessel, you bring her home, to celebrate with us."

Ahmad felt his eyes begin to well up. He fought off his thoughts of sadness for their loss—sadness for what *might have been* for him, and sadness for the struggle of his homeland. He held the match to the vessel's flame then touched the wick of the second candle. When the flame took hold, he blew out the match and placed it on the edge of the vessel.

He bent his head for a brief moment, as if in prayer, then lifted his eyes to the candle. "I light this candle, that its light may bring peace to this long-suffering region, and to all our families, whether Jewish, Muslim or Christian. That we may live together as we once did…not so long ago. And that a mother's peace—a wife's peace—may always find its home here, for all time."

Tears burst from Esty's eyes and poured down her cheeks. She dabbed them with her cloth napkin and turned away. Her father looked at Ahmad and nodded ever so slowly.

"You bring love and comfort with you to our home, Ahmad. Thank you."

"Love was already here, sir."

Esty escaped into the kitchen without saying a word.

Ahmad glanced at her father with a look of apology.

"She'll be back in a minute. She still has difficulty, especially at times like this." He passed the dish of flatbread to Ahmad. "Here, let's get started. You have a long drive back."

Liyah and Morningstar entered the kitchen, startling Liyah's mother as she stood stirring something on the counter, the whir of mixer blades drowning out their footsteps.

"Goodness! You'll give me a heart attack, creeping up on me like that."

"We weren't *creeping,* Mama," Liyah protested.

"What did you girls do all this time, after bringing your father back from the office?" She lifted the mixer from the bowl. "Seemed awfully quiet up there."

Liyah didn't answer. Standing by the sink and staring out the window, her mind drifted, replaying the movie reel of the past couple of days—being with her friends, this time at her home in Palestine. Getting to know Ahmad better. Meeting Esty. Seeing Ooray at the Mount of Olives. Desperately searching for Khalib. So many thoughts spinning around in her head.

"Liyah?. . .Liyah!"

Huh?. . .Oh, what?

"Gracious, child. What's come over you lately?"

"We were chatting about Ahmad, Mrs. Rahim," Morningstar chimed in, rescuing Liyah, temporarily. "He's a nice boy, isn't he? Even quite handsome on top of it all, I'd say." She laughed nervously.

When Liyah's mom looked over at Morningstar, Liyah pressed her finger to her lips and shook her head at her friend.

"Only him? All this time?" Liyah's mom replied in a surprised tone, setting Morningstar back on her heels.

"Just talk, Mama," Liyah insisted. "You know. Nothing much."

"You barely know him."

Liyah looked over at Morningstar, lifting her palms and shrugging her shoulders before turning back to her mom. "I'm almost seventeen."

"What does that mean?" her mom replied. "You haven't been formally introduced. And don't disrespect me with that shrugging business, young lady."

"Seriously Mama? In this day and age?" Liyah glanced again at Morningstar for some reassurance, then faced her mom again. "Besides, we *have* been introduced…don't you remember what Baba said the other day at his work?"

"Don't fight me, Liyah. You know I'm the one who should be approving your relationships. I know this is a special time while we try to find your brother, and Ahmad's help is appreciated. But when this is all over, and Khalib is finally home, we need to return back to normal."

"Normal? What does *normal* mean?" Liyah shot back, releasing her pent-up frustration. She stared at her mother, locked in the moment until she felt the tears pour down her face. She brought her eyes to the floor.

Her mother moved toward her, touching her shoulder, then lifting her chin and hugging her. "I'm sorry, dear. It's these times, and the loss of Khalib. It's all too much. We'll figure something out." She used her thumbs to wipe away Liyah's tears. "Now go tell your father to finish up on his work. Dinner is almost ready."

Forty-Four

AHMAD PICKED UP his knife and pasted the unleavened bread with the *haroset*, then took several large bites. "Very good," he said, his words almost indecipherable from his mouth half full of crackers, and a day without water. He gulped down half of the water from his glass, coughing in between gulps.

Esty's dad laughed. "It's good though, right? If I do say so myself."

As Ahmad collected himself, Esty reentered the room.

"So sorry," Ahmad managed.

"No, it's me," Esty replied. "That was nice, Ahmad." She sat back down.

Ahmad listened as Esty's dad shared some of his meeting at the IDF—the likely closure of the borders, the concern for possible attacks from Gaza, chaos in Jerusalem...things Ahmad was already concerned about himself. It made him wonder if he should stay up all night and write his article so it would be released before any trouble began. He sensed his mind drifting off again, then felt Esty kick him from under the table, snapping him back into the conversation.

Rising from her seat, Esty took the remainder of *haroset* into the kitchen. She removed the brisket from the slow cooker on the counter, then retrieved the potatoes au gratin and baby artichoke dishes from the warm oven. In two trips, she filled the water glasses and placed the serving dishes on the dining table.

As they ate the main meal, Ahmad felt his hunger recede. He suddenly realized he had barely looked up as he shoveled the food down. He gazed over at Esty and her dad, relieved that they seemed focused on the meal as well.

"You must learn a lot about the different religions, Esty," he said. "Doing so many tours in Jerusalem, I mean."

"Yeah, I enjoy them. Lots of people from all over the world come here. But I'm afraid my knowledge of Islam and Christianity is pretty superficial. I naturally learn about some of the history of Jerusalem and Israel, and the details behind the construction of the Old City - the churches, synagogues, mosques, and temples. And I also pick up a few things about the religious teachings found in the books like the Bible, Quran, Torah, and Talmud. But since I don't practice all the religions, my knowledge is limited. And people within each of these religions practice and believe differently, too."

"But you do have a sense of the common beliefs of all these," her dad replied, "like compassion and forgiveness. What you were saying the other day. The things you talked about in the Garden of Gethsemane and on the Mount of Olives with your new friends from America and Hong Kong."

"Ahmad was there, too," Esty added.

"Yes, of course." her dad replied. "And what did you think of that, Ahmad?"

He had missed a few details of the conversation, his mind wandering once more to his yet-to-be completed article. *What's wrong with me,* he thought, looking like a deer caught in the headlights. Had she told her dad about what went on that day on the Mount?

"Ahmad?" Esty prompted.

He looked at her, a forkful of potatoes au gratin poised to enter his mouth. "Uh, you mean the powers?"

"Powers?" asked her father.

Ahmad felt the heat of Esty's glare.

"I have no idea what you're talking about, Ahmad," she said, a sharp edge in her voice. "He wants to know about the things we talked about." She softened her tone a bit. "You know…the spiritual things that all religions share, like love and connectedness."

Ahmad sensed a touch of uneasiness as if he was now under a spotlight. "Oh," he replied, turning to her dad. "Yes. And each seems to also have a mystical side as well. For Islam, it's called Sufism. It's kind of like trying to understand your life and the universe through your own personal connection with Allah, and the giving up of what you might call *worldly things*. It's what I identify with the most."

"I visit the Mosque and pray five times a day, and fast…well, at least I try." He let out an abbreviated laugh, still trying to ease the situation and gauge her father's reactions. He continued. "I see the good that having a belief, and gathering with others of the same belief, can do. And the caring that some of these groups show for others in the world. But a part of me also sees the history of great harm caused by these same religions…the fostering of the wrong notion that any person is better than another...or *different* from each other. The chains of structure and power can often be the breeding ground for the ego...for hatred, wars, and persecution. It blinds people. Somehow, they lose the ability to see the harm they are causing others, the harm that is happening still to my Palestinian brothers and sisters."

He caught Esty's eye, seeking a hint of approval, wondering if he had recovered her favor, or perhaps faltered even worse. After all, he really didn't know her dad, did he? Only what he had learned during the interview.

A warm smile crept over Esty's face, much to Ahmad's relief.

"Very well said, Ahmad," Esty's dad noted. "I can see why you want to be a journalist. You have the eye of an independent observer."

"Yeah, I agree, Dad. And I completely get that mystical connection." She shifted her gaze to Ahmad. "I feel the same way about my own religion sometimes. Maybe it's why I don't follow all the guidelines either or attend Synagogue as much as I should. But I have been reading a lot about Kabbalah, the mystical part of Judaism found in the Zohar. *Zohar* means *radiance* in Hebrew." She glanced to her right, "Did you know that, Dad?"

Before her father could answer, she turned back again to Ahmad. "Kabbalists believe their main mission is to restore God's light, the light that has been lost by humanity. I see it as a path for me, and for all of us. I talked to Liyah and Morningstar about the situation here, and Morningstar said it seemed much like what had happened to her tribe, when settlers moved west across America and claimed the land for themselves without considering those who had already been there a long time. She said their mission is to restore the light to the world. It seems much like the message of the Kabbalists to me."

Ahmad smiled at her. Her bubbly enthusiasm had returned, something that attracted him to her, acting on him like a gravitational force of some sort. But he couldn't tell if her dad was concerned about her newly announced interest in the mystical side of her religion. He had noticed her father's expression become more serious as she spoke.

Esty's dad cleared his throat. "The world these days seems to be darkened by fear, and that fear is the fuel for extremists everywhere. The vast majority of people in Iran, Palestine, and other Arabic nations do not hate Jews, but many have been conned by the extreme elements around them. Similarly, Jews do not hate Muslims, but live in fear of being pushed into the sea. So, we overreact and allow the small minds of some of our own leaders to wave the fear card before us and cloud our judgment.

"We need both a wise head and an open heart. I may be from the old school, but because we live in these imperfect minds and bodies,

I believe we need structure at times too. Don't you think? We need both the heart and the head—empathy, and connection as well as the knowledge and awareness of our collective human history."

Esty's dad reached out, gently grasping his daughter's hand. A huge smile captured his entire face. "At this moment, sweetie, your mother has never been more proud of you, nor have I."

The love between the two was palpable to Ahmad. It radiated like the sun and warmed everything in its path.

Yes, he thought. *Love indeed resides here.*

SUNDAY

Forty-Five

KHALIB HAD SPENT a restless night worrying about what was going to happen when the morning came. Finally dozing off, he was immediately reawakened by voices from the other section of the tent. He strained his ears to hear to decipher the discussion.

Mabood, head of the Khalib's group in the tunnel, was talking to two other men. Khalib couldn't quite get all the details of the plan, but he had previously overheard enough to know that a group of them were going to slip into the outskirts of Tel Shiva to steal food, and maybe a couple of vehicles. After that, sometime, perhaps mid-morning, they would break down the camp and make the journey through the hills and into Jordan, and then to Syria. Once there, he and the other captives would become part of a larger camp, before being shipped somewhere more permanently. *Maybe a country like Ethiopia or Somalia in Africa,* he wondered, *or even Afghanistan…or who knows where?* What he was sure of, though, was that this would be his last day in his homeland and that his slim hope for going home, of being rescued, was evaporating.

"All right, let's get a move on," Khalib heard Mabood say. "You two will be in charge. Take one of the two vans parked in front of this tent and leave one here. Choose one guard to go with each of you. And pick one prisoner each too. We'll need them to help pull this off. On the way back, two of you will be in each van, one to drive and one to watch one over this guy." He pointed to Khalib. "With four of you gone, we'll have just enough of us left to keep an eye on the others here at camp. If anyone tries to escape, shoot them. We can't afford to mess this up now. We need to get to the border by the afternoon. The two men we have planted there will get off duty at four, and we can't stay in this country one more day. The noose is narrowing."

A few minutes later, Khalib heard the flap between the two sections of the tent being pulled aside. He clamped his eyes shut, pretending to be still asleep. He picked up the sound of footsteps approaching him. A boot slammed into his ribs.

"Get up!"

Khalib tossed the blanket to the side and stood up, holding his side.

"You're coming with me. We have a job for you."

Khalib didn't recognize the man. He thought he must have been already in the camp when he was brought there. "Where are we going?" he asked.

"Never mind that now. Let's go."

Khalib brushed his wavy hair with his fingers, rubbed his tired eyes with his fists, and followed the man out of the tent. They stopped at the side of a van. Another man was waiting there. As the two men spoke, Khalib looked out into the darkness. It was not yet dawn, and the moon still cast a shadow of his form on the ground, although less defined than it would be from a full moon. He glanced up at its light in the cloudless sky. It was in its crescent phase, providing enough light to make one's way around without tripping, but not enough to see anything in great detail. He gazed at the starry sky. There were more stars than he recalled ever seeing. *Perhaps because this is the edge of the desert?*

He tilted his head back, looking straight up, and focused on what seemed to be a kind of small, foggy group of stars. *Part of the Milky Way,* he imagined. *Or maybe the Andromeda Galaxy?* He had just learned more about them at school. The brightest star in the sky then caught his attention, sitting right above the thin crescent of the moon, poised as if it might drop at any moment into its scoop. *Not a star at all, but a planet,* he recalled. *Venus.*

The combination of the crescent moon, with Venus close by, reminded him of the symbol of Islam…of his homeland…and of his people. It trapped his mind and sent it reeling. With hope dangling by a thread, worry crept into the remaining vacuum of his thoughts. He felt it grab him by his throat, and squeeze. The muscles in his body begin to quiver. He brought his eyes down from the heavens and clamped them shut. *I am never going to see my family again, am I? I am going to be lost forever.*

A sudden "Hey, you!" jolted his eyes open. "Get in the van!"

Khalib obeyed, climbing in and sitting between one of the guards and another prisoner he knew from the journey through the tunnel. One guard sat behind them in the third seat of the van. One more guard sat shotgun to the driver. Both carried repeating rifles, and an extra belt of bullets over one shoulder.

It seemed to Khalib that the trip to Tel Shiva took almost no time at all, but he knew his mind was racing, trying desperately to fight off the urge to panic.

The driver pulled the van into a large parking lot at a dealership on the outskirts of the city. No one was around. He drove through a few rows of used vans until he found one similar to the one they were in. He shut off the lights and signaled to the man next to him. They both jumped out and approached the other van. The driver carried a long flat tool that he used to force open the door while the other man kept guard. There was no movement anywhere nearby.

Once in the empty parked van, the driver bent down toward the ignition. A few minutes later Khalib heard the engine start. The man with the machine gun returned, motioning to the guard sitting next to Khalib to move into the driver's seat. The guard behind Khalib told the other prisoner to get out, then took his seat while the guard with the machine gun led Khalib's fellow prisoner to the stolen van.

Khalib's van followed the other one out of the dealership to a small shopping mall a few blocks away. The van stopped by the curb at the entrance to a supermarket. The guard waved the driver of Khalib's van past. Khalib's van then stopped in front of a sporting goods store three buildings down.

"Out!" said the driver, peering at Khalib through the rearview mirror.

Khalib got out and stood next to the man who had been guarding him. The guard motioned for him to follow. Approaching the main entrance, he smashed open the window with his rifle butt, reached past the glass, and unlatched the door. He did the same to the inner door, entering the store. He shot off several rounds, disabling the alarm system before the motion detectors could kick in. Then returning quickly with a couple of heavy objects, he set them down to prevent the doors from closing.

Once both of them were inside, he handed Khalib a list and pointed to the items checked in red. "Get these and put them in the van!" he demanded. "Do it fast. And then get your ass back in your seat. Don't even think about anything else!"

Khalib scanned the list: twelve sleeping bags, twelve backpacks, six canteens for water, two compasses, and five boxes of energy bars. Items checked in blue were what the guard would apparently get: blankets, binoculars, zippered running jackets, dozens of sets of hiking pants, and a handful of other items.

"Get moving!" ordered the guard.

Hustling through the aisles, Khalib made trip after trip to the van. All the while he wished he was older, or at least bigger, so he could carry more things and make fewer trips. Or even overpower the guard. He felt angry and frightened at the same time. On his final trip into the store, he had difficulty locating the energy bars, but finally caught a glimpse of them on display near the cash register. He moved behind the counter to see if there were more of them underneath. Bending down, he slid open the door to a cabinet and found a number of boxes. He grabbed several and started to stand up to place them on the counter. As he did so, his eye caught the silent alarm button, set under the lip of the counter.

Khalib paused for a moment, his mind swirling. *There is really nothing to lose anymore, is there?* He reached to press it.

CRACK!

The sound of a rifle butt smashing into the side of Khalib's head echoed through the store. He collapsed onto the tiled floor, motionless.

Forty-Six

AT EARLY MORNING light, after eating his breakfast in preparation for the day's fast, Yusuf lightly jostled Zack and Kai Li awake from their cozy sleeping quarters where they were lying on hand-made carpets, amongst soft pillows, and wrapped in cotton quilts. Once they were functioning, he served them bread dipped in olive oil and thyme that was called za'atar, along with eggs, cheese, and yogurt.

"Sorry, boys. I wanted to get an early start. I could use your help with the falcons this morning. I want to make sure they're ready for their performance in Jerusalem, and I promised Ahmad that I'd have you back to Bethlehem late morning. Ahmad said he needed some time to work on something and asked me if I could have someone get you there."

After washing the dishes using the sand from outside the tent along with a small amount of water, he took them to the field. Dawoud was waiting with Taliq and two other falcons.

"*As-Salaam-Alaikum*," Yusuf called out as they approached. "What have you got there?"

Dawoud turned. "*Wa-Alaikum-Salaam.* How is everyone this morning?"

"Hello, Dawoud," replied Zack. "Really great, my man. Never knew you could be so comfortable sleeping on the ground." He smiled over at Yusuf.

"Hi, Dawoud!" echoed Kai Li.

"Hi guys!" replied Dawoud. "Hassan thought it might be interesting to fly a handful of the drones with the falcons during the event. So I've been working on seeing if I could teach the birds to recognize them, and think of a few routines."

"A little chancy with all the security there today, don't you think?" Yusuf cautioned.

"Perhaps, but it sure would be interesting. The falcons are approved by Israeli security and Hassan said the drones will not be an issue. I'm thinking we should act now and apologize later…if we have to." He let out a short laugh. "Best to not say anything until after the show is over."

"What are you teaching them?" asked Yusuf.

"So far, I've taught them a few signals to identify the drones and to perform a couple of exercises. You know, using special signals like the combinations of short and long whistle blows that we use to send them out, attack their prey, and get to their positions in the Old City for the entertainment…the usual. But I need help getting the drones up in the air and programming a few simple routines." He picked up one of the drones and looked at Kai Li. "Akeem isn't here today. I was hoping I might get some assistance from you."

"Lucky day," Kai Li replied. "Jamal transfer programs to me after we work on problem yesterday, in case he need more help. We can figure somethin' out."

Over the next few hours, the four worked together, practicing a few routines the birds were to perform once in the Old City, including chasing and killing prey, circling and flying in patterns with the drones, taking off and landing, and sending them swooping over the heads of the spectators.

By midmorning, they had completed their exercises to the satisfaction of all. Dawoud remained in the field with the falcons and drones while Yusuf took the boys to the road where a car was waiting to take them into Bethlehem. Before closing the car door, he leaned in.

"Dawoud will need both of you boys this afternoon to help make sure this goes off well. He'll be in charge of the activities. I won't be able to make it. And won't be seeing you before you go. Nice to meet you. Go in safety and peace."

"We'll let Ahmad know," replied Zack. "*Salaam*."

Yusuf laughed. "Well done, Mr. Zack. I texted him a little while ago. He'll pick you up at the Inn around noon. Dawoud will meet you all in the plaza by the Dome of the Rock…a little after one. *Salaam*." He swung the door shut.

Fifteen minutes into the ride, Zack snatched his phone from the pouch of his hoodie and glanced over at Kai Li. "We better check in with the girls." As he switched his phone to his other hand to make the call, a piece of paper fell in his lap. He picked it up.

"What's that?" asked Kai Li

"It's a drawing of an Arabic letter…*K* or something. Must 'a been stuck to the back of the phone."

"Let me see."

Zack passed it to him, then clicked on Liyah's name in his contacts list.

Kai Li studied the piece of paper. "Not Arabic," he said. "Something else."

"Yeah? I wonder how it…"

Liyah's voice from the speakerphone interrupted him. "Hi, Zack. We were wondering when you guys might call. We didn't want to wake you."

"Not wakin' us, girl. We put in a whole day already."

"Right!" Morningstar said in light sarcasm from the background.

"Tell Star I liked her better when she was quiet, and not sarcastic."

"I heard that, Zack. We're on the speaker together."

Zack chuckled. "So, what's the plan for today? We'll be at the Inn in about an hour."

"Ahmad is working on his article at the Dawn this morning," Liyah replied. "We're kind of stuck here at the house. Did you hear anything more about leads for Khalib? We're all pretty down about yesterday."

"Sorry. No word."

"I 'member this," Kai Li mumbled.

"What was that?" asked Liyah.

"Oh, you know," Zack replied. "It's Kai talking to himself again."

"Morning, Kai Li," said Morningstar. "Ignore Zack."

"He's studying a piece of paper I found in my pocket," Zack continued. "You know how he gets. He probably doesn't hear you."

"I hear. Seen this before." He handed the paper back to Zack. "We see this in the tunnel...same thing. You forget? I say look like the Chinese symbol for water, but not exactly."

"Tunnel?" asked Liyah.

Zack looked at it again. "Oh, yeah. I do remember this. He's talking about the tunnel, Liyah. The one we thought maybe the terrorists had used to escape. Near that old airport. What was left of it. The same tunnel where Ahmad got stuck. This sign, or symbol, or whatever it is, was scratched into a stone in the wall, near the entrance."

"You saw the same writing on the wall as the one on that paper?" Morningstar asked.

"Yup," replied Kai Li. "Very strange."

"Can you take a picture and send it to me?" Liyah asked.

"Sure." Zack focused the camera on it, clicked, then forwarded the picture to her.

When the image appeared on her phone, Liyah gasped. "Allah!"

"What?" Zack said loudly into the speaker. "What's the matter?"

"I know what this is. It's sort of a K, but…"

Zack cut her off. "That's what I said."

"This symbol is a little different. It's like a fancy English *K,* but made to look more like a symbol. When we were little, Khalib and I made up symbols that stood for our names, so we could pass notes to each other. And if our parents got hold of them, we would lie and say we found them. That they weren't from us. It was a game we used to play so we could say things and they wouldn't know what we were up to. That symbol represented his name."

"Are you sure?" Zack questioned. "This exact sign?"

"Yes. This is it. Exactly."

"Jesus!" shouted Zack. "He must have been in that tunnel. But then how did that paper get in my pocket?"

"In tent," Kai Li said, his voice growing anxious.

Zack looked confused. "Tent?"

"Yeah. That boy spilled water on you, then he cause big stir wiping it off."

"Oh my God! You're right."

The sound of Liyah crying came through the speaker. Zack paused for a moment, staring at Kai Li. "Star. Call Ahmad and tell him what we found out. We're stuck here on our way to Bethlehem. But maybe he can get in touch with Yusuf and figure out what to do. We can't waste any time."

"Okay," Morningstar replied, her voice calm, steady. "I've got it. We'll let you know how we make out."

"Please. And good luck!" He hung up, turned to Kai Li, and sighed heavily. "I just hope, for Liyah's sake that we're not too late."

Forty-Seven

ESTY TURNED HER father's car into the parking lot on the outskirts of Tel Shiva and waited, with Liyah next to her and Morningstar in the back. An SUV pulled up beside them. A bearded man in a white ankle-length robe, wearing a red and white checkered headdress with a black cord bound atop, stepped out. Esty put down her window as he approached the driver's side.

"*Shalom*. I'm Yusuf. You must be Esty?"

"Yes, I am. *Salaam*."

"Ahmad had nice things to say about you." He peered in at Liyah, then Morningstar. "And your friends. Good morning, ladies. *Salaam*. I was thinking he might make it here with you, and maybe Kai Li and Zack. I sent them on their way quite a while ago."

"We convinced Ahmad to stay and work on his article for the paper," Liyah replied. "He's trying to meet a deadline. Zack and Kai Li didn't have a way to get back this way."

Yusuf stroked his beard, as he glanced at the Ministry sticker on the car window. "This might turn out to be dangerous." "Not something for young women like yourselves."

"We'll be fine, Mr. Yusuf," replied Morningstar, leaning forward.

"Besides, we don't have much choice," Liyah added.

"So, I see."

"Do you know where Liyah's brother is?" Esty asked.

"Not really. But I do know two things. One is, I walked through the camp this morning…the one we were at yesterday where the note was likely stuck into Zack's pocket, and I'm sorry to say the camp has already been abandoned. The second is that there are only a couple of ways they would likely leave to get to, say Syria or even Iran. Both would begin by heading north."

"Oh…but, so, how will we ever find them?" Liyah complained, her words tripping out from a sudden rush of anxiety.

"It's a long shot," Yusuf admitted. "But I was informed by my sources that a couple of stores in Tel Sheva were broken into for food and other supplies early this morning, and a white van stolen from a dealership—one that resembled two others we saw in the camp. Those vans are also missing, so we have something to look for."

Liyah watched him study the car sticker again. "Does anyone else know you have come to me?" he asked Esty.

"No," Liyah assured him emphatically, before Esty was able to reply. "Don't worry, sir. We are all working together. No one knows about your meeting us, except Ahmad."

"Okay." Yusuf replied. "To continue then, there are fewer towns on the main road north, into the Yatir Forest. It's likely they'd head that way. I called ahead after I left the abandoned camp and asked a couple of my scouts to park on the side of the two main roads leading to the forest. My feeling is we barely missed the vans leaving the camp, since the tea in the tent was still warm." He glanced at Morningstar and Liyah. "We better get going. Do you have any money with you to buy them off, since we don't have any weapons? I have some, but I don't carry much around with me."

"Oh!" Liyah gasped. "I didn't even think of that. How stupid of me. I have a little, and I'm sure my dad would have given us some, but he was with Ahmad at the office today…so much is happening so fast. In Jerusalem, news-wise, and for us."

"Thank you, Yusuf," Esty replied calmly. "I have some. Everything we have, combined, will have to be enough."

Yusuf nodded to Morningstar. "Why don't you come with me? We should take two cars, and you can communicate with Esty and Liyah on your phone. That way we won't get separated."

Morningstar got out and joined Yusuf. In five minutes both cars were on the main road out of Tel Sheva. A few minutes later they were on Rte. 60, heading northeast.

Yusuf took in a breath, letting his shoulders relax. "So, Morningstar," he began, keeping his eyes on the road, "Ahmad told me a little about you and your friends, but he was rather rushed. I understand you're all leaving in the next day or so."

"Yes, sir," she replied. "As long as we find Khalib."

"Kind of a long trip for just a few days here, yes?"

"It's an even longer *story*," she replied, smiling over at him.

"I see. Well, I hope to hear it if we—"

Yusuf's phone rang through the car speakers. He pressed the button on the side of the steering wheel. "Yes, Ali."

"I tried to reach you about ten or fifteen minutes ago. Had to leave a message, so I thought I'd try again," the voice answered over the speakers.

"Sorry, Ali. Must have been right before I got back into the car. What have you got?"

"I saw three white vans pass by here at that time."

"Where exactly are you?"

"I'm parked on the shoulder of the road on Rte. 31, just southwest of Hura."

"Any other possibilities?"

"No, not so far. Those might be the only ones I will see. Definitely fit your description."

"Okay, thanks. We're about ten minutes from you. That would put us about twenty-five behind, if that's even them. Let me know if anything changes."

Yusuf hung up, then dialed another number. The call was picked up before it had a chance to ring through the speakers.

"Yusuf?"

"Checking in, Elyas. Anything yet?"

"No. Not yet. If they came this way, there's a chance I missed them. But I've got someone else up by the entrance to the forest. We'll see. Might be the last chance."

"Okay. We'll be at the intersection with 316 shortly. I'm going to take the chance that they'll take the same route I would. 316 through the forest then along the West Bank border. Keep me posted."

Yusuf hung up and turned to Morningstar. "Can you send a text to your friends? Tell them to set the GPS to follow Rte. 316 to the Anim Synagogue…that's A-N-I-M…in case we lose them."

Morningstar did as directed. Two minutes later Yusuf exited off 31, merged onto 316, and headed towards the Yatir. Morningstar checked behind to make sure they were still following, then nestled back in her seat.

Yusuf stole a quick glance at her. "I like what you're wearing, Morningstar. Especially the hijab tied around your neck." He laughed. "What tribe are you from in America?"

"Lakota," she replied, a bit surprised by the question. "Sioux. Do you know of us?"

"I heard of the name. I do know some things about our Native American relatives."

She studied him. "Relatives?"

"The Iranian people are not all born terrorists, as often painted by the Western press. We certainly have our share of bad leaders, but our people have good hearts. We are all humans. Some more *directly* related than others."

"It's true everywhere," Morningstar replied. "We're all connected through history."

He glanced at her again, then brought his eyes back to the road.

"Ahmad speaks highly of you. At least during the brief time I had the opportunity to ask about all of you. This morning he told me *I was in good hands*. Not sure what he meant. Do you know?"

"We like Ahmad, too," she replied, dodging the question.

"Hmm." Yusuf said, a grin forming at the corners of his mouth. "Well, anyway, you're right about all of us being connected, young lady. How wise of you. That is what I meant by *relatives*. In Iran, near where I live, they found ancient cave paintings and symbols carved into buried clay tablets that were tens of thousands of years old. And in America, they found the exact same pictures and symbols in Native American cultures…in Kentucky, California, New Mexico, and Iowa."

"My Lakota family is from South Dakota," Morningstar replied. Our sister tribe, the Dakotas, are also from the Sioux family. Some are from Iowa."

"See," Yusuf replied. "That's exactly what I mean. My ancient relatives traveled through Asia and crossed the land bridge to Alaska, then spread out in America. In that way, my family is tied to yours. We might even be *directly related*." His grin grew larger.

The phone rang again through the car speakers.

"Got something, Elyas?"

"I think so. I received a report that three vans, similar to your description, just entered the Yasir Forest along 316 a short time ago."

"Great. That means we're only about fifteen to twenty minutes behind. Thanks." He hung up.

Five minutes later he handed his phone to Morningstar. "Why don't you call Liyah or Esty? We can catch them up on what's going on."

Morningstar clicked on her phone.

Liyah was right on top of it. "What's up?"

"Go ahead and plug into the car so we can all talk," said Morningstar.

After a pause, Yusuf spoke. "All set?"

"Both here," replied Esty.

Yusuf updated Esty and Liyah on the recent conversations, and his plan to try to catch up to the vans before they made it to the West Bank border. "Not sure what we can do once we catch up except maybe warn the border guards if they take us that way. Don't think they're going to be very afraid of us, if you know what I mean."

Yusuf kept the line open, and in a short time they passed the sign:

Welcome to the Yatir Forest

"I hope they stop before we lose them crossing the border, or slipping off in another direction," Yusuf reiterated into the speaker. "There's no road other than 316 going through here. So if they stop, we should see them."

"I've never been here," Liyah said. "We hardly ever get to cross into Israel. There are a lot of trees. So unusual, since we are still in the Negev."

"Technically, we crossed the edge of the Negev desert when we started up into these small hills," Esty replied. "Over four million trees have been planted here over the last fifty years. Most of them are conifers, like Aleppo pine and cypress but many are broad leafed too, like Olive, fig, and Eucalyptus. There are also a lot of vineyards here."

"Spoken like a true tour guide," Liyah joked, her voice cracking with nervousness, her whole being trying to ward off a feeling of dread that kept creeping into her thoughts.

Esty smiled over at her. "Soon, Liyah. Fingers crossed."

"This road takes a hard right about a mile ahead," Yusuf noted. "We're running out of time. The forest ends at the Anim Synagogue. That's our GPS point. I've been here before, and I know several escape routes into the West Bank. However, I don't think they'll go there. It's more likely they'll head for shelter in Jordan, and cross over the Red Sea somewhere with some help."

"So we're going to lose them?" asked Morningstar. " I haven't seen one person since we entered the forest."

"Perhaps. But it's a long haul on the route that I think they'll take, through desert-like conditions. My guess is they'll regroup before then, check supplies, and rest a bit. They've been up a while already."

Yusuf made a sharp right angle turn and a few minutes later, the forest ended. He slowed his car as the paved road turned to dirt, and they entered a large, rock-strewn, open area. A short distance ahead, beyond a few scraggly trees, three parked vans came into view. Yusuf stopped and signaled Esty to back up to the tree border. He followed her.

Once hidden, Yusuf stopped again and got out of the car. He approached Esty's window.

"Leave your car behind these trees. It's best they don't see any Israeli stickers, especially from the Ministry. And you may need another car to get out if something happens to mine…or me, for that matter."

Before Liyah and Esty stepped out of her car, Liyah slipped her bracelet off and handed it to Esty. "Put this on. You will feel its energy. If you hold it out in front of you and point your hand, you can create a force field that will protect you. The more you concentrate, the bigger the field, and the more accurately you can channel it."

Esty put it on. "Oh, my. I see what you mean," she said, caught by surprise and appearing a bit worried. "My whole arm is tingling."

"Not sure I get what you girls are up to," Yusuf said quietly, "but let's go."

Yusuf got back into his driver's seat while Liyah and Esty climbed into the back. He pulled the car onto the dirt road and cautiously approached the vans, stopping a few hundred feet away. As he stepped out of the car, he turned back to the girls.

"They probably won't harm me, since I have both Iranian and Saudi identification papers. They may have even heard of me. But we don't know if they have Khalib or not. If something happens, you'd best get back to your car and get out of here. Esty, get behind the wheel of this one just in case."

As Yusuf walked toward the vans, one of the men standing at the back of the last van saw him coming. He called out to another. Both men, equipped with semi automatic rifles, stepped forward to meet him. Liyah noticed words being exchanged but could hear nothing. One of the men then left, disappearing behind the small knoll next to the vans.

A few minutes later the man reappeared, waving his hand to the other to join him. The other man held the rifle to Yusuf's back as they went up the hill, disappearing down the other side.

Forty-Eight

Bethlehem

ZACK AND KAI LI arrived at the Inn in Bethlehem late morning, freshened up with a quick, much-needed shower, then entered the dining area. The peak breakfast crowd was gone but the ambient noise level, created by the random chatter and clanking of porcelain plates and dinnerware, remained high.

"Good morning, you two," their favorite server said with enthusiasm. She picked up a couple of menus and moved into the dining room. "You're in luck. Your usual booth is open. It's been crazy here this morning…I'm sure you can imagine with it being Easter and all. A party just left, but we'll be inundated with people coming out of church services any moment now."

Zack slid into his seat, his back to the next booth and Kai Li sat across from him.

The waitress handed each a menu. "Take your time. We had a server call in sick, so I'm a bit slammed. I'll be back as soon as I can."

"No worry," said Kai Li.

"Yeah, no problem. Thanks," Zack added.

Zack raised his menu and leaned his head against the back of the booth. "Feels like it should be nighttime," he said into the menu. "I'm exhausted."

Kai Li snickered. "Not use to get up so early, huh?"

"Every day it seems," Zack complained again.

"Not sorry. I get up in dark every day to go to factory."

"Yeah…well good for you," Zack replied, briefly slipping into his old sarcastic tone.

"Feel better when we eat," said Kai Li.

"Yeah. No idea how they do this fasting crap…and for a whole month. Insane."

"To make us think of how other people suffer, you know?"

"Okay, okay. Yeah, I get it. Sorry I brought it up." He studied the menu some more. "What do ya think? They serve breakfast all day here. Some special deviled eggs for Easter I see and–"

The waitress returned. "If you're ready I can squeeze in your order now before I deliver the meals to the next table." She filled their glasses with water.

"Sure, sure." Zack replied. "I'm all set. I'll have those deviled eggs and a big order of blueberry pancakes with strawberries and whipped cream on top. Let's see…and some toast. Oh, and do you have hot fudge to pour on the pancakes?" As he leaned forward to hand the menu to the waitress, he noticed Kai Li staring at him over the top of his glasses.

"What? What!" Zack said defensively. "You eat like a bird. No wonder you're thin as a rail."

Kai Li ignored him, sliding his glasses back up on his nose. "I like banana yogurt, some granola, and glass of orange juice. Thank you."

The waitress took the menu from him.

"Make that two glasses of orange juice…big one for me."

Kai Li frowned at Zack as the waitress retreated.

Zack took out his phone and rested his head against the booth again. A moment later he turned his ear to the back of the booth and listened.

Kai Li checked to see if there were any messages on *his* phone, expecting to hear from Ahmad about when he would be there. He saw only one, and it was from Liyah. "We get text." Kai Li said, looking over at Zack. He paused, then raised his voice. "I say…Liyah, send–"

"Shh, shh," Zack hissed sternly, bringing his finger to his lips. He pointed repeatedly behind himself using his thumb, then whispered. "Pastor is sayin' somethin' to this guy, Billy Kane."

Kai Li looked curiously at him and waited.

Zack finally returned his attention to Kai Li. "Sorry," he said, speaking quietly in a low tone. "There's something strange going on next door, here. Sounds like Kane has been planning something and the pastor is getting cold feet." Zack scratched his chin. "And Kane sounds a lot like that other guy, Murtaza."

"Cold feet?" Kai Li asked.

"Shh!"

"Okay, okay." Kai Li whispered back. "So?"

Before Zack could answer, the waitress showed up with the food and set their meals in front of them.

"Thank you," Kai Li whispered.

She glanced down at him then over to Zack, shaking her head. "At least you two are entertaining, although I haven't a clue what you're up to."

"So, what they say," Kai Li continued in a whisper.

"I'll tell you later," Zack said. "I'm starved. Let's eat."

Midway through finishing his pancakes, Billy Kane and the pastor settled their bill and slipped out of the booth, passing by Kai Li and Zack. Kai Li was looking down, but Zack glanced over, getting only very quick glimpse of them. He tapped the table next to Kai Li and pointed to them.

"Did you notice those guys?"

Kai Li turned around, only to catch their backs as they walked away. "No."

"I only saw the side of Billy there, myself, but I did notice he had a big mustache. I'm thinkin' he could pass for Murtaza's brother with that…and his voice and all."

"Not likely," Kai Li mumbled, as he turned his attention back to the table. "Not think Murtaza get out here a lot, 'cept maybe time we meet him."

Zack's voice took on a more serious tone. "Well…I heard them discussing something going down today in Jerusalem. Do you remember all that talk about the end of times when we met them?"

"Sure."

"They were talking about it again. And the pastor was arguing that what Kane was planning was not a good idea anymore. That people were going to get hurt. And even if it did speed up the Rapture, the end of days would happen anyway. He said there was no need to hurry it...and not on Easter Sunday when so many innocent Christians would be in the Old City."

"But what could happen? Not hear of any problem today...anywhere."

"I don't know," Zack replied, turning back to finish his pancakes. "But I told you before...I don't trust these guys."

Zack's phone rang. He picked it up.

"Hello…Yes…Okay, we'll be ready."

"Ahmad?" asked Kai Li.

"Yup. He'll be here in fifteen minutes. Enough time for us to finish eating."

"I already finish," Kai Li replied, grinning at Zack. "Not a farm animal with head in trough like you."

Forty-Nine

AFTER A WHILE, not seeing Yusuf return, Liyah checked her phone. "It's been fifteen minutes, Star" she said. "I'm worried something has happened."

"Me, too," Morningstar replied. "I think we should go help him."

"That's crazy," Esty objected. "How can we help? He told us to stay here then leave if it got dangerous."

"But what about Khalib?" Liyah protested.

"He might not even be here," Esty countered.

"Okay!" Morningstar said. "This isn't helpful. Etsy, you stay here and honk if you get in trouble. Liyah and I will go check things out."

Liyah's stomach churned as she and Morningstar approached the crest of the very small hill. She remembered being with Morningstar in the cave after they first met, and how afraid she was. It was that same feeling of paralyzing fear clutching at her, tightening her throat, making her joints feel weak. But this wasn't because of closed-in places, like before. She had overcome that. Now it was more not knowing what to expect. Her mind was spinning out of control. *Would I end up captured, too? Will I be tortured, like I've read they do to women and girls? Will I never get back…like Khalib? Khalib! That was it, wasn't it…back then in the cave with Morningstar that day. Think of someone else, Liyah, Ooray once said. Put someone else before you, and the fear will pass…Khalib! He is the one for this moment.*

Morningstar signaled to Liyah to duck down. They crept on their hands and knees toward the ridge where they could look down undetected. She glanced over at Liyah. "You okay?" she whispered. "You look pale."

"That's because I probably am," Liyah replied. "I'll be okay. Just forgot myself for a minute."

They poked their heads above the ridge and looked out over a small flat plateau, piles of boulders strewn about the sandy ground. In the middle stood what looked like the remains of some old building, only a section of a portico made of large square stones was left standing.

"What is this place?" asked Morningstar in a hushed voice, staring at the ruins.

"Must be the Anim Synagogue," Liyah replied. "Esty told me before we got here that it was in the Bible, and was in use a few hundred years after the death of Jesus. Then it became a mosque. Not many people come here apparently, but close by there are both Christian and Jewish settlements. She told me that for centuries they all lived together in the area, in peace. So this is kind of a sacred site, in the middle of nowhere."

"Probably why your brother's captors chose it," Morningstar replied.

"You'll be taking my job soon as a guide, Liyah." Esty said, catching them by surprise.

Morningstar grabbed her arm and pulled her down. "Shh…What are you doing here?"

"I didn't want to be left out," Esty replied. "Not being much help sitting in the car. Why are you shushing me? I don't see anyone around. I wonder where Yusuf went."

"Voices carry out here," Morningstar replied. "Just bein' careful. I thought I saw something, but I guess not."

They studied the ruins for a few more minutes. Morningstar started to get up, but then crouched back down, pointing to the stone portico. "There. See them? Just on the other side of that high stone thing. I think I saw movement between the gaps in the stones."

"Yes. Yes. I see it," Liyah responded.

The three were suddenly startled by a deep voice coming from behind them. They jerked their heads around. A man in hiking pants and tan zip jacket was pointing a gun at them and speaking in Arabic.

"He wants us to stand up," said Liyah.

After rising to their feet, the man waved the barrel of the rifle in the direction they had been looking. They turned and moved slowly towards the broken stone pillars.

"Don't do anything, Liyah," Morningstar said under her breath. "Not now. We need to find out what's going on."

"*Sah-kah'-teh!*" the man said, angrily.

"He wants us to shut up," Liyah whispered.

"*Sah-kah'-teh!*" he repeated.

The man took them around the side of the stone portico. Two men sat with their backs against the stones, eating. One had a weapon next to him, braced against a pillar made from three large limestone blocks stacked one upon the other. Two others were standing, one speaking to Yusuf. Liyah noticed all the men were wearing the same kind of hiking clothes. Yusuf's face dropped when he saw the guard bring the girls in front of the men.

"What's this?" asked the man who had been speaking to Yusuf.

The guard said something in Arabic, addressing him as Mabood. The men on the ground stopped eating and looked up.

Mabood faced Yusuf. "They're with you?"

"No. But you need to leave them alone," Yusuf replied.

The guard shook his head and said something again to Mabood.

"You're lying to me, Yusuf. I thought you were going to help us?"

"No, I'm telling the truth. You said others know of me. So, you know that I speak the truth. I was at your camp looking for the boy. I just want him to be released. This is his sister." He pointed to Liyah. "As I said, they are not with me. I'm headed back to Iran. I can get you substantial funds from Hezbollah or other groups when I return home…It's the boy in exchange for the money, as I told you."

Mabood looked at him suspiciously, not saying anything.

The guard brushed the muzzle of his gun against Esty's blond braided pigtails, flipping them back and forth, and smiling. The men sitting against the stones laughed.

The other man standing next to Yusuf whispered into Mabood's ear. Mabood nodded.

"Where are you from?" Mabood asked Esty.

"Don't answer," Liyah cautioned.

Mabood put his finger in Liyah's face. "You shut up!"

He returned to Esty. "Well?

She didn't say a word.

"You're not wearing a hijab, like that boy's sister." Mabood pointed his thumb at Liyah. "So, you're not Palestinian…Jewish, maybe?" He narrowed his eyes.

Esty kept silent as Mabood circled them.

"I don't think so, Yusuf." he finally said. "I can get a lot of money for these three and the boy, especially this blond Jew. All you offer me is a promise. And I can trade *you* to the Israelis for an even bigger prize."

"Sorry, Yusuf!" said Esty. "It's my fault."

"Nonsense," Yusuf replied. "It was never going to work out. I was trying to buy time so you three could get out of here. These are bad men. They are apparently not funded by Hezbollah, and they care nothing–"

"*Sah-kah'-teh!*" shouted Mabood.

The guard brought the butt of his rifle up using both hands, preparing to bring it down on Yusuf's head.

Morningstar grabbed hold of her necklace with her left hand and pointed the fingers of her right hand at the rifle. A beam of bright red light shot from her fingertips. The gun flew from the guard's hands onto the ground. Morningstar then kicked it away.

The man sitting on the ground scrambled for his rifle, propped against the limestone pillar. Morningstar turned, held out her hand, and blasted the topmost block with another beam of intense light. It blew apart as if hit by a rocket, showering chunks of heavy rock down on the man, knocking him out.

"Stand back, Yusuf!" Morningstar yelled. "Liyah, keep Esty safe."

Yusuf stepped back, appearing shell-shocked.

Morningstar took several steps back, then held her palm out, casting a net of light that surrounded all the men. They struggled unsuccessfully to move, frozen in place.

"I'll keep them here. You guys have to find Khalib. He must be close. But be careful Liyah, they have three vans. There must be more men around, and some might have weapons."

Yusuf picked up one of the rifles and joined Liyah and Esty. They spread out, keeping in sight of each other, moving outward and scouting the area.

Suddenly, a shot rang out. The girls jerked their heads toward Yusuf, who was running in the direction of a group of hand-hewn stones at the perimeter of the synagogue site. Another shot rang out.

Yusuf dropped down.

"Oh, Allah!" cried Liyah. She and Esty ran toward him.

As they neared Yusuf moved, signaling them to get down. He pointed the rifle at the stones and fired a shot. A man's head disappeared behind the rocks.

They crept closer, keeping their heads low. When they neared, Yusuf stood up quickly, pointing the rifle, ready to shoot. But no one was there.

A few feet past the base of the rocks was a small depression area in the ground. At the right end of it was a cave-like entrance, supported by two walls of limestone bricks.

"Looks like a mine or tunnel down there," Liyah said,

They moved carefully down the rocks and stood to the side of the dark entrance.

"It's probably an old room. Like maybe the basement of the synagogue, or a storage area."

"Well, we know one thing," replied Yusuf. "There is at least one man with a rifle in there. It's probably where they're keeping their prisoners until they were ready to leave for the border."

"There's no way to go in there without getting killed," Liyah cautioned.

Esty looked over at Liyah. "Maybe we don't have to," she said anxiously, shaking her wrist with the bracelet. "I was practicing with this like you said, when I was waiting for you guys. I got out of the car and played around with aiming at a tree, to sort of see what I could do to create that force field you talked about. And…"

She stopped talking and faced the opening of the underground tunnel.

"And?" Liyah urged.

"And I accidentally set the grass on fire. Had to stomp it out before someone noticed." She stared at the dried bushes at the side of the entrance. "I was just thinking, we could sort of *smoke them out.*"

"Smoke?" Liyah questioned. She paused. "Oh, I get it. Yeah, great idea! You start it. I'll do the rest."

Esty felt the band on her wrist, pointed her hand at the dried shrubs and closed her eyes. In seconds they burst into flames. A thick black cloud of smoke began to rise up.

Liyah clasped her necklace, took a deep breath then blew as hard as she could. Smoke poured into the opening between the limestone walls.

A moment later, men began to run out, coughing. First came two carrying weapons. Liyah pointed at the lead one, instantly heating his gun to the melting point. He flung it aside. Yusuf tripped the second, retrieving his gun after he fell.

Eight more bodies flooded out of the underground cavern. The last, a boy with curly dark hair and a gash on the side of his head, finally staggered out, coughing.

Liyah thought her heart would burst into flames like the bushes. She ran to him, crushing him in her arms. "Khalib! Oh, Khalib!" She kissed the side of his head by his wound.

Khalib hugged her until she thought she would break in two. He helped identify those who were the actual prisoners and those who were the guards. Yusuf gave the intact gun to the prisoners and kept his. They marched the two guards back to where Morningstar held the others captive. He then gave the two remaining rifles to the prisoners and relieved Morningstar of her duty.

The prisoners herded the guards to where the three vans were parked. They waited for Yusuf and the girls, who joined them a few minutes later with their cars. Yusuf instructed the guards to get in one of the vans but removed the keys and stuck them in his pocket. He gave the keys for the other two vans to the prisoners. "Just split up in two groups and head back home," he said. "Keep the guns so these guys don't get them."

"The border is only about fifteen minutes from here," Yusuf continued. "After I cross safely, I'll use my contacts to notify the guards of what happened here. I'm sure they'll enjoy picking up these charming lads and hauling them off to jail. You will all have a good head start and should be able to get wherever you need to go."

"We heard the borders are now closed," Morningstar noted. "More trouble brewing I think. But Esty's father has contacts with the Israeli Prime Minister and Liyah's dad with the Ministry of the Interior. They will make the calls to watch out for you should you get picked up by mistake."

Yusuf moved toward Esty's car, but halted, turning his head around toward the men again. "And you better ditch those weapons once you're safely out of here. Don't want any accidents after all this, right?"

Esty sat in the driver's seat of her car with the window down, along with Liyah, Morningstar, and Khalib. Liyah got out and walked up to Yusuf.

"We heard what you said. Does that mean you're not coming back with us?"

"That's right, Liyah. It's too dangerous for me here now. I was planning to leave anyway. Guess I didn't think it would be quite this soon."

Liyah's eyes welled up. "I don't know what to say. Thank you is not enough. I owe you the world."

He held her hands in his. "You owe me nothing. I'm not even sure what just happened here. I've become tired of how I've had to play this game, trying to save a homeland for Palestinians. Extremists on both sides seem to be fueling the fire with their own desire for power and revenge. I'm getting too old for this."

Liyah slipped her hands from his, then hugged him.

Yusuf smiled. "Who would have guessed it would be three girls. Our own culture has a lot to learn. But from the little that you told me of your mission, and from what I saw today, hope might finally take root through you and your friends. *Light Passers* I think you said?"

Liyah let him go, clearing her eyes of the tears.

"Go in peace, my child," said Yusuf. "And go with Allah. *Ma'a Al-Salmah.*"

"*Salaam*," replied Liyah, looking gratefully into his eyes.

Liyah returned to her seat in the back, next to Khalib and they all waved to Yusuf. As Esty pressed down on the accelerator, dirt and pebbles kicked up under the tires of Esty's father's car.

FIFTY

Beit Lahia

RANIA AL-RAHIM finished tidying up the kitchen then took the linen basket that was full of clean clothes upstairs. She pushed the door open to Liyah's room, stepped inside, and set the basket on the end of the bed. As she folded the clothes for her daughter and Morningstar, her always active mind was slowly captured by the quiet solitude of her surroundings. The edge of her thoughts softened. She felt her shoulders relax.

Busy work kept her from thinking too much. From feeling too much. Now, caught in the present moment, the sadness began to seep in again. It seemed to her it was always there, waiting—waiting for a crack, the smallest crevice, a singular moment of calm that allowed it back in.

After placing the last of the items she was holding into the drawer of Liyah's dresser, she sat down in the chair in the corner of the room. She glanced over at the desk her husband had restored. *Liyah's most favorite possession,* she thought. *How grown up she had become. Especially the last few weeks.*

The sun's rays, breaking away from the edge of a cloud, poured through the window panes, striking a picture of Liyah and her brother, and catching her eye. Khalib was little. He was walking next to Liyah, holding her hand. *Liyah asked her for it,* she remembered, *shortly after he had gone missing.*

She dropped her head into the palms of her hands. She felt a pain in her heart. An ache in her very soul. *I've lost them both, haven't I?*

She began to weep.

Gathering herself together, she finished her work in her daughter's room and moved to her own bedroom. She placed her items in her bureau then opened her husband's top drawer. As she began placing his socks to one side, the upstairs extension next to her rang, catching her by surprise. It was at times like this she was glad they still kept the old phone system, along with the cell phones. She hated having to hustle down the stairs when she was in the middle of something. She sat on the bed and lifted the receiver.

"Hello?. . .Liyah? Where are you? You never tell me exactly where you're going anymore! I thought I–"

She stood up. "What is that you're saying? I don't understand…Liyah? Where'd you go?"

"Hello, Mama," came the voice at the other end.

She dropped back onto the bed, wide-eyed. "Khalib?"

As she listened, Khalib sounded like a machine gun, excitedly sputtering a string of details about what happened—his capture, the tunnels, his rescue. Her mind began floating. She gathered nothing. Understood nothing. She only heard his voice. The voice of her only son. *He was alive. And he was coming home.*

She hung up the phone and dialed her husband's work number. It seemed like forever before someone picked up.

"Hi. This is Mrs. Rahim," she said, breathless. "Is David available?"

"Is everything alright?" asked the receptionist.

"No. I mean, yes." I mean, well can he come to the phone?"

"Just a moment. I'll check."

The silent interval felt like a torture test. *I have to tell him right away,* she thought. *Before they take it back. Before I have to give him up again. Now!* She sensed her nerves fraying. She didn't think she could make it. *You have to answer…NOW!*

"Hello," came the voice, as her husband picked up the line in his office. "Something wrong, dear?"

"Wrong? Oh, David!"

"What? What's going on?"

"It's Khalib." She began crying.

"Oh, no. Tell me it isn't true. Not our son!"

"Yes…I mean…no," she managed between sobs. She took a deep breath. "He is okay, David. He is fine." She took another breath. "He was rescued…David? Did you hear me?"

"Yes. Certainly," her husband replied, sounding stunned before finding himself. "That's wonderful news, Rani. The best!…But by whom?"

"By your daughter. Oh, David. Oh, Allah…Come home, dear. Can you? Please."

"Of course. I'll be right there. I'm sort of hiding out here today, anyway. I guess I won't have to avoid things anymore. It's a happy day, my love."

She heard the click at his end. Resting the receiver gently back in its cradle, she sat back down on the bed and let the tears flow freely.

FIFTY-ONE

IN THE SEMI-ARID, desolate landscape at the southern end of the Gaza Strip where it meets the border with Egypt and the remains of the old Arafat Airport tunnels could be found, preparations were underway for the launch of the drones.

Five desert-brown vans bearing no markings sat parked in a semicircle. A short distance away, two mobile rocket launchers rested, anchored deep in the sand, each capable of sending four missiles simultaneously into northern Israel. Ten men in army camo jackets and pants divided their time between readying the launchers and unloading one hundred boxes from each of the vans. A single box contained twenty-four small drones, all equipped with a rectangular explosive packet. Twelve thousand drones in all.

Hassan left the launchers and joined Jamal and Nasir near the vans, which were being unloaded, boxes organized into groups according to their markings.

"How are we doing here?" he asked as he approached.

"Pretty much on schedule, Hassan," Nasir replied. "Jamal and I completed all the last-minute coding changes yesterday. The software was reloaded into all the drones during the night, and the final target maps stored in their memory based on their missions."

Hassan glanced at his watch. "I believe it was estimated it would take several hours to complete the release of all of them, correct?"

"That's right," Jamal replied, placing the final drone in its position with the two hundred and forty-nine others of that batch. "With the help of your men it will take another hour to get half of the groups…or should I say swarms positioned along this part of the old landing strip, and ready to take off. So, the plan is to keep releasing swarms as we complete the setup of the remaining groups."

"It's a lot of drones." Hassan noted, his eyes scanning the many groups already lining the pockmarked runway. "It was hard for me to imagine as we talked about it, but seeing them…well, it's like a miniature invasion force."

"Exactly," Jamal replied, standing up and stretching his back. "Because that's what it is."

"Will we be able to get the first group up and out soon?"

"We actually set the first swarm off quite a while ago," replied Nasir. "They're on their way to the Ovda Airbase near Eliat. We figured about a five hour flight south from here." He rubbed his chin. "It will be the longest of the missions. Might be close on the energy side from batteries, but we're hoping the slightly larger ones will work fine for that group. We released the second wave a half hour later."

"When will the others begin hitting their targets?" Hassan pressed.

Jamal bent down and picked a large notepad up off the ground. He flipped back to the first section and shared it with Hassan, moving his finger down the page as he spoke.

"This part here lists the first target areas. Nine to be exact, all air bases. The idea is that we hit each of them in the first wave within a total time span of only thirty to sixty minutes. The goal is the dismantling of the military jets and helicopters on the airfields, or close by. The second wave will hit the same targets twenty minutes later, in an attempt to hit those that were missed, or were in the hangars and would now be taken to the airfield to fight the invisible invaders. A third wave will follow this but will only be sent to the three primary bases where most of the jets and helicopters are stationed. Ramat David Airbase in the north near Haifa, and Palmachim and Tel Nof air bases located in between Tel Aviv and Jerusalem."

"And the other bases?" asked Hassan.

Jamal flipped the page. "These are the rest of them: Hatzor and Sdot Micha near Jerusalem, Hatzerim and Nevatim near Beersheba, Ramon in the Negev, and Ovda near Eliat, where some are already headed."

Hassan studied the drones already in place. "You are varying the size of the swarms, I see. Why is that?"

"Simply because of the number of aircraft or weapons in a given target area. The largest ones include extra drones intended to smash into the hangars, blowing a hole in the sides to allow other drones access to the planes or copters."

"And you've incorporated the latest photographs of the targets and probable specific locations? I mean of the planes and helicopters."

"Yes," Jamal said firmly. "The drones will continue to look for them if they fly by or don't see them right away. They're on autopilot, as you know, using video and images to locate terrain and the targets. They also communicate via infrared to share information once there, so they don't go after the exact same targets." He looked over in the direction of Nasir and checked his watch, finally bringing his attention back to Hassan. "Subsets of the drones will, however, be intentionally searching for the same targets. For instance, at the large airbases smaller groups will break off to go after specific jets, like the F-15 Eagles, F-16 Fighting Falcons, and stealth enabled F-35 Lightning IIs. And other groups will go after the Apache, Black Hawk, and Panther copters."

"And what about the artillery?"

Jamal opened the notebook to another section. "The last swarms will be sent out to the Israeli artillery locations posing the greatest threat to attacking Gaza in retaliation." He slid his finger down the page. "And then to these other secondary locations, and to scan the skies for the Israelis own large drones and UAVs—unmanned aerial vehicles—used for reconnaissance and special ground attacks. We believe the time delay to start on the artillery is acceptable, since we need to disable the planes first, before most of them leave the bases. The artillery is largely in the open, won't know what to expect, and are not easily moved to shelters anyway."

"They may also try to use the artillery against us, regardless," Jamal continued, "not knowing where the drones originated but wanting to counterattack us anyway they can. In fact, we're sending most of the drones on a bit of a circuitous route, through the West Bank then circling back, so that if anyone sees them it will look like they are all coming in from the north, and not being launched out of Gaza."

"Speaking of launching," Hassan added. "We'll be sending about a hundred rockets from the launchers here toward Israel, then moving them to a new location to hide. The IDF will be able to calculate our original location from the trajectory of the missiles. But we feel more of these will get through to their targets because of the disabling of much of their artillery, and the added accuracy of our rockets…thanks to help from Iran."

"I was thinking that those would not be very much more accurate than the last attempt a year ago," Jamal replied. "None of those hit any targets. So, what you're telling me is that you believe you'll hit a few targets this time?"

"Absolutely. More than a few."

"Military, right?" Ahmad questioned, raising his eyebrows suspiciously.

"Yes…well, for the most part. Largely the same targets as the drones, but also a few soft ones."

"You said no civilians would be hurt," Jamal said, his tone stern. "No general attacks on the public like you've been trying, right?"

"Well, it's inevitable some people will be hurt, but not intentionally. We agreed to *minimize* the collateral damage, not guarantee zero casualties."

Jamal wrung his hands. "What kind of soft targets?"

"Sorry, can't say, but no people. Only structures. You should understand it was going to happen whether or not we sent any drones. The drones add a distraction value and make the possibility of hitting the targets more probable as well by eliminating some of their ability to destroy our rockets once they're in the air."

"And what about the fifty drones we gave you as a reward for your financial and other support?" Jamal asked.

"They'll be used to distract the Israelis from our joint mission. Akeem learned a lot from that tech nerd, Kai Li. He installed some images in the drones and programmed their flight patterns. We should be all set. So, what's the final timing of all this from your side?"

"The entire duration of the attacks is estimated to take no more than two and a half to three hours. Beginning only a few hours from now."

"Good," said Hassan. "And Hamas has undercover agents placed near the various targets. I'll advise them to be aware of information relating to the possible attacks in their area, and report back."

"Well, don't say anything specific," Jamal warned. "And not before we start sending out the second wave. You never can be one hundred percent certain of who you can trust, and we're so close…don't want to blow it now. It will be too late to stop us shortly, or compromise the surprise."

"Got it," agreed Hassan. He shook Jamal's hand, then turned and headed back over to the mobile missile launchers.

Jamal grabbed a box of drones sitting along the runway and rejoined Nasir in putting the swarm teams together. He started to focus on his task, but a corner of his mind was unable to let go of his discussion with Hassan. A knot began to form in the pit of his stomach.

FIFTY-TWO

Old City

AHMAD PULLED INTO the lot across from the Jaffa Gate entrance to the Old City. He located a spot at the far side and began swinging into it. A man in a car approaching from the opposite end of the row blasted his horn in anger.

"*Sorry!*" Ahmad mouthed to the man, realizing he had cut him off. Ahmad completed his capture of the space and shut the engine off. Exiting the car with Zack and Kai Li, he clicked the lock from his key fob. They headed across the lot toward the gate. Finally pushing through a throng of people funneling into the narrow passageway into the Old City, Ahmad stepped to the side and stopped.

"What a zoo!" he shouted. "I thought it was bad along the highway from Bethlehem, but this is ridiculous. I've never seen so many people."

"I wouldn't know," Zack replied. "We get plenty of traffic jams in Detroit at rush hour, but I have to say this is worse than that. A ton more people crammed in here, for sure."

"Look like Chinese New Year at home," Kai Li added. "Except people more serious here. Lot of flags and signs. Not everyone happy."

"It's been getting more and more that way lately," Ahmad explained. "Sometimes violence even erupts. It used to be rare, at least here in the Old City part of Jerusalem. Now they even close it off from time to time. I'm kind of surprised they didn't shut more things down this weekend with the growing uneasiness, but then it's an exceptional weekend for all the faiths. People have come a long way."

"They are closing some of the borders already," Zack said. "That's what we heard at the Inn."

"Yeah!" Ahmad replied. "To Gaza and the West Bank. Not to the city itself. Our passes still seem to be good. So where do you need to be for the falcon thing?"

Yusuf said Dawoud would be in the plaza between the Dome of the Rock and Al-Aqsa Mosque about one o'clock."

Ahmad checked his watch; it was 1:15 p.m. "Okay, let's get a move on."

They proceeded through the crowded narrow streets of the Old City toward the Temple Mount, jostled by a dense sea of humanity under a clear blue noonday sky. Ahmad had been here only a few times as a kid with his madrasa class. In his older years, it had become too difficult to get there from Gaza because of the restrictive border into Israel. But he still remembered the aromas of the food wafting through the air, the colorful garments being sold at the many kiosks, and the chatter of so many different languages. Even at this speedy pace to get to the Temple Mount he could still sense those smells, feel the excitement, and take in the energy.

Ahmad made a left along the street parallel to the Western Wall, then a right at the major walkway that led up the stairs to the Mount. His pace slowed to a crawl with being bounced this way and that, and having to turn around every few seconds to make sure his friends didn't get lost in the crowd.

At the top of the stairs, they made their way to the middle of the square. Ahmad glanced over at the Dome entrance, then scanned the crowd, slowly rotating his view until he faced the Al-Aqsa Mosque.

"You guys see him?"

"Not yet," Zack replied. "I forgot how big this place is. He said something about a fountain."

"Purification Fountain probably. I vaguely recall it. But you can't see clearly more than twenty feet in any direction with all these people. Let's try over there, down those wide stairs toward the Mosque, near that small group of trees."

They weaved their way across the wide stone plaza and down the stairs. As they moved closer, they could see the small fountain where Muslims purify themselves before prayer. There, in his best white *thawb*, red checkered headdress, and black headband, stood Dawoud.

"*Salaam*. Welcome my friends. Such a wonderful day for an exhibition."

"Hi!" returned Zack, studying the area around them. "Where are the birds?"

"And drones!" added Kai Li, brimming with excitement.

Dawoud laughed loudly. "Patience, patience. The falcons are in the minaret, with a couple of Yusuf's pupils I found to assist me." He pointed to the open walkway surrounding the top of a tall narrow stone tower at the side of the Mosque. "We brought five falcons up there. Two you helped train, Zack, and three that will do some special routines, including hunting prey…always a favorite of the people."

"What about Taliq?" Zack asked.

"Ah, well he is over there, at the top of the Tower of David by the Jaffa Gate. You probably walked in right underneath him. The Israelis were nice enough to let me use it for this special occasion. I've got him hooded and guarded and will join him shortly. We'll get started in about thirty minutes."

He handed Zack and Kai Li three stapled pages each. "Here's a copy of the plan for the show."

"And the drones?" Kai Li pressed again.

"Yes, sorry. There are nine drones on the roof patio of the Church of the Holy Sepulcher with Akeem. He's waiting for you." He turned to Ahmad. "I thought maybe you could take Kai Li over there then come back and help Zack."

Ahmad completed texting something on his phone, then nodded. "Sure, I can do that. Sounds great. Something to add to my article perhaps, before it goes to print - cooperation amongst the concerned parties." He chuckled. "We even have America and China involved in this."

Dawoud turned back to Kai Li and Zack. "On the first page, you'll see the locations of the birds and drones, along with the call sequences for the whistles in order to identify objects and command the birds. On page two, you'll see the order and details of events starting with the preliminary *fly-bys* with the falcons, the hunting of prey, the flyover with the drones, and then the joint maneuvers. The last page is the phone numbers of all of us, so we can stay in contact…Oh, and this is for you, Zack." He reached into the breast pocket of his *thawb*, pulled out a gold whistle and handed it to him.

"What am I s'posed to do with this? Looks like you've got it all covered."

Dawoud grinned. "Yusuf decided you're going to be the star, along with Taliq, of course."

"Star?"

"Yes. You're becoming famous with the falcons, us, and even the Bedouins."

A broad smile swept over Zack's face.

"Don't get a big head. Or should say *bigger*," Kai Li commented. "Must be sweatshirt."

"Yes. That must be it," Ahmad joked.

"Jeez. Not you too, Ahmad. I get enough of that from Mr. Kaibo, here."

Dawoud pointed to the large yellow stone platform next to the fountain, raised two steps above the limestone squares of the courtyard. "Best to stand up there. This is the one place you can be seen from all the important places—the entire Temple Mount, the Mosque, the Dome, the Tower of David, and the Church of the Holy Sepulchre…especially in that sweatshirt."

Kai Li laughed. "Told you!"

Zack frowned at him.

Dawoud bent down and reached into a duffle bag at his feet, removing a leather arm protector. "And you'll need this as well. You'll be a central point for everyone, and at times the falcons will rest here with you, so people can see them up close before they take back to the sky. The keepers of the Mount know this will be happening and told me that they'll make sure the platform remains clear of others - those who might want to jump up there, crowd you in, or even try to touch the falcons."

Dawoud picked up the duffle and motioned to Ahmad and Kai Li. "Okay, let's make it happen. We can walk together to the end of the Muslim Quarter, then Ahmad can bring Kai Li to the church to be with Akeem. I'll continue to the tower."

"Am I supposed to just stand here in the meantime?" Zack asked sarcastically.

"I'll be back in no time," Ahmad assured him. "Besides, the others will be joining you soon."

"Who?"

"Morningstar, Liyah, and Esty. I spoke with Esty on my way to pick you guys up at the Inn. Told her about the event you were helping out with. I received a text from her a little while ago saying it would be a great treat to take Star and Liyah into the Old City to see it before you all have to leave. I texted her our location as we got here. They're bringing Khalib, too…Kai Li's request."

As the three headed out of the square, Zack stepped up onto the platform so he could be recognized if the girls showed up before Ahmad returned. He scanned the horizon, hoping he wouldn't have to wait long, given the curious stares already focusing on him.

Kai Li turned slightly, looking over his shoulder as the crowd quickly filled in around them, obscuring his view. In between the moving bodies, he caught a last glimpse of Zack, appearing like a red fire hydrant next to the small cupola of the fountain.

Fifty-Three

Southern Negev

AT 1:40 P.M. on Easter afternoon, twenty minutes ahead of schedule, two hundred drones flooded into the airspace over Ovda Airbase near Eliat, the southernmost point of the Negev. No one could see them coming, not even in their single swarm formation with less than ten feet separating each drone from its nearest neighbor. They slipped in between the black-brown rocky hills and descended into the sandy desert valley toward their targets, maintaining an altitude of only one hundred feet above the ground.

A mile from the control tower, they shifted over to a parallel runway where most of the jets were lined up in neat rows, like perfect soldiers waiting for orders to march into battle. Closing in on their targets, the drones split into three groups. One hundred and twenty-five continued on the path to the planes, while a group of fifty proceeded toward several hangars, the rest seeking out the small number of helicopters stationed on the perimeter.

The drones slowed as they neared the jets, swinging around in a quarter circle, aligning with the engine intake manifolds, then continuing forward. Only a few pilots and mechanics were on the tarmac checking out their planes. At the last second, several of the men lifted their heads, picking up the low buzzing sound of the drones as they approached. It was too late.

Bang!...Bang!

The two engines of the first fighter jet in line exploded almost simultaneously with an ear-splitting sound, blowing metal parts back out through their intakes, and causing the pilots and workers in the area to drop to their knees, ducking away from any possible line of fire. One after another, the drones slammed into the twin turbine engines of each plane. The resultant explosions ripped through the line of jets like artillery fire chasing a tank. Some of the engines dropped immediately from the plane to the ground while others dangled precariously from the wings. Those that remained fixed in position billowed black smoke and spewed fire…all incapacitated.

The small number of pilots and mechanics who had been servicing the planes rose cautiously to their feet, gawking at each other. Silence had instantaneously returned. Except for the odd scrap of metal still falling from some of the engines and hitting the tarmac, they heard no gunfire, no whirring drones, no vehicles, no spinning up of a jet engine. *Nothing.* The only thing they could see was the dual plumes of smoke rising from all the planes down each of the lines, like smoke stacks filling the air in an old mill town.

One of the mechanics, wearing grease on his green, baggy overalls yanked his walkie-talkie from his belt and called the operations center. His words tripped over his lips as he tried to explain what had just happened. As he handed the phone over to the pilot next to him, a second set of explosions went off a short distance away, crippling a group of helicopters, some bursting into flames.

The two ducked down again. The pilot handed the phone back to the mechanic without answering. She then scrambled up into her jet and radioed the Command Tower.

"Mayday! Mayday! This is Captain Shira Weiss. We're under attack. Code Red! Tarmac position B9. Send support. NOW!"

Moments later, the tall glass windows at the top of a hangar shattered into smithereens…then the next hangar, and the next. This was followed by a series of loud blasts, as trailing groups of drones flew in through the blown-out windows and crippled the aircraft inside.

A small number of remaining drones proceeded toward the control tower.

"Southern Command," came the gruff male voice of the main operator.

"Hello. Yes. This is Ovda Tower. We have a reported Code Red. We're checking it out, but none of the planes here are reporting back to the tower. We're even unable to contact the copters. Smoke is–"

Ten drones rammed into the communication beacons at the tower, exploding like a series of artillery shells, and severing the cables to phone and Internet lines.

"Hello, hello…Southern Com here. Come in…Come in Ovda…Ovda?"

The operator tried unsuccessfully to reconnect with the base. He rotated in his swivel chair and threw up his hands to the operator next to him. "No idea what that was about. We seem to have lost all connections. I see no problems with the radar units there...clear skies on the Ovda screen. But they mentioned Code Red, so we better check it out. Call the Nevatim base at Beersheba and have them scramble a couple of Apache copters and F-16s for reconnaissance."

Fifty-Four

Temple Mount

ESTY, MORNINGSTAR, AND Liyah, holding hands for safety, emerged from the horde of humanity milling about the Temple Mount. Upon seeing Zack over by the fountain, Liyah began waving her arm high above her head and calling out but was unable to get his attention.

"Zack! Zack!" she repeated as they made their way around the fountain and to the platform.

"Ah, there you are. I was beginning to think I was going to be swallowed up here before any reinforcements arrived. C'mon, up here." He reached down, helping each of them past the people blocking the steps, and up beside him.

"Wow!" Esty observed, scanning over the heads of the people in the square. "At least you can see from up here. You could get lost down there. I've seen masses of people here during holidays, but nothing like this. You came at a great time to catch the best of the Old City."

Zack grinned. "I think we already saw it, by the best tour guide in Israel."

"Ha! Very funny."

He chuckled. "Not kiddin' you, girl."

"Well, this is going to be a real treat, Zack," said Liyah. "We heard you were doing well with the falcons."

"We'll see. Kai Li is over on top of the Holy Sepulchre church. He's gonna release some drones at some point. He was expecting Khalib to help."

"We dropped him off. I'm sure he's already there," Liyah assured him.

"What drones?" asked Morningstar.

"Yeah. Last minute thing. I'm not sure myself what's exactly going to happen…except we'll have a bird's eye view." He laughed, appearing pleased with himself. "You can stay up here with me, but keep back a little. The birds have really sharp talons and can freak you out when they fly right at you before landing."

"Enough said, Zack," replied Liyah. "Don't worry about that. I'll keep my distance!"

Zack laughed. "Yeah, haha, I get that. I bet old *eagle eye* isn't afraid, though." He pointed to Morningstar. "Our fearless leader." He laughed again.

"Oh! I almost forgot her nickname," Liyah said, chuckling.

Morningstar shook her head at the two of them.

Ahmad suddenly slid through a group standing close to the platform.

"I was getting worried about you," Zack said.

"Akeem has some good things planned," Ahmad said excitedly, his gaze drifting to each of them. "He and Kai Li were discussing the routine, and also some tech stuff I have no clue about."

"Nerd speak," Zack laughed. "Two peas."

"Stop it, Zack." Liyah scolded. "You've been regressing since you came here."

"Gotta have *some* fun," he said as he pulled his phone from the pouch of his sweatshirt. He suddenly felt a lump forming in his throat. These types of things drove him crazy. He wasn't afraid of anything he could see…no problems dealing with that at all. *But this anticipation,* he thought, *the not knowing…this is something else. Being the center of attention is one thing, but being 'on stage'?...well that was another matter altogether.*

"Khalib is also with those two," Ahmad added. "It was good to find out he was okay."

Zack glanced at the paper in his left hand. "Any minute, guys. Keep your eyes on the tower by the Mosque."

They picked up the series of clear, shrill staccato blasts from a whistle.

"Now!" he said, pointing to the minaret.

Two dark dots appeared near the arches at the top of the tower. They began circling high above the square, slowly descending, maintaining their circular pattern until they were easily visible about forty feet overhead. People in the crowd began looking up and pointing. The number grew organically, rapidly, until much of the crowd's attention was on the sky.

A whistle sounded again—another message, understandable only to the birds, Dawoud, and Zack. The birds rose higher, narrowing their distance apart from each other. *Another command.* They dove down at a sharp angle toward the end of the plaza, on the other side of the Dome, picking up speed as they neared the ground. At less than twenty feet above the crowd, they leveled off, sweeping across the plaza at over fifty miles per hour.

Everyone near the flight path ducked quickly as the falcons flew by, side by side, like two jets at a military fair. From the viewpoint on the platform, the dipping heads and bodies of the crowd mimicked a grain harvester cutting a swath through a fresh field of wheat. The falcons made several passes to the *oohs* and *aahs* of those below, then returned to the minaret of the Mosque. Applause rippled throughout the square.

The whistle blew again. This time Dawoud released all five falcons from his location. They dove together, crisscrossing the plaza, rising up, and diving again. The crowd responded with cheers and more applause as the birds returned to their roost in the Mosque.

"This is amazing!" exclaimed Esty. "Best performance ever here!"

Zack checked the paper again in his hand. He swallowed the lump that was caught in his throat. His stomach knotted. "Over by the Tower of David," he said, his voice noticeably quivering. "Here we go."

A sequence of whistle blows sounded. The crowd, now trained, looked to the skies. They swiveled their heads round and round…searching…waiting.

Zack imagined Taliq perched on the brick sill at the top of the open stone tower. He fixed his eyes in that direction. Not a muscle twitched.

Suddenly, high above, Taliq came into view. He drifted down closer, soaring fifty feet above the crowd then outward over the walls of the Mount, disappearing over Jerusalem. In a few minutes he returned, circling over the Church of the Holy Sepulchre, dipping down over the people praying at the Western Wall, then rising suddenly above it. He passed over the Al-Aqsa Mosque and finally the Dome of the Rock, where he rose high once more, circling slowly, flapping his wings occasionally then gently gliding along.

Tens of thousands of onlookers, crammed together throughout the Old City and even in Jerusalem proper, craned their necks in an attempt to follow him. For a short time, the flag waving of protesters, street spats, and the buying at the outdoor markets ceased. Everyone waited breathlessly for whatever would come next.

Taliq rose even higher until he was a dot in front of the sun. People screened their eyes from the rays but continued to look up. Suddenly a loud *thupp!* came from the direction of the church. It sounded to Zack like a muffled military cannon. He recognized it.

They had used this in the training exercises—a small portable launcher that shot balls and other objects into the air for the falcons to seek, minimizing the difficulty and complexities of using live prey.

The sound was also a call to Zack. He removed the whistle from his pocket and blew out a code as the birdlike object passed high above the plaza, before reaching its peak directly over the center of the square.

Taliq began his dive, his wings beating rapidly as he headed down toward his target, then pulling in his talons and wings, morphing into the shape of a bullet. He accelerated downward, passing speeds of one hundred, then one hundred fifty miles per hour. At seventy-five feet above the crowd, he hit close to two hundred miles per hour, swooping down on the fake falling bird, smashing into it, then latching onto it with his talons. His momentum carried him just above the crowd as he unfurled his wings, pumping them with his great strength, changing the arc of his trajectory, then rising once more.

Zack blew another code into the whistle. Taliq swung around and closed in on him, dropping his prey on the platform, then rising, and circling again.

Zack raised his leathered arm.

Taliq banked and dove. He entered the plaza again, only ten feet overhead, reaching close to seventy miles per hour. Even Zack thought he wasn't going to be able to stop in time. But a hair-raising short distance out, he applied his brakes, leaning back, exposing his brown underside with its white dots and yellow streaks, pushing hard against the air with his powerful wings, and elevating his legs. What Zack felt was sure to be a disaster this time, turned once more into a soft landing. Taliq's talons gripped onto the protector. A second later he stood quietly, content there on Zack's arm, his head nodding and tilting this way and that at the crowd…like a circus performer taking in the adulation.

Ahmad, Esty, Morningstar, and Liyah, all having ducked to the ground in fear of their lives, slowly rose to their feet.

Zack grinned at them like the cat that ate the canary, pointing to Taliq with his free hand.

"My kinda guy."

Fifty-Five

"IS THAT IT?" asked Hassan, as he neared the end of the runway where Jamal and Nasir were assembling the final drone groups.

Jamal stood up. "Yeah. All of the drones have been sent on their missions. These will make up the last wave. They're headed primarily for all artillery locations."

"Are we ahead of schedule?"

"A bit. The first ones hit early at Ovda and we're trying to make sure everything happens on the shortest time interval across all the targets."

Hassan looked surprised. "You mean we've already hit the main air bases at Tel Aviv and Haifa?"

Jamal checked his watch. "Any minute now, I suspect. And the follow-up waves should arrive at all the bases within the next thirty or so minutes…except these, of course, which will hit the artillery shortly after that." He waited, studying Hassan. "Is that a problem? You look concerned."

"Ah, not really. Can't believe it's finally happening, I guess."

"Well, you *better* believe it. And you *better* do whatever you have planned pretty soon, because whatever is left in their arsenal of aircraft and guns is going to be focused on where they need to retaliate. Your launchers should be put back underground somewhere. And all of us should clear out of here pretty damn soon."

Jamal stooped down to help Nasir, then cocked his head up at Hassan. "So, now that there's no stopping this, tell me…what are those *soft* targets you are aiming the rockets at?"

Hassan hesitated. Jamal stood back up. "They are soft, right? You agreed to that…no one is to be harmed intentionally."

"We're not aiming them at anyone. I already told you…if that's what you mean."

Jamal narrowed his eyes. "Yes. That is exactly what I mean."

"Okay, then we agree. But you're naïve to think people won't be harmed, even by your drones. There is always *collateral damage* in war. And you know that. You just don't want to think you caused it."

Jamal pressed. "What are the targets?"

"Usual ones, you know, mostly communication and radar towers to prevent them from locating and destroying the missiles before they hit. And a few other things."

"Like?"

"Ah, well maybe a possible historical site or two…just as punishment. Not any buildings with people in them. But what do you care, anyway? I heard someone in your family died in an artillery attack on Gaza some time ago."

"Yeah, Hassan, that's right. There's not a day that goes by that I don't think of that. And at times I have hate in my heart…still. But I just can't take revenge that way. I want to honor my father. He wouldn't do that." He stared hard at Hassan. "And what about the drones we gave you for your financial assistance?"

"Soft targets."

"Who programmed them?"

"Akeem."

"Where is he now?"

"Not sure."

Jamal frowned. "Not sure?"

"Well, he finished his tasks for us, so I don't need him. Last I knew he was by the falcons and planning something for this afternoon in the Old City."

Hassan turned his attention back to the missile launchers, talking as he walked away, his back to Jamal. "This is it, Jamal. It will all be over soon…and then we just have to lay low."

Nasir rose to take the strain off his knees "What's up, Jamal?"

"I don't know. Something is not sitting right with me. I need to get within cell range. Can you finish up here?"

"Sure, I've got help. But we best not communicate for a few days after this goes down."

"Yes, for certain," agreed Jamal, as he started to walk toward his car parked on the other side of the vans.

"Commander Korrin here."

"This is Lieutenant Peretz at Palmachim. I've been asked to contact you directly. Sorry to bother you on your home line. I don't have access to the emergency one."

"Yes Lieutenant, no problem. What is it? You sound out of sorts."

"I am. We've been hit!"

"Hit. What do you mean?"

"I mean exactly that. It's bad, sir. Not many injuries, but most all of the planes and copters are out of commission."

"What?" the Commander boomed into the phone. "What the hell are you talking about?"

"Sir. Sorry, sir. The engines have been hit on all of the aircraft on the field. Even many of the planes in the hangars. A couple of the mechanics reported sighting drones…like hundreds of them."

"That's impossible, Lieutenant. What about radar and countermeasures?"

"Nothing reported on radar, sir. No countermeasures could be taken. The drones seem to be very small. They came in undetected."

"Preposterous!"

"I'm calling you from my cell, sir. They've knocked out the line communications at the tower. We've ordered any planes available to scramble up and scout the area."

"Any damage assessment yet?"

"Too early. But from the calls I've been handling so far, it seems maybe seventy-five percent."

"Well, get them all up!"

"I don't mean left. I mean damaged."

There was a long silence. "Sir? Sir? Are you there?"

"My God, Lieutenant! I'll call you back. Do whatever you can. I need to check with the other bases."

As the Commander hung up, the Israeli-blue emergency phone in his office rang. He crossed the hall, walked to his desk, and picked it up.

"Commander Korrin here."

He listened in silence, then dropped into his black leather swivel chair.

"Holy Shit!"

"What are they doing next, Zack?" asked Liyah. "That last one with the drones flying around was cool. The people in the square seemed to love it, too. Was it called something special?"

"It just says *drone flyby* on my paper. It's Kai Li and his new buddy there, Akeem. Who knows with those two? I'm waiting for the falcons and the drones to do something together."

"Really? Wow. My dad insisted Khalib and I stay out of town, especially Khalib." Liyah searched the skies for whatever might come next. "He's dreadfully afraid something might happen again." She brought her attention back to Zack. "I don't blame him. We only just got Khalib back. But I'm really glad we did come…you can't hide away your whole life."

Ahmad tapped Liyah on her elbow. "Your phone is buzzing."

Liyah slipped it out, raising it to her ear. "Hello?...Oh, hi Jamal…Thanks. Uh-huh, yeah, we're in the Old City watching an exhibition. He's here but over by the church, the Holy Sepulchre, working on some drones that…Uh-huh…Sure. Is everything alright?...Yes. Okay, I'll text it right away. Talk to you later."

Ahmad caught her eye before she started to text Kai Li. "What was that all about?"

"It was Jamal. He said he was calling from some remote place and needed to get a hold of Kai Li right away."

"That's odd," said Zack. "I wonder what it could be about? It's not like they're best friends."

Liyah typed Kai Li's number and sent it to Jamal, then returned her phone to her purse. She looked up at Zack. "Odd indeed."

The Pastor's phone *binged.* He tapped on the incoming message.

Just got word from contact. Underway. Taking action on my side.

He typed his reply, Don't know, Kane. Have second thoughts. then waited.

Too Late. It's what we have been waiting 2,000 years for. I have even fooled the IDF. They are still waiting for info from me that they will never receive. We're in with both feet now.

"Mr. Prime Minister. Thanks for joining on this video link."

"Hello, Deputy Minister. What's the urgency, Saul?"

"I've reconvened the emergency group that met yesterday under your direction. We're all here online—Air Force Commander Korrin, Major General Levi of Aman Special Ops, Director Cohen of Shabak, and Dr. Blum."

"So I see."

"We'll get right to it. We have a critical situation underway. Let me turn it over to Commander Korrin. Commander."

"Gentlemen. I'll put it simply. We're under attack. All nine major air bases, all jets, all helicopters, and even air defense and communications systems."

"From whom, Commander?" asked the Prime Minister.

"Don't know the source. But drones…and not the regular ones we use. These are very small. I just received word from five of those bases that a second wave is already hitting. And a major artillery location called into Central Command that all their guns have been disabled."

The Prime Minister's countenance stiffened. "All?"

"Yes, except for a few in for repair and in underground bunkers. It appears these drones are attacking the guns by flying right into the muzzles. They are blowing up in the turbines of the aircraft. From the stations already reporting, it looks like we're losing about eighty to ninety percent on average across the board."

"God!! And Air Defense?" asked the Prime Minister, visibly shaken.

"Nothing was picked up, sir. We only know that it's definitely a drone attack. Thousands of them, very small but equipped with pretty powerful explosive devices. Hundreds at a time. Swarms of them. The second waves are taking out the aircraft not hit by the first wave, and even those remaining in the hangars."

"Holy crap! Hamas?"

"No, sir," replied Director Cohen. "Internal Security here at Shabak categorically deny that. Hamas does not have the technology to pull something like this off. And ground reports from visible sightings indicate most came in from the north.

"""North? Syria?" The Prime Minister's face grew visibly pale. "Are you serious?"

"It's not Syria, Mr. Prime Minister," Major General Levi interjected. "It would be unlikely, and Russian Intelligence has assured us of that."

"Thank you, General Levi," replied the Prime Minister. "I would suspect not. Then who?"

"That's just it, sir," said Commander Korrin. "At this point, we have no idea."

"Adam?"

"Hello, sir," replied Esty's father. "Our diplomatic counterparts in Iran and Saudi Arabia also deny any activity. And that makes sense to me. We were making headway with assuring them of our intent to loosen recent restrictions on Palestine. But that's not to say it couldn't be Hezbollah out of Lebanon, or even the radicals from Iran operating under everyone's radar. We all agreed to clamp down on border entry this weekend, to protect Jerusalem from outside influencers and keep a lid on this cauldron that has been heating up. Only special passes are allowed through at this point."

The Prime Minister paused briefly. "Okay. So, Director Cohen, what is the position of Shabak?"

"Sir, Dr. Blum is correct. The borders, for all intents and purposes, were sealed. However, there have been rumors about internal threats over recent weeks, and this time of year there are always threats and uprisings, as you know. We are waiting on a report from our top agent, William Kane, who infiltrated Hamas a few years ago. Kane is known as Murtaza by them. He has been working on uncovering a new terrorist plan, possibly intended for this weekend."

"Well, get him on the phone."

"We've tried."

"Tried? This is more than critical!"

"I know sir. It's just–"

"Just what? Demanded the Prime Minister.

"He's gone dark."

Fifty-Six

HELLO?" QUESTIONED KAI LI, not familiar with the number showing on his phone.

"Hello, Kai Li. This is Jamal. Liyah gave me your number."

"Okay. About to send out drones. Can I call back?"

"Only take a minute," Jamal assured him. "Before you let them go, can you tell me who did the programming?"

"We did. Me and Akeem. I help with any difficult tech stuff, but he already input almost all data. And Khalib, Liyah's brother, is with us, too."

"Can I speak with Akeem? It's important."

Kai Li handed over his phone. "It's Jamal."

"Hi Jamal…Yes…No, *I* did. We have only nine here...What?...Just a minute." He put it on speakerphone. "Okay. Go ahead."

"I know you're in the middle of this," Jamal apologized, "but I need to know where all the drones are. I gave fifty to Hassan."

"He has all of them." replied Akeem. "Well, except for these."

"And you programmed those?"

"Most of them. Kai Li helped me check things out the other day, and the three of us checked again a little while ago. For the ones we have here."

"Are they equipped with the boxes?"

"These are. The *boxes* on these are different, though. A little bigger and lighter and they have confetti in them. Don't know about the others."

"What in those?" Kai Li asked. "Hassan say he did have extra ones. From some test he did with you."

"Did he say where those were destined?" asked Jamal, deflecting the question.

"No," replied Akeem. "We got them all set for him the other day. Checked out the communications, infrared, you know. He said he'd put the final maps in with help from another technician. I helped that other guy, too."

"What other guy?" asked Jamal.

"A friend of Hassan's. I think his name was Murtaza."

"Murtaza?" questioned Kai Li. "Zack and I not see anyone else yesterday."

"No, because he came after you and Zack left," Akeem replied. "Hassan said it was okay to show him how to use the drones."

Jamal paused before speaking. "Does he have the black boxes?"

"He brought some with him. Much heavier than the test ones we used when we found out about the infrared issue. What's in them?"

Jamal didn't answer.

Akeem continued. "He said he'd get someone to load his own more detailed maps for whatever he is doing. I thought he'd be here."

"There?" Jamal asked, sounding confused.

"Yeah, well I mean, Temple Mount. I was expecting both him and Hassan would be here, since this is the general location they both mentioned. The Old City is programmed in. They just have to select a route and stick in any added pictures or coordinates they need."

"Allah," Jamal whispered under his breath.

"Somethin' wrong?" asked Kai Li.

"The black boxes…the real ones," Jamal replied, then paused. "They're high power explosives."

"What?" came the reply, in stereo.

"I've got to go," Jamal said, his voice hurried. "Let me know if you see them. Sorry to drag you into this, boys."

Akeem and Kai Li gawked at each other before refocusing on their task. A few minutes later, they released the six drones from the roof above the entrance to the Church of the Holy Sepulchre. Attached to each, in place of the explosive devices, was a similar rectangular box, but filled with sparkles in all the colors of the rainbow.

The drones rose up, circled the large gray dome covering the tomb of Christ, then spread out over the square. On the platform, Ahmad, Esty, Liyah, Morningstar and Zack all stared up into the sky as they approached.

All at once, high above, the drones opened the packets they were carrying. Colorful metallic confetti rained down over a mesmerized crowd. Cheers went out as if it was a New Year celebration. Then the audience went silent, waiting in anticipation for what might come next.

In the relatively quiet interval, Esty heard her phone ring. She bent down and slipped it out of a pouch in her backpack she had set on the platform next to her.

"Hi Dad. What's up?...I'm in the Old City, with Liyah and everyone. There's a fantastic show going on here, and Zack and Kai Li are part of…What do you mean? I can't leave now. Okay, okay, I'll go as soon as I can. But I've got to get Liyah and Star back to Liyah's for dinner…Yeah, I get it."

"Sounds like that was your dad," said Ahmad.

"He wants me to leave. Said there's something big going on…an attack on the airfields, including the ones in between here and Tel Aviv, and that the riot police have been ordered to secure Jerusalem and the other big cities."

"I hope they don't get here before the next routine," Zack replied. "Don't want them spoiling that."

"He sounds dead serious," Esty insisted, "Said he was in on an emergency call with the Prime Minister. Something about being betrayed, and small drones. I don't know, maybe we should go before something happens, like he says."

Three drones suddenly appeared overhead, in close proximity to each other, crisscrossing the square. Taliq then flew into view high above, with two other falcons slightly behind him in a small vee formation. Once they were dead center over the square, a whistle sounded. They began to dive, picking up speed, and aimed at the drones.

The falcons quickly closed the gap on their prey to only fifty feet, but the drones suddenly split apart, circling back at a sharp angle, rising rapidly. Unable to change direction fast enough to overcome their accelerating downward motion, the falcons swept underneath the drones, like missiles flying beneath a squadron of planes. The crowd cheered enthusiastically, as if they were at a bullfight in a coliseum.

The falcons then rose high once more and began circling. They dove again, but with the same result. Dawoud's whistle from the Tower of David blew a different code. The falcons then split their formation, each approaching the drones from a different direction and a different angle. They zeroed in, speeding about fifty feet above the plaza, screaming over the heads of the onlookers. The drones, sending confusing, mixed messages to each other, were unable to determine the right path out.

As the drones continued on a straight, horizontal trajectory, the falcons shifted into attack mode, joining closer together, and swooping in from behind—the most vulnerable angle for the drones. The falcons smashed into them, each taking a different drone.

Confetti again blew out of the packages that were the payloads of the drones, sprinkling down above the crowd as the drones themselves went into freefall. The falcons dipped, flapping their broad wings, and catching up to the drones less than ten feet above the crowd. They latched their talons around the rotors and pulled their prey back into the air, disappearing back toward the tower, to Dawoud.

"Totally awesome!" shouted Ahmad.

"Really unbelievable!" agreed Morningstar.

"So I guess that's it. We should get going," added Ahmad. "Don't want to piss off your dad, Esty."

Zack's phone buzzed in his sweatshirt pocket.

"Kai?"

"Yeah. We pack up drones. Take about twenty minutes. Meet you somewhere."

"Okay. What was it Jamal wanted?"

"He say this guy Murtaza has drones, and explosive packs. And Akeem thinks maybe target is here, in Old City."

"Well, let's get out of here, then!" Zack replied. "Esty's dad says the police are on their way. I'd like to go to the Inn, get some sleep, and go home. No need to get stuck here. Meet you at the Jaffa Gate."

Zack stepped off the platform, still wearing the leather arm protector. Esty slipped the straps of her backpack over her shoulders and followed him and the others as they began to move towards the stairs next to the top of the Western Wall.

Ahmad took his buzzing phone from his shirt pocket, bending his head to shelter it from the noise around him, continuing to walk slowly along.

"Hello?...Yes, we're looking out for her. I've agreed to take the girls to Gaza so she can get home…Really? Let me think…I don't have any contact with him, the main guy I met with is named Yusuf, but he's gone, headed back to Iran…Uh-huh…Zack is here with us and mentioned that name. Let me check."

Ahmad called out as he tried to catch up. "Zack! Hold up!"

Zack turned and stopped, along with the others. "What?"

"It's Esty's dad. He wants to talk to you."

"My dad?" asked Esty. "What's he want with Zack?"

"It's about some guy," Ahmad said, handing the phone to Zack.

"Yes, sir? This is Zack…Murtaza? What does he look like? Yes, Kai Li and I met someone who looked like that…big curly mustache, that's right. Might be the same guy…No, I have no idea where he is or how to get ahold of him. We met him through a guy named Hassan, but we also saw him in Bethlehem, when he was with a Pastor…Kane? No. Don't know him by that name…You say he might go by both….Yes, I guess it might be the same person. I should also tell you, Dr. Blum, that Kai Li knows that he has some number of small drones we've been using here for the show, except they may be equipped with explosives. And I hate to say it, but the target might be here in the old part of Jerusalem…Sir?...Sir?"

Zack glanced over at the others and shrugged.

"Oh, I thought I lost you, sir…Yes, don't worry. We're leaving now."

"Yes, Prime Minister."

"Hello, Commander. What's the latest?"

"We just heard that a couple of our main communication towers have been hit by rockets."

"How is that possible? We always take those out long before they hit anything."

"I know sir, but not only have our aircraft and artillery systems been compromised by the drone attacks, these missiles seem to be more accurate. Still no idea where the drones originated, but the two missiles we think came from the south, so we have some manned drones out scouting now. They are on their way to Gaza, but the attack may be over by the time they arrive."

"Anything else?"

"Although the drone attacks appear to have ended," Commander Korrin replied, "I regret to report that every airbase was hit with multiple waves of them. Looks like over ninety percent of reconnaissance, airstrike, and artillery capabilities have been compromised." He paused. "There is some good news, though."

"And what is that?" asked the Prime Minister, sounding both irritated and defeated.

"No deaths so far. Some injuries…but no one has been killed."

"That's incredible. Just lucky?"

"Well, yes, I'm sure luck is a factor. But the drones attacked the engines not the aircraft themselves, so a few mechanics and others were slightly injured. And the artillery housings were blown up from inside the barrels of the guns when most were unmanned. It looks like it was intentional."

"Odd. Well, scramble everything you have left, Commander. I've put the Army on notice, and all the major cities are being flooded with police and S.W.A.T. teams as we speak."

"Yes, sir. Consider it done!"

S.W.A.T. teams in dark blue riot gear began infiltrating the Old City from all directions, through the Jaffa Gate, Lion's Gate, Zion Gate, and the Damascus Gate—the gate that had been temporarily closed during riots the previous year when twenty-two Palestinians were injured.

Groups of protesters waving Palestinian flags, along with regular Easter celebrants, pushed against the police as they poured in the gates.

A loud explosion suddenly rocked the waning afternoon. On the other side of the plaza, in the center of the Jewish Quarter, a drone slammed into the roof above the Hurva Synagogue, the stunning showcase of Jewish life and beliefs. Chunks of rock and plaster tumbled down to the square below. A moment later, another drone hit the Golden Menorah display in the cobblestone plaza in front of the synagogue, shattering the bullet proof glass enclosure and toppling the seven-candle gold symbol of the Jewish faith. Those standing nearby either dropped to their knees or scattered, pushing their way between the bodies around them, seeking a way out of the city.

An instant later, several more drones blew apart a couple of the upper windows of the synagogue, raining stained glass down on pews packed with people. The crowd outside started fleeing for their lives as worshippers flooded out the main doors and into the plaza.

From their position, walking alongside the top of the Western Wall, Esty and her entourage had a bird's eye view of the destruction and the panic gripping the tens of thousands of people tripping over each other to find a way to the exit gates.

"Oh my God!" Esty gasped, turning to Ahmad. "We need to get out of here. You take Liyah, I'll go with Star. Meet you outside the Jaffa Gate if you get lost…Follow me, Zack!" She grabbed onto Morningstar's hand and rammed her way through the crowd in the Al-Aqsa Plaza.

It only took a few seconds for the crowd to engulf them. As Ahmad and Liyah disappeared into the mob, Zack saw another drone smash into the tower next to the Church of the Holy Sepulchre, far across in the Christian Quarter. It was followed by the sound of another detonation. He reached over and yanked Esty to a stop.

"You and Star go!" he demanded. "The church where Kai Li and Khalib are has been hit."

"Oh, no!" Esty exclaimed. "There are probably over five thousand people in that building today, worshiping and milling about."

"I know my way out of here through the Lion's Gate from when I met you the other day," Zack assured her. "I'll get them. When we make it outside the gate, I'll call and we can regroup."

"Okay, I'll meet you later. But be careful! There's something really bad going on, and I fear it's gonna get a lot worse."

Zack slipped his hand into his sweatshirt, removed his phone, tapped Kai Li's name, and began forcing his way through the crowd using his leather protected arm as a wedge.

FIFTY-SEVEN

LIYAH AND AHMAD searched in vain to reconnect with Esty. Bodies jostled hard against them from every direction. Every inch of the stone plaza was crammed with people. Ahmad looked up to get his bearings and located the Tower of David near the Jaffa Gate. He yanked Liyah's hand. "This way."

Ahmad tripped and bullied his way to the edge of the Temple Mount square, still not far from the Al-Aqsa Mosque. He finally pulled Liyah to the side to get some breathing space near the top of the Western Wall.

"What's the matter?" Liyah asked.

"Just needed to stop. It's hard to fight this crowd and we have a long way to go to get out of here." He pointed over the top of the wall to the Jaffa Gate, catching his breath. "And I get this feeling of suffocating in the middle of that mob."

"I know just how you feel. I get that too, but I try to overcome it by slowly taking a few deep breaths and focusing my mind. I learned it from Kai Li and Morningstar."

Ahmad managed a chuckle. "Yeah. Kai Li also helped me when I was stuck in the tunnel. I'm trying, but let's rest a minute. I'm afraid we'll get lost again until the crowd thins out." He turned and gazed out over the square below.

"It's awful." said Liyah, placing one foot on the wide stone brim that capped the top of the wall. She stared down at the mass of people still praying at the base of the wall, fifty feet below her. Some were ignoring the chaos and tucking their messages into the cracks between the large stones like so many others had done for centuries.

"They don't seem to be leaving down there by the wall," Ahmad noted. "They might even be praying harder than before.

"No better time," Liyah replied.

"Hey!" said Kai Li. "You okay?"

"Me? You're the one sitting on the roof next to the tower which I just saw get hammered."

"We safe," Kai Li replied. "Scary stuff, though. What happen?"

"Don't know. Someone is using drones to attack the city. I think it's Murtaza, or Kane or whatever his name is and …Ugh!"

"Something wrong?"

"No, sorry, just got elbowed in the chest. Do you remember that conversation at the Inn with him and Hassan about the Rapture. The end of times?"

"Of course…you pretty pissed at me."

"Well, it all ties together. That conversation and the ones I heard when Kane was talking to the pastor. They said something was going to happen any time now. I think they meant the Rapture. Murtaza is trying to start it. I'm sure of it."

"Not possible. Need a big war or something, and Jesus to return."

"That's just it," Zack replied. "Murtaza must think that by attacking the Mount, especially the most important Christian, Jewish, and Muslim holy sites, he can cause both the West and the East to bring on the final war that will destroy the world."

"Huh? That is crazy!"

"Well, no one ever said he was sane," Zack continued, "and if you think of it, it's really not so far-fetched. We all know this is a tinderbox here, and has been for a while. Everyone is walking on eggshells. Countries that hate Israel will take it as an excuse to finally attack. Western countries like America will have to respond, and so will Russia. No one will know who is killing who and blowing up the sites. It will be total turmoil. An inferno! And that is the definition of the end, isn't it?"

"Jeez. Seem crazy. Can't believe it," Kai Li said in astonishment. "But still, what about Jesus?"

"Don't you remember the Eastern Gate? The one Jesus is supposed to come through when he returns to Jerusalem at the end. They talked about it. Not everyone believes it, but people like Murtaza do, and like some Evangelicals, he's willing to do anything to make it happen."

"Jus' seem crazy," Kai Li repeated.

"Yeah, but look what's already happening. This is part of our mission, Kai. Don't you see? We have to stop it."

"B-b-but how?" Kai Li stammered, his old stutter haunting him.

"We have to save the two Christian sites that would make a difference, the church where you are, where Jesus' tomb and crucifixion site are, and the Eastern Gate. I'm convinced they will be the places which will be attacked. It's already beginning - right where you are."

"But how?" Kai Li repeated.

"Use the drones you have. Program them as fast as you can to attack only drones carrying the packets with the explosives. The drones will be lost in the collisions, but the explosives will go off in mid-air so they can't harm anything or anyone. Get them up in the air fast, to guard the church!"

"What about you?"

"I'm headed up the Via Dolorosa to the Lion's Gate, the same route I took before, that goes toward Gethsemane. Maybe there's something I can do. Keep me posted. I'll come back for you and Khalib."

As Esty and Morningstar neared the stairs that led down to the plaza below, a string of heavily armed and helmeted police ascended, spreading out toward the Dome of the Rock, and the Mosque.

"This is bad, Star," Esty said. "Last year, they raided this area and overran the Mosque. Looks like they're doing it again. It's becoming more frequent, and they use any excuse. I guess they think whoever is attacking the city is hiding here somewhere. This has to stop! Come with me."

Esty led Morningstar the short distance across the plaza to the Dome, where police were encircling the entrance. She made her way around the side of the group, dragging Morningstar with her. She stepped up on the stone step between the giant red marble pillars framing the entrance.

The captain of the police stopped her from entering the Dome. "Where do you think you're headed, ladies?" he growled.

"You and your men can't go in there, Captain. This is a sacred space for Muslims."

"I have orders to secure the city."

"That doesn't mean you need to go in there. Stay out!"

The Captain laughed. "Is that an order?"

"If that's what you need!" Esty replied, defiant.

"Step aside, young lady."

Esty slipped her backpack off and placed it next to her. Unzipping one of the large pockets, she extracted her puffy blue newsboy cap and her badge. She then stood back up, placed the cap on her head, and handed the badge to the Captain. As he glanced at it, Esty turned to Morningstar and whispered. "My dad is not going to like this at all if he finds out, but I feel it's time to take a stand. If I get hauled into the station, just call Ahmad and get his GPS location so you can find him."

The Captain chuckled. "What am I supposed to do with this?"

"I just wanted you to see that I am Jewish, and that I have credentials from the highest levels of the State, and connections to the Prime Minister."

He laughed again. "That's exactly where my orders came from."

People taking pictures of the confrontation with their cell phones moved in closer as the imam stepped out of the mosque to join Esty and the Captain.

"What can I do for you, officer?" asked the imam.

"We need to search the property."

"Well, unfortunately I can't allow that. But I can assure you that if you're looking for someone with a bomb or weapons, no such person is inside."

"I can't take your word for it, Imam. Sorry, but you'll have to step aside, too."

A drone suddenly flew over the top of the Western Wall and across the plaza, smashing the side of the Dome near the entrance, exploding with terrific force, and blowing open a hole in the glazed ceramic tile mosaics that adorned the spectacular building.

The Captain pushed the imam to the side and knocked Esty down as he brushed past her, ordering his men to storm the Dome.

Morningstar, still standing in the entranceway, held up both hands and set forth a wave of energy that stunned everyone within fifty feet of her and held them motionless, including the imam.

Esty rose to her feet. "You're really good at that, Star. How long can you hold them there? I need to make some urgent calls."

"Quite a while, but not all night," she responded, her voice steady.

"Okay I'll be as quick as I can," Esty replied as she disappeared into the alcove of the Dome.

Akeem helped Kai Li reprogram the drones remaining in their possession. Khalib then sent out the new instructions to the drones using Kai Li's cell phone. Right before they completed the programming, another drone hit the church, this time flying in through one of the large stained-glass windows above the congregation. When it crashed through, the explosive device detonated, blowing apart a chandelier and scattering its remnants over the churchgoers, along with shards of the stained glass. Although close to it, they could barely hear the explosion, muffled by the enormity of the church and its thick stone walls.

A few minutes later he, Akeem, and Khalib released the first two drones above the patio of the church where they were stationed, then the next, and the next, until all drones were safely in the air.

Kai Li nodded to Khalib and Akeem. Picking up his phone he called Zack. "All up! Nothing I can do now. Where are you?"

"Headin' down the road from Lion's Gate toward the Eastern Gate. I need to check on this before coming to get you. I'm almost to the cemetery in front of the gate. Don't see any–"

BOOM!...BOOM!

"Zack, what was that?. . .Zack?"

"Jamal, what's going on?"

"Nura?"

"Yeah. We said no injuries. I don't know of anyone dying, but we have people here getting hurt."

"I was afraid of that. Hassan has some drones, but he said if he used them, he'd only hit soft targets where no one would be hit. I'm more afraid of the missiles he's launching. We knew Hamas had their own plans that we couldn't stop. If he uses the drones, he'll probably hit Jewish targets, maybe some water treatment plants or something. I don't really know."

"He's already hit the Church of the Holy Sepulcher, the Hurva Mosque, and the Dome of the Rock with the drones."

"Not possible," Jamal stated.

"Well, it's true, Jamal. I'm here in the Old City. I'm telling you they've been hit."

"Can't be. I mean it can't be Hassan. None of those are Jewish sites. He wouldn't hit a mosque, and certainly not the Dome. And what benefit would it be to attack the church? He'd only piss off the Christians."

"Seems like maybe that's what he's trying to do."

"It has to be someone else, Nura."

"Hold on a second. I'm getting a text. Damn Jamal!"

"What?"

"A rocket just hit halfway up the Western Wall."

"Hi, Esty."

"Ahmad! Where are you?"

"Liyah and I are still in the plaza. We're at the top of the wall. A rocket just hit the wall below us, and people are scattering around down below. The whole city is a crazy mob scene. We're just trying to wait it out a little until things ease up."

"Star and I ran into a little trouble, too. We're at the Dome of the Rock. Stay there. We'll be over soon."

Esty hung up and dialed Zack. The phone rang a few times before he answered

"Hel..lo?" he said, groggy.

"You okay? This is Esty."

"Oh, hi Esty. I guess I got knocked out by a couple of blasts. I fell down and hit my head on one of the gravestones in the cemetery here, by the Eastern Wall." He surveyed the wall briefly, rubbing the back of his head. "There are two big holes in one of the giant doors. Looks like they're trying to destroy them."

"Who?"

"I think it's a guy named Murtaza. The one I just spoke to your dad about. He must have crashed a few drones into it. The doors are super thick, but he also has more drones. I've got to find him."

"Forget it," Esty pleaded. "Go around to the Jaffa Gate. We'll meet you there."

"Okay, but I still have to do something first. And then there's Kai–Wait...I think I see a few people with drones in the cemetery a short distance away."

"Zack?. . .Zack?"

Ahmad crept back onto a limestone walkway along the top of the wall and peered down below. A handful of people, injured by the falling of stone fragments, were being carried to safety. He studied the large crater in the ancient stone wall below him. *It will still take a number of missiles to bring the whole thing down*, he thought.

Liyah joined him on the cap of the wall. "Who called?"

"It was Esty. She said to wait here. They'll be back over shortly."

"You think this is a good place to be? What if we see another rocket?"

"I don't think anyone would send two rockets to exactly the same spot," Ahmad responded. "This might actually be the safest place."

A partially muffled explosion resounded from across the way. They looked toward the Church of the Holy Sepulchre. Smoke rose a short distance above its dome. Two small objects tumbled to the square below.

Liyah squinted. "I think there are drones flying around over there! And more over there." She pointed halfway between the church and the Dome of the Rock.

"And over our heads," Ahmad said, looking up. "Some seem to be attacking others. Maybe the show is still going on?"

"I doubt it," replied Liyah. "There are more headed right toward the wall below us. Look!"

They watched as two drones crashed and blew up, carving smaller craters into the wall, closer to the base. Two other drones were intercepted by other drones, causing them to explode before hitting the wall.

Ahmad stared in disbelief. "It looks like a dogfight between drones! This is crazy. What the hell is happening?"

"I don't know," Liyah replied, "but the drones that are saving us are outnumbered." She immediately focused her attention on the drones that eluded the others and were heading to the wall below. Using her braceleted hand to point, she mustered her energy. As the drones closed in, a red laser-like beam shot from her fingertips hitting the first drone, and then the second.

Blam!...Blam!

Both drones exploded in the air before hitting the wall.

"Ahmad! There are more coming. Hold onto my other arm. The power will be shared between us. All you have to do is to *will* the concentrated light to hit the object you point to."

"I'll try," he said, grabbing onto her wrist.

As half a dozen more drones appeared, they began to fight them off. Ahmad failed at first, creating weak beams, then missing his target even when he was able to concentrate better. One drone hit the wall right below him. Taken to his knees, he let go of Liyah's wrist, but reached up and latched back onto it. He rose to his feet. Together, they began to counter the drone attack on the wall, knocking them out of commission before they could hit their target.

During a brief pause while still anticipating another wave, they both gazed down at the wall to assess the damage, then looked to their left along the top of the wall toward the Mosque. There, on the top of the wall, not twenty-five feet away from them, and staring out over the square below, stood Nura…her eyes steady, her black and white keffiyeh rippling lightly in the cool afternoon breeze.

Fifty-Eight

Zack worked his way from the outer edge of the cemetery toward the base of the gate, keeping low and ducking occasionally behind the gravestones until he could finally see more detail. There were two men dressed in jeans and light gray sweatshirts, and a third in a suit standing off to the side between two trees. One of the men in jeans was trying to launch drones while the other stood by.

He squinted to get a clearer view and noticed one of the men had a machine gun strapped across his chest. Unsure that his powers could reach that far to disarm the man, he crouched down behind the stone. After a minute of pondering what to do, he pulled the gold whistle out of his pocket along with the instructions from the show. He studied the paper for a moment, put the whistle to his lips, and blew out a code. Resting his back against the stone marker, he returned everything to the pocket and sat, waiting.

The men gazed around trying to track the source of the whistle, then returned to their task.

Zack scanned the sky until he saw a falcon circling above. The effortless and rhythmic push of its wings and side to side easy glide of its body were unmistakable. It was Taliq. Zack's throat clenched around his windpipe as his nerves began to rattle him. *I've got to get up so he can see me…but they'll see me, too.*

He stood up from behind the gravestone anyway, pretending to casually walk through the cemetery in the direction of the men, looking at the stones now and then as if searching for a family member. As he moved closer, the man with the gun called out to the others. Then all three brought their attention to Zack.

Zack kept walking, trying to get within a comfortable range to do something.

The man with the gun moved toward him." Hold it right there," the man shouted.

Zack stopped, still doubtful he was close enough. *Do something,* he told himself. *You have to do something…now!*

He aimed his hand at the gun. A beam of intense white light burst from his fingers, missing the mark.

He tried again. This time it hit the gun, but wasn't strong enough to melt it, or knock it from the man's grip.

The man panicked and began firing. Zack ducked behind another stone as the bullets ricocheted off it. As he peeked back around, more bullets peppered the stone. The man advanced.

Zack felt trapped. *Just a little closer,* he thought. He jumped up, running for the next stone. The man fired another stream of bullets, missing him as he dove for the cover of the stone.

He waited a moment before finally peering around the edge of the gravestone. He could see the man just standing there, aiming his rifle. When the man caught a glimpse of Zack's red hood, he started firing again.

Taliq emerged into view, diving out of the sky at an incredible speed, then smashing into the man, knocking him out and sending the rifle flying.

As Taliq rose back into the sky, Zack wove through the stones, rushing at the man who was trying to launch more drones. As he neared, the man saw him coming. He stood up.

Zack lunged for his legs, tackling him. They began rolling on the ground, fighting.

Murtaza, hiding near the trees, ran over and picked up the gun. He pointed it, waiting for a clear shot at Zack. Suddenly Taliq swooped down again, widening and cupping his wingspan to break his speed as he flew toward his target. He raised his legs in attack.

THWAP!

Taliq's talons sank into Murtaza's eye sockets. The momentum of the great bird carried both Taliq and Murtaza fifteen feet before he let go, flapping his wings wildly to rise again.

Zack overpowered the man on the ground. He reached into the pocket of his running pants, pulled out his knife, and flipped it open. Holding the blade against the man's throat, he yelled in his face. "You freakin' guys would never survive a day in Detroit!"

A group of riot police scouting the area around the Old City rushed over, guns drawn. They had witnessed everything, from the attack on the wall, to the gun being fired, Taliq, and the scuffle, but had been too far away to intervene.

Zack closed the knife and stealthily returned it to his pocket as the officers separated the two. One of the officers tended to Murtaza, calling in an ambulance, while two others surveyed the drone area and radioed the bomb squad.

As the lead officer questioned both of them, Zack pulled out his identification pass and handed it to him. The officer scanned it. "You've got some friends in high places. What's that thing on your arm?"

"Leather protector," Zack answered. "Part of the show today."

"What show?"

"In the Old City…the falcons." He reached into his pocket and took out the whistle. "I'll show you."

Zack stepped back and lifted his arm. He signaled Taliq, still circling a short distance above.

In no time at all, Taliq dove, making a sudden but soft landing on Zack's arm, startling the officer. "That's astounding!" he said, recovering. "What were you doing out here by the gate?"

"Just saw these creeps trying to break it down."

The officer studied him closely, turned to the wall, then handed back the pass along with a card from his breast pocket. "You're quite brave, young man. Just be sure to call the number on this card within the next forty-eight hours. We'll need a full statement from you."

Zack nodded. "I'll be sure to do that, sir."

Nura reached into the inside pocket of her black trench coat, clicked a number, and lifted the phone to her ear.

"Hello?"

"This is Nura, Hassan. Tell them to stop!"

"Nice to speak with you, too," Hassan said, sarcastically. "Tell who?"

"Stop sending the drones and missiles. Hitting the Western Wall was never part of anyone's plan."

"It was part of mine," Hassan said, flatly. "It's time to do something. Not sit here and take more abuse."

"The attacks on the weapons of war were enough," Nura insisted. "No harm."

"We are not attacking people," Hassan reminded her. "The aircraft was your plan, not Hamas'. It just allowed us to finally strike back, by affording us some protection."

"Well it's time to stop. People are getting hurt from falling debris. One of your missiles has already hit the wall. Go ahead. Send the message…Stop it!"

"I don't know," Hassan replied.

"I'm standing on the top of the wall, Hassan. All the people can see me. You know my reputation with all Muslims in Palestine. If you send a missile, and it kills me, what do you think is going to happen to you?"

There was a long pause.

"I'm not at the launch site anymore. I can relay the message by radio."

"Do it then. And call me back immediately."

Nura glanced at the two next to her on the wall. Liyah was typing something on her phone as Ahmad scanned the sky. Below, in the square, chaos still ruled, pouring out into the other areas of the Old City. The exit gates were jammed, only a trickle of the tens of thousands of human beings were getting out.

———

Zack held Taliq out before him and smiled. He removed a snack from his pants pocket and fed it to him.

You're a lifesaver, my friend. I've got to help save my other friends now, so go home. Fly away to Yusuf and *your* friends." He smiled again, then winked at the great bird. "And may Allah go with you."

Zack signaled with his free hand. Taliq tilted his head several times, blinking his eyes, then launched himself off Zack's arm, flapping his wings slowly yet with great strength. He rose steadily, his silhouette moving across the light of the dimming sun, until he disappeared behind the Tower of David.

Zack's phone vibrated in his sweatshirt pocket. He took it out and tapped on the incoming text. It was a group message from Liyah to him, Esty, Morningstar, and Kai Li.

At the Western Wall with Ahmad
Meet here instead of Jaffa Gate
Need help…Come quick!

Zack turned and headed back toward Lion's Gate, the fastest route from where he stood.

———

Nura looked down at the message on her phone.

Couldn't stop all missiles.
Stopped ones not yet launched.
Five coming in your direction.
Packs of drones coming, too.
All others halted.
Twenty-two minutes to first strike.
Get out of there!...H

She slipped the phone back in her pocket, then gazed down again over the square below, and out over the rest of the Old City.

Morningstar was losing her stamina to hold the force field in place. *Where is Esty?* She reached in the hip pocket of her jeans for her phone while still holding up her other hand as she read the message from Liyah. *What could Esty be doing in there?* she wondered. *They need us.*

She backed up slowly until she could look over her shoulder into the wide hallway encircling the actual rock from where Muslims believe Mohammad ascended into heaven, and where Jews believe Abraham, father to all three religions, prepared to sacrifice his son.

No Esty. In fact, no one at all. *Did everyone flee for safety during the time she held the police at bay*? She dialed Esty on her phone using her one free hand. It rang, but Esty didn't answer. *Could she be with the others?*

Concerned and confused, she moved forward, passing through the group of frozen police and the imam. When she was a safe distance away, she released the force field and mixed in with the crowd while heading across the plaza to the wall.

Angling her way through the mass of people, she bumped into Kai Li, who was walking near the wall, approaching from the direction of the stairs.

"Where are they, Kai Li?" She called to him, urgently.

"Up ahead." He pointed. "See?"

Morningstar caught a glimpse of Ahmad and Liyah standing on the edge of the wall.

"What about Khalib?" she asked, her face dropping.

"Khalib is okay. Akeem took him to Jaffa Gate...will wait for you. Safest place."

"Good!" she replied, letting out a sigh of relief, as she and Kai Li made their way over to the others.

A few minutes later Zack joined them. "I ran all the way here," he said. "Sorry, Kai, thought maybe you were still tied up with the drones."

"I use GPS location," Kai Li replied.

"Well, what's going on?"

"Did you see Esty?" asked Morningstar.

"No," Zack replied. "I thought she was with you."

Morningstar turned to the others. "Anyone?"

She received nothing but blank stares.

"What's the emergency?" asked Zack.

Liyah explained what she and Ahmad were facing with the drones, how they barely handled it, and that she believed the only way to save the wall from the next onslaught was if all of them worked together.

"Did you see Nura?" Liyah said, finally. "She's famous in Palestine for helping the injured and standing up to Israel. I don't know why she's here at the wall."

"Where?" asked Kai Li.

"Right over there." Liyah turned and pointed further along the top of the wall. She then searched near the crowd, but Nura was gone. "Uh, well, she *was* there."

Ahmad spotted a large group of drones in the near distance. The five of them readied themselves along the wall, each about ten feet apart, except for Ahmad who still needed Liyah next to him to share her power. As the drones approached, they all focused their attention. Powerful beams of red and white light crisscrossed the sky, seeking out the drones and detonating the explosives they carried in midair.

Once the wave had been destroyed, they turned and gathered back together, stepping off the wall. Esty was now standing right there, her pack slung over her shoulder, and her bright blue cap sitting above her long blond pigtails.

"Where have you been?" asked Morningstar.

"I was in a room at the Dome, trying to get some peace and quiet to make some calls. It took me longer than I expected."

Morningstar gave her a look of disbelief.

"What?" Esty demanded. "Ask Zack and Ahmad."

Both nodded in agreement. "But that was a while ago," Zack added.

Liyah explained to Esty what had been going on - the missile, the drones, Nura.

"I see," Esty said, "but we have to get out of here, now."

"No one else can help but us," Liyah countered.

"Yeah, but more missiles are coming," Esty warned. "And we can't stop those."

"How do you know that?" Ahmad asked. "Why would *whoever is doing this* send more missiles to this one location?"

"Well," Esty began to reply, "I, ah–"

"To start a war." Zack interrupted.

"War?" asked Ahmad.

"Yeah, attacking these holy sites would cause confusion and bring on a big retaliation from all sides."

"Who would want that?" asked Esty.

"Some very bad dude," Zack replied, looking out over the square. "But no time to explain now. Here they come!"

Three clouds of drones, with a space between each group, moved more clearly into view. Only a short distance away, they were headed directly for the wall.

"Stand with Zack!" Liyah blurted out to Esty. "He'll show you what to do. Back on the wall everyone!"

They rushed to their positions and readied themselves as the first handful of drones closed in. They focused on them, sending pulsating beams of light crisscrossing again above the square, below the top of the wall. The drones began exploding above the heads of those in the plaza, until the last one was demolished.

Another swarm was upon them seconds later. They fought them off ferociously, destroying all but one, which hit twenty feet below Kai Li's feet, exploding and knocking him down, his head jutting out over the top of the wall. He stood back up, visibly shaken, and glanced down at the deep indentation created in the thick wall.

The third cloud of drones was quickly upon them. They tried desperately to get them all, but several made it past their beams, blowing up small parts of the wall and showering rock debris down on those stubbornly still praying below, now on their knees.

Exhausted, they dropped down on top of the wall right where they had been standing, their legs dangling out over the square. Then it happened.

"Look," shouted Kai Li, staring out toward the Jaffa Gate. "Missile!"

They scrambled off the wall, flattened themselves down on the rock surface next to the cap of the wall and covered their heads. There was a huge explosion as the missile disintegrated into a cloud of small particles. The tiny bits of debris flew harmlessly against the wall, and swished over their heads, a swirling eddy of dust. They slowly lifted their heads and stood up, looking around.

"What the hell was that?" Zack said, looking down the wall then out at the panic-stricken crowd.

"Another one!" shouted Ahmad.

"Four," added Esty, pointing.

"We done for," Kai Li whispered under his breath.

But just as they prepared to take cover, two wide beams of bright red light raced overhead, striking the first missile and pulverizing it into fine dust. The next missile in line was destroyed in the same way.

In the short gap, waiting for the third missile, they sought the source of the beams. Turning, they looked over their shoulders, back towards the Al-Aqsa Plaza.

A large eagle sat perched atop the golden crescent moon that capped the Dome of the Rock. From the eagle's eyes, red laser-like beams shot out, coursing through the sky. Locking in on the last missiles, the beams destroyed each as it approached, one after the other.

"Awesome!" Zack yelled out.

"What's happening?" Ahmad asked, dumbfounded.

"I called him after I texted you guys," Liyah replied. "I didn't think we'd make it through this on our own. It was my prayer at this wall." She pointed to the eagle.

"It's Ooray!"

FIFTY-NINE

THE EAGLE SWOOPED down over the entire crowd packed into the Temple Mount, locking in everyone's attention before returning to its crescent perch. With all eyes focused on the majesty of the great bird, a sudden flash of white light from the eagle's eyes lit up the Old City, freezing everyone in place, and stopping time.

Ooray then took the minds of all the multitude on a journey through history. Back…back…back in time, all of them soaring in the body of an eagle…to one hundred thousand years ago, flying over the Levant, the present-day home of both Israel and Palestine. As they circled high above, the years then began to roll forward. Ten thousand years flew by in a matter of seconds. The first humans appeared from out of Africa, finding shelter in the caves below.

Thirty thousand years in ten seconds—still circling in flight, humans are forced out of the area by adverse climate changes. After ten thousand more years pass, they return again to the Levant. Stone tool users, probably from Iran or Iraq, and Egypt, slowly replace the Neanderthal groups, and develop a successful culture in Palestine.

As the flight above the Levant continues, a thousand historical years are condensed into every single second, the migratory tribal hunter-gatherers move about, blending, coming, going, still arriving from Africa in the south, from the east, and the north…into Palestine, into Haifa, into Jordan.

Now it is fifteen thousand years ago. Early pagan tribal settlements start to pop up below in several regions. Cultivation of cereals begins along with the making of beer, and the domestication of dogs.

Seven thousand more years fly by in a few seconds. Stone houses dot the landscape. More waves of humans flow out of Africa and into the region. More tribes arrive from other directions…they fight but also mix, as it always has been throughout history in the aftermath of war and conquest, and even times of peace.

They fly lower. It is now just over three thousand years ago. The Israelites are expelled from Egypt. Moses leads his followers through the hostile environment of the Sinai Peninsula. At the same time, the Philistines—sea people from the island of Crete in the Aegean Sea, move south across the Mediterranean Sea into Egypt, and east into what is now the Gaza Strip.

Four hundred years later, after the Babylonian departure from the area, the descendants of Moses finally find a home, appearing in the hills around Canaan along with the Philistines. They begin to fight as each group expands throughout the region and more people flood into Judea, the land east of Jerusalem which includes the current West Bank of Palestine. Groups of people from Syria, Jordan, and Arabia continue to move into the region. Their descendants become known as the Palestinians.

As Ooray continues to lead his Temple Mount flock in a flyover of the old Levant, all of this history is captured in the most minute detail and stored in their minds.

More Palestinians arrive from the Arabian Peninsula. Over the next five hundred years, waves of foreign armies move in and out, claiming the land, capturing and enslaving the people.

Time begins to slow. Jesus is born in Bethlehem. The Romans rule.

Six hundred more years fly by, and it is now fifteen hundred years ago, a time soon after the death of Mohammad. Arab Muslim forces conquer the region. More waves of armies invade the region—the Christian Crusades, the Turks, and the British. Then, for hundreds of years of recent history, both Jews and Palestinians, as well as Christians, live together harmoniously, sharing the city of Jerusalem. But after 1948, things began to change.

Ooray brings everyone back into the present, releasing the friends standing on the cap of the Western Wall, but still holding all others in suspended animation. Ooray's form as an eagle, again perched on top of the Dome of the Rock, begins to transform, becoming a shimmering crystal object with its facets reflecting light in all the colors of the rainbow and pulsating with the frequency of Ooray's spoken words.

"I come before you, from a great distance. What has been happening here over the years now threatens the Earth itself. If it were not for my friends who stand upon your wall, I might have let you disappear into nothingness…the result of the catastrophic events you bring upon yourselves.

"Those on the wall have saved you. Their mission is to help save humanity. It is a tall task. They have chosen to start here, in Jerusalem, the ancient cornerstone of civilization and religious freedom. But they need your help. And now, you owe it to them.

"Based on the journey you just took, who would you say owns the land you all call your home? You Jews? You Palestinians? You Christians? What about the Babylonians, Assyrians, Persians, Greeks, Romans, Arabs, Turks, British, and Crusaders? No?

"Who was the first one here you ask: the Jews or the Palestinians? Well, I must turn around then and ask you: Of which parcel of land do you speak? The entire Levant? The currently occupied region of Israel? The Gaza Strip? The West Bank? Jerusalem? The Temple Mount? Tell me! Or perhaps it is I who must tell you?

"It should be clear to you. No one owns the land. Not here in the Levant, the land of Israel and Palestine…nor anywhere else. No one ever has. You witnessed this with your very own eyes. The land belongs to everyone—to the universe to which we are all connected, one to another…to all things.

"The first humans came here in small numbers. They were migrants, they came and left, then some came back and left again. They followed the food, not a religion. Some formed tribes, and more tribes entered from the outside. They mingled, they fought, they shared. Some formed settlements, or left again, or were conquered. More mixing. Even the Neanderthals were in this region before your ancestors. Many of you have their DNA in every cell of your body, as do people all over the world.

"You are entitled to your own religions and your own beliefs, if those seem to temporarily keep your fears at bay. But not when you use them to subjugate, control, or harm others. And by bearing false witness to others, you not only harm your true self, but you also harm the future generations. The *bearing of false witnes*s simply means not speaking the truth…giving power to a lie. It is against the commandments Moses brought from the mountain, against the betterment of all mankind. It is the darkness before the light."

"Following rituals, worshiping idols, building statues, and writing history books do not make something true. Truth resides in your heart and is spoken by the small still voice within you…your true self. It is the same for all humans, and in all the universe. It is a constant.

"When you give power to those few who seek to feed their weak egos, afraid of the truth, you dim your own light. The heart of a child, whether Christian, Jewish, or Muslim…or of any belief or non-belief, is still the heart of a child—and all children seek love and truth above all else. Leaders with weak egos harm the children.

"Those who feed on fear and power, and do not put others first…whether just a believer, or a self-indulgent priest, imam, rabbi, or born again pastor, steal that true voice from the child instead of feeding it. True leaders speak and act for others, not themselves. The real spiritual leaders of all religions and all beliefs understand this. There are many still out there who can help restore this earthly home for you all. But it is up to you as well. To do your part. To lead."

Ooray paused, the beams of his being crisscrossing and flooding the Old City like search beacons. "The prayers slipped between the old stones of the Western Wall are messages of hope and love. Look over, look up…to those who adorn that wall of the Temple Mount, which has now been saved. This wall has never been so honored, nor been more precious with their presence. They come from America, Asia, Israel, and Palestine. They believe in the basic goodness that is central to all spiritualities—the common lessons of what it truly means to suffer, to surrender, to have, to fear, to forgive, to lead, and to love."

Ooray continued to stretch the minds of the onlookers again, taking them on one last journey…that of Liyah, Ahmad, and Esty. They first find themselves in the sandals of a young Arab girl, two thousand years ago, born from generations of the mingling of ancient Syrian and Arab settlements in the Levant. She travels to the Mediterranean coast with her father, a trader of cloths. She meets, then marries a darker skinned man of Egyptian origin and moves into a simple home in the region that later would be known as Gaza. Ooray speeds them through thirty generations in a mere five seconds, witnessing the world through the eyes of the direct descendants of that one girl…to the occupation of her homeland by the British, to 1948 and the years after, as growing Jewish control of the region crushes the hopes of the Palestinians. And finally, to the recent missile attack by Israel on Liyah's hometown.

It is now present time. Ooray stops and casts a beam of white light to the top of the wall…on Liyah. He silently informs them she is part of that direct line of descendants, her father the great grandson of a Palestinian newspaperman, like himself. Ooray tells them this week that she and a Muslim boy named Ahmad worked together, with the help of all the others on the wall, to locate her lost brother.

Ooray shifts the spotlight to Ahmad and channels the minds of all to *his* history.

In a flash, they become him, standing on the wall and looking down on themselves. Time begins to slowly reverse itself. They are fighting off the drones, then watching Zack with the falcons, then trapped in an underground tunnel searching for Khalib; they taste the dust with their hearts pounding as the fear of suffocation snatches their thoughts. Back they go, to his meetings with Yusuf, to Gethsemane and the Mount of Olives with his new friends. And then to his childhood, as he grows up abandoned.

In an instant, they are thrown back twelve hundred years. The Christian Crusaders storm Jerusalem and Palestine, pillaging the homeland of Ahmad's direct ancestors. Now further back in time, they are living under Roman rule in the hills of Judea. They are herding sheep.

Still further back, they find themselves in a Bedouin tent on the edge of the Sinai Peninsula, just inland from the Gulf of Suez. It is three thousand years ago. A band of Israelites led by a man named Moses passes through. The Bedouins provide water for them, and to a young girl, whose descendants will find a new home in the Levant, and eventually bring forth another young girl into the world…Esty. The white light shifts briefly to her.

Time continues backwards twenty-five more years, and suddenly they are enslaved Jews in Egypt. Ooray explains that a plague has just ended, and the Pharaoh has cast them out. Moses will lead the followers in search of a new home.

Time now shifts forward again. Four hundred years pass after Moses' death. They arrive in Canaan, and they settle there. They see everything through the eyes of a young woman. A water bearer at the ancient temple at the Temple Mount, the descendant of the young girl who was given water by the Bedouins, by Ahmad's ancestors.

Jesus arrives through the Eastern Gate, and they watch him knock the coins of the money changers to the ground.

Time moves five days ahead. Through the woman's eyes, they witness Jesus bearing his cross along the Via Dolorosa. The young woman recognizes him and bends down to touch the cross. She feels a magnetic force as her hand brushes against his cheek. They feel it, too.

It is suddenly six hundred years later. Muslims have conquered the land. They watch as most Jews flee the region for Europe, Poland, Hungary, and Russia. For over a thousand years, the Jewish population flourishes in those countries.

Now it is November 1938. They are in Berlin. They have the eyes of another young girl, watching as her father tries to protect his business from a storm of angry Germans. They break the glass windows in the front of his store and set fire to the inside. Her father is beaten, just for being a Jew. It is *Kristallnacht*. The beginning of the horrendous end of the lives of six million jews.

Four years pass in a moment. They are still *her*. She is only twelve. She has been separated from her family and is on a train to Poland.

They are packed into open berths like cattle, with nothing to eat, no place to go to the bathroom except for the hay they lie in with all the others. They, and over a million other Jews, arrive in Poland, at a prison camp called Auschwitz. It is the middle of the Holocaust.

Slightly more than two years go by. The camp has been liberated from the Nazis. She is one of only seven thousand left at the camp still alive. Over one million perished. Tomorrow will be her birthday—she had kept count of the days by using her fingernails to make scratches into the wood slat frame in the barracks which had become her home for more than two years. She will be fifteen. She weighs seventy pounds. Her cheeks are sunken, her eyes hollow, her skin yellow, her bones protruding. Ooray's followers can feel her frailty in its full measure. There is no energy nor muscle tissue left to walk on her own. They feel a soldier lift her limp body and carry it like a sack of beans to a medical tent.

They weep. It is all they can do.

It is one year later. They are still that girl. She is back in Berlin. She is stronger. She has searched for her mother and father but will never find them. She is certain of their fate, but she will never know, even on her dying day.

Ooray moves seven years ahead. She is married. She is preparing to move to her new homeland, Israel…to Tel Aviv. She raises a family. Years later, her grandson is educated in America. He will have a daughter. Her name will be Esty.

Ooray shifts the beam one last time. It shines upon Esty again, standing proudly at the top of the wall with her new friends, her Israeli-blue newsboy cap atop her head. He then shines the light on Morningstar, Kai Li, and Zack. Ooray's full voice returns.

"These young people are trying to give you one last chance. Together, they have saved this old city for everyone: its wall of hope, its Eastern Gate, and its cherished monuments to Moses, Jesus, and Mohammad, who like all of you sprang from the same source. They have united to help you find yourself by first honoring others—to redeem that inner light within you by helping others find *their* light, that will then be shared with others.

"Cast your light out over this troubled world! And then into the universe, so that I may see it as well.

"Find the light for the other! Only by its glow will you then find your own."

Ooray's image transforms again into the form of an eagle, pulsating pure white light. Taking flight, Ooray circles high above the Temple Mount, climbing, and finally shrinking into a single small dot. Then, in the blink of an eye, Ooray disappears.

Sixty

Beit Lahia

THE DOORBELL CHIMED, sending Liyah's mother scurrying from the kitchen into the front hall. She unlocked the safety bolt, pressed down on the latch, and pulled open the door.

"Good evening, Dr. Blum. Nice to see you. Please come in and join us. We've been anxiously awaiting your arrival."

Esty's dad bowed, then entered. "Good evening. So nice of you to host us."

"Our pleasure. Sorry you had to get a ride."

"Not a problem at all," he assured her. "I apologize for being late. I had some important calls to handle. But I was able to get an escort, and he'll wait for me in the car until we're done with the evening…no rush." He smiled. "The Prime Minister apparently wanted to keep me safe."

He set the box he was carrying down on the floor next to the wall, catching a glimpse of his daughter's backpack leaning against a leg of the bureau in the hall. "And Esty was pretty excited to get here. Are you sure it's all right for her to stay over tonight?"

"Yes, yes. Of course. All the kids have plans to go to the airport together in the morning to say goodbye to each other, without us around."

He smiled again. "Who can blame them?"

"Quite the day," she replied, taking his coat and hanging it in the closet. "Come. They're all in here," she said, leading him into the dining room.

"Everyone, this is Esty's father."

David Al-Rahim rose quickly from his seat at the end of the table and moved toward him. "Adam!" he said, grasping his hand firmly. "It's a pleasure. I've heard so much about you, I hoped someday I would have a chance to meet you. Who would have imagined it would be casually, in my own home, and after…well, the odd events of today."

"David," Esty's dad replied, nodding. "Likewise. But much of my work, one might say, is *across the table*…in secrecy. It is you whose reputation precedes you."

Liyah's eyes were fixed on her dad, standing there next to Esty's. Her heart swelled with pride. She glanced over at Esty and caught her attention. Esty winked.

"I understand you have met my daughter Liyah, and her friend Morningstar."

"Yes, they visited the other day. Hello, ladies."

"And I'm aware Ahmad interviewed you."

Ahmad reached over to shake his hand. "Hello, sir. Nice to see you again."

"And," Liyah's dad continued, "at the end of the table down there is Zack, sitting to the right of my chair, and Kai Li across from him."

"Gentlemen," Esty's dad said, breaking into a broad smile. "The stories abound about you two."

The two boys glanced at each other, appearing unsure of how to react until Esty's dad broke into a laugh. "It's all good, boys," he said. "Quite good in fact. There's so much to thank you for." He scanned faces at the table. "All of you."

"And last," continued Liyah's dad, "but of course not least, is our son, Khalib."

Esty's dad reached across the table and shook his hand. "Well, I suppose you are the most honored of the guests, Khalib, for if it weren't for you, I understand we would not be having this gathering at all. We are all so very glad you made it home safely. And in time to be part of the defense of the Old City."

Liyah watched the expression on her brother's face shift in seconds from doubt to insecurity, to acceptance, and finally breaking into a smile—transformed by the sincere tone of Esty's dad's voice, and the kindness in his eyes.

As Esty's dad took his chair and the others nestled back into their own, Liyah's dad returned to his seat at the head of the table near the window; immediately on the right of him, was Kai Li, followed by Esty, Khalib, and Ahmad—sitting on his wife's left. Moving from her end of the table and going back up the right side, was Star, Liyah, Esty's dad, and finally Zack—sitting on his left, across from Kai Li.

"As a quick note," Esty's dad offered, "before we settle in to eat, I wanted to give you an update on the events of the day from the perspective of the Prime Minister. I spoke with him about my plans to join you here at Liyah's home. He was initially horrified at the attack by drones on the Israeli military targets. It's still a mystery to him, and all of us, how that was accomplished without greatly harming anyone.

"He'll be looking into it but it's pretty clear the Palestinian people likely had nothing to do with it…at least, that is his opinion. The news came to him that it was Palestinians and Israelis," Esty's dad continued, glancing at Ahmad, Liyah, Khalib, and finally his daughter, "who, along with our foreign guests, saved our most precious Western Wall…not to mention the Old City itself. So, he is not of the mind to look for people to punish, except for maybe a few members of Hamas, and others who seem to have had the total devastation of the Old City in mind."

He took a sip of water and continued. "The Prime Minister was so overwhelmed by calls from his Cabinet representatives who had attended the festivities, the police forces who tried to secure the city, the imam of the Al-Aqsa Mosque, the Bishop of the Church of the Holy Sepulchre, and thousands of others, that he declared a temporary moratorium on all restrictions; he will open the city for more celebrations over the next few days as Ramadan comes to an end."

He shifted his eyes to Liyah's father. "While there will still be some kind of investigation, out of necessity, I'm sure, David, we can arrange a representative of your paper to help report the story. The Prime Minister also invited all sides to join hands in cleaning the debris from the street and Temple Mount. This will be followed by a feast for everyone, paid for by the Israeli government, and a review of many long-standing restrictions on the Palestinian people."

"Now, thanks to Esty, I may have a better idea than most, about what really happened at the Temple Mount today. But I know that much more will be unraveled over the coming weeks, which I hope we can all learn from. And some of this, like the eagle and lasers destroying missiles, I'm certain will never be fully understood at all." He winked openly at his daughter.

Liyah's mom began serving small side dishes of fruit to the guests then took her seat. Her husband raised his water glass and scanned the faces around the table.

"Welcome everyone!"

After the water glasses around the table clinked against each other, he continued. "I thank my daughter for putting this event together on last minute notice, and Esty and Ahmad for getting most of you here."

More clinking of glasses.

"Given the short time available, we don't have a five-star meal to present to you. However, my lovely wife, Rani, has prepared a number of dishes and side plates which represent a mix of the traditional foods of both Passover and Ramadan. We'll be serving them shortly. But first, I understand that some of you have brought some gifts you acquired during the week, in anticipation of handing them out before our honored guests leave for their home ports. So, I'll just stop talking and let my daughter take over from here." He looked over at her. "Liyah?"

"Sounds like I'm at a business meeting at the Filastin Dawn," Liyah responded, her comment met by light laughter.

Liyah felt the muscles in her body tense up. She wasn't used to speaking off the top of her head to a group, even if she knew most of them. Public speaking was a daytime nightmare of which she had a deadly fear. She paused, shifting in her seat, not wanting to mess up this important opportunity. She took a deep breath, gathered herself, then glanced towards her father. "Thanks Baba. I'd like to say something before we get to the gifts."

She paused, looking around the table, before resting her eyes on her brother, sitting directly across from her. "First, I want to acknowledge Esty's dad's mention of Khalib. We got so caught up in things today it's easy to forget how this all started. Not everyone here knows the exact details of how I met Kai Li, Zack, and Star, or what is going on with some of the wild things that have been reported in the news the past few hours…like the appearance of the eagle in the Old City, strange light rays hitting missiles and drones, time seemingly stopping, and other weird stuff." She smiled at all the faces around the table and gave a subtle nod to her dad.

"I hope things will become clearer over time. There's no need to go into them now nor worry anyone unnecessarily. I just wanted to say that I am so fortunate to have met these three, and now Esty, and to get to know Ahmad better. And of course, to meet Esty's dad, who seems to be getting famous with the Israelis. And now us." She grinned, bowing to him.

Liyah returned her gaze to her brother. "So, like I was saying, before we got mixed up in all this other drama of the business of saving the Western Wall and maybe the Old City, or even preventing a worldwide catastrophe," she continued, chuckling, "all I was trying to do was to find Khalib and bring him safely home."

She sensed her eyes welling up. "I felt it was my fault that he was taken. I didn't know if he would be hurt, or maybe never come home, an-and how I was ever going to live with that." She lowered her head slightly to avoid direct contact, as tears began to collect in the corners of her eyes and trickle slowly down the ridge between her cheeks and nose. Morningstar touched her hand.

Liyah wiped the tears away with the sleeve of her blouse, then looked back up, studying each face at the table, one by one. "My family has been so understanding, even though I knew they were feeling the same pain, the same loss. You have all been so good. It took all of us to find him, to bring him home, and in the process, these other good things happened. As if by magic, it might seem." She exhaled slowly, heavily. "So, thank you…all of you…for the gift of my brother."

As some of the others wiped the moisture from their own eyes, Khalib, who had been so quiet since his return, so caught in his thoughts about his journey, rose from his seat, circled the end of the table behind his mother and Morningstar, and moved towards his sister. Liyah stood as he approached and wrapped her arms around him, squeezing him with all her might, tears now pouring down uncontrollably.

Liyah then bent down and removed an article from beneath her chair. "This is for you." She handed him the t-shirt she had purchased in the market with Morningstar, the one with the golden eagle—the symbol of strength, courage, wisdom, and freedom—set against the red, black, white and green of the Palestinian flag. "You remind us that this is what we Palestinians are fighting for. Not to harm others, but to stand tall, for ourselves, and for everyone."

Khalib broke out in a broad grin, accepting it with great enthusiasm, and kissing his sister on her cheek. He held it up against his chest for all to see as he made his way back to his seat next to Esty.

Before taking her own seat, Liyah looked over at him once more. "Maybe that will distract you, little brother, so you can stop gawking at Esty."

As laughter filled the room, Liyah felt the stress of her speech, the day, and the week melt away, like snow from branches in the spring sun.

"Next?" Liyah's father broadcast to the table.

"I'll go," said Morningstar. She reached into the pocket of her tunic and pulled out a small colorful object, less than half the size of her small palm. She looked at Liyah's mom, sitting on her left. "Mrs. Rahim, I wanted to thank you for your kindness to me during my stay here, and that of your husband as well." She glanced over at him, then back, surprised to suddenly notice that Liyah's mother wore her hijab more loosely than any of the previous days, her clothing a bit more casual. "I couldn't have asked for a better host. Not only did you make great meals during the important evenings of the fast for Ramadan, but you graciously accepted the different customs and behaviors that my friends and I brought with us. We are not Muslims, but I know I speak for the others in saying that for this week, we were."

Morningstar presented her gift: a handwoven X enclosed in a circle, to Liyah's mom and rested it in her palm. "I didn't know what to get you. This is all I have. I carry it with me always. It is what my Lakota tribe in America, and other Plains Indians tribes, call a medicine wheel…sort of like a pie cut into four parts. It represents all the knowledge contained in the universe. The lines that form the X separate the circle into four equal parts: one yellow, one white, one black, one red. Each part, or color, represents a direction; moving counterclockwise and starting with yellow we see east, north, west, and south. The four colors are also seen in the mix of the colors of the skin of all people. The seasons of our lives and mother earth are reflected by the colors too, with yellow for growth and spring, white for death and winter, black for maturity and autumn, and red for birth and summer. In addition to other things, the four elements are also represented: yellow for fire, white for air, black for earth, and red for water."

Morningstar gently closed Liyah's mother's fingers around the wheel. "You now have all the truth of life within the palm of your hand. May it bring to you a life of love without fear, and the feeling of connectedness to all things."

Liyah's mom's eyes softened. She sat quietly for a moment looking at Morningstar. She rubbed the medicine wheel between her forefinger and thumb before setting the wheel next to her plate. She caressed the side of Morningstar's head with her hand and smiled. Thank you, my dear one. I could not be more honored by receiving this. But I don't want to take this from you, because it is something so special to you."

"I'll find another just like it. Don't worry. Maybe I'll even mail one to Khalib." She looked over at him. "It often has an eagle feather attached to the center of the X. Maybe he'd like that?"

"Damn straight!" Khalib blurted out.

"Khalib!" cautioned his dad.

"I know, Baba, but that is so cool."

Liyah's mom stood up. "My turn now," she said, handing a small cloth sack to Morningstar. "Go ahead and reach in and take one. Then pass the bag down to Dr. Blum, Zack, Kai Li, and Esty. When I found out there might be some gifts, I hunted through all the drawers and found these. They are called subha…Islamic prayer beads. They come in different colors and numbers of beads. You can use them for prayer, or simply fiddle with them as a way to relieve tension. Like you Morningstar, I can get some more anytime."

"Thanks," Morningstar replied, taking one and passing the pouch along.

Each of the others fished out a string of beads and gave their thanks, ending with Esty. "We don't have anything like this in Judaism as far as I know," she said, holding up her string.

"Some Christians use what are called rosary beads," said Zack. "Pretty similar I think."

"Yeah, and Buddhist have worry stone," Kai Li replied.

"Many Native American tribes also use worry stones," Morningstar added.

Ahmad had stepped out for a moment to use the bathroom in the hall and was making his way back when he noticed the end of a black and white checkered cloth caught in the large, zippered pocket of Esty's pack. He leaned down to get a better look, with one hand holding onto the bureau for stability. With his other hand, he began to unzip the pocket.

Esty caught a glimpse of him in the corner of her eye, pushed her chair back, and stepped quickly into the hall to intercept him. "Ahmad," she whispered loudly as she approached. "Don't!"

Morningstar, with the closest view into the hallway, noticed Liyah's eyes follow Esty. She turned her head just enough to see what was going on, trying not to cause attention.

"Anyone else with a gift, or message they'd like to convey?" Liyah's dad asked.

Esty's dad was finishing his fruit salad. "Yes, I do. One minute."

As Esty's dad began to stand up to retrieve his box from the foyer, Liyah saw Esty grab Ahmad's hand to stop him from unzipping the bag. He let go of the scarf-like cloth and looked up at Esty. Stuffing it back fully into the pocket, he stood up, Esty still holding onto his hand.

"Nu…"

Esty pressed her finger against his lips. "Shhh..."

Their eyes locked briefly…then Ahmad kissed her.

Liyah felt her heart sinking like a stone to the bottom of the sea.

Morningstar turned her head to look at her friend. She watched Liyah's jaw drop and her face turn pale. Reaching her hand out, she placed it on Liyah's leg, catching her eye. "Sorry," she mouthed silently, squeezing Liyah's knee gently.

Liyah turned away as Esty's father walked behind her, heading into the hall. Ahmad and Esty re-entered the dining room, passing on the opposite side of the table. Liyah avoided eye contact with them.

A few moments later, Esty's dad returned, set his box on the table next to his place setting, and remained standing. When he had everyone's attention, he began to speak.

"My family came here to Israel, after the devastation of World War II—after the torture and massacre of six million fellow Jews. I am a student of history. I was educated in America. I understand the similar persecution that Native Americans must have felt as the United

States pushed west, and the enslavement that generations of black people from Africa had to endure." He glanced at Morningstar and then Zack.

"In 1937, about the same time that the Germans were opening the first concentration camp of the Holocaust, something else was happening in China." He looked over at Kai Li. "It is known as the Rape of Nanking. In a matter of six weeks, invading Japanese soldiers raped and slaughtered eighty thousand women and a quarter million soldiers and citizens of that city…half its population."

Esty's dad then brought his attention to Liyah's mother, her father, and finally Ahmad. "Since that time, here in the heart of the Levant, in Palestine, a group of people is still under siege who continue to suffer the indignity that comes with no power and no voice, and who still strive for the return of their homeland."

He tapped the table with his finger. "When will all this suffering of humanity stop? I guess that is the question for all time, isn't it? For this kind of suffering is not new to any period of human existence, or any country, or culture. We have all been victims at one time or another, but we have also been guilty of inflicting such suffering as well. No one can claim the high ground."

"I have tried to influence the leaders of Israel to see the truths of which I speak, so that their policies could be changed to foster the safety and harmony of all people. I often feel my words have not found fertile soil, and that I have failed in my mission. I believe most of my Jewish friends are simply afraid. Afraid of losing their homeland once more. Of being cast out on another long journey through the desert. Or packed in like cattle in a freight car. Perhaps this fear causes us to overreact."

He cleared his throat. "The extremists from all sides use fear to stir things up and to drown out my voice. My time to influence change is getting shorter. Yet, I have learned something interesting these past few days."

"Esty has shared with me some things that seem unbelievable: about energetic powers, of great change that awaits over the horizon, of the strange things that happened in the Old City today. But mostly she has told me about a mission of her own, how the change we seek can be found simply by believing in and helping others first, above ourselves. And I am coming to believe she is right. It is the only way to disarm the extremists, share the land in harmony, fight racism, break the division between those who have and those who have not, and raise us all up together."

Glancing across the table to Ahmad again, he continued. "But this will take the courage of a new type of soldier, like those sitting at this table, who saved Khalib, protected a city, and who can lead the mission to return the light to humanity. I had the opportunity to speak with Ahmad. I see in him that new warrior. His pen is ready, and his heart is boundless." He nodded to Ahmad. "I tip my hat to him…and to all of these new young friends. Through them I have renewed hope."

He opened the box and removed eleven silver candle stands, placed a short white candle in each base, and set them in front of him.

"Since my daughter had better things to do than pick me up, I had the driver stop while I ran into a store to get these." He laughed. "Sometimes things just work out right."

He selected one of the candles, placing it in front of him. "This one is for Esty's mom." He struck a match and lit it. "Esty and I always want her to share our times together, whenever possible. Her mother would be very happy this day. So, I thank you all for that too."

From her candle, he then lit each of the others, passing them out until everyone had one in front of them.

"When I light the candles in remembrance of her, I always use her flame to ignite the others. I was thinking of that on my way here tonight…I mean why I do that. It has been subconscious, I guess…that I always knew I got *my light* from her. But it suddenly became clear to me after Esty explained one of the messages that…*Ooray* I believe the name was, sent out to those in the Old City today. That we need to find our light so we can share it with others. Yet, in a twisted sort of logic…finding our own light means first getting out of our ego and putting others ahead of ourselves.

"I see now, that it was in this way, she and I found *ourselves*, unknowingly helping ourselves by giving tribute to the beautiful light already existing within the other. I then honor her, and myself, by remembering that my light came from the love I gave to *her*…not because she loved *me*. By sharing her light with you, not only do I keep her forever present, I also keep my own light alive. Let us seek to help others shine their light, so their light…that *other light*…can then re-ignite our own."

Sitting back down, he held his palms out to everyone. "The light has found this table, these families, these friends. We are now the firekeepers…and the passers of that light."

After a brief silence, and a few tears, Liyah's father stood up.

"Well said, Adam. I think I speak for everyone here in that regard. I have just one more thing to say, and one more gift to give, before we begin our delayed dinner." He scanned each face at the table. "I know you must all be starving so I'll keep it short. For Ahmad, I just wanted to say that you now have an open job as a full journalist at the Dawn.

You can claim it when you're finished with your studies…or whenever, for that matter."

While all the others clapped, the CEO of the Filastin Dawn slipped out of his chair. Lifting a twine-bound stack from the floor, he tossed copies of the Monday morning edition of the paper onto the middle of the table, bearing the headline:

THE FILASTIN DAWN

The Light of Hope: Alive in the Levant
—A Perspective —

By Ahmad Aziz

"Now…Let's eat!"

Monday

Sixty-One

Mount of Olives

IT WAS MID-MORNING. The boys sat on the stone wall in front of Gethsemane, waiting for the girls. Zack checked his phone.

"Where the hell are they?"

"Esty said they needed to stop and pick something up," Ahmad replied.

Zack stuffed the phone back in the pocket of his sweatshirt. "Figures."

Chatting and laughing, the three girls finally approached. "Hey guys!" Esty called out. "Hope you haven't been waiting long."

"Get any sleep last night, or have you not stopped talking?" Zack asked half sarcastically, his smile betraying him.

"Not fooling us, Zack," Morningstar replied.

"Where's your pack?" Ahmad asked Esty.

"Don't need it for this…left it in my car. We found a spot right next to yours."

"Okay then," Liyah said. "I guess it's time to get this done. I think my dad knows we're not going to any airport, and Esty's dad is probably at the Ministry, but I'm sure my mom is keeping track of the time. Lead the way, Esty."

The sun had risen above the top of the Mount into a clear blue sky. Esty swung open the small iron gate and they entered the gardens. Weaving along the cement path they passed by the tomb of the Virgin Mary, merged onto the stone path, then the trodden earth one. Stepping up onto the wall that led between scattered bushes and olive trees, they made their way up the steep incline and into the glen near the top of the hill…to their spot.

A light intermittent spring breeze filled their noses with the sweet smells from the blooming bushes and olive trees and the scents of pine, fruit, smoky wood, and the sea. They gazed down the hill and out to the Temple Mount.

"Seem calm," Kai Li noted.

"Yeah," Zack agreed, "but you can see the two holes in the Eastern Gate even from here."

"A reminder for us," Esty said.

They stood in silence, taking it all in until Liyah spoke up.

"I hate goodbyes."

"Well, there's no point in waiting," replied Ahmad.

"Before we go," said Morningstar, "I have something for Esty." She squeezed Esty's hand and removed the red and white bandana from her head. "Here you go. A gift from the Lakota Nation. I have this hijab from Liyah, not that I won't buy another bandana as soon as I get home." She grinned at Liyah.

"Oh my God, Star!" Esty gushed. "Thank you so much. I'm sure I'll be the only one here with one." She hugged her new friend, then took a small white box from her purse. "Okay, well I have a gift, too," she said. She turned and handed it to Zack.

"Me?"

"Zack's always surprised when someone offers him a gift," laughed Liyah.

"No su'prise," replied Kai Li. He likely not get many."

"Wise ass. Did I say I was going to miss you again?. . .I take it back."

Zack opened the box and removed the top half of a fluffy cotton protector. He stared at the small gold cross resting on the bottom part. Briefly eyeing Esty, he removed it, placing it in the palm of his left hand.

"Liyah and Star told me all about your journey together, and how you gave your prized possession to another boy. I thought you might like to replace it with this one. It's from a little shop not too far from the Eastern Gate. When I told them whom I was buying it for, they just gave it to me. Their way of thanking you. Word travels fast."

Zack placed the stud through his ear and attached it to the cross. He smiled at her then looked down over the hill, at a sight very similar to what Jesus would have seen only days before giving his life for his beliefs...for others. When he turned back around, he had tears in his eyes.

Esty wrapped her arms around him.

"Okay, that's enough," said Ahmad, before breaking into a laugh.

Liyah faced Ahmad. "One more gift. It's for both you and Esty." She took a box slightly bigger than Zack's from her jacket pocket and handed it to Esty.

Esty opened it, showing it to Ahmad. They looked at each other, then at Liyah. Esty removed two silver chains, each with a half-heart attached. A single silver heart pendant had been cut in two in a zig-zag pattern. On the back of one was the letter E, and on the other, was the letter A. Both letters were hand-scratched into the silver.

"When you and Star were getting the cross for Zack," said Liyah, "I found it. I pressed both halves in my hands to give them the energy we all rely on. You two will have to experiment on how to use them, like Star and I showed Esty in her bedroom last night. There was no time to get them engraved, so I scratched the letters in myself, using the edge of the stone from my necklace." She chuckled. "So, I guess you'll both have to think of me when you look at them."

They all laughed, then Liyah turned to Morningstar. She could feel the honor radiating from her friend's eyes. "I'm okay, Star," she whispered. "It was the right thing to do…for them, for the people of Israel and Palestine, for the future. I should have seen it earlier."

Morningstar burst into tears and hugged her friend with all her might.

"Wow," said Esty, "shouldn't it be us doing that? I don't know what to say, Liyah, but thank you so much!"

"Ditto," Ahmad added.

"Time to go," said Kai Li.

They handed out one more round of hugs before Zack, Kai Li and Morningstar moved a short distance away. Clasping their original gifts from Ooray, they focused their attention on their destination: home. In a few moments, their bodies transformed into sparkling facets of multi-colored particles, slowly fading into the morning rays of the sun. A high whining sound arose, becoming louder…and louder, until…

Pop!

In simultaneous flashes of pure white light, they vanished completely.

About the Author

After a career as a corporate executive, and technology start-up founder, Bruce Campelia decided to apply his life experiences toward developing the Light Passers Chronicles series. In his books, he incorporates his educational background in engineering, physics, business, and health, with knowledge gained from his extensive world travels and an insatiable curiosity for learning. He weaves together mystery, history, philosophy, culture, spirituality, and technology, into modern-day adventure-thrillers…with a touch of fantasy.

Through masterful storytelling, he invites us all, ages 12-102, to find the light in ourselves and others, and "pass that light" throughout the world.

Born in Boston and living in St. Paul, Bruce holds degrees in engineering and business, as well as a Ph.D. in health. When not stressing out over the next novel, he likes to hike mountains, play the piano, and visit his three daughters and five grandchildren who live in Boston and Seattle. He is also Co-Founder and Executive Director of One for Health Foundation, a nonprofit that is focused on wellness, and helping kids become their "best selves."

Find out more at www.lightpassers.com

Lightning Source UK Ltd.
Milton Keynes UK
UKHW012010301222
414659UK00014B/291/J